THE SECRET TO HAPPINESS

JESSICA REDLAND

Boldwood

First published in Great Britain in 2019 by Boldwood Books Ltd.

Copyright © Jessica Redland, 2019

Cover Design by Charlotte Abrams-Simpson

A CIP catalogue record for this book is available from the British Library.

Paperback ISBN 978-1-83889-212-8

Ebook ISBN 978-1-83889-214-2

Kindle ISBN 978-1-83889-213-5

Audio CD ISBN 978-1-83889-210-4

MP3 CD ISBN 978-1-83889-362-0

Digital audio download ISBN 978-1-83889-211-1

Boldwood Books Ltd
23 Bowerdean Street
London SW6 3TN
www.boldwoodbooks.com

To my dad, Peter, with love xx

1

It had to be time to get up for work. Surely. Alison stretched her arm out from under the duvet and retrieved her mobile from the bedside drawers. The bedroom briefly illuminated as she checked the time. 5.38 a.m. Not time for work, then.

She turned her head towards the window. It had been raining for three hours and forty-seven minutes now. Starting with a torrential downpour at 1.51 a.m., it had now settled into a slow but steady rhythm. And she'd been wide awake for every single drop.

Beside her, Dave was in a deep untroubled sleep, punctuated by the occasional grunt or snore.

She slowly turned over to face him, but he had his back to her as usual. He muttered something when she gave him a gentle nudge, but didn't wake up. She was about to give him a harder shove but stopped herself. What was the point? He'd only tell her to go back to sleep. Sleep? If only she could. And he'd tell her that getting upset about it wasn't going to change anything. No, it wasn't. But a hug and comforting words might help her find the strength to face the hardest day of the year.

Peeling back the duvet, Alison pulled on her fluffy dressing gown and padded downstairs to the kitchen.

The familiar feeling of despair enveloped her as the fluorescent tubing flickered then burst into life revealing the concrete flooring, bare plaster, and dilapidated dark wood units. Oh, the joys of living with a builder: a house full of unfinished projects because Dave couldn't bear to spend his evenings and weekends doing what he did all day. Of course, paying someone else to do it was completely out of the question. She'd stupidly suggested that once. Never again.

The dining room had been out of action for four years because it was packed out with boxes containing the new kitchen. It wasn't good to moan about that either. Besides, they had no social life, so who would they invite round for a meal even if it was in use?

He'd promised this would be the year for sorting it, though, and had even booked a week off work next month to finally fit the kitchen. She wouldn't hold her breath.

Alison placed a giant mug of milky, sugary tea on the coffee table in the lounge and took a few deep breaths. It was time.

Crouching down, she opened the cupboard on her grandma's old dresser. There it was, nestled under Trivial Pursuit, a guidebook for Corfu, and a pack of playing cards. She lightly ran her fingers down the navy spine of the large photo album, goosebumps pricking her arms, then carefully removed it.

Curling up on the large tub chair with the unopened

album resting on her legs, Alison closed her eyes and breathed in and out slowly, trying to steady her racing heart. Fifteen years. Had it really been that long?

As she slowly turned page after page, photos first, then newspaper clippings, the rain continued its patter against the front of the house and Alison's tears kept in time with the slow and steady rhythm of the drops.

* * *

Alison was in the kitchen eating breakfast when she heard Dave thunder down the stairs. She glanced at her watch, tensing. He was running late as usual, which would somehow be her fault.

'Where've you put my phone?' he demanded as he strode down the hall, sounding more like an army sergeant than a loving boyfriend. A hefty six-foot-three rugby player, he dominated the kitchen doorway, blocking out the natural light from the glass either side of the front door.

'I think you might have plugged it in to charge in the lounge,' she said softly, knowing full well that he had.

When Dave returned to the kitchen, phone in hand, she looked up at him expectantly, but he didn't even glance at her. She willed him to look at her, to hug her, to tell her he was there for her. He'd forgotten last year but surely he wouldn't do that again.

'What were you doing up so early?' he asked, his voice still gruff.

Alison felt herself deflate. 'I couldn't sleep,' she muttered. 'Too much in my head.'

He yanked open the fridge. 'Where's my butties?'

Alison's shoulders drooped even further. 'In the blue

container.' She picked up her second warm croissant and slathered it with butter, blinking back the tears. He'd forgotten it again; he was more concerned with his sandwiches than her, as usual.

Pushing a stray dark curl behind her ear, Alison took another deep breath. She'd have to prompt him. Last year, she hadn't said anything until the following day and he'd had a go at her for not reminding him on the day. She wouldn't make that mistake again.

'So, it's the 11th of May today.'

He closed the fridge door and stared at her. 'And…?'

'And… well… it's… you know…'

'Ali! I'm late. Spit it out or shut up.'

His eyes bored into her and she felt that momentary burst of confidence ebbing away. 'Never mind. It's nothing.'

Dave dropped his packed lunch into his toolbox. 'Where's the bananas?'

Damn! She *knew* she'd forgotten something. 'Still on the shop shelves? Sorry. There's pears.'

'Bloody hell, Ali,' he snapped. 'When have I *ever* liked pears?'

She continued eating while he wittered about pears being the devil's fruit. Why did he have to make such a fuss about little things like that? Especially today.

Watching him choose a pear from the bowl – with such a disgusted look on his face it could just as easily have been a decaying mouse – Alison shook her head and bit into her croissant again, closing her eyes as the melted butter oozed onto her tongue. Heaven in pastry format.

'Jesus Christ, Ali!'

She snapped open her eyes, startled to find him right next to her.

'No wonder.' He shook his head. 'No *bloody* wonder.'

She flinched as he grabbed his toolbox and stormed out of the kitchen.

As the front door slammed, she ripped off a piece of croissant and crushed it between her thumb and forefinger, a mixture of guilt and frustration flowing through her. She hadn't needed to ask him what he meant. She could fill in the rest of the sentence for him. *No wonder you're so fat. No wonder you keep ordering bigger uniforms. No wonder the stairs leave you breathless. No wonder we never have sex.* She surveyed the plateful of pastries, the full-fat butter, the luxury jam, her third giant mug of milky, sugary tea. All for one person. Yes. No wonder.

She had a good excuse for the feast that morning, though, not that Dave had acknowledged it.

As she cleared the table, tears welled in her eyes once more. How could he have forgotten again? Maybe he'd remember that evening. Maybe he'd come home with flowers and a hug. Alison wiped the table with such a furious swipe that crumbs scattered across the concrete. Sod it! They could stay there.

* * *

'Morning, Ali! Morning, Chelsea!'

Alison couldn't see her, but she knew that Sarah the florist was hidden behind the enormous floral arrangement travelling past the reception desk of Whitsborough Bay's only five-star establishment, The Ramparts Hotel.

'Morning, Sarah!' they both called.

Alison inhaled the fresh, heady scent. 'Ooh, they're gorgeous.'

'They weigh a ton.' Sarah placed the vivid orange, purple and cream arrangement on the end of the granite desk then rolled her head and shoulders. 'I swear I get a better workout from my contract here than I would from any gym membership.'

'I've never set foot in one and wouldn't want to,' Alison said. 'How I maintain this sylph-like figure is a complete mystery.' She ran her hands down her curves and shimmied, making Sarah and Chelsea laugh.

Watching Sarah reposition a couple of violet Calla Lilies, Alison sighed. 'I love flowers. Shame the only place I get to enjoy them is at work.'

Sarah looked up. 'Dave doesn't buy you flowers?'

'Not even supermarket ones.'

'Not even today for the anniversary?' Chelsea asked.

If only! Alison picked up the day's visitor schedule and scanned down the names, the words blurring on the paper as tears pooled in her eyes. She would *not* cry. She was stronger than that. Besides, she'd already cried a reservoir that morning so there couldn't possibly be any water left in her body.

'He gave me nothing,' she admitted. 'Not even a hug.'

'Do you think he forgot?' Sarah asked.

Alison shook her head. 'He'll mention it tonight. He's always running late on a morning.' The thing was, in the early days, it was because he couldn't resist her, pulling her back to bed or joining her in the shower. Not anymore. What had happened to them? Where had the intimacy gone? Together since they were seventeen, the first six years had been so good. As for the last four... But every couple had rough patches, didn't they? That's all this was.

'I bet he'll have a surprise planned for when you get home,' Sarah said. 'How many years are you celebrating?'

Tears under control, Alison looked up from the paper-work. She took in Sarah's eager smile and her stomach clenched. Another person who didn't know. She'd have to tell her. 'It's not that kind of anniversary. It's actually—'

'I'd like to check out. Room 387.' A heavily pregnant woman accompanied by two nursery-aged girls stood in front of the reception desk.

'I won't be a moment.' Alison tapped a few keys to retrieve the guest's bill. 'Was everything all right with your stay, Mrs Hanson?'

'It was lovely, thanks.'

'Ask her,' said the older child, tugging on her mum's skirt.

Mrs Hanson frowned at her daughter. 'Shh!'

'*Ask her!*'

'Shhhhh!'

'Is there something I can help with?' Alison asked as she printed the bill.

'No! It's nothing. She's being silly.'

'I am not,' cried the child. 'Ask her.'

'No.'

Leaning over the desk, Alison smiled at the girl. 'I'm here to help. You can ask me anything, sweetheart.'

'Honestly, it's nothing.' Mrs Hanson tried to put her hand across her daughter's mouth, but the girl wriggled from her grasp.

And then it was too late.

The child looked up at Alison, all blonde curls, chubby cheeks, and innocent big blue eyes. 'Is your baby a boy or a girl?'

Alison's stomach churned as though on a spin cycle. *Smile. Must keep smiling.*

'Olivia!' her mum cried. She turned to Alison, clearly mortified. 'I'm so sorry.'

'It's fine.' With shaking hands, Alison passed her the bill. 'If you'd like to—'

A MasterCard was thrust into her hand.

'You haven't said,' Olivia wailed. 'Mummy's having a baby too and I want a brother this time. If she has a girl and you have a boy, can you swap?'

Mrs Hanson jabbed her PIN into the card machine then stared at it, snatching the card the second the transaction completed. 'I'm sorry,' she muttered again.

Alison plastered a smile on her face and turned to Olivia. 'I'm not having a baby.'

Olivia's face scrunched up with confusion. 'But you have a big tummy like my mummy's.'

The heat in Alison's cheeks cranked up another notch and she felt sweat pooling under her arms. 'Yes, I know, but that's because I'm... I'm just fat.'

Alison had never seen a pregnant woman, two kids, and a large suitcase move so fast.

Grabbing her blazer, she indicated to Chelsea that she was nipping to the loo. She escaped from behind the reception area and dashed across the palatial lobby, through the empty bar, and into the ladies'.

Moments later, she slumped down onto the seat in the furthest cubicle, her head between her hands, gulping in the bleach-tainted air. It wasn't the first time it had happened. A teenager had given her his seat on the bus. She'd smiled and thanked him, thinking he was being chivalrous, until he'd said, 'My sister's having a baby next month. When's yours due?' She hadn't found the strength to correct him so had mumbled, 'The month after,' and prayed the conversation was over.

She took a chocolate bar out of her blazer pocket. Hands shaking and stomach gurgling, she ripped open the wrapper, the intense aroma of cocoa soothing her. Biting off a large chunk, she closed her eyes as the chocolate melted on her tongue, easing the tension in her shoulders. She eagerly took another bite, then another, until she'd devoured the whole bar, barely tasting anything after that first divine mouthful.

Staring at the empty wrapper, Alison shook her head. How many times had she done that? Sat in the same cubicle, surrounded by opulence, secretly scoffing chocolate? She glanced down at her uniform, stretched across her body. Dave was so right. No wonder.

When Alison emerged from her hideout, her heart raced when she spotted she wasn't alone. 'Sarah! I didn't hear you come in.'

Sarah rose from the deep-rose chaise longue. 'I wanted to check you were okay.'

'Me? Why wouldn't I be?' she responded innocently. 'Too much tea this morning.' She moved to the sink and squeezed luxury lavender soap onto her hands, cursing that she hadn't flushed the toilet.

'But you haven't been to the loo, have you? You've been eating chocolate.'

Alison stopped mid-rinse. 'How...?'

'Because it's exactly what I'd have done. Exactly what I *did* do. Frequently.'

'Yeah, right. Because you're so enormous.'

'I used to be,' Sarah declared proudly.

Alison turned back to the marble sink and finished

rinsing her hands while trying to find the right words. She didn't want to offend Sarah but the last time somebody had said, 'I used to be fat' to her, it turned out that they'd gained half a stone and 'ballooned' from a size eight to a ten. Hardly the 'obese' category into which Alison fell on those hideous height-weight charts. She turned off the taps and wiped her hands on a sumptuous cream guest towel.

'I lost five stone,' Sarah said.

No! Alison spun around to face Sarah. 'Really?'

'Really.'

'How?' She tossed the towel into the laundry basket.

'I dumped my useless boyfriend. I was a comfort eater so I needed to get rid of what was causing me discomfort. With Jason gone, I didn't need to turn to chocolate, cake or kebabs so the weight came off. And I go running on the beach. Never thought I'd get into that.' She smiled gently. 'Are you a comfort eater?'

Alison shrugged. 'I think I'm just an eater. Full stop.'

'Do you *want* to lose weight?'

Alison shrugged again. 'I'm not sure.'

'If you're happy, then don't change a thing. Personally, I think you're amazing exactly as you are.' Sarah paused and cocked her head to one side. 'But people who are happy don't usually hide in the toilets, troughing chocolate. Remember, I've been there, done that. I know it doesn't help.'

'It's fine. I'm fine. I just...' Alison voice cracked and she shook her head, tears welling in her eyes. Who was she kidding? 'I hate the way I look, Sarah. I hate the way I feel. I hate the way other people make me feel, like that little girl just now. Yet I can't seem to stop eating. What's wrong with me?' Tears tumbled down her flushed cheeks.

Sarah held her arms out and Alison gratefully accepted

the hug. She was used to Dave's grumpiness and could usually laugh off incidents like the one at reception. Just not today. She clung onto Sarah as sobs wracked her body.

'Thank you,' she said when she'd calmed down.

Sarah nodded. 'Anytime. If and when you're ready, I'd love to help you.'

Alison wiped at her smudged mascara. 'Thanks, but I think I'm a lost cause.'

'No, you're not. I believe in you. You just have to believe in yourself. You can do this, Ali.'

Someone believed in her? For that brief moment, Alison felt inspired. 'Okay. You're on.' She removed another chocolate bar from her blazer pocket and handed it to Sarah. 'Amnesty time.' She *could* do this. She really could.

'Chelsea told me what anniversary it is,' Sarah said. 'I'm so sorry. I remember it happening. You must have been quite young.'

'Twelve.'

'I'm here for you if ever you want to talk about it.'

'Thank you. It means a lot.' Especially since Dave clearly didn't care.

* * *

Back home that evening, Alison found Dave sprawled on the sofa in front of the TV, shouting at the football and guzzling lager. The house smelled of the lasagne she'd prepared the night before. Had he actually taken the initiative and put it in the oven? Wow! Wonders would never cease.

'I'm home,' she said, when he didn't look up. 'Did you have a good day?'

Dave punched his fist in the air. 'Thank you, ref! Told you that was offside.'

She coughed loudly.

'Did you get my lager?' he asked, eyes still glued to the TV.

'No. Was I supposed to?'

'I texted you. Told you to get a case on your way home.'

'I didn't get a text.'

He sat upright, jaw clenched. 'Jesus, Ali! You're winding me up, right?'

She shook her head. 'Why didn't *you* go on your way home?'

'Because you always do the shopping. This is my last one.' He took a final glug from his can then crushed it and dropped it onto the threadbare carpet. 'I can't watch the footy without a drink.'

She hesitated in the doorway. Stay? Go? Either way, she'd ruined his evening and he'd be in a foul mood for days. In all honesty, she couldn't bear to be near him right now. The old Dave would have held her while she sobbed and reassured her that he was her family and he'd never leave her. But the old Dave had barely been around for the last four years.

'I'll go now if you like,' she said, trying to sound cheerful.

He'd already turned back to the TV. 'Damn right you will,' he snapped. 'You can take the van,' he added in a gentler tone, as though he was doing her a huge favour. 'And you might want to get something for your tea while you're there.'

'What about the lasagne?'

'I've eaten it.'

Alison's eyes widened. '*All* of it? That was four portions.'

'Shoot! No! You pussy. You kick like a girl.'

Her throat tightened. Had he forgotten or was it simply that he didn't care anymore? She wasn't sure which was worse.

Thirty minutes later, Alison sat in Dave's van in a deserted corner of the supermarket car park and prised open the flap on a five-pack of custard doughnuts. Saliva filled her mouth as she breathed in the sweet vanilla scent.

She paused as she pictured Sarah's eager expression when she'd reassured Alison that she wasn't a lost cause. Closing the bag, she took a deep breath. She could do it. Starting now, she was taking control back. Then she pictured that familiar look of contempt on Dave's face that morning and that tiny flicker of self-belief fizzled out. *Sorry, Sarah. Maybe another day.*

'To family,' she whispered, taking a doughnut out of the packet. 'I miss you all so much.'

Six minutes later, Alison licked her sticky fingers and stared into the paper bag. All that remained was a small dollop of custard and a sprinkling of sugar.

No wonder.

2

DANNIELLA

Danniella crept down the stairs of Sunny Dayz Guest House, eyes fixed on the front door, ready to sprint back upstairs if necessary. Pulling her loose dark cardigan across her slender frame, she peeked around the corner into the spacious dining room. Seated in the bay window were the elderly couple from Liverpool who stunk the place out with their daily kippers. At the other end, a woman in her mid-twenties tucked into a bowl of cereal while a toddler mashed banana into a highchair food tray.

Releasing the breath she'd been holding, Danniella tucked her dark brown bobbed hair behind her ears and tiptoed across the room towards her favourite table by the fire exit.

The proprietor, Lorraine, burst through the door from the kitchen, holding a cafetière. A curvaceous woman in her mid-fifties, she beamed at Danniella as she poured the coffee. 'Have you seen that gorgeous sunshine, my dear? I was beginning to think the rain was never going to stop. I was just saying to my Nigel last night that we might have to start building an ark.' She giggled at her own joke.

Danniella smiled politely. 'Can I have some wholemeal toast, please?'

'There's nothing on you, my dear. Are you sure I can't tempt you with something more substantial? A poached egg, perhaps? Some beans?'

'Just the toast, thanks.'

'As you wish.'

Danniella pulled her cardigan across her chest again and closed her eyes for a moment, biting her lip. Poor Lorraine. Every morning she tried her best to open up a conversation only to be cut off. Danniella hated being aloof towards such an affable woman, but she had to maintain that distance. If she didn't, there'd be questions and she couldn't go there. Not yet. Possibly never.

Opening her eyes again, she spied a copy of *Bay News* abandoned on the next table and flicked to the properties section.

Lorraine re-appeared and placed a rack over-loaded with triangles of thick toast on the table. 'Enjoy your breakfast, my dear.'

'Thank you.' If Danniella managed to get half a slice down her throat, she'd be doing well. She pushed the paper aside, selected a triangle, then froze, heart thumping, at the creak of the front door opening. Straining to listen, she could make out heavy footsteps in the lobby.

'Delivery for Lorraine Thorpe,' called a woman's voice, and Danniella breathed again. Every morning. Every single morning. She couldn't go on like this.

After buttering the toast, Danniella took a bite, but it felt like gravel scraping down her throat. She managed about two-thirds before giving up and picking up the paper again.

The woman with the toddler left, followed soon after by the kipper couple.

'The property section, eh?' Lorraine asked as she cleared the vacated tables. 'Buying, renting or browsing?'

'Renting, hopefully.' Sod it. She could talk about flat-hunting and, if that led to questions about the past, she'd simply make an excuse to leave. 'It's not going very well. Apparently, I'm being too fussy.'

'Who says?'

'Estate agents.'

Lorraine stopped stacking pots. 'What are you looking for?'

'Only three things and one of those is negotiable.' Danniella counted her needs off on her fingers. 'One- or two-bed flat. Not ground floor. Ideally with a sea view. One of the agents actually laughed at me. Turns out it's more lucrative to rent to tourists for part of the year than a longer-term let. Who knew?'

'How long a lease are you wanting?'

Until my past catches up with me. Danniella's insides twisted. 'Three months initially. Hopefully longer.'

Lorraine picked up the pots. 'I've got an idea. Give me five minutes.'

Sipping on her coffee, Danniella leaned back and gazed round the empty dining room. Lorraine seemed to have taken the cringe-worthy seventies-throwback name 'Sunny Dayz' as licence to go crazy with the colour yellow. White and yellow gingham cloths adorned the tables, the crockery was bright yellow, and the walls were pale lemon. Danniella's tastes were neutral and minimalist, but there was something about the explosion of colour in Sunny Dayz that lifted her dark mood each morning and gave her the much-needed strength to face the day. After eight months of running, she felt so lost, so lonely, so weary. There was also something about Whitsborough Bay that felt safe and she really hoped *this* was the place where she could start afresh. But she'd experienced that before, in other towns, and had ended up moving on.

Lorraine bustled back into the dining room. 'Are you free at eleven?'

'I can be.'

'My son, Aidan, has a top-floor flat to rent on Sea View Drive, overlooking North Bay. I think you'll love it.'

* * *

A couple of hours later, Danniella squinted up at the row of pastel-coloured Victorian five-storey terraced properties on Sea View Drive, then turned to look down the cliff gardens and at the North Sea beyond. Aidan's flat was in the blue building: Cobalt House.

'Danniella?' A tall dark-haired man, probably in his late-twenties, appeared in the doorway at the top of a flight of stone steps.

'Yes. Aidan?'

'That's me. Come on up.'

He shook Danniella's hand as she reached the top, held the door open for her, then indicated that she should follow him up the stairs. 'The flat's empty. A friend was renting it but he's relocated to New York with work, as you do. It happened so fast that I haven't had time to look for a new tenant. If you like the place, your timing's impeccable.'

'Are all the flats rented?' Danniella asked.

'It's a mix but I know all the neighbours and can give you the full lowdown later if you want.'

'Yes, please, if you don't mind.'

'So, what do you do?' Aidan asked. 'Mum said it's something to do with writing.'

'I'm a proofreader and copy editor. Mainly crime or thrillers but I work with some romance writers too.'

'That's a bit of a contrast.'

'True, but when the body count gets a bit high, it's good to have some light relief.'

He unlocked number six and they stepped into a light hallway with stairs ahead of them. She widened her eyes, not expecting a duplex.

'There's a video intercom system there.' Aidan pointed to the technology by the door. 'The lounge is to the right and the kitchen's to the left.'

Danniella walked towards the huge bay window in the lounge, taking in the sweeping views from the Sea Rescue Sanctuary in the north round to the castle in the south. 'It's stunning.'

'It's not too shabby, is it?' Aidan said, the pride in his voice obvious. 'Kitchen?'

She reluctantly tore her gaze away from the window and crossed the landing to the kitchen.

'It was re-fitted in February,' he said.

The high gloss cream units, cranberry-coloured range cooker, and real wood worktops and flooring were unexpected in an old property. It was exactly to her taste, not that she'd have cared if it had been decked out in seventies' Formica; the security arrangements had met the fourth requirement that she hadn't mentioned to Lorraine. It was safe.

They ascended the stairs. 'There's a bathroom through there and a separate shower room. Two of the bedrooms are the same size so it depends on whether you want a sea or park view.' He pointed to another door. 'Third bedroom. Smaller, but still a good size.'

Danniella ran her hands through her hair and shook her head. Damn! And it had been going so well. 'Sorry, but I think three bedrooms will take me over my budget.'

Aidan smiled. 'You might be surprised.'

Wrinkling her nose, she told him what she'd hoped to pay. 'There's some leeway, but not much.'

'Then we're good,' he said. 'Steve paid £20 a month more than your ideal. If you can match that, it's yours.'

'I can, but are you sure?'

'Mum's a good judge of character and she rates you. No pets, non-smoker, tidy, pays on time. You sound like a dream tenant, so you'd be doing me a favour. Bedrooms?'

Stepping into the master bedroom, Danniella turned on the spot, taking in the stylish cream shabby-chic bed, wardrobe, drawers and dressing table. 'I love it. You've got good taste, Aidan.'

He smiled. 'I can't take credit for it. The flat and furniture belonged to my wife.'

'Belonged?'

'She died in a car crash three years ago.'

Car accident? Danniella felt the ground shift beneath her and the blood rush from her head. She grabbed hold of the door to steady herself. *Don't faint. Don't be sick. Please.* A few deep gulps of air helped slow her racing heart.

Aidan had stepped out onto the balcony and, thankfully, didn't appear to have noticed her reaction. 'There's a table and a couple of chairs out here,' he called. 'Perfect for morning coffee.'

By the time he stepped back into the bedroom, she'd managed to compose herself. 'I'm sorry about your wife. That must have been tough.'

'Thank you. It was but Elizabeth was terminally ill so we were expecting it. The accident made it a little sooner, but only by a couple of weeks, if that.'

Imagine knowing your spouse was going to die and preparing for that, only for them to be killed ahead of their time? One of those scenarios was bad enough, but how could someone even begin to recover from both?

Looking at the bed in the second bedroom, it struck her that nobody would ever sleep in it. No family. No friends. Nobody. This was it. This was her life from now on. Sadness enveloping her, she followed Aidan out and closed the door.

'I didn't ask you what you do,' she said.

'Similar field to you. I'm a travel writer. No dead bodies, though, unless you count the occasional unwanted cockroach.'

She probably wouldn't see much of Aidan once she'd settled in but, if she did, at least she could steer conversations towards work; anything to avoid talking about the past. Or death.

'Why don't I leave you to look round on your own?' Aidan said. 'I've got some calls to make so I'll meet you outside.'

He disappeared down the stairs and Danniella headed for the small balcony off the first bedroom. Leaning against the metal railings, she closed her eyes and gulped in the salty air. Gulls squawked overhead, the occasional engine revved, and she could just make out the gentle lapping of the waves.

She opened her eyes again, looked towards the sea twinkling in the unexpected sunshine and, for the first time in eight months, she relaxed. Properly relaxed. This was it. This was *the* place.

At last.

3

KAREN

'Breathe in, lift your arms...' Karen swooped her arms in a wide arc and held them above her head, her gaze sweeping around the group of fourteen bootcampers stretching out on North Bay's promenade. 'Breathe out, lower your arms... and give each other high-fives or fist-bumps because you smashed that bootcamp. The Awesome Award goes jointly to Becky and Jayne for some seriously impressive planking so it's photo time for you two. Everyone else, have a great weekend and I'll see you again on Tuesday.'

The bootcampers said their goodbyes and set off along the promenade while Becky and Jayne posed for their photo holding a bright yellow branded Bay Bootcamp flag. They'd been great supporters of Karen's business, being personal training clients for six years and the first to sign up when her bootcamps started two years later.

'Where do you think Ryan will take you tonight?' asked Becky, as they walked towards North Bay Corner together.

'I'm hoping for Salt and Pepper Lodge. We haven't been there for ages,' replied Karen.

'How many years is it?' Becky asked.

'Thirteen since our first kiss at the end of college party, which is when we started seeing each other, and five since he proposed.'

'I can't believe you still haven't set a date,' Jayne said. 'It was one of the first things we did.'

Karen shrugged. 'Developing the PT business had to be the priority at first, then bootcamp. To be fair, we'd probably have set a date by now if Ryan and Steff hadn't started that bloody running club last year. I can't believe how much time we've spent apart thanks to that.'

'Why are they still doing it?' Jayne asked. 'I thought it was just for the London Marathon and that was, what, three weeks ago?'

Karen nodded. 'Tell me about it. It was the Hemmerby Half on Sunday so they snuck that in too. It's finished now though, thank God. Tonight will be our first proper evening together in about eight months and I can't tell you how much I'm looking forward to it. It's been a strain but normal service is about to be resumed.'

Reaching North Bay Corner, they paused in front of Blue Savannah. A few brave punters were seated outside the café bar, huddled over their drinks, seemingly determined to take advantage of the rain-free evening despite the chill still hanging in the air from a late-afternoon downpour.

'We'll see you on Tuesday,' Becky said.

'With big news,' Jayne added. 'Pin him down to a date tonight before he sets up another sideline like coasteering.'

'Oh God, don't mention that to Ryan. He'd love it.'

Karen waved them off then jogged towards the car park next to Hearnshaw Park, smiling to herself. Becky and Jayne were right about it being the perfect opportunity to talk

about the wedding. Five years was a long time to be engaged
with no timescale in mind. When Ryan proposed, she'd not
been too bothered about rushing up the aisle; for her, the
proposal had been more about the gesture of commitment
than the big day itself. Lately, though, she'd started to think
about weddings. Her best friend, Jemma, had moved in with
her boyfriend, Sam, and it was only a matter of time before
he popped the question. A few of her regular bootcampers
were tying the knot over the summer, as were a couple of her
PT clients. Weddings were definitely in the air. It was time
that hers was too.

* * *

'Ryan?' Karen called, kicking off her trainers in the hall.
'Ryan?'

She ran up the stairs of the three-bed townhouse that
they'd rented for the past eight years. Pausing on the top floor
landing, listening to the shower running in the wet room, she
stripped off her sports gear before gently pushing the door
open. Perfect opportunity to make up for lost time.

Ryan was rubbing shower gel over his chest. Karen
tiptoed behind him and pressed her naked body against his
back. 'I think you missed a bit,' she said, wrapping her arms
around him and rubbing the suds on his washboard stomach, getting lower with each circle of her hands.

He moaned softly. 'How was bootcamp?'

'Good. They worked hard.' Her hands reached lower still.
'Ooh, speaking of hard…'

Ryan turned around, rubbing the suds from his eyes. 'You
know you always have that effect on me.' He kissed her and

she wrapped her arms around him, pressing her body close to his.

'So where are you taking me tonight?' she asked between kisses.

Ryan tensed. 'Tonight?'

'Yes, tonight. You're taking me out.'

'Since when? I've made plans.'

Passion flowing down the drain with the suds, Karen dropped her hands and stepped back so she could see Ryan's face. 'You're pranking me, yeah?'

One look at his expression told her he wasn't. 'Remind me...'

She stared at him for a moment, then shook her head, not daring to speak because after months of patience, what she wanted to say wasn't going to be pleasant. How could he have forgotten? How? She snatched at a towel.

'Kaz...'

Wrapping the towel around her, she fixed him with a hard stare. 'Come on, then. What have you got on tonight that's so important?'

'Steff and I are planning the next steps for Bay Runners.'

'What next steps? You promised me it was temporary and we'd return to PT and bootcamps as normal.'

'I know, but we think Bay Runners should become part of the core business.'

Karen folded her arms. 'So basically the two of you have made a decision about *our* business without consulting me?'

'It wasn't like that.'

'From where I'm standing, it was. Go on, then. You'd better rush round to your best friend's and get planning, hadn't you?' Karen stormed out of the bathroom to their bedroom where she pulled on her PJs and clambered into bed, not caring that she was still wet.

Ryan appeared in the doorway a couple of minutes later with a towel around his waist. 'What are you doing in bed?'

'Watching TV and having an early night, seeing as the plans you have with our business partner are far more important than the ones you had with me.'

'Bloody hell, Karen. Stop being so cryptic. Hands up, I've forgotten what we had planned for tonight and I'm sorry, but it's been a crazy few weeks with the marathon then the half. I've had a lot going on.'

'It's fine. Forget it.' She picked up the remote control and switched the TV on.

Ryan turned around and switched it off so Karen picked up the remote and switched it back on again.

'You're being childish now.' Ryan switched if off and stood in front of the receiver so she couldn't connect with the remote.

'Really? And you're not?'

'No. I'm trying to reason with you. I've admitted I messed up and I've apologised, even though I don't know what for. You've stormed off to bed and you won't tell me what I've done wrong.'

'You want to know what you've done wrong?'

'That would be helpful.'

'You *really* don't know?'

'Do I look like I know?'

To her horror, Karen felt tears burning her eyes. She *never* cried and she certainly didn't want to let him see how much he'd hurt her. He was usually good at this sort of stuff. How could he not have registered the date?

Ryan was still staring at her, frowning. She desperately

wanted him to leave her alone before she either broke down sobbing or yelled at him. Swallowing hard, she said, 'You said we'd have a date night because we haven't spent any time together recently. That's all.'

Ryan rubbed his hair on a towel. 'I can ring Steff and cancel.'

Too little, too late. 'No. You and Steff do what you've planned. I've got a headache anyway. I could do with an early night.'

'Are you sure?'

'I'm sure. Now shift so I can put the telly on.'

She pretended to be absorbed in a programme about building flat-pack homes while Ryan wandered around the bedroom pulling on his clothes.

'I'll see you later,' he said, leaning over for a kiss.

Karen turned her face slightly so that he could only kiss her cheek. 'Hope your planning goes well.'

'I'm sorry,' he said again.

She didn't trust herself to speak so merely nodded. She managed to hold it in as he ran down the stairs but the moment he closed the front door, a loud, agonised wail escaped from her and she clung onto the duvet, sobbing.

4

ALISON

'What are you doing this afternoon?' Chelsea asked as they approached the end of their shift.

Alison hesitated. Chelsea – early forties, divorced – had a strong opinion on anything and everything, especially other peoples' relationships, and was never shy about voicing it. She was also like a tracker dog when it came to sniffing out a lie. 'Food shopping then preparing a roast dinner for Dave,' she responded, trying to sound casual.

Chelsea tutted. 'Spoiling Dave for a change? Why do you bother? He never spoils you. He forgot the anniversary and your birthday. Why not have an afternoon for you instead of that idiot?'

'He's *not* an idiot.' Cheeks burning, Alison grabbed the handover log and pretended to check it. What gave Chelsea the right to criticise Dave all the time? She'd never even met him so why did she hold such a low opinion of him? Alison nearly laughed out loud as the irony struck her. It was her fault. Chelsea's opinion came from what Alison had told her and clearly she hadn't painted him in a favourable light.

'And he didn't *forget* my birthday,' she added in a calmer tone, keen to redeem Dave. 'He got the dates mixed up. That's all. He was only a day late with his gift and it was exactly what I wanted.'

Chelsea's shriek of laughter ricocheted off the marble walls, drawing curious glances from guests seated in the lobby. 'A gift card?' Chelsea cried. 'So much *deep* thought must have gone into that.'

'You know I love reading so it was the perfect gift for me. Anyway, there's an ulterior motive for the roast. I'm hoping to persuade him to go abroad when we're off next month.'

'I thought Dave was finally fitting the kitchen.'

'He was, but it's waited four years already, so what's another few months? Besides, I'm used to the chaos.' She wasn't. Drawer fronts coming off in her hands, cupboard doors hanging from their hinges, and a cold concrete floor had turned her creative space into a place to avoid.

'You hate your kitchen, though,' Chelsea said. 'Why not get the kitchen done and book a holiday for later?'

A guest approached the reception desk, ending their conversation.

Alison completed some paperwork while Chelsea checked the woman in and answered a barrage of questions. Was Chelsea right about prioritising the kitchen over a holiday? Dave had never hidden his resentment at spending his free time on home improvements. Only last night, they'd spent an hour checking through the flat-pack boxes filling the dining room when he'd muttered, 'Can't believe I'll be spending my week off doing what I spend my working days doing. Some bloody holiday. I wish we were going abroad instead.'

She'd looked up from her checklist. 'Ooh, me too. Where would you fancy?'

He smiled then winked at her. 'Do you remember Corfu?'

'Best holiday ever,' she said, pulse racing at the memory of the last-minute deal they'd taken to celebrate turning twenty-one. It was six years ago but she could remember every detail like yesterday.

'Why don't you open that bottle of Rioja?' he suggested.

'But it's a school night.'

'I feel like living dangerously.'

Giggling, Alison headed for the kitchen. The last time he'd suggested sharing a bottle of wine was the last time they'd been intimate. Maybe...?

Curled up together on the sofa, they spent the next hour or so reminiscing about Corfu. Lazy days by the pool had transitioned into nights filled with hot, passionate sex everywhere: the beach, a dark corner of a club, the pool, their balcony.

'I never wanted that holiday to end.' Alison gently stroked Dave's thigh.

'Me neither.'

He leaned towards her and she held her breath. He was going to kiss her. He was going to... But he placed his empty wine glass on the lamp table beside her and yawned. 'I'm done in. Early start. Night.'

'Oh. Okay. I'll finish this, then I'll be up.' Her voice sounded small and distant, but Dave didn't seem to notice. Without so much as a peck on the cheek, he left the room.

Alison swigged the last of her wine, sighed, and sank back into the sofa, shoulders slumping. Not like Corfu, then. Never like Corfu.

She put her glass down and picked up an A5-sized photo frame.

'What happened to us?' she whispered, running her fingers across the image of the pair of them sipping cocktails at a swim-up bar, tanned, happy, and besotted with each other. 'You promised me you wouldn't change. You said we were family. Just the two of us, always and forever.' Alison swiped at her damp cheeks. 'I need you to be my family, Dave. You're the only one left.'

Mercedes arrived for the next shift just then, bringing Alison's focus back to the present. Chelsea was trapped answering a guest's questions so Alison ran through the handover log then escaped, keen to avoid more of Chelsea's Dave-bashing.

Five minutes later, standing outside Bay Travel, Alison deliberated. Holiday or kitchen? She desperately wanted the kitchen fitted but she also desperately wanted the man she loved to look at her the way he used to, to touch her, to kiss her, to tell her how much he loved her, to tell her she was his family, always and forever. She wanted intimacy. She wanted conversation. She wanted Corfu. Sod it. She pushed the door open and strode towards the section labelled: 'Greek Islands'. Holiday one, kitchen nil.

Rushing home from the supermarket, travel brochures weighing her bags down, Alison prepared the joint of beef then popped it in the oven. She peeled and chopped vegetables, mixed Yorkshire pudding batter, and set the kitchen table.

She lightly brushed her fingers over the gorgeous cerulean Denby dinner set; a housewarming gift from her grandma. 'It'll be quiet without you,' her grandma had said when she presented it to Alison. 'But it's time for you to have a new home and start a new family.'

'I miss you, Grandma,' Alison whispered, holding one of the plates close to her chest. 'Why did you have to leave me too?'

Swallowing the lump in her throat, she took a deep breath and re-focused. Special plates, posh cutlery, real material napkins instead of kitchen roll and... this shit-tip of a kitchen. But it was fine. She could cope with it. The holiday would be more than worth the sacrifice if it helped them rekindle what they'd lost. Maybe she should make an effort too? Put a bit of slap on? Wear something nice?

After showering, Alison slathered herself with some expensive body lotion she'd received from Secret Santa at work. Gazing into the small mirror above the sink, she carefully applied her make-up then spritzed herself with perfume. Looking good. Smelling divine.

Back in the bedroom, she opened the wardrobe door, angling her body so she could ignore her reflection in the full-length mirror. One glance was all it usually took, but not today. She was feeling positive today. She was taking control.

Running her hand along the hangers from right to left, Alison's jaw tightened as she rejected each item. Baggy. Frumpy. Black. Too tight. More black. Out of fashion. Dave hated it. Grey, dark grey, navy, black. She screwed up her eyes, stamped her feet, and released a frustrated squeal.

When she opened her eyes, she was facing the mirror. The unforgiving mirror. She slammed the door shut and strode across the landing to the bathroom, shaking her head. What was she thinking? If Dave even noticed – a big if – he'd probably wrinkle his nose and say, 'What's that stench?' or curl his lip and say, 'What's that muck on your face?' Or both.

She wiped her face clean, scrubbed at her wrists and neck to remove all traces of perfume, then returned to the bedroom where she pulled on a comfortable greying bra, a pair of giant belly-warmer knickers, some leggings, and a baggy grey T-shirt. She'd made his favourite meal and brought out the Denby. That was more than enough.

Dave arrived home shortly after six. 'Something smells good. Is that what I think it is?' he called from the hallway, a rare note of pleasure in his voice.

'It might be,' Alison called as she spooned hot fat over the roast potatoes, which were crisping to perfection. 'How was your day?'

'Shite.'

One of these days he'd surprise her and say 'good'. Or perhaps he'd ask her how her day had been. Yeah, right.

When Dave re-appeared fifteen minutes later, he sat down at the kitchen table without even looking at her.

'What's this?' His voice was terse as he picked up the brochure she'd laid on his placemat.

Draining the water from the pan of carrots, her heart raced. It could go one of two ways. Please let it go well. 'Holiday brochure.'

'Why?'

'Because you said we should book a holiday.'

'I didn't.'

Alison put the carrots down and picked up the pan of peas. 'Maybe not book one, then, but you said you'd rather go abroad instead of doing the kitchen and it got me thinking that—'

'Jesus, Ali, make your mind up,' he snarled. 'You keep nagging me to fit the kitchen, you've got a million other jobs you want me to do too, and now you want to go off gallivanting to Greece. You can't have it all. And how do you think we're going to pay for a holiday? With fairy dust?'

'We've got plenty of savings.'

'Which was your idea in case of emergency. "Not for extravagant holidays," you said.'

'I know, but Corfu was six years ago. I think we need a break.'

Silence.

Alison dished up the food. Should she push it again? No. Clearly, he'd had more of a 'shite' day than usual. Maybe tomorrow. Forcing herself to smile, she placed his loaded plate in front of him. 'And for dinner tonight, the chef is delighted to present all your favourites.'

Placing her plate down opposite him, Alison pulled her chair out but stopped when she clocked his expression: eyebrows knitted, lip curled in apparent disgust.

'What's wrong now?' she demanded, her patience worn thin.

Dave pointed at his plate. 'This. I thought you said it was *all* my favourites.'

Had she forgotten to dish up something? Alison scanned the plate. Nope. She looked up at Dave, shrugging.

'Horseradish,' he prompted.

'Sorry. Of course. I'll get it.'

But as she opened the cupboard door, Alison had a sinking feeling she'd forgotten to add it to her shopping list. She shuffled a few jars and bottles around, stomach churning. Crap. Slowly closing the door, she turned to face Dave. 'We've run out. Sorry. All your other favourites are there.'

'Which will taste like absolute shite without horseradish.' He pushed back his chair, making an ear-splitting screech across the floor. 'Nice one, Ali. I'll have to order pizza instead.'

After she'd slaved away all afternoon? No way. 'You're not going to die from horseradish deficiency,' she snapped. 'Get it eaten and stop being so bloody childish.'

His eyes widened. 'Childish? I'll show you childish.'

It seemed to happen in slow motion. Dave knocked his plate with his hand as he rose to his feet. It spun across the table, crashing into hers, jettisoning both plates towards the floor. Gravy flew in every direction, covering the floor, the units, and Alison. Peas and carrots dispersed, and dollops of mash and roasties splatted onto the concrete floor like islands in a sea of gravy.

Her precious plates shattered, fragments scattering across the floor.

With an anguished cry, Alison sank to her knees, reaching for the nearest shards.

'My plates,' she sobbed, looking up at Dave helplessly. 'My beautiful plates. What...? Why...?'

Dave stared at her, his eyes cold and uncaring. He picked up the travel brochure and tossed it towards the recycling crate by the back door. 'Greek Islands? You in shorts or even worse, a bikini? You've got to be fucking kidding me.'

When he slammed the front door, the whole house seemed to shake. Alison slumped back against the fridge-freezer, heart thumping, hot tears rolling down her cheeks. What the hell had just happened? He was grumpy and he had a short temper, but he'd never been violent. Never.

She stared at the pieces in her hand. Had Dave pushed the plates off the table deliberately? No. He wouldn't do that. He knew how much they meant to her. It had been an accident.

Hadn't it?

5

DANNIELLA

'Here you go, 6 Cobalt House is officially your new home,' Aidan said.

Danniella smiled at the 'I love Yorkshire' keyring he handed her. 'Thanks, Aidan. For everything.'

'As I said before, you're doing me a favour. Good tenants are hard to find.'

'How do you know I'm going to be a good tenant? I might be planning to set up a cannabis farm or bury a few bodies under the floorboards.'

Aidan raised an eyebrow. 'I think someone's been editing too many crime novels.'

Danniella laughed out loud at Aidan's comment. The sound seemed so unfamiliar. She hadn't laughed since... She shook her head. 'I'd best start moving in then.'

Aidan nodded. 'I was thinking we could take a couple of bags or cases up now, I'll run through a few things with you, then help you bring in the rest.'

'I couldn't ask you to do that. You've done so much already.'

'Honestly, it's not a problem. Unless you really want to do ten trips up three flights of stairs on your own.'

She smiled once more. 'When you put it like that... Thank you. Again.'

* * *

Lorraine stopped by later that afternoon. 'I won't stay long, my dear, as I'm sure you've loads to do. I couldn't let you move into your new home without some flowers, though.' She handed Danniella a large yellow bouquet.

'They're beautiful,' Danniella said. 'Thank you. Have you got time for a coffee?'

'Only if you're having one.'

'I was just about to.' Danniella indicated for Lorraine to follow her into the kitchen. She put the kettle on to boil and rested the flowers in the sink, making a mental note to add a vase to her ever-growing shopping list.

'It's a lovely flat,' Danniella said as she placed a milky coffee in front of Lorraine and sat down opposite her at the kitchen table. 'I'm so grateful to Aidan.'

'Did he tell you it was his wife's?'

'Yes. He told me she died.' Danniella sipped her drink, part of her wanting to know more. Had Aidan been in the car at the time? Had it been his fault? How was he coping? Did the pain ever go away? But she was equally afraid to explore that avenue in case the conversation steered round to her own past. That was the problem with conversations; they were meant to be two-way.

'She was such a wonderful girl, was Elizabeth,' Lorraine said. 'He met her on one of those internet dating sites and they'd only been seeing each other for a couple of months when she found out she had leukaemia. Once the doctors confirmed it was an aggressive form and terminal, she tried to push Aidan away. She told him to meet someone new, but he was having none of it. He's such a caring lad is my Aidan, always has been. He made it his mission to make her remaining time as happy as it could be. He told you he's a travel writer, yes?'

Danniella nodded.

'He stopped the overseas assignments,' Lorraine continued, 'rented out his flat and hired a campervan. They travelled round the UK seeing all the places she dreamed of seeing. Aidan wanted to take her abroad but Elizabeth said there were too many places and not enough time. She wanted to die knowing she'd explored every part of her home country instead of barely scratching the surface of the world. When the travel became too much for her, they came back here to prepare for the end. Elizabeth had only one regret: that she'd never been able to get married and have children. He couldn't do anything about the kids but, God bless my boy, he arranged a wedding for her. He said he was taking her on one last weekend away and he drove her to Sherrington Hall where all her friends and family were waiting to give her the wedding of her dreams.'

Lorraine produced a handkerchief from the pocket on her cardigan and dabbed her eyes. 'It was such a beautiful day. She only had a couple of weeks left at that point. They were on their way back here the following day when a young lass failed to stop at a crossroads and ploughed straight into the passenger side. They say Elizabeth died instantly and sometimes I wonder if that was kinder than another two weeks of her body failing her.'

'So Aidan was driving?'

'Yes, my dear, but there was nothing he could have done. There was nothing any of us could have done. Of course, at the time, I kept thinking that if only I'd given her one more hug that morning, it wouldn't have happened, but Aidan said we couldn't think like that or it would drive us crazy. If he'd been driving faster or slower, if he'd been longer in the shower, if she'd not had a second cup of tea, if the council had cut the hedge back so the stop sign was more visible... any one of a million things could have brought a different outcome but, at the end of the day, Elizabeth had a terminal illness and she died having had the most incredible day of her life. We all had to focus on that and stop trying to find someone or something to blame.'

Lorraine made it sound so easy: no guilt, no blame, just one of those things. But it wasn't, was it? It was always someone's fault.

'Was Aidan hurt?' Danniella asked.

'A few broken bones but he was very lucky.' Lorraine took a gulp of her coffee. 'Anyway, Elizabeth left the flat to Aidan. He tried to give it to her parents but they insisted he kept it. The friendship and sunshine he brought to their daughter's darkest days, meant everything to them.' She sighed as she smiled ruefully at Danniella. 'You can't choose who you fall in love with, can you?'

Danniella shook her head. 'There'd be fewer broken hearts in the world if we could.'

And then it happened; the inevitable question. 'Is there someone special in your life, my dear?'

Stiffening, Danniella stood up and took their empty mugs to the sink. 'It's a bit complicated,' she said with her back still turned, praying that Lorraine wouldn't ask anything more.

Silence.

Danniella only relaxed and turned around again when she heard Lorraine push back her chair. 'That's life for you. Always complicated. Well, my dear. It's been lovely to see you again, but I'd best be getting back.' Lorraine lifted her bag onto her shoulder. 'I'm sure my Aidan's already said this but do shout if you need anything doing.'

'He has. Thanks again for the flowers and for recommending me to Aidan.'

'An absolute pleasure, my dear. I'm thrilled we've got you all settled although I do miss your pretty face around Sunny Dayz. Don't be a stranger, will you?'

Danniella smiled. 'I'll try not to be.'

* * *

Sitting on the balcony later that afternoon, Danniella reflected on the amazing thing that Aidan had done for Elizabeth. What a great premise for a book. Perhaps she'd feed the idea to one of her romance writers. One name immediately sprung to mind, but that wasn't an option. She shuddered.

Speaking of romance, she needed to think of a better way to respond to questions about her relationship status although when would anyone ask? She had no intention of making new friends. No way could she risk letting anyone in. If she bumped into any of the other residents of Cobalt House, she'd smile and say hello, but make it clear that she wanted to keep herself to herself. Nobody was going to challenge that. From now on, it was Danniella, her flat, her work, and the occasional interaction with Lorraine and Aidan. This was her new life. This was how it needed to be.

She stayed on the balcony, watching the activity on the seafront. There were cyclists, dog walkers, joggers and what looked like some sort of fitness club or bootcamp running along the promenade.

At 7 p.m., she stood up and stretched. She hadn't intended to devote the whole day to settling in, yet somehow the time had escaped her. She'd better put in a few hours of work before bedtime.

As she fired up her laptop at the lounge table, she felt that familiar tension across her shoulders and neck. Would he have emailed again? A couple of weeks had passed since his last contact so it was certainly possible.

Seventeen unread messages filled her screen and she scanned down them, grinding her teeth, letting out a shaky breath of relief when none of them were from him. Right, it was time to focus on work and finish proofreading a thriller for one of her regular clients.

'Another coffee then I'll get cracking,' she muttered to herself, wandering across the hall into the kitchen. She reached for a banana and ate it while waiting for the kettle to boil. As she threw the skin into the bin, it struck her that she'd just eaten something without having to force it down her neck. Eating unconsciously? That was a first.

Coffee made, she returned to her laptop and her pulse raced. He'd emailed.

Where are you? Why are you doing this to us? I've said I'm sorry. Why don't you come home and we can talk about it? You can't keep running. Surely you realise that?
E xx

Danniella's breathing came thick and fast as she dived for the toilet, making it over the bowl just in time. She'd been foolish thinking she might actually be able to put her past behind her and start rebuilding her future. Clearly, he wasn't going to let that happen.

She crept back towards the lounge, then changed her mind and took the stairs. She clambered under the duvet, shivering.

'Leave me alone,' she whispered, curling into a protective ball. 'Leave me alone. Please. I can't do this. Just leave me alone.'

6

KAREN

'Thank you so much for changing the day,' Pippa said when she met Karen outside Blue Savannah for a PT session. 'I felt awful asking if you could do a Friday evening but with me working away, it was either Fridays or skip PT for a month.'

'Honestly, it's no bother.' Karen knew she'd have spent the evening stewing over Bay Runners so Pippa's call had been a welcome diversion.

'As long as I'm not ruining the start to your weekend.'

'Far from it. Come on, then, let's start with a gentle jog round to the beach huts.'

As they jogged, Karen tried to take in most of what Pippa was saying, but her mind was elsewhere. After their row last Thursday, Ryan hadn't returned until the early hours. He'd whispered her name and even prodded her but, unable to face another argument, she'd pretended to be asleep. The following morning, she'd been up early to run bootcamp and, when she returned, Ryan had left for his PT sessions. They'd both been working over the weekend and, in the brief moments they'd been together, the atmosphere had been tense.

On Sunday night, Ryan had wandered into the lounge. 'We need to talk,' he said.

Karen's heart sank. That sounded like the opening lines to an 'it's over' conversation. It couldn't be. Not after thirteen years together. Not after one stupid row and a weekend of sulking.

'Go on, then,' she said, hoping her voice sounded stronger than she felt.

'What happened on Thursday night?' he asked.

'You went out with Steff because you forgot you'd made plans with me.'

Ryan shook his head. 'That's not what I mean. It's your reaction that I don't understand. I've forgotten about plans before and you've laughed about it. You haven't stormed off to bed.'

'I only did that because you'd screwed up so spectacular-ly.' She was aware that she was shouting. What was happening to them? They never rowed. Bay Runners had done this to them. Ever since he'd started that bloody running club, it had been all work and no play and it had stretched them to snapping point.

'How?' Ryan demanded. 'How did I screw up spectacu-larly? What was so special about Thursday night?'

'You *really* don't know, do you?'

'Not a clue. And don't go all cryptic on me again because we need to sort this out.'

Karen stared at him for a moment, then stood up. 'Wait here.' She ran up to their bedroom on the top floor and retrieved a small package from her bedside drawer. Running back down the two flights of stairs, she sat down and handed the wrapped gift to Ryan. 'This is why I was so pissed off with you.'

'Do you want me to open it?' he asked, looking puzzled.

'If you want to know how badly you screwed up, that might be a good idea.'

Ryan ripped open the paper. Prising open the lid on the watch box, his eyes widened. 'What's this for?'

'Take it out and turn it over.'

On the back of the watch was an engraved message: *13 years. Unlucky for some, but not for us. Always yours, Karen xxx*

'Shit,' he said. 'Thirteen years together and five years since I proposed.'

'*Now* he gets it. Give the man a trophy.' She winced at the sarcasm.

He took her hand in his, guilt written all over his face. 'I'm so sorry. I'll make it up to you. I promise.'

Yet, so far, the promise had come to nothing. There'd been no suggestion of going out for a meal or even a drink. There'd been no flowers. There'd been no gifts. In fact, nothing had changed. They were still like two ships passing in the night.

'... and I was wondering what you thought about that.'

Karen glanced across at Pippa. She'd completely zoned out. 'Sorry, Pip. I was deciding whether to keep running or do some core work and I missed that. What did you ask me?'

For the rest of the session, Karen concentrated hard. The focus and attention she gave her clients was what generated repeat business and recommendations, yet here she was switching off when one of her more interesting and committed clients was talking. Sessions with Pippa were usually filled with laughter and fascinating conversation, yet Karen couldn't remember laughing once and that was all thanks to Ryan. He might have lost interest in PT and boot-camps in favour of distance running, but they were still Karen's passion and the reason the three of them had established Bay Fitness. She wasn't going to let him spoil it for her or for her clients.

* * *

'You did really well tonight,' Karen said to Pippa when they'd finished stretching out after the session. 'I can see some big improvements. How do you feel?'

'Amazing. Six months ago, I couldn't have run for a bus and now I can run... I'm not actually sure how far I can run, but the point is I *can* run. I've got strength and stamina and it's all thanks to you.'

Karen smiled. 'It's thanks to you, Pip. You're the one who's put in the hard work. All I did was give you some structure.'

Pippa shook her head. 'And you motivated me, and you made me believe in myself, and you pushed me when I thought I had nothing left and made me achieve that little bit more. It's definitely thanks to you.'

Karen waved her hand. 'Aw, stop it. You'll make me cry, and I *never* cry.' Her smile faltered as she thought about last Thursday and the sobbing mess she'd been after Ryan stormed out. 'I'll see you at the same time next Friday.'

As she set off back to her car, Karen's thoughts returned to the situation at home. Not only was Bay Runners going to remain a regular Friday evening fixture, but Steff and Ryan were also hoping to fit in another couple of evenings, perhaps after bootcamps. Great. Evenings on her own were about to become the norm.

Driving home, her stomach was in knots. When did Ryan

think they were actually going to see each other? Or was that the point? After all these years, had he gone off her? Was he pulling away because he didn't want to be with her anymore? No. That couldn't be it. Until the non-anniversary, he'd still kissed her every day with passion – not just a perfunctory peck on the lips. They still made love regularly, despite the time apart, and it never felt like just-a-quickie-because-perhaps-they-should. So what was it? If it wasn't for Steff being gay, Karen might have been worried that they were having an affair. How did Steff's girlfriend, Mia, feel about all the time Steff and Ryan were spending together? Was she finding it a problem or was she supportive of the new business venture? Perhaps that's all there was to it: Ryan was distracted with the work involved in making a success of something new and he wasn't impressed at Karen's lack of support. She'd try to make a bit more of an effort, but he had to accept that some compromise was needed on his part too or there was no point in being together.

Karen shuddered and turned up the volume on Bay Radio, trying to push the idea of life without Ryan firmly out of her mind. They'd been together for so long. Facing the future without him didn't bear thinking about.

Ryan's car was parked on the drive when she arrived home and, for a brief moment, hope filled her that he'd have told Steff to manage Bay Runners on her own. As if. Steff would have picked him up and Karen would be spending the night in front of the TV eating a microwaved jacket potato and salad for one. Whoopee.

With a heavy heart, she unlocked the door, hung her backpack up on a peg and kicked off her trainers, inhaling the unmistakable aroma of Ryan's special chicken Balti. He must have made it ready for his return. Her stomach growled and she hoped he'd made enough for her. Shower time first, though.

Halfway up the stairs, she stopped. What was that on the carpet? She bent down and picked up what looked like a pale-pink rose petal. A few stairs further up, there was another one and, when she reached the first-floor landing, there was a trail of them, mixed with red ones, leading to the bathroom door.

'Ryan...?'

No answer.

Karen tentatively pushed the bathroom door open and gasped. The blackout blind had been pulled down and there were lit tealights and church candles everywhere. The bath itself was full of bubbles and rose petals, and there was a glass of white wine perched on one corner with a square cream envelope propped up against it. Karen reached for the envelope and ripped it open. Within a circle of tiny red hearts were the words: *I've been a complete and utter idiot! I really am very sorry.* A cartoon bird holding an olive branch made her smile. She opened the card and read Ryan's scrawling script: *The card says it all. Please forgive me. Relax and enjoy the wine. Dinner is ready when you are. No coming down before your bath or you'll spoil my surprise! Happy 13 years and 8 days' anniversary. Looking forward to the next 13. And the 13 after that. And... well, I think you get the picture! I love you always. Ryan xxx*

Karen sighed contentedly and shook her head. The soppy git. She wasn't really into the whole romance thing. She didn't need cards and flowers and couldn't bear cuddly toys. For her, the important things in a relationship were the things you couldn't touch: honesty, respect, trust, compromise and commitment. However, the card was sweet, and the bath was definitely a winner, especially as there'd been a chilly wind down on the seafront.

'Thank you,' she called, stripping off and sinking beneath the bubbles.

* * *

She wasn't sure what to expect after her bath. Would they be eating then going out, or would they be staying in? She pulled on a loose blue summer dress and added a silver pendant, reasoning that she could easily bling it up with a pair of sparkly heels and grab a jacket if they were going into town.

More rose petals now littered the hall downstairs, leading her to the kitchen-diner at the back of the house.

Ryan, dressed in a tux with a frilly pink apron over it, stood by the kitchen table, which was covered in more rose petals. A bottle of champagne rested in an ice bucket.

'You look gorgeous,' he said.

'You're looking pretty hot yourself. I'm liking the tux. Not quite so sure about the apron.' She wandered over to him. 'Very James Bond, and you know I have a thing for Daniel Craig.'

'I know. So does that make you my Bond Girl?'

Karen giggled. 'I'll see what I can do.'

'I'm so sorry,' he said, putting his arms round her. 'Can you forgive me?'

'Yes. But don't do it again. You really hurt me by forgetting.'

'I know. I really am sorry.'

Karen stepped back from his embrace and nodded. They needed to talk about the reality of their demanding schedules but now wasn't the time. He'd apologised and, even more important to her, he'd obviously asked Steff to manage Bay Runners on her own that evening which was a huge sign of his commitment to their relationship. 'Fancy showing me how sorry you are?' She unfastened his apron and lifted it over his head.

'The curry...?'

'Food can wait.' She unbuttoned his shirt and ran the tips of her fingers down his muscular chest. 'This Bond Girl would like to play with James Bond's loaded weapon. What do you say to leaving me shaken, but not stirred?'

Ryan laughed. 'Go on then.' He unzipped his trousers. 'But this is for your eyes only.'

7

ALISON

'Are you sure I can't tempt you with anything else?' The waitress at Waterfront Lodge passed Alison her takeaway cup of tea.

'Just the tea, thanks.' Alison glanced at the glass cabinet loaded with sumptuous cakes and traybakes and her stomach rumbled appreciatively. *Must be strong. Must be strong.*

'The salted caramel shortbread is freshly made and to die for,' the waitress added. 'Perfect mid-afternoon snack. But, if you're sure...?'

Alison's mouth watered. But she had to say no. It had been three weeks since she'd handed over her chocolate to Sarah and made a commitment to take control of her eating. And how long had that commitment lasted? Five hours? Six? What was wrong with her? *Don't do it. You don't need it.* But it looked so delicious.

'Oh, go on then,' she said. 'Two slices please.'

Alison handed over the money and took the paper bag with a smile. It was a Saturday and what person in their right mind dieted on a weekend?

She'd barely stepped away from the counter before she opened the bag and took her first bite. Mmm. Closing her eyes, she savoured the buttery crumbliness of the shortbread, the saltiness of the gooey caramel, and the rich sweetness of the chocolate. Divine.

The warm early June weather had brought out dog walkers galore on the beach below her. Crossing the road and looking back towards North Bay Corner, she could see that the beach in front of the colourful beach huts was alive with kids playing and people soaking up the sun.

Finishing her first piece of shortbread, she took a sip from her tea, then reached into the bag for the second piece. No. Stop. If this was going to be her last weekend of indulgence, she was going to savour the second piece at her favourite spot: Stanley's bench. The giant rusted steel sculpture of a local fisherman from the fifties, Stanley Moffatt, had been donated by an elderly resident as her legacy to the town she loved. Alison found something very comforting about sitting beside the colossal structure, relishing a rare opportunity to feel petite. Plus, it was above the rock pools; her special place.

She sat down on Stanley's bench, sipping her tea, devouring the second shortbread, and absorbing herself in the buzz around her. Locals brushed shoulders with day-trippers and holidaymakers. There were families, groups of giggling teenagers, couples taking romantic strolls, and dog walkers. Mobility scooters travelled alongside cyclists, and joggers weaved in and out of the crowds. She really was fortunate to live in such a beautiful place that so many people wanted to visit and, looking at the North Sea twinkling in the sun, who could blame them?

She slipped off her jacket and closed her eyes as the sun kissed her bare arms and face. It was the most relaxed she'd felt in weeks. Dave had barely spoken to her since the plate-smashing incident but that was fine because Alison had nothing to say to him. She'd replayed that scene so many times. Although she wanted to believe it was an accident, that one statement – 'I'll show you childish' – suggested a deliberate act. The lack of remorse had floored her and that parting shot about her in a bikini? Why had he felt the need to hurt her again? That night, she'd come so close to packing a bag and leaving, but where would she go? With no family and no close friends, even Dave in a foul mood was better than being alone.

Frantic barking interrupted her thoughts and drew her gaze to the left. A couple of dogs were chasing each other in a circle, ignoring the shouts of their owners who were attempting to untangle their leads. A tall, slim woman running towards them tried to avoid the chaos but it seemed that, wherever she moved, the dogs moved too, their leads stretching across her path.

Alison leapt off the bench as the woman screamed and tumbled full-length onto the pavement. One of the dog walkers rushed off and the other stood by, looking helpless.

Alison crouched down beside the woman. 'Oh my God! Are you all right?'

'A bit winded.'

'Take it slowly,' Alison said. 'Let me help you.'

The other dog walker disappeared too. What was wrong with people? She helped the jogger to her feet and over to the bench, wincing at the blood trickling down both the woman's legs.

'I'm Alison. What's your name?'

'Danni... Er, Danniella.'

'Did you hit your head?'

Danniella put a shaking hand up to her forehead and frowned. 'I don't think so.'

Removing a packet of tissues from her bag, she nodded towards Danniella's bloody knees. 'Do you mind?'

Danniella looked down and released what sounded like a sob mixed with a groan. 'I'm not good with blood.'

'It probably looks worse than it is.' Alison mopped at some of the dribbles. 'But we do need to get you cleaned up. You've got some grit in there. If you wait here, I can get a bottle of water from the café.'

Danniella shook her head. 'Don't worry about it. I think I'll just head home. Thanks for your help, though. Alison, was it?'

'Yes.' She frowned. 'Is home close?'

Danniella nodded, but didn't share any further information.

'You've scraped your arms too. I can help you home and clean you up. I'm a first-aider at work so I'm used to it and I promise to be gentle.'

Danniella bit her bottom lip and stared at Alison, as though weighing her up.

'I promise I'm not a mad psychopath,' Alison said, 'and I won't steal all your stuff as soon as I know where your spare key's hidden.'

Danniella smiled, her shoulders relaxing. 'Don't you have anywhere that you need to be?'

Alison shrugged. 'I'd love to say that I have an exciting life full of plans for a sunny Saturday afternoon but, sadly, I don't. Except first-aid duties, of course.'

'Okay. Yes please,' Danniella said.

Alison stood up and helped Danniella to her feet. 'Where are we going?'

Danniella pointed to a row of flats on the cliff above them. 'Not far. It's the blue one.'

A hill. It had to be up a hill, didn't it? On a hot day too. 'Great. Let's do it. But I think we should take it really slowly because of your knees.'

Danniella nodded. 'I don't think I could take it quickly even if I wanted to.'

8

DANNIELLA

Danniella's stomach was in knots as she crossed the road and slowly limped up the zigzagging cliff path with Alison by her side. *Calm down. Stop panicking.* It had been an accident and Alison had simply been the closest person. It was good that there were still people around who were prepared to help strangers, especially as the dog walkers who'd caused the accident had fled the scene. She needed to focus on that instead of being instantly suspicious that Alison would demand to know her life story.

She winced as she stretched her right knee too far.

'Painful?' Alison asked, puffing beside her.

'Agony. I don't think I've fallen over like that since I was a little kid.'

'I went splat a couple of months ago in the middle of the hotel lobby where I work. Tripped over my own feet and went arse over tit.' Alison held her hands to her cheeks. 'I still go red thinking about it.'

Aware of Alison's increasingly laboured breathing beside

her, Danniella slowed her pace. 'Do you mind if we take it a bit slower? It hurts.'

'We can go as slowly as you like.'

Ten minutes later, Danniella let them into her flat. They'd chatted about their jobs on their way. When Danniella shared that she was a proofreader and copyeditor, Alison said that she was a prolific reader. It transpired that she'd read books by most of Danniella's clients, giving them plenty to talk about, much to Danniella's relief. Books, like conversations about work, she could cope with. Good subject. Safe subject.

Sitting at the kitchen table a few minutes later, she winced and looked towards the window, biting her lip, while Alison gently cleaned her wounds.

Rummaging in her enormous bag, Alison pulled out a first-aid kit. 'It drives my other half mad that I carry so much stuff, but you never know when it'll come in useful.' She squirted some antiseptic spray. 'All done. The spray just needs a minute to dry.'

'Thank you. Would you like—?' The sound of the buzzer ringing stopped Danniella mid-sentence, eyes wide, pulse racing.

'Are you expecting anyone?' Alison asked.

She shook her head.

'Shall I check who it is?'

'Please. You need to hold the button to speak.'

'Hello?' Alison said into the intercom.

'Hi, it's me. Mum's been on a baking frenzy again. Scones this time. Don't feel you have to.'

Danniella smiled. Lorraine seemed to have made it her mission to feed her, regularly bringing round home-baked goodies. She'd been wary of Lorraine's visits at first but she had a gift for making small-talk, never asking Danniella about her past, and she no longer dreaded her calling.

'It's my landlord,' she called to Alison. 'You can let him in.'

'Come up,' Alison said. 'I'll leave the door open.'

Moments later, there was a knock and Aidan called out, 'Hello?'

'In the kitchen,' Danniella called back.

Aidan appeared holding a bag for life. 'Sorry for disturbing your weekend. I'll just leave...' His eyes widened. 'Alison?'

'Oh my God! Aidan?' They hugged each other briefly. 'Wow! It's been...'

'Nine years. How are you?'

Danniella looked from Aidan to Alison and back again. Sparkling eyes. Shy smiles. If she was a betting woman, she'd have put money on a story of love lost. Perhaps first love.

'I'm good, thanks,' Alison said, her hand clasped across her mouth, a look of astonishment on her face. 'You?'

'Really good. I can't believe it. The last time I—' Aidan's phone rang and he grimaced. 'Sorry. I'm running really late and I've got to go. It was great to see you, Ali. Hopefully see you again if you're a friend of Danniella's.'

Alison nodded. 'Hopefully.'

'Enjoy the scones. Bye.'

'Would you like a drink?' Danniella asked after Aiden closed the flat door. She wanted to ask about Aidan, but that would inevitably lead to questions in return. Alison seemed chatty. Maybe she'd volunteer the information.

'Some water would be great, thanks,' Alison said. 'But let me do it.'

Danniella pointed out where the glasses lived. 'I could do

with putting my feet up,' she said. 'Do you want to come through to the lounge?'

After easing her legs up onto the sofa, Danniella twisted them from left to right so she could see the extent of the damage. Both knees were covered in grazes, with several more down her right leg.

'I hope I'll be okay to exercise again by Tuesday,' she said. 'I'm supposed to be starting bootcamp.'

'Bootcamp?' Alison shrugged. 'I'm going to show my ignorance now...'

'Instead of going to the gym where you'd probably exercise on your own, you work out as a group and you do it outside. There's one that runs on the seafront.' Danniella nodded towards the window. 'I've been watching it and was tempted but the group was a bit big for my liking. I spoke to the owner, Karen, and she's starting a new mid-morning one from Tuesday which she reckons will be low numbers so, injuries permitting, I start then.'

Alison stood up and wandered towards the window. 'Is everyone who goes to these bootcamp thingies really fit?'

'Mixed ability from what I've seen. Karen says a competitor runs one aimed at the super fit. I've seen them running up the cliff holding weighted backpacks above their heads.'

Alison turned from the window, mouth open. 'Seriously? People do that for fun? That sounds like some sort of mediaeval torture.'

Danniella laughed. 'It probably is but each to their own. Karen says she'll push people if she thinks they're not pushing themselves, but she welcomes all levels.'

Alison returned to the armchair and gulped down the last

of her water. 'She wouldn't be able to do anything with someone like me, though, would she?'

'What do you mean, someone like you?'

'Twice my ideal body weight, not exercised since college, can barely make it up a flight of stairs without oxygen, likely to create craters on the beach.'

Although Alison laughed as she spoke, Danniella didn't miss the wobble in her voice and the glint of tears in her eyes. 'Don't be so hard on yourself. Are you interested? I'm not very confident around new people so it wouldn't be so nerve-wracking if there's a friendly face there.'

Alison sighed. 'I need to do something.' She ran her fingers through her dark, curly hair. 'I'm not sure, though. A bootcamp?'

'What's stopping you?'

'I don't own a pair of trainers, for a start.'

'Then buy a pair.'

'And I don't have a sports bra.'

Danniella raised an eyebrow and Alison laughed again. 'I know, I know, I can buy one. But I can't run. I can barely walk at pace.'

'Everyone has to start somewhere,' Danniella said. 'When you started work, did you know how to do your job?'

'No, but—'

'But you learned how to do it. Someone showed you. You might have taken a while to learn, a step at a time, until one day you realised you could do it easily. This is no different. Honestly, it isn't.'

'Yeah, but I didn't have to wear lycra and a sports bra for work.'

'And you don't have to wear lycra and a sports... actually,

you probably do need the sports bra. But wear what's comfortable. Go for leggings and a baggy T-shirt.'

'A polar bear onesie?' Alison suggested. 'That's comfortable.'

'I'd love to see that, but it might be a little hot and sweaty.' She smiled. 'What do you think? Will you hold my hand on Tuesday?'

Alison paused for a moment. 'I don't start work till two so I'm free that morning. I could get some trainers tomorrow. I... No. I can't do it. This body is *not* built for running.'

'Then don't run. Focus on the other stuff. Tell you what, why don't I give you Karen's number so you can talk to her? I'm sure she has a plan for those who are new to exercise.'

'I'm not sure...' Alison held her head in her hands and released a little squeal. 'Okay. You're on. But if I'm going to do this, I need to do it now or I'll have chickened out before I get down the first flight of stairs.'

'Are you sure? I don't want to push you into something you don't want to do.' She knew exactly how it felt to be in Alison's situation, out of breath and uncomfortable, experiencing a daily battle with willpower. She also knew that finding the strength, determination and courage to do something about it was like panning for gold; what you were looking for was in there somewhere, but it was almost impossible to find amongst the dirt. She'd never actually won her battle; the move from food as a friend to food as her enemy had been a fallout from what had happened.

Alison smiled weakly. 'It's only a phone call. I can always say no.'

Danniella handed over her phone. 'Use this. Karen's number's loaded in.'

When the call connected and it was clear that Karen was

available for a chat, Danniella picked up the empty glasses and hobbled into the kitchen, smiling at the thought of wearing onesies at a bootcamp. She hoped Alison would sign up for bootcamp. There was something warm and engaging about her and it had felt so easy and natural chatting with her just now; something she hadn't done in so long. She could imagine them becoming good friends. Rinsing the glasses, butterflies danced in her stomach. Friends? Was she doing the right thing? Friends talked. Friends opened up. Friends didn't keep dark secrets locked away.

Deep in thought as she stared out the window towards Hearnshaw Park, she jumped when Alison spoke.

'It's done. I'm signed up. Spookily enough, I know Karen. I never made the connection.'

Danniella's pulse started racing. She tried to keep her voice light and breezy. 'You know Karen and you know Aidan? Is Whitsborough Bay smaller than I realised?'

'Sometimes it feels like it, but it's pure coincidence really. Aidan was a friend at college. He was...' She paused and smiled, a wistful expression on her face. 'He was the one that got away, I suppose. As for Karen, I live next door to her mum and little sister. There's an eighteen-year gap between Karen and Eden so Karen had already left home before I moved in. I only really know her to say hello to, but she seems lovely.'

Feeling calm again, Danniella wiped her hands on a tea-towel and took her phone back from Alison. 'Excited?'

'Hmm. That's probably not the word I'd choose.' Alison sighed and shook her head. 'I have to do something, though, because I can't go on like this. You saw me puffing and panting up that hill. I know you slowed down because of me and not because you were in pain.'

'I *was* in pain. I...' Danniella shook her head. 'Okay,

you've got me. I could tell you were struggling and I wanted to help.'

Tears filled Alison's eyes again. 'A few weeks ago, I got upset about my weight when a little girl thought I was pregnant. Someone offered to help me get my act together. I said yes, then ate an enormous bag of doughnuts and talked myself out of it. I've been offered help again and, this time, I'm going to accept it because I have to. I can't...' Alison's voice broke and so did her tears.

'Aw, don't cry.' Danniella reached out and hugged her new friend, swallowing hard on the lump in her throat. How amazing did it feel to hold someone again after all this time? 'We'll do this together. It'll be a new start for both of us.' She hoped so because she so desperately needed that new start.

9

KAREN

'Yes! I've got another punter for my mid-morning bootcamp,' Karen cried, dashing into the kitchen-diner after Alison's phone call. Ryan was at the table, scowling at something on his laptop, paperwork strewn round him. She flung her arms around him and kissed his neck.

'How many's that?' he asked, not reacting to her kiss. 'Two?'

She gave him a playful shove. 'Six.'

'Is it really worth it for six people?'

Bristling, Karen released her hold and stepped away. Taking an apple from the fruit bowl, she bit into it. 'Did you really just ask me that? That's like saying one-to-one PT isn't worth it.'

He didn't even look up from his laptop. 'Don't be daft. Of course it is. But we get paid a decent amount for it being one-to-one. You've got six people on this mid-morning bootcamp paying the same amount each as the fifteen to twenty clients on the morning and evening ones. The return is significantly less.'

'Yes, I know that, Mr Mathematical Genius.' Karen sat down opposite him and took another bite from her apple. 'But six people for an hour's bootcamp brings in more money than an hour's individual PT and, if you cast your mind back, we only had a handful of clients for the first few bootcamps but you didn't seem to think they were a stupid idea. It takes a while to grow these things.'

'It's pointless. There's no way you'll grow to those numbers on a mid-morning session.' Still not looking up, Ryan flicked through some paperwork, releasing an exasperated sigh.

Karen shook her head. 'I'm not expecting to. I want it to remain small and friendly. I'm hoping that...' Why was she even bothering? Ryan wasn't listening and, even if he had been, he wasn't going to change his mind about it. She was convinced there was a gap in the market for people who worked from home, those who had kids in part-time nursery or school, and those who perhaps felt intimidated by a large group. Danniella had joined for two of those reasons. Alison had voiced concerns about her lack of fitness and her weight, but said the idea of working out in a small group wasn't quite as terrifying as a large one. Why couldn't Ryan understand that?

He released another exasperated sigh and banged his fist on the table.

'Anything I can help with?' Karen asked.

'A bit of peace and quiet would be nice,' he snapped.

Fine. You struggle on your own, stupid arse. Did he need to be so rude? Her fist tightened around the apple. How tempting it was to hurl it at him. She stood up. 'I need to head out for PT with Becky and Jayne in five anyway, so peace and quiet will be restored.'

'Good.'

Not wanting to start another argument, her voice softened. 'I don't suppose you fancy Blue Savannah for drinks tonight? We haven't been there in ages.'

Ryan's head snapped up. 'Did we have plans?'

'No, but I thought it might be nice to go out for a drink and spend some quality time together.' Karen sighed. 'But you've already made plans with Steff, haven't you?'

'We need to talk about the Great North Run.'

There was always something, wasn't there? 'And you couldn't have chatted about this after, say, Thursday's bootcamp?' Karen stamped on the bin pedal and tossed her half-eaten apple into it – better there than at Ryan's head.

'Steff has karate on a Thursday night,' he said in an annoying sing-song voice. 'You *know* that.'

Karen's phone sounded with a reminder alarm. Time to go, which was just as well, because there'd definitely be an argument if she stuck around. 'I guess I'll see you when I see you, then.' She didn't wait for a response.

* * *

'I knew something was up,' Jayne said as the three of them sat on the promenade wall after an hour's PT session, legs dangling over the edge, a foot above the sand. 'I said so, didn't I, Bex?'

Becky nodded. 'Not that we've been gossiping about you, of course. We just had a sense that you weren't yourself. Wondered if you wanted to talk.'

'Looks like I did,' Karen said. 'Thanks for letting me offload.'

They sat in silence for a few moments, the gentle breeze from the sea cooling their faces.

'You don't think...?' Becky began. 'No. Forget I said it.'

Karen smiled. 'You're wondering if Ryan and Steff are seeing each other? No. They're just good friends. Besides, Steff's gay.'

'Is she?' Jayne frowned. 'She's always flirty with the men at bootcamp.'

'It's just her way. She'd be flirty with the women too if she was single, but she's not. She lives with a lass called Mia. I haven't met her but I've seen photos and she's stunning. She's like a brunette version of Steff.'

'You haven't met Steff's girlfriend?' Becky said. 'I thought you and Steff were great mates.'

Karen sighed. 'Not really. She's always been Ryan's friend rather than mine. There was some awkwardness at college when Ryan and I got together. We got past it but there's always been this undercurrent.'

'I'd never have guessed,' Jayne said. 'Shows what a professional you are.'

Karen smiled gratefully. 'We don't meet up outside of work but we're fine when it comes to the business. Other than the Bay Runners thing, we've always been on the same page.'

'I'm sure it'll settle down soon,' Becky said. 'It sounds like this running club is still a novelty. I bet you put loads of time into planning bootcamps when you first set them up.'

'About six months,' Karen admitted.

'There you go, then,' Jayne said. 'Once they've worked out a routine for the club, Ryan will be back to giving you the attention you deserve.'

'And you'll set the date,' Becky added. 'We expect invites to the wedding.'

Karen laughed. 'Thanks, you two. I'm sure you had better things to do this evening than listen to me whinging.'

Becky shook her head. 'The only place we needed to be was here with you. That's what friends are for.'

* * *

As she drove home, Karen smiled to herself. How amazing were Jayne and Becky? It was easy to think of them, and others, as clients but they were so much more than that. These men and women who she trained, pushed, motivated and sweated buckets alongside had become like her family – her fitness family – and, no matter how dismissive Ryan was about it, she was excited about growing a new branch of her family with the mid-morning bootcamp.

Jayne and Becky were right, too. New initiatives took planning and organising and perhaps she'd been unfair in forgetting that Bay Runners needed that time if it was going to be successful. She'd apologise to Ryan and also to Steff next time she ran a bootcamp with her because, if she was honest, she'd been snippy with her recently, which hadn't been fair.

Having the house to herself that evening was going to be no bad thing. She could have a glass of wine and run over the plans for the mid-morning bootcamp in peace. She'd make a success of it. She was determined to prove to Ryan that it was a good idea.

10

ALISON

When Alison arrived home from Danniella's, she started preparing a chilli for dinner. What an unexpected afternoon! She'd made a friend and she'd signed up to bootcamp. How would Dave react to that? Would he be proud of her? She sighed. No, he'd probably laugh.

And what about seeing Aidan again after all these years? He hadn't changed at all. A few more laughter lines around his eyes and creases on his forehead perhaps, but still gorgeous.

While most of her classmates had continued their education at the local sixth-form college, Alison had taken a BTEC in Travel and Tourism at Whitsborough Bay TEC. Fed up of being a loner at school, she'd hoped to put the past behind her and finally make some new friends – ones who didn't know what had happened. Waiting in the corridor before her very first class, though, everyone seemed to know each other and Alison felt sick with nerves as she pressed herself against the wall, fighting the urge to flee.

A tutor appeared and announced that the seat they chose

would be theirs for the next two years so they should pick carefully. Alison sat down and watched with a sinking heart as the other seats filled and the one beside hers remained empty. And then it happened. The most attractive boy she'd ever seen stood over her and smiled. 'I'm hoping that seat's got my name on it,' he said.

'What's your name?' she asked, butterflies stirring in her stomach.

'Aidan.'

She grabbed her pen, scribbled his name on her pad, ripped the page off and placed it on the seat beside her. 'Wow! Look at that. Destiny.'

Aidan laughed. 'Definitely destiny. Looks like I'm all yours for the next two years.'

The butterflies in Alison's stomach danced. All hers. She could live with that.

Only he never was hers. They spent every moment at college together, becoming steadily closer, but Aidan had a girlfriend who went to the sixth form. When they split up over the October half-term break in the first year, Alison wondered if she stood a chance, but nothing ever happened. By the time she met Dave in the May, she'd resigned herself to only ever being Aidan's friend. If he'd seen her as anything more, he'd have made his move. Over the past few years, though, she'd occasionally wondered what if...?

* * *

'Are you still playing rugby tomorrow?' Alison asked Dave over their evening meal.

He gave her a withering look as he scooped up a forkful of chilli and rice. 'You know I am.'

She speared a kidney bean with her fork and pushed a few grains of rice round the edge of her plate with it. 'Do you think you'll always play rugby?'

'Oh yeah. I'm sure I'll still be playing in my seventies cos it's such a gentle game,' he said, his voice dripping with sarcasm. 'Perfect for old gits.'

'I didn't mean that,' Alison protested. 'It's just that you loved rugby at school and college and you still play now, but I loved hockey just as much and I don't play it anymore and—'

'That's because you're too fat.'

'Dave!' She could have laughed it off if he'd said it jokingly, but his tone was cruel, just like when he'd talked about her in shorts or a bikini. If he was trying to hurt her, he was certainly succeeding.

'What?' He shoved another forkful of food into his mouth and showered bits of rice onto the table as he spoke. 'You want me to lie and say that you're curvy or cuddly instead? You were when we met but you're not now. You're a right chubba now.' He took a swig of his lager. 'You're not thinking of joining a hockey club again, are you? Jesus, Ali, they'd need an ambulance on standby. Imagine if you fell on one of the lasses in a bad tackle. You'd crush them. Unless you bounced.' He laughed loudly. 'Oh, what an image that is.'

'It's not funny.'

'It is. You bouncing around the hockey pitch? Boing, boing.'

She stared at him, open-mouthed.

'Come on, Ali. What's wrong with you? You used to have a sense of humour.'

'And so did you.' Alison pushed her barely-touched plate of chilli aside and stood up. 'I'm going next door. I'm babysitting for Eden.'

'You've hardly touched your tea.'

'I wouldn't worry about that,' she snapped. 'After all, a chubba like me has plenty of fat reserves to keep me going.' She stormed out of the kitchen, grabbed her bag from the hall, and slammed the front door.

Standing on the doorstep, she shook with rage. How could he possibly think he was being funny? She used to laugh at comments about her weight. She'd giggle senselessly and tell him he was hilarious. She'd even made jokes herself. It wasn't funny anymore, though, and he'd definitely crossed a line this evening. Had he crossed it long ago and she'd never realised? Had her absolute devotion and adoration of him helped create the man he'd become? A man who thought fat-shaming was funny? A man who, as Chelsea had quite rightly pointed out, didn't treat her well?

* * *

'I couldn't remember whether you were going out at seven or half past,' Alison said when Rachel answered the door at ten to seven, though she knew full well it was the latter.

Rachel smiled. 'Half past but feel free to make yourself at home while I finish getting ready.' She opened the lounge door then called up the stairs, 'Eden! Alison's here.'

Alison heard a door open and footsteps on the stairs. Eden had recently turned twelve and was nearly as tall as Alison, but she wasn't averse to a bear hug. 'Our Karen says you're starting her new bootcamp,' Eden said, hurling herself at Alison.

'Yeah, but I'm not sure it was a good idea.'

Eden let go and pulled Alison over to the sofa. 'Why not?'

Biting her lip, Alison hesitated. She'd always been careful

not to put herself down in front of Eden, not wanting her to be affected by hang-ups over body image at such an impressionable age. 'I'm not very fit,' she said eventually. 'I couldn't even run for a bus.'

'Isn't that, like, the point of bootcamp? To get you fit and help you run?'

Alison shrugged. 'Maybe.'

'Totes! I bet you a new lipstick that, in two months' time, my sister will have you running at least half a mile. Maybe even a mile.' Eden held out her fist towards Alison who laughed and bumped it with her own. A twelve-year-old girl supported and believed in her. Would Dave? Highly unlikely, considering his cruel comments earlier.

* * *

As soon as Eden had settled in bed, Alison found herself replaying the ugly scene with Dave and the doubts set in. Damn him! She reached for her phone. She'd felt guilty that she hadn't taken Sarah up on her offer of support but there was no time like the present. Right now, she needed it.

✉ To Sarah

Sorry I haven't been in touch since the chocolate amnesty. My willpower didn't make it to the end of that day. Thought you might like to know that I've signed up to a boot-camp starting on Tuesday. Not sure what possessed me and panicking I can't do it but I've paid my money so bring it on! Xx

Sarah rang moments later.

'Oh my God! Bootcamp? I am *so* excited for you. Tell me more.'

So Alison did and, as she chatted, she realised that she was excited too. This was new. It was different. It *was* exciting.

'If I can lose weight, so can you,' Sarah said. 'Repeat after me, "I can do it!"'

'I can do it.'

'And now say it as though you actually believe it.'

'I can do it!'

'Again. Louder.'

'I CAN DO IT!'

Sarah laughed. 'Yes, you can. And don't let anyone tell you otherwise.'

* * *

When Rachel returned, they chatted over coffee and she was just as supportive as Eden and Sarah had been. Alison left the house on a high but, as soon as she stepped onto her own doorstep, she felt the positive energy slipping away and running down the street. He was going to ruin it. He'd have a field day talking about her starting a tsunami by running along the beach or something equally nasty. She hated the thought of keeping secrets but she wasn't going to tell him about bootcamp. Why give him the ammunition? He'd find out eventually but, for now, she'd keep it quiet.

Taking a deep breath, she unlocked the front door and tiptoed up the stairs. Dave was in bed and his breathing was deep and regular. Asleep. Phew!

Getting ready for bed as quietly as she could, Alison crept under the duvet, taking care not to knock into him.

'You went to Rachel's half an hour early,' he said.

Damn! Awake. 'How do you know that?'

'It was on the calendar.'

'Oh.' Since when had Dave ever paid any attention to what was written on the kitchen calendar?

Silence. Alison could feel him staring at her but she refused to turn over.

'Why did you go early?' he asked.

'I got my times mixed up.'

'You're usually good with stuff like that.'

'Yeah, well, I can't be perfect all the time.'

Silence.

'Why did you *really* go?' Dave asked, his tone gentle. 'Was it because of what I said?'

Alison lay in the darkness, pulling the duvet up to her chin.

'It was, wasn't it?'

Silence.

'Ali?'

She turned over to face him, her eyes adjusting to the gloom. 'If you must know, yes. I know I'm fat and I hate myself enough for that without you calling me names.' She went to turn over again but he placed his arm on hers, stopping her.

'I had a shite day,' he said. 'You got the brunt of it.'

She sighed. 'I always do, Dave.'

'I know. I shouldn't have said those things about your weight.'

Her eyes clouded with tears. 'No, you shouldn't. You were nasty to me. *Really* nasty.'

'I'm sorry.' He reached out and gently stroked her cheek. 'I don't know why I said it. I didn't mean it. You're still my favourite girl.'

Butterflies fluttered in her stomach. Still his favourite girl? Raised in a dysfunctional family full of animosity, Dave had always struggled to voice his emotions. Calling her his 'favourite girl' was his way of saying 'I love you'. Yet he hadn't said it for months. Possibly years.

'Even though I'm a chubba?' she whispered.

'You're beautiful.'

He drew her face closer to his and gently kissed her. Alison's heart started to race and she felt her whole body react to his tender touch.

'Dave, I...'

'Shh,' he whispered, moving in for another kiss. He stroked his hand down her arm, his palm grazing her breast.

A soft moan escaped from Alison's lips. This was the Dave she remembered; the tender, loving Dave from the early days and that holiday. Every time he lashed out at her after a bad day at work, or simply because he was in a bad mood – which was nearly all the time – she thought about that man who she'd fallen in love with when she was only seventeen, the man who'd been there for her at a time when she'd so desperately needed someone. Occasionally she got glimpses of him and those rare moments were what kept her going.

As he pushed her nightshirt up over her breasts so that he could gently kiss and caress her, she pushed aside his cruel words. As his kisses trailed down to her stomach, she pushed aside his laughter. And as his tongue slipped between her legs, sending jolts of electricity through her, she focused only on the good times. Long ago. This rare glimpse of the man she adored wouldn't last long so she needed to make the most of it and completely surrender to him.

But as Alison lay awake in the early hours, listening to Dave's gentle breathing, a thought popped into her head that simply wouldn't go away: what did he want from her? He'd gone from cruel to attentive in the space of a few hours; something didn't add up.

Even more disturbing, why was she thinking that way?

11

KAREN

Karen was dozing on the sofa when she heard Ryan's key turn in the lock. Her head felt fuzzy from the bottle of wine she'd downed. So much for one glass. What time was it? It had to be really late because she remembered still drinking after midnight. Squinting towards the clock, she tried to focus her tired eyes. 2.37 a.m. What the hell had Ryan and Steff been doing for that long?

She ran her hands through her hair and looked down at the rumpled midnight-blue satin and Chantilly lace slip that she'd bought for their anniversary.

Curled into a ball on the sofa, she listened to him trying to walk up the stairs, tripping up and clattering against the wall. So that was what they'd been doing: drinking. She looked down at the empty bottle and glass on the floor and sighed. Why couldn't he have come home to a few drinks with her instead?

Shivering in the coolness of the early hours, she pulled a throw off the back of the sofa and snuggled under it. When Ryan discovered she wasn't in bed and came looking for her, at least he wouldn't be able to see the stupid satin slip. The humiliation of lying seductively on the sofa, bathed in candlelight, waiting for him to come home and participate in some steamy make-up sex, could remain hidden under a couple of square metres of chenille. Actually, best blow out the candles too, removing all evidence of her failed seduction attempt.

Back on the sofa, the throw pulled up to her chin, she listened to Ryan's footsteps on the second flight of stairs and waited for him to come downstairs to find her. Her eyes were heavy and she fought to keep them open. Perhaps if she closed them and concentrated on listening out for the door opening…

* * *

'Karen,' said a voice. 'Karen!'

She rolled over and squinted at the figure towering over her. 'Ryan?' She opened her eyes a bit further then blinked as he moved aside and she was blinded by the sunlight streaming through the lounge window. 'It's morning?'

'It's nearly ten.'

'Ten?' She rubbed her eyes and stretched her back out. A night on the sofa certainly wasn't what she'd planned.

'Why are you sleeping down here?' Ryan asked, crouching on the floor beside her.

'I was waiting for you. I wanted to say sorry for being funny about the amount of time you've spent with Steff.'

Ryan shook his head. 'It's my fault. I *have* spent too much time with her. We had a lot to do and it was important stuff, but you're more important.' He gently stroked her cheek and tucked a strand of hair behind her ear. 'I'm sorry.'

Karen smiled weakly. 'I should have been more supportive about Bay Runners. If it's going to make Bay Fitness even more successful, I should be encouraging it instead of fighting it.'

'Right back at you about the mid-morning bootcamp. It's good that you're trying to attract a new audience.'

Karen smiled properly. 'What a pair we are, eh?'

As she sat up, the throw slid down to her waist, revealing the slip.

Ryan's eyes widened. 'What's that you're wearing?'

She looked down, her cheeks burning. 'Pathetic and wasted attempt at an apology through seduction.'

He stood up. 'It's a nice colour.'

A nice colour? *Nice*? Was that all he had to say?

'Cup of tea?' he asked, heading for the door.

'Er, yes please.'

Karen slumped back against the sofa. What just happened? If there was anything guaranteed to send Ryan wild with desire, it was satin and lace. Had he really walked away from her when she was wearing it?

12

ALISON

✉ From Karen

Really excited to see you for your first
bootcamp this morning. This is the first
ever session in the mid-morning slot so
we're all newbies together. I've been
running bootcamps for over 4 years now. My
philosophy is fitness through fun and
friendship. Don't worry about what size you
are or what your fitness level might or
might not be. You've taken the first step by
signing up and I'll help you with the other
steps — fast, slow and sometimes backwards.
I'm sorry I couldn't convince the sun to
play today but don't let the drizzle put
you off

Looking in the full-length mirror, Alison felt sick. She pulled the navy T-shirt away from where it clung to her lumps and bumps and tried to suck her stomach in but it had little impact.

'Bootcamp? What the hell was I thinking?' She shook her head at her reflection then slammed the wardrobe door closed. Enough.

Perching on the end of her bed, she pulled on her new sports socks and trainers. When she'd finished fastening the laces, she took a moment to get her breath back.

'I used to be fit,' she muttered. 'Now I can't even bend over to fasten my bloody laces without getting breathless so there's no way I'm going to be able to run unless they want to cart me off in an ambulance.' She stamped her feet. 'Oh my God! I can't do this.'

⊠ From Danniella
Are you as nervous as me? So glad you're coming or I might have bottled it!

⊠ To Danniella
That makes two of us. About both points. I feel sick! I'm definitely coming but I'm not sure I can do it

⊠ From Danniella
You can and you will. I'll be right next to you cheering you on xx

Alison nodded then stood up tall. Danniella was right. Karen, Sarah and Eden were right. It was going to hurt but she could do this.

On the first stair, she muttered, 'I can.' On the second, she said, 'I will.' With each step down, her voice grew louder until she stood in the hall and shouted, 'I can and I will!'

13

KAREN

Karen switched off the car wipers with a tut. Grey skies, drizzle, and the threat of heavier rain was not the ideal start but hopefully nobody would be put off at the first hurdle.

She grabbed the kit she needed out of her boot, zipped her neon pink Bay Fitness branded waterproof up to her chin, and jogged down to North Bay beach. There were a few dog walkers, runners and cyclists on the promenade but the beach was pretty much deserted.

She planted a neon orange flag in the sand then distributed some plastic marker discs across the beach to create workout stations. Ready. All she needed now was bootcampers. She took a few deep breaths to calm the butterflies that always paid a brief visit when she was meeting new clients.

By 9.50 a.m., nerves settled, she had a full complement of six and she could almost smell the fear.

'Good morning, bootcampers,' she said, stepping back so that she could see everyone. 'A massive welcome to Bay Bootcamps. It's great to meet you in person and I'm glad the weather hasn't put you off. I'm Karen Greene, one of three owners of Bay Fitness, which encompasses Bay Bootcamps, Bay Runners, and personal training or PT. I see a few nervous faces. Hands up if you're nervous.' Karen raised her hand and smiled as everyone followed suit. 'It's completely understandable when you haven't done anything like this before. Despite the nerves, who's a little bit excited, even if only a tiny, weeny bit?'

Karen thrust her hand in the air again and laughed as one of the bootcampers copied but most of the others did a tentative half-raise accompanied by a grimace. 'My aim for today is to take away the nerves and start building excitement. Before I explain what we'll be doing, I want to emphasise something. You're all starting from very different places and I want you to remember that you and your goals are unique. This means you'll all go on very different journeys. Please don't compare your progress, or what you may feel is a lack of it, to that of anyone else in the group. The only person you should be comparing yourself to is the person you were before you signed up. Simply by being here, you're already a winner.'

Karen smiled at the group again. 'Let's have some introductions. If you can give your name and tell me if you know anyone here, that would be great.'

She moved around the group: a PT client of hers called Bryan, a mother-and-daughter team called Dawn and Hailey, and a woman in her late-twenties called Melanie who jokingly said that anyone who shortened her name to Mel would have to eat sand.

'Melanie it is, then,' Karen said, smiling. 'I get it. The only person allowed to call me Kaz is my fiancé. Anyone else has to drop and give me twenty so be warned, you lot. Moving on...'

'Hi. I'm Danniella and I'm going to continue with the name preferences thing. I know that Danniella is a mouthful but I'd rather nobody calls me Danni or Dan. Sorry.'

Karen smiled at Danniella who looked like she wished the beach would turn to quicksand and swallow her up. 'Thank you, Danniella. And do you know anyone?'

'Alison, but we only met on Saturday. I fell over on the seafront and she patched me up.' She looked at the woman next to her and smiled warmly.

'Hi, I'm Alison. I'll answer to that or Ali, although I've been known to respond to Fatty, Jabba, Porky, Chubba...' She said it with laugher but Karen had seen the same self-deprecating approach in so many of her previous clients and wasn't fooled by the bravado.

'I think we'll stick to Alison or Ali, eh? Welcome. Let's get started, then.'

Karen ran through the structure, demonstrated each exercise, then asked the group to copy. After a warm-up, the session started. She walked amongst the group, giving tips on technique, ways of making the exercises slightly easier for anyone who was struggling or harder for those who could push further, and encouragement to everyone.

She loved teamwork and it was a joy to see it in action through the support that Danniella gave Alison. Working out next to each other, Danniella regularly encouraged Alison to keep going, even trying to pace the exercises she was doing to keep time with her. With Danniella's encouragement, Alison really pushed herself. She'd told Karen that she'd been a keen hockey player in school and college but hadn't done anything for the nine years since leaving education. She was Karen's favourite type of client; those who came from zero fitness often achieved amazing things.

'I hope you enjoyed your first bootcamp,' Karen said to the group after they'd cooled down, feeling a stab of pride that it had gone smoothly and that they'd all worked hard. 'Before you go, I'd like to get a photo of you all with the flag.' She unfurled a bright yellow branded flag and assembled them into a group, those in the middle holding the flag. She'd previously checked they were happy to have photos posted on social media. Danniella said she'd prefer not to, so she stepped discreetly to one side. Alison had said it was only okay if she could always hide behind the flag. Sure enough, she positioned herself so her whole body was covered by the material. Karen couldn't wait for the day when Alison felt proud of her body and didn't feel the need to hide like that. Hopefully it would be soon. Alison had joked on the phone that she wanted to lose half her body weight but Karen planned to keep a close eye on that. Success didn't need to mean a particular weight or dress size; it simply meant that Alison was happy with herself and felt fitter.

Photos taken, Karen draped the flag over her arm, and smiled at the group. 'If you have any questions or concerns before the next session, please get in touch. If you haven't exercised for a while, you will probably hurt so I'm going to put some information on the Facebook page about how to ease that. Take on plenty of fluids, eat well, and I'll see you on Thursday.'

'I loved that,' Danniella said, hanging back with Alison. 'So much fun.'

'Thank you,' Karen said. 'What about you, Alison?'

'I wouldn't say that love has sprouted but there's a seedling there that may grow into something.'

Karen smiled. 'You did really well today, Alison. I was impressed with your determination.'

'Really?' Alison raised an eyebrow.

'Really. And you were a great support for her, Danniella, so thank you for that.'

'Pleasure,' Danniella said. 'Do you want a hand with anything?'

'If you've got time, I'd love it if you could collect the markers.'

Karen folded the photo flag and packed it away, then pulled the flagpole out of the sand, watching Alison and Danniella giggling as they raced to pick up the marker discs. Considering they'd only just met, they looked like a strong friendship in the making. How lovely that her bootcamp had the power to bring strangers together and create bonds. There probably weren't many people who could say that about their jobs.

As she walked up the beach with the two women, chatting about the exercises they'd liked the most, and joking about sand in every crack and crevice, Karen sighed contentedly. It had definitely been the right decision to set up the mid-morning bootcamp and this small cosy atmosphere was exactly what she'd had in mind. Bollocks to Ryan.

* * *

Back in the car park, Karen placed her kit in the boot and was preparing to drive off for a PT session when her phone beeped with a text. It was from a private number but that wasn't unusual because her mobile number was displayed on the Bay Fitness website and on social media.

 From Unknown

```
I'm impressed. You're certainly very open-
minded
```

She laughed. Okay. Strange. Obviously a wrong number, though.

```
✉ To Unknown
Sorry but I think you've got the wrong
number
```

```
✉ From Unknown
No. It's meant for you, Karen
```

Karen's heart raced. What?

```
✉ To Unknown
Who is this?
```

```
✉ From Unknown
Wouldn't you like to know?
```

```
✉ To Unknown
Yes. That's why I asked! I've no idea what
your message means
```

```
✉ From Unknown
Didn't think you would. But you will. Soon
```

Karen shuddered, her heart thumping rapidly. What the hell was that all about? Who was it? They obviously knew her, but the message made no sense. Open-minded? About what? She shook her head. She should just ignore it. It was somebody playing silly games. She didn't know who, she didn't know why, but she did know they weren't worth it. Switching the phone to silent, she zipped it into her pocket and drove across town for her 11.30 a.m. PT client.

All the way through the session, though, it felt like the phone was burning a hole in her pocket. As soon as she got back to her car, she checked it but there was nothing: no more texts, no mysterious phone calls. It was just a stupid prank, it meant nothing, and she needed to forget about it.

But something deep down in the pit of her stomach told her that it wasn't nothing. It wasn't nothing at all.

14

KAREN

Two days later, Karen sat down on the edge of the bed, smiling, as she listened to Ryan singing in the shower. Ed Sheeran he wasn't, but it still warmed her heart to hear him sing the wrong words out of key because that meant things were back on track. Ryan never sang when he was stressed and she hadn't heard his warbling for quite some time.

Bending down, she pulled on her socks. Much as she'd love to strip off again, return to the shower, and give him even more to sing about, she had to work.

'I'm off,' she called through the door of the wet room. 'Are you going to tell me where you're taking me tonight?'

'No,' Ryan called back. 'It's a surprise. See you after bootcamp.'

Karen ran down the stairs and headed out to the car. She wasn't a fan of surprises but Ryan had promised her she'd love this one so she'd have to go with the flow.

Driving to Hearnshaw Park to meet her first PT client, Karen couldn't stop speculating about her evening. Where could Ryan be taking her? She'd asked him what she should wear but he'd said her outfit would be waiting for her when she got home. Most intriguing. She shook her head. She needed to forget about it or she'd be distracted all day.

The two PT sessions went well, and the second mid-morning bootcamp couldn't have gone better. Everyone paired up perfectly: Melanie and Hailey, Dawn and Bryan, Alison and Danniella. She loved that last pairing. Watching them crease up with laughter in front of the second tier of beach huts because Alison couldn't co-ordinate her arms and legs for a set of jumping jacks, a warm feeling swirled in her stomach. She was about to run up the steps to see if she could give Alison any tips but Danniella was already breaking down the move, showing Alison exactly how to seamlessly move from a crouched position into a leap with arms and legs stretched out in a star-shape. It took a few attempts but Alison eventually nailed it and the two of them hugged each other, squealing. It was only bootcamp two but Karen could already tell that the friendship emerging between them was going to be powerful. Individuals could achieve a lot but groups could achieve so much more.

'That's your second bootcamp smashed,' Karen said when they'd finished their cool-down stretches. 'At the end of each session, I'll give an Awesome Award. It's given to one or more bootcamper who's pushed extra hard, overcome obstacles, or demonstrated great teamwork. The award is that you get to have your picture taken with the flag. Yeah. I know. No expense spared. Today's Awesome Award goes to everyone, though, so let's get another picture of you all on the steps with the flag.'

As before Danniella stepped aside and Alison hid behind the flag again, but she was smiling and that was enough for

Karen for now. The day would come when she felt proud of her body.

'Goodbye,' Karen said. 'Have a great weekend, and I'll see you all on Tuesday.'

As they thanked her and headed off in different directions, that glow of pride warmed her again. It was early days but she had a strong feeling that this small and cosy bootcamp was going to be her favourite.

She took a swig from her sports bottle then settled onto the sea wall to wait for her newest PT client, Jay. She'd phoned him several times to chat about his fitness goals, but had only managed a conversation with his voicemail so far.

A tap on her shoulder five minutes later made her jump. Twisting round, she looked up at a man in his early-thirties with strawberry blond hair gelled back from his forehead, and a stylish beard. Hair colour aside, he bore a remarkable resemblance to James Corden.

'Are you Karen?' he asked.

'I am. Jay?' Karen scrambled to her feet and shook his hand. 'Great to meet you.'

'I'm early so please don't feel you need to stop what you're doing.'

She shook her head. 'Early is perfect because we can have a chat about your fitness goals before we start. Fancy sitting down for a bit?'

He nodded and they both sat down on the sea wall.

'So, Jay, what's prompted you to sign up for PT?'

Jay looked down and twiddled with his watch strap in silence, his shoulders hunched. With a sigh, he looked up again and shrugged. 'I might as well be honest. It's embarrassing, though.'

Karen gave him a reassuring smile. 'Whatever you say

will stay between the two of us, but you don't have to say if it makes you uncomfortable.'

Jay looked down again. 'It's my fiancée, Sophie. She won't set a date for our wedding unless I lose at least three stone.' He patted his stomach.

'You're kidding me, yeah?' Karen asked, desperately hoping he was.

He looked her in the eye again. 'Nope. I've been issued with my ultimatum. I can lose the stomach or I can lose Sophie, so here I am.'

Realising her mouth was agape, Karen quickly closed it. Oh my God! Was it possible to feel so much contempt for someone you'd never met? Who issued an ultimatum like that? Who refused to marry someone because of their weight?

'I bet you weren't expecting that confession,' Jay said. 'You probably want to tell me to dump her for being so shallow.'

Karen smiled. 'I'm not here to judge. It's between you and Sophie. What I will say, though, is that you have to want to do this for you too. I've worked with hundreds of clients and the ones who succeed are the ones who want it for themselves. Do you want this for you as well as for Sophie?'

'I don't want to lose her,' he said.

'That's not what I asked. PT is a big commitment and it's hard work. Do you want to do this for you?'

Jay fiddled with his watch strap again. 'I think so.'

'You *think* so?'

'I know so.' He looked up and thrust his shoulders back. 'Yes, I want to do this for me.'

'Good. Keep focusing on that. So, you said in your email that you haven't exercised for a few years...?'

'That's right. I've never been into sports or the gym but I

used to be fairly fit and several stone lighter. I'm a geography and history teacher and I would spend weekends hiking up mountains with some mates or wandering round historical sites, but...' He tailed off as he stared towards the sea.

'But you don't do that now?' Karen asked.

He shook his head. 'Sophie isn't much of an outdoors person. She doesn't do hills or castles or bad weather.'

'What does she do?'

Jay grimaced. 'Shopping and drinking mainly.'

'Do you miss the hiking?'

'Yes. But things change, don't they? We can't spend our lives doing the same things we've always done. Sometimes we need to develop new habits.'

'Wise words. So, are you ready to develop your new PT habit?'

Jay grinned, revealing cute dimples. 'I'm willing to try. Bring it on.'

'You do realise that once a week won't make much difference, don't you?'

Jay's face fell. 'You mean I won't lose three stone in two months from doing this?' Then he grinned again. 'It's okay. I'm realistic about how hard I'm making this for myself. The thing is, I'm hoping to make it a surprise for Sophie so that rules out evenings and weekends. I don't work on Thursday mornings, though, so here I am, raring to go.'

Karen scrambled to her feet and dusted some sand off her leggings. 'Let's get going, then.'

Throughout Jay's PT session, Karen's thoughts kept returning to what he'd said about his fiancée. What sort of person stopped the man they supposedly loved from pursuing his passions and then complained when the result was weight gain? Didn't Sophie realise the irony of what she'd done? And where was the compromise in their relationship? It sounded like he'd given up everything he liked for her and was doing all the things he hated. Which then got her thinking about her own relationship with Ryan. Where was the compromise in their relationship? Jay had made sacrifices so that he could be with Sophie, whereas she and Ryan were pursuing their passions separately, leaving no time to be together. It wasn't sustainable. At the risk of starting another argument, she was going to have to insist on them sitting down, looking at their busy work schedules, and finding time for each other. It might mean some tough decisions for the business, but something was going to have to give. And soon. Otherwise their relationship was going to be the casualty.

* * *

After she'd finished with her final PT client of the day shortly after 7 p.m., a ball of excitement grew in Karen's stomach. What had Ryan got planned?

Back home, she kicked off her trainers, dumped her bag, and ran upstairs to find her outfit. A large brown paper bag sat on her side of the bed. She pulled the handles apart and lifted out a note:

Are you ready to have the time of your life? Pick you up at 7.30 p.m. prompt xx

Smiling, she picked out the first item: a white vest top. Under it, there was a thin long-sleeved pale-pink shirt and, under that, a pair of white cropped trousers. No way.

She washed quickly then pulled on the clothes, pulse racing. Despite being released before she was born, *Dirty Dancing* was Karen's all-time favourite film. She loved the music, the era, the dancing, the chemistry between Jennifer Grey and Patrick Swayze and that uplifting ending that made her heart soar. Last July, one of her birthday gifts from Ryan had been a special Blu-ray anniversary boxset to replace her well-worn DVD. Moaning about 'stupid girly dance films', she'd insisted they watch it together and he begrudgingly admitted that it was pretty good. Snuggled up to him on the sofa, she told him that the scene where Johnny and Baby practised their iconic lift in the lake was her ultimate fantasy. Ryan had laughed and said, 'It'll have to stay as a fantasy, then, cos there's no way I'm freezing my bollocks off in any of the lakes round here.' And she thought no more about it.

Until now.

She read the note again then looked at herself in the full-length mirror. It was definitely a copy of the outfit Jennifer Grey wore and, coupled with the reference to the song...

A horn honking outside drew her to the window and she gasped. Leaning against a black classic car was Ryan, dressed in black trousers and a black vest, a leather jacket casually slung over his shoulder. He looked up at the bedroom window, removed his dark glasses, and indicated with a nod of his head that she should join him. Giggling, Karen raced down the stairs and flung open the door.

'Hi Johnny,' she said.

'Would Miss Frances Houseman like a ride?' he asked.

'She certainly would.' Karen slipped on a pair of cream Converse, locked the door, then ran up to Ryan. 'You look amazing.'

He tossed his jacket through the open window into the back seat then wrapped his arms around her and kissed her, taking her breath away. 'So do you. And you'll look even better in about an hour.'

* * *

'No way! How on earth did you find this place?' Karen asked, gazing at the dark water of the lake in front of her, a light breeze causing small ripples to fan out across the surface. Trees surrounded the lake, broken up by the occasional clearing like the one they'd parked in.

'One of my PT clients is a photographer and he told me about it.'

Ryan took her hand and led Karen along the shore, past a copse of trees, to where the lake opened out into a small pond. Across the pond lay a wide log.

'I know it's not exactly over a ravine like in the film,' Ryan said, 'but at least a fall would give us wet feet instead of broken bones. Shall we?'

He kicked off his trainers and carefully walked across the log in his bare feet, then turned around and beckoned to Karen. Smiling at the extra bit of detail from the film, Karen stepped out of her Converse and followed him.

They stood on the log, wobbling slightly, grinning at each other.

'What now?' Karen asked.

'I'm not really sure,' Ryan confessed. 'You know I'm no dancer.'

'Let's just try walking back and forwards a bit and wiggling our bums,' Karen suggested. 'They do that in the film.'

'Nice. I can manage walking.'

'Is this working for you?' Ryan asked after they'd paced up and down a few times.

After the effort he'd gone to, Karen didn't feel she could say that it wasn't turning her on in the least. It felt weird, awkward, uncomfortable. The rough bark was digging into the soles of her feet and she suspected she might have cut herself.

'Maybe the lake?' she suggested, smiling at him. 'That's my proper fantasy moment.'

Ryan grimaced. 'It's going to be freezing, isn't it?'

'I reckon so. But we're here now. Might as well give it a go.'

Karen stepped off the log and picked up both pairs of footwear. Barefoot, they made their way back to the car and she removed her shirt. Ryan looked at her questioningly.

'Baby doesn't have the shirt on in the lake scene,' she explained. 'If we're going to do this, we need to do it properly. Which means you need to take your top off too.'

Ryan obliged and a ripple of desire ran through her. Fantasy time. Bring it on!

Holding hands, they tiptoed into the water.

'Shit!' Ryan cried. 'It's freezing.'

'I think we might need to just run for it.' Taking a deep breath, Karen ran forward until the water was up to her waist. 'Come on, 'fraidy cat.'

'I can feel my balls shrinking already.'

Karen laughed as he sprinted towards her, squealing like a small child on a rollercoaster.

Ten minutes in the water was as much as they could bear. During that time, they didn't manage anything resembling the lift. They bumped chins, hit each other in the face, and went splat several times before agreeing that it was a lot harder than it looked in the film. Karen wouldn't have minded if they'd giggled their way through it, but Ryan had become increasingly agitated with each failed attempt and he made her feel like it was her fault. On top of that, her eyes were stinging and her torso felt bruised from where he'd tried to hold her. Some fantasy!

'You'd think that two fit people like us could have mastered this,' Ryan muttered as they trudged out of the water. 'Especially you with your yoga crap.'

So he was blaming her after all. She knew it. And why couldn't he have just called it yoga or Pilates instead of belittling it simply because it wasn't something he'd ever embraced?

Ryan put his arm round Karen and pulled her close as they stepped out of the water, shivering. 'I've got some towels in the boot.'

'And a change of clothes?'

'No. Just the towels.'

Why did he never fully think things through? Karen sighed. 'You've got a dry vest and I've got a dry shirt. Looks like it's those with towel skirts.'

'I'm sorry,' Ryan said as he passed her a beach towel. 'It didn't work, did it?'

'What didn't?'

Ryan rubbed a towel over his wet hair and shrugged. 'This. Epic fail. It wasn't your fantasy re-enacted, was it? It was more like two idiots pissing about in a freezing lake. We'll probably pick up some dodgy stomach bug from swallowing the water.'

She'd never lied to Ryan and she wasn't about to start. 'I like that you tried, though. And I enjoyed the dressing up and the drive.'

He smiled weakly. 'Yeah, the car's great. Wish I could keep it.' Ryan leaned against the boot. 'That bloody log killed my feet.'

'Mine too. But the water was so cold that I can't actually feel my feet right now.'

They looked at each other for a moment then both laughed. Ryan reached out and gave her a soggy hug. 'I genuinely imagined it going so much better in my head.'

Karen kissed his bare chest, cringing at the chill of his skin against her chapped lips. 'I think that's why they're called fantasies. They're great to dream about but the reality is never quite the same as the fantasy.'

Ryan held her tightly. 'Some fantasies live up to expectations. Just not this particular one.'

'True. The James Bond thing was good.' Karen nuzzled against his neck. 'You can wear that tux again any time.'

'And that blue lacy thing you were wearing when you fell asleep downstairs was good,' Ryan said. 'You can wear that again.'

Could have fooled her. He'd rejected her when she'd worn it so she'd tossed it in the back of her wardrobe, never to see the light of day again.

Karen's teeth started to chatter.

'Come on,' Ryan said. 'Let's get you home and forget all about this.'

As they headed back towards Whitsborough Bay, Karen stared out of the window at the passing countryside, fighting back an overwhelming desire to cry. Why? Ryan had tried to do a nice thing and it hadn't quite worked. Did that warrant tears? If anything, it warranted a celebration that he cared enough to try and make her happy. So why did she have this sense of foreboding?

15

ALISON

A clattering noise awoke Alison with a start. Who was being loud? And on a Saturday morning?

She rolled over but the bed was empty. Where was Dave? Had there been a last-minute change of plan and he'd gone to work?

She sighed. Day one of their week off together and she had no idea how they were going to spend it. There'd been no more mention of going on holiday since the night of the smashed plates, not that she'd expected there to be. She wasn't convinced that fitting the new kitchen was on the cards either as there'd been no talk of emptying the cupboards in preparation.

It had been such a confusing week and she'd found herself treading on eggshells, wondering whether she was going to wake up next to Jekyll or Hyde. She'd grabbed the moments of affection with both hands, determined not to burst the bubble by talking about holidays or the kitchen, or telling him she'd started bootcamp. On those few good days, she fantasised about him producing travel tickets or suggesting they go for a drive which happened to end up at the airport. On the dark days, she knew there was as much chance of that happening as there was of her ever fitting into a pair of size twelve jeans.

* * *

'Do you want some toast?' Dave asked when she made her way down to the kitchen.

Alison stopped dead in the doorway. Dave offering to make breakfast? That was a first. 'Yes, please.'

Dave smiled at her. Actually smiled. Wow! If he was in a good mood again, she wouldn't initiate any conversation. He could pick the topics and she'd go with the flow.

'I've got a present for you,' Dave said when they'd finished eating. He handed her something wrapped in newspaper. 'I think I've got the right ones.'

She peeled back the paper, gasping as she revealed two cerulean Denby dinner plates.

'Don't tell me I've got the wrong bloody colour,' he said.

She slowly shook her head. 'No. It's right. It's just that... I can't believe you did that.' As she said the words, she wasn't sure whether she meant about him replacing them or about him smashing them in the first place.

'Yeah, well, I'm sorry and all that. I know your grandma gave you them and you were a bit precious about them.'

Precious? No. She wasn't precious *about* them; they were precious *to* her. He of all people should have understood that. They were the last gift she'd ever received from a member of her family. He *knew* that. He *knew* that was why they meant so much to her. He got it. Or she thought he did. Maybe he didn't. Maybe he never had. Maybe she'd just dreamt that he understood her because she'd needed him to.

Silence.

Dave cleared his throat. 'So, erm, I was thinking about what you said before about going on holiday this week instead of doing the kitchen...'

Alison's heart started pounding. 'Yes...?'

'And I think you're right.'

'You do?' She fought hard to contain the squeal of excitement building inside her. He didn't like it when she was 'giggly and girly'.

'Some of the lads from work are going to Ibiza this week and I've always wanted to go there.'

Ibiza? She'd been hoping he'd suggest Corfu again but, hey, it was a holiday and Ibiza might be even hotter and steamier than Corfu. Yes!

'Ibiza sounds good,' she said, already mentally working her way through her wardrobe and trying to think what she had in light colours rather than her signature black.

'I know I said that stuff about not spending the savings on a holiday, but I was thinking it's been so long since Corfu—'

'Yes. Go for it.'

Dave screwed up his nose. 'Actually, I already have.'

'Oh my God!' Alison clapped her hand across her mouth. 'That's amazing. When do we go?'

Silence.

'Dave? When do we fly?'

He suddenly seemed very interested in a groove in the table, scraping toast crumbs out of it with his thumbnail.

'Dave?'

'The flight's late tomorrow so we're driving down early afternoon, but it's er… it's not we as in you and me.'

Alison's stomach churned. 'What do you mean?'

He looked up, his expression guilty. 'I said the lads were going and they've invited me.' He laughed nervously.

He was going on holiday. Without her. Using their savings. Without her.

'How long have you been planning this?' she whispered.

'Not long. Greavesy called while you were out babysitting last weekend.'

Oh my God! He'd been nice to her when she'd got home. He'd apologised about calling her fat. They'd made love. And it had all been because he'd been trying to sweeten her. She'd known it. She'd known he was up to something, but she'd never imagined something as low as this.

'Why didn't you tell me before?'

He shrugged apologetically. 'I'm telling you now, aren't I? We're not leaving till tomorrow.'

Replacing the plates. Making her some toast just now. All pathetic attempts at easing his guilty conscience. He'd obviously chickened out of telling her during the week, probably knowing he was bang out of order.

She watched him dump his mug on the table for her to clear away before making his way towards the door. Then he stopped and turned around.

'Was that sports gear I saw in the washing basket?' he asked.

Heat rushed to Alison's cheeks.

'You've never gone and joined a hockey team, have you?'

'No.' She straightened her shoulders and stared at him defiantly. 'I've joined a bootcamp.'

He laughed out loud. 'Yeah, right. You? At bootcamp? That's hilarious.'

'Why's it hilarious?'

'Have you looked in the mirror lately? Jesus Christ, Ali. Bootcamp? That's classic.' He left the kitchen, chuckling to himself.

16

DANNIELLA

'I'm so sorry. I know we've only just met, but I didn't have anyone else to turn to...'

Danniella held out her arms and hugged Alison. 'Hey, don't cry. You came to the right place.' She led Alison into the lounge and sat beside her on the sofa.

'You're sure you don't mind me staying here? It's only for one night. If I'd had to stay there a moment longer, I might have smashed one of those damn plates over his head.'

'How about I make us a cuppa then you can tell me all about it?'

Alison blew her nose. 'That would be great. You're sure I'm not stopping you from working?'

Danniella paused. 'I do need to do some work today but I'm okay for the moment.'

'Just say the word and I'll bury my head in my Kindle. I really, really appreciate this. You're a true friend.'

Friend. Danniella repeated the word in her head as she made the drinks. It had been a long time since someone had referred to her as their friend and, for a brief moment it made her feel normal. Normal person, normal life, normal friends. Except nothing about her existence was normal. She breathed deeply and slowly, trying to calm the rising anxiety.

Over the phone, Alison had said that Dave was setting off early afternoon tomorrow so Alison would be heading home then. That meant a full day with her. Would it be possible for them to spend that long together and not talk about Danniella's past? She liked Alison very much and suspected she was the sort of person who could be trusted. Was she the sort of person who'd understand, though? Only time would tell. For now, it would need to be small talk. She could ask Alison about Dave and if that led to questions about Danniella's past, she'd play the work card. Tonight, they could watch a film or go the cinema; good tactic for avoiding conversation. Or Danniella could pretend she had a bad head and needed an early night. It would be fine. She'd find a way to cope. Alison needed her and, after nine months on the road, she knew exactly what it was like to need someone.

'Here you go,' Danniella said, handing Alison a mug of tea a few minutes later. 'From the beginning?' Alison had given her some details over the phone but it had been a garbled rant about plates and holidays and kitchens that really hadn't made much sense.

Danniella listened, sipping on her coffee and trying to maintain a poker face, as Alison talked about Dave, her partner of ten years. Going on holiday without her, paying for it using their savings, and only telling Alison when the deed was done? What a git! The offences kept stacking up as Alison told her in more detail about the plate-smashing incident, the insults about her weight, and the continued failure to fit the new kitchen or do anything else around the house.

'It's been a difficult few months,' Alison finished.

'A few months? It sounds like this has been going on for a lot longer than that.'

'A difficult few years, then.'

'What are you going to do when he gets back?'

Alison picked up a scatter cushion and cuddled it to her chest. 'I honestly don't know. What would you do if you were me?'

Danniella sighed. 'Oh, Ali, it would be so easy for me to sit here and say walk away, but we both know that things are never that simple. Ten years is a long time to invest in a relationship, but perhaps that's the point. Do you and Dave even have a relationship? I know you're angry and hurting, quite rightly, which may have skewed what you've just shared with me, but all I heard was negative stuff. I'm so sorry.'

Alison nodded. 'You know what? So did I. As I was telling you all about it, I tried to throw in some positives, but I was struggling to find any.'

'Can I ask you a question?' Danniella asked. 'But when I ask it, I want you to say the first thing that comes into your head, no matter how it might sound.'

'Okay.'

'Why do you stay with Dave?'

'Because he's the only family I've got,' Alison responded immediately.

'But do you love him?'

Alison didn't answer for a moment, then she closed her eyes and shrugged. 'Is it possible to love someone but not actually like them?' She opened her eyes again and looked at Danniella.

'I'd say it probably is.' Oh yes. Definitely. Danniella knew that feeling well.

'After Corfu, we both changed jobs which meant more

pressure, longer hours, weekends, shifts. We adjusted to our new work routines but forgot to create a home routine. It seemed that, whenever Dave was home, I was working, and whenever I was home, he was working, playing rugby or out with his mates. We muddled along for a couple of years, but, by then I'd become so lonely that I started over-eating. When he started criticising my weight, I felt so angry with him because if he'd occasionally put me first, I might not have been lonely and I might not have turned to food. How can you have a relationship with someone you hardly ever see? How can you be affectionate when all you feel is anger and hurt? And how do you even start to talk about what's happening when you've let it go on like that for four years and every conversation seems to generate an argument?'

Danniella's heart raced as she thought of her own situation. She could relate to everything Alison was saying. Everything. 'I'm so sorry. It must have been tough. I get why it would have become too hard to talk to him. Was there nobody else you could talk to about how you were feeling?'

'My family...' Alison stopped and sighed. 'Let's just say they're not around. Long story. Maybe another time. As for friends, Aidan was really my only friend. After I met Dave, we didn't hang around so much and we didn't stay in touch when we left college. Now I know a lot of people through work but there's nobody I'd call a proper friend. We go out occasionally and we chat at work but it's all superficial stuff. You could probably have guessed that I'm a Billy No Mates, though, given that I need somewhere to stay and the only person I could call has been in my life for less than two weeks.' Alison exhaled. 'Oh my goodness, I've just registered what a liberty that is. I'm so sorry. Where's my head at? I'll leave you to it and check into a guest house.' She rose from the sofa.

'Sit back down. You'll do no such thing. You came to the right place. I don't have anyone to turn to either so I know what it's like.'

'You're sure it's okay?'

'I'm sure.'

'Thank you. I really appreciate it,' Alison said. 'You've got work to do and I've kept you chatting too long so how about I earn my keep and make us some more drinks while you do whatever you need to do? I'll read and I promise not to disturb you.'

'Sounds good. Thank you.'

When Alison left the room, Danniella moved across to the table and opened her laptop. She did have work to do but none of it was urgent. None of it *needed* to be done that weekend but the conversation with Alison had hit that inevitable point where it was appropriate for Danniella to share something about herself. She couldn't do it. She wasn't ready. Saying it out loud would make it true and she still couldn't face the truth.

Alison opened her eyes in the second bedroom at Danniella's the following morning. She reached for her phone to check the time and tutted. Six missed calls, eight texts, and two voicemails, no doubt all from Dave. She unlocked the screen to check. Yes. All Dave. Bollocks.

Grinding her teeth, she scrolled through the texts, starting with the earliest, sent about an hour after she'd stormed out the house:

✉ From Dave (11.51 a.m.)
Where are you? How do I work the tumble dryer?

✉ From Dave (12.35 p.m.)
Why aren't you answering your phone? Where's my passport?

✉ From Dave (2.17 p.m.)

Still can't find my passport. Answer the
bloody phone!

✉ From Dave (4.44 p.m.)
I've found it. Cheers for your help on that.
Not. Are you in a strop?

✉ From Dave (6.52 p.m.)
Will you be home for tea? Fancy a takeaway
for our last night together? x

✉ From Dave (11.21 p.m.)
This isn't funny. I'm getting worried. Where
are you? I'm sorry. I should have told you
about the holiday sooner. Please come
home xx

✉ From Dave (2.03 a.m.)
Please call me. I miss you. The house is
empty without you xxx

✉ From Dave (8.50 a.m.)
Been awake all night worried about you. I
know I screwed up big time and I'm sorry.
Greavesy's picking me up at 1.30 I don't
want to leave without saying goodbye. Please
come home xxxxxxxxx

Shaking her head, Alison listened to the voicemails. The first
had been left mid-afternoon and was a frantic tirade of abuse

about her leaving him on his own with his washing to sort, unable to find his passport, struggling to find a beach towel, wanting to know where to buy currency... She didn't bother listening to the end.

The second message had been left in the early hours and was the complete opposite, begging her to come home because he was sorry and he missed her. Apparently he'd come across the commemorative album during his passport search and registered that he'd missed the fifteen-year anniversary. 'Why didn't you say anything?' he asked. 'No, scrub that. I should have remembered. Shit! You tried to tell me, didn't you? It was the day you were up early. You even told me what date it was and all I did was moan about the pears and... oh, Christ... that's the night I ate all the lasagne and sent you out for lager. You must have hated me for that. You probably still hate me. Come home, Ali. Please. Or call me. I just... I'm really sorry. I know I've been a crap boyfriend and... it's just that... Forget it. It doesn't matter. You're still my favourite girl. Always will be. Please call me. I need to know I haven't lost you.'

Warm tears cascaded down Alison's cheeks as she listened to the second message over and over. She'd never heard Dave sounding so emotional. And he'd called her his 'favourite girl' again.

'He still loves me,' she whispered.

Wiping her cheeks, she peeled the duvet back, then hesitated. Did she really want to rush home after what he'd done? Did one soppy message mean instant forgiveness? Yes, it had been a lovely message, but... Maybe one more listen before she dashed home to reassure him that he hadn't lost her; that they were fine.

Dialling back into voicemail, she connected to the first

message by mistake. The abusive message. The message full of venom. Her hands scrunched the duvet and her jaw clenched. No, they were *not* fine, and she was *not* going to rush home and pretend they were.

'What do you think?' Alison asked Danniella. They'd wandered down to the seafront for a takeaway breakfast, eaten on Stanley's bench.

Danniella handed the phone back to Alison. 'It's like listening to two different people.'

Alison sipped her tea. 'And if you'd only listened to the second one?'

'I'd say Dave's had a light bulb moment and he's genuinely sorry. But you can't ignore the first one, Ali. He was so rude to you.'

'I know.'

'Is he like that at home?'

'Sometimes.'

A young couple walked past them, giggling, arms wrapped round each other. It had been like that with Dave at first. No, not just at first. It had been like that for six years. Not anymore, though. Her shoulders slumped as she forced back the tears.

'Have you ever been rock-pooling?' Alison asked, looking down onto the beach. It had recently been high tide, leaving only a narrow stretch of sand interspersed with freshly-filled rock pools.

'Erm... no, I don't think so. Maybe as a kid. I don't specifically remember, though.'

'My whole family loved rock-pooling. I had a younger

sister and brother, Fleur and Max. We used to compete to see who could find the biggest starfish or crab, or the brightest coloured shell. It was so exciting, wading through the pools in our wellies, carefully turning over stones and hoping to find something special. My parents and my grandma would join in too. Grandma always found the best stuff, but would call one of us over and make out that we'd found it.'

'Sounds like fun.'

Alison nodded. 'It was. There are lots of rock pools in Whitsborough Bay but we liked the ones below us the most.' Her breath caught as she visualised the photo in the commemorative album of the six of them posing in front of those very same rock pools, brightly-coloured fishing nets in their hands, buckets at the ready to see what they could catch. Such happy times. When her dad had accosted a dog walker to take that photo, none of them had a clue that it would be their last ever family snap.

Tears dripped down her cheeks and she swiped at them. 'Sorry. It's been fifteen years, but sometimes...' Alison shook her head and took a deep, shaky breath. 'I was twelve when it happened. It was Fleur's tenth birthday. We'd planned a cinema trip to York then a family meal, but I came down with a stomach bug. Fleur, bless her, said we could do it the following weekend, but I said they should go without me.' She paused and shook her head as more tears spilled down her cheeks. 'Biggest regret of my life. If only I hadn't insisted.' She turned to face Danniella, that familiar feeling of guilt enveloping her, threatening to suffocate her. 'I stayed with Grandma while the four of them went to York. But they...' Her voice cracked. Oh, God, this was so hard, even after all this time. The memories, the guilt, the loss. Deep breath. 'They never made it home.'

Danniella's eyes widened. 'What happened?' she whispered.

'They were nearly home. Ten minutes away, fifteen tops. But a lorry coming down Branning Bank had brake failure and ploughed through the lights straight into our car. They didn't stand a chance.'

18

DANNIELLA

Danniella felt like she was caught in a whirlpool, spinning out of control, trying to breathe. The horizon wouldn't stay still as she clung to the bench. *They didn't stand a chance. They didn't stand a chance.* Rain pouring down. The squeal of tyres. The screech of brakes. And that sickening thud. *She didn't stand a chance. She didn't stand a chance. She...*

'Danniella? Are you okay?' Alison's voice sounded so distant, as though at the end of a long tunnel.

'Didn't stand a chance,' Danniella whispered, gasping for breath.

'The paramedics said it happened so fast, they wouldn't have felt anything,' Alison said. 'I'm not sure I...'

But Danniella wasn't listening. Alison was right. So fast. So very fast. Screaming. Blue lights. Thunder. Bella Bunny lying in the middle of the road. Torrential rain and...

Danniella leapt to her feet and staggered across the path. Clinging to the metal railings, she vomited onto the beach below. Instantly, Alison was by her side, holding her hair back as she vomited again.

'I'm sorry,' Danniella gasped, pressing a trembling hand against her lips. 'I'm so sorry. Your poor family. I didn't mean to...' She closed her eyes for a moment. 'I just felt...'

'We need to get you home,' Alison said. 'Take my arm.'

Slowly, silently, they made their way back up the cliff path. Sweat trickled down Danniella's face and back, despite the goosebumps covering her arms. Her arms shook, her stomach churned, and her legs felt too weak to support her body.

When they finally made it to the flat, her hands were shaking so much that she couldn't fit the key into the lock. Alison gently took it from her and unlocked the door. 'Nearly there,' Alison whispered. 'Nearly home.'

* * *

'I'll get you some water,' Alison said when they'd made it up the stairs and into Danniella's bedroom. 'Will you be okay on your own for a minute or do you feel sick again?'

Danniella sank onto the bed. 'I'm okay. Just tired.'

With Alison gone, she tried to lift her T-shirt over her head, but couldn't find the strength. Crawling under the duvet, fully dressed, she groaned. What had just happened? *Oh my God. Poor Alison. What must she be thinking?* There she'd been, pouring her heart out and... Danniella shuddered and pulled the duvet more tightly round her. She was going to have to explain her reaction. But how? There was no way she could tell Alison the truth and risk losing her only friend. Think! But her head was fuzzy and her thoughts confused.

'I've got your water.' Alison placed a glass on the bedside drawers. 'How are you feeling?'

'Like the worst friend in the world.' Danniella pressed her fingers to her lips. 'I'm so sorry. I can't believe I—'

'Hey. It's fine. I'm more worried about you than me.' Alison crouched down beside the bed. 'The good news is there was nobody on the beach below. Round here we're used to being crapped on by seagulls. Projectile vomit is a new phenomenon.'

Danniella gave a weak smile. 'Must have been something I ate.'

Alison raised an eyebrow.

'Or one of those twenty-four-hour things. I'll be fine after I've slept.'

'Which should be my cue to go, but I'm not sure about leaving you.'

Danniella smiled weakly again. 'You need to see Dave before he leaves and I need to sleep.'

Alison stood up slowly. 'Okay. I'll pack my stuff then leave you in peace. But if you need anything, I'll have Dave's van, which means I'm less than ten minutes away. I mean it. Anything.'

Tears pricking her eyes, Danniella reached out from under the duvet and took Alison's hand. 'Thanks. You're a good friend.'

'It's mutual,' Alison said, gently squeezing Danniella's hand. 'You've been a better friend to me this past week than most people I've ever met. You're stuck with me now.'

'I'm so sorry about your family,' Danniella said, releasing Alison's hand. 'So many questions and—'

'Which you can ask me another time,' Alison interrupted. 'And you can tell me what happened to you before you moved here. Or not. No pressure.'

'What do you mean?' Her pulse quickened.

'We both know it wasn't something you ate. When I was telling you about the crash, you weren't on the seafront with me. You were in another place, in another time, reliving something pretty horrific.'

Danniella's heart thudded like a drum. She knew. Alison knew. 'I wasn't. I had a funny turn. That's all.'

Alison held her hands up as though in surrender. 'We're friends, right? My friendship isn't conditional on you telling me about your past. But if you ever want to talk, whether that's tonight, next month or next year, you only have to say the word.'

'There's nothing to tell.'

Alison nodded then turned towards the door. 'Get some rest and call me if you need me. Promise.'

'I promise.'

When the door closed, Danniella released a long, shaky breath. Shit, shit, shit! What now? Run again? Where to? And what would she do when she got there? Hide away in a grotty B&B, avoiding conversation, avoiding eye contact, avoiding life. She'd been there, done that, and the loneliness had nearly destroyed her. Those first few months had been the hardest, especially Christmas. A bottle of vodka had got her through Christmas Day, but waking up on the bathroom floor in a pool of her own vomit had been a clear message that alcohol was not the answer. Constantly running wasn't the answer either. Was she strong enough to tell Alison, though? She liked her, trusted her... but would Alison still like her if she knew the truth?

'I'm off,' Alison called. 'Speak to you later.'

When the flat door closed, Danniella crept across the bedroom, opened her wardrobe door, and retrieved a fabric storage box from the top shelf. With shaking hands, she lifted the pink butterfly-covered lid, reached inside, and felt for the soft fabric. Bella Bunny.

Danniella cradled the soft pink rabbit against her heart as she sank to the floor, her body shaking with anguished sobs.

'I'm sorry,' she cried. 'I'm so sorry.'

19

ALISON

Alison hesitated as she set off down the cliff path. Had she done the right thing in leaving Danniella alone? She took a few paces back towards the flat then paused again. No. Danniella needed to be left in peace. The offer to talk was on the table and Danniella could accept it as and when she was ready. And if she was never ready, that was fine too. Alison had meant what she said; her friendship was not conditional. She, of all people, knew how hard it could be to talk about the past.

What could have happened to Danniella? Her reaction on the seafront had been pretty extreme even before she'd decorated the beach. Pale face. Tormented eyes. Fear. Confusion. Just like looking in a mirror fifteen years ago.

She'd known something was wrong that day. Her parents and siblings weren't expected back for a couple more hours but Grandma seemed to be on edge, constantly checking her phone, peering out the window, wringing her hands, before disappearing into the kitchen. Alison turned the TV down low, listening to her grandma's worried tone, 'Martin, it's me.

Where are you? If you were giving the meal a miss, you should have been home by now. Presumably you're driving. I'll try Lily again.' And, moments later, 'Hi Lily. Can one of you give me a call? Hopefully you decided to stay for a meal after all. Or maybe it's bad traffic. I'm getting worried, though.'

A film of sweat covered Alison and she felt nauseous again as she listened to Grandma repeatedly calling, sounding a little more desperate with each message. Then she muted the TV, heart thumping, as she heard Grandma saying, 'Who is this...? I'm Valerie Jenkins. This is my daughter-in-law's phone...'

She dashed into the kitchen to find Grandma gripping the phone with one hand and the edge of the sink with the other, tears rolling down her cheeks. 'All of them?' she whispered. 'Are you sure...? It's a dark-blue Ford Mondeo... My son, Martin, and his wife Lily... Yes, Max is seven and Fleur is ten today... *was* ten today.'

And at that moment, everything went black for twelve-year-old Alison.

* * *

On the bus, Alison rested her head against the window. She hadn't allowed herself to think about that day for years, or at least not in that level of detail.

Alison's friends had gradually drifted away from her after the crash. The friends she'd known since primary school were discovering boys and fashion. They wanted to have fun and didn't know how to deal with someone who'd lost their parents, their siblings, their home, and had moved in with their grandma. The fledgling friendships she'd made in her first year at senior school weren't strong enough to survive her absence. So it really was just Alison and her grandma; a close-knit family of six suddenly depleted to two. And that was how it remained for the next five years until Dave came into her life.

Dave. Alison sighed. On the fifth anniversary of the crash, shortly after Alison turned seventeen, there was a lecture at college on changes in what constituted 'family' and the impact of this on the tourism industry. Her peers shared stories of being on holiday with a single parent, as part of blended families, or with same-sex parents. Alison felt as though she was having an out-of-body experience as she listened to them talk about the 'absolute nightmare' of being split up on airlines, the astronomical cost of trips for large families, and the challenges of finding something to please everyone. Didn't they realise? Didn't they have any idea how lucky they all were? One parent, two, three, four, step, foster, gay... at least they had parents. They had siblings, half-siblings, step-siblings, cousins or friends with whom they holidayed. Alison would have sold her soul to be sitting in a different row to her family on an aeroplane if it gave her one more family holiday.

She hadn't meant to stand up. She hadn't meant to scream it out loud. The shocked expressions. The whispers. The nudges. Ignoring her tutor's anxious calls for her to come back, Alison had grabbed her bag and fled along the corridor, down the stairs, round the perimeter of the playing fields and into the copse where the smokers hid at break-times. Tears blurring her vision, she beat her fists, then her palms, against the rough bark of an old oak, yelling and sobbing. It wasn't fair. It wasn't right. She wanted her family back. She needed them. Reeling at the pain in her hands, she sank to the ground, shaking.

'Jesus! Are you okay?' Someone knelt down beside her and she looked up, startled.

'It's Ali, isn't it?' he asked.

She nodded numbly.

'I'm Dave,' he said.

She knew. Dave Goddard, seventeen, flanker on the rugby team, studying construction. The changing room gossip suggested half the hockey team had a crush on him and, looking at him now, she could see why. Tall, strong, and with the bluest eyes she'd ever seen, bright like the sky on a summer's day but with a navy outline like the contrasting sea. Her heart raced.

'Let's see your hands,' he said, gently.

They shook as she held them out in front of her, curled into loose fists.

'Tell me if I hurt you.' He carefully unfurled her fingers and she winced at the blood and splinters. 'Ow. That looks painful.' He rested her hands in his and looked up at her with sympathy. 'Those splinters need removing.'

Alison glanced back towards the college buildings and shook her head. 'I can't go back in there. Not today.'

'Why? What's happened?'

'I... erm... I can't...' She started crying again.

'Hey, don't cry. It's okay.' Dave put his arm round her and she gratefully rested her head against his chest as she sobbed.

She'd never had a boyfriend; not even a date. As he held her closely and whispered 'shh' soothingly, her heart raced, the pain in it easing for a moment.

'Do you want to come to my house?' he asked, still holding her. 'I'm only ten minutes' walk from here.'

'Don't you need to be in a class?'

'No. I need to be with you.'

Butterflies swarmed in her stomach as Dave helped her to her feet then picked up his backpack and hers, slinging them both over his shoulder.

In his kitchen, he was so gentle as he carefully removed the splinters and washed away the blood that she could barely feel the pain.

'You're like a gentle giant,' she said, immediately cursing herself for saying something that sounded so childish.

He smiled. 'You wouldn't say that if you saw me on the rugby pitch.'

'I have.' She blushed. 'You're really good.'

His smiled widened. 'And so are you. At hockey, that is.'

She smiled too. 'Thank you.'

'Have you got a boyfriend?' he asked shyly, rubbing antiseptic cream into the cuts.

'Not at the moment.' She didn't like to admit she'd never had one.

'I was wondering if you'd like to go out with me?'

Her eyes widened. 'Really? I'd lo...' Then she stopped, self-doubt taking control. 'You could have your pick of the hockey team, you know. Why would you want to go out with me?'

'Why wouldn't I?' Tilting her chin upwards, his lips brushed lightly against hers, sending the butterflies in her stomach swooping and soaring. 'Yes or no?'

'Yes,' she whispered. 'If you meant it.'

'I meant it.' His lips met hers again and he ran his hands through her curls as he kissed her fervently. Her first kiss; everything she'd dreamed of and so much more. Her heart raced and her legs felt weak as she clung onto him.

A couple of weeks later, they sat on towels in front of the caves on the beach at South Bay. As darkness fell, Dave lit a small fire and draped a blanket around their shoulders. They'd been inseparable since their first kiss. She'd fallen in love and it was time to show him how much she trusted him too. Between sobs, she opened up about her family tragedy and how it had affected her in obvious but also in unexpected ways: losing her friends and turning to food for comfort. He told her about his hostilities at home: how his stepfather, Keith, verbally abused him every day and wasn't averse to turning physical either.

'It's not fair,' he said. 'I hate my family but they're still around making my life hell. You loved yours and they were taken from you.'

'I miss them so much. I want my family back,' she sobbed.

'I can't bring them back,' Dave said, 'but I can be your new family and you can be mine.'

'You mean that?' she asked.

He kissed tenderly. 'You and me. Family. Always and forever.'

And, for six years, that's how it had been. Six happy, laughter-filled years.

* * *

The bus pulled into Alison's stop and she set off on the short walk home. She hadn't texted Dave to let him know she was coming, and there'd been no more texts or calls from him. It was pointless planning what to say to him as it depended on what sort of mood he was in. If he really had been awake all night, worrying about her, he'd be in a foul mood because he

loved his sleep. And, of course, it would be her fault for aban-
doning him in his hour of need.

She unlocked the door, expecting to find a suitcase inside,
but the hallway was empty.

'Dave?' she called. 'Hello?' Alison cocked her head to one
side and listened. Absolute silence. 'Anyone home?'

Placing her bag and keys by the door, she checked the
lounge and kitchen but they were both empty. Upstairs was
deserted too and there was no sign of a case anywhere. Dropping onto the edge of the bed, her heart sank. She was too
late. He was going away for a week and she hadn't even said
goodbye. What if something happened to him? What if there
was a plane crash or a quad bike accident? What if he was
taken from her too? Still emotional from Danniella's, she
threw herself onto the bed, sobbing into his pillow.

'Ali?' Dave stood in the doorway, unshaven and looking
exhausted, a bouquet of lilies in one hand.

'I thought you'd gone without saying goodbye. I couldn't
see a suitcase' she said.

'It's in the garage, I'm going soon though. I was going to
leave you a note with these.' He lifted up the lilies, but then
the tone of his voice changed from gentle to aggressive.
'Where the hell have you been all night? Would it have killed
you to text or phone me?'

'Staying with a friend.'

'Who? You haven't got any friends.'

Ouch. 'Danniella.'

'Never heard of her. Are you sure it wasn't a male friend
giving you a bit of comfort because your nasty boyfriend
forgot the crash anniversary?'

Jaw tightening, Alison leapt off the bed and shoved past

Dave, grabbing the bouquet from his hands. 'I'd better put these in water. Don't you have a flight to catch?'

'Ali...'

Ignoring him, she stormed down the stairs. How dare he? As if she would *ever* be unfaithful to him. Didn't he know her at all? She yanked open one of the kitchen cupboards to retrieve a vase and squealed in frustration as the door came off in her hands. With another squeal, she hurled it against the wall, not caring that it took a chunk out of the plaster. It wasn't like it was fresh plaster waiting to be painted. It wasn't like anything in their home was shiny and fresh. Including their relationship.

She grabbed a vase and rinsed the dust and cobwebs out of it before shoving the lilies in it. How had he changed so much? Where was that gentle, loving individual who'd promised to be her family, always and forever?

'I'm sorry.' Dave leaned against the side of the fridge-freezer.

'What for?' Alison spun round to face him and started counting off his misdemeanours on her fingers, her voice getting higher and louder with each. 'For accusing me of seeing someone else? For having a go at me for walking out after you booked a holiday for *you* with *your* mates using *our* money and only telling me about it the day before? For forgetting about the fifteenth anniversary of my family being killed? For leaving me with a shit-tip of a kitchen for four years? For all the other half-arsed jobs? For never helping out around the house? For expecting me to do the shopping when you have a van? For being a miserable, grumpy, opinionated arse? For calling me a chubba? For deliberately breaking my grandma's plates?' Alison paused as she ran out of fingers. 'Do you want me to go on?' she yelled, holding up her hands, fingers splayed.

She waited for Dave's reaction, breathing rapidly. Was he going to shout back? Storm out? To her horror and surprise, his eyes filled with tears. 'Why do you do it then?'

'Do what?' she snapped.

'Stay with me?'

Alison stared at him, jaw clenched.

'There must be a reason,' Dave continued, his tone subdued. 'You've just listed ten selfish, inconsiderate things I've done and I bet you could have easily listed ten more. But could you have listed ten good things? Or even five?'

Alison pulled out a chair, sat down at the table, and indicated for Dave to do the same.

'If you'd asked me five years ago, I could have listed hundreds.'

'And now?'

'You're right. I'd struggle with five. Really struggle.'

'Christ, Ali. What happened to us?' He sounded defeated.

Alison took a deep breath. 'You changed, Dave.'

'So it's all my fault?'

'That's not what I said, is it? But you *did* change. You must realise that. And if I changed, it was in reaction to how you started treating me.' Alison paused but Dave didn't speak – just kept staring at the table, shoulders slumped – so she continued. 'That's partly my fault because I should have pushed back on lots of things but, by then, you started commenting on my weight which made me eat even more and... well, you know how that cycle goes.'

Silence.

'Are you going to say anything?'

Dave looked up, his eyes bloodshot and the rims red. 'I think you've said it all.'

A car horn sounded outside followed by a beep on Dave's mobile. 'That'll be the lads. I've got to go.' He pushed his chair back. 'Will you still be here when I get back?'

'Where else would I be? Unless you don't want me to be here?'

Standing up, Dave rubbed his hands over his eyes then down his cheeks and across his stubble. 'You don't get it, do you?'

Alison shrugged. 'Get what?'

'From the moment I saw you, it was only you. Always has been. Always will be. But my tosser of a stepdad was right. I was never good enough for you. *He* knew it. *I* knew it. The only person who didn't know it was you and I kept waking up each morning, wondering if that would be the day when *you'd* finally realise it.'

The horn sounded again.

'I'm sorry, Ali. I've got to go.'

She looked up at him, frowning. 'I'm confused. Are you saying you've been trying to push me away to prove Keith right?'

'I don't know what I've been doing. I don't know what I want anymore.'

She stood up, tears pricking her eyes. 'Then I suggest you spend this week working it out, because if you don't want me anymore—'

'No! Of course I still want you.' He pulled her to him and held her tightly. 'You're still my favourite girl.'

'Are you sure about that?' The tears started flowing again.

'Like I said, it's always been you.'

He bent down and kissed her with such passion that it took her breath away, filling her with desire for him.

The horn sounding again broke them apart. He cupped her face in his hands and gave her one more tender kiss. 'I'm sorry. For everything.'

Then he was gone.

She sat back down at the kitchen table, holding her fingers to her lips, the tears in freefall. Was it over? Did she want it to be? Quite honestly, she wasn't sure what she wanted. She glanced at the lilies. Guilty flowers, just like the replacement plates. Yet he'd seemed so sincere just now, same as on that early morning voicemail.

Shaking her head, she stood up. A week stretched ahead of her, all alone in the house with only her thoughts. It was going to be hell.

20

KAREN

'Thanks for this.' Jay said when Karen met him at North Bay corner on Sunday evening. 'I didn't expect you to be free on a Sunday.'

Karen smiled. 'I'm not normally but my fiancé, Ryan, has squeezed in a PT session with a client who's going away so I thought I might as well squeeze you in.'

Jay bounced from one foot to the other and she noticed the beads of sweat on his forehead. 'Have you been working out already?'

'I ran from the car.'

'Did you warm up first?'

He shook his head and Karen tutted good-naturedly. 'Ready for a steady jog past the huts?'

'I'm ready for a sprint.'

'Well, we're not sprinting. We'll take it easy.'

They set off along the promenade, past a long stretch of bright red, yellow, orange, blue and lime-green beach huts. More huts were set into the hillside, clustered into smaller groups, all positioned to make the most of the view over

North Bay. Outside some huts were people relaxing in deckchairs with hot drinks or a glass of wine and a book. Outside others were large families or groups of friends gathered together, laughing, drinking and eating. The delectable aroma of barbequed sausages and steaks wafted towards them, making Karen's stomach rumble. It all looked so inviting and she felt another pang of regret that so much time and energy had gone into building the business to the detriment of time with each other and time with friends. She definitely needed to pin Ryan down for that conversation. It hadn't felt right to have it immediately after the disastrous *Dirty Dancing* evening, but time was passing and she was going to have to bite the bullet.

'Slow down a bit,' she said to Jay for the third time.

'It's busy down here tonight,' he said, as they weaved their way in and out of walkers, dogs, joggers and cyclists. 'I hardly ever come down. Sophie doesn't like sand.'

Why didn't that surprise her? 'I love it down here,' Karen said. 'Especially when the weather's like this. There's so much going on. The place feels alive.'

It really was a perfect evening. The blue sky was tinged with pink and a gentle breeze scudded small fluffy clouds towards the sea. The breeze was cooling without being cold; the ideal conditions for a workout.

'How did you escape without Sophie knowing?' she asked.

'She's gone to the cinema with a friend. Girls' night.'

They reached the end of the beach huts, jogged past the ice-cream kiosk, and made their way to a raised grassy area.

'We'll stretch out here, then we'll use the benches and the grass for our session,' she told Jay. 'We're going to mainly work your leg muscles, but we'll finish with some work on your triceps and abs.'

'Sounds good. Push me hard.'

'I always push my clients hard,' Karen said, 'but pushing too hard isn't effective.'

'I can take it.'

'It's not about whether you can take it or not. It's about getting the most benefit from the exercise.'

Karen demonstrated each exercise and checked Jay had the technique right before each round of reps. He'd been chatty throughout his first workout but remained silent this time, only pausing to ask the occasional question about technique. His reps got faster and faster until sweat poured down his face and into his eyes, and he was quite literally gasping for air on each intake of breath. Like she'd done when they'd jogged there, Karen had to keep reminding him to slow down, which he would do for a few reps, then he'd be back up to a frantic pace moments later.

'Seriously, Jay, slow down,' she insisted when he lost his footing stepping up onto the bench and nearly fell. 'It's not about speed. It's about technique. As soon as you try to go faster, you lose the technique and you risk injury.'

'But I need to go faster to burn more calories and lose weight,' he panted, starting again.

'Jay, please stop and listen to me.'

But he ignored her and continued frantically stepping up and down.

'Jay! You need to stop.'

He continued stepping.

'STOP. RIGHT. NOW!'

Jay stopped dead, looking startled.

Karen took a deep, calming breath. 'I'm so sorry. I have

never had to shout at a client before but I wasn't getting through to you. I *want* to help you but I *can't* if you won't listen to me. We have two choices. Either you follow my guidance or we part ways because I cannot and will not put myself in a position where I know a client's going to hurt themselves.'

Jay's shoulders slumped. 'I'm sorry. That was stupid of me. It won't happen again.'

'Promise? Because I won't be happy if I have to raise my voice again.'

He smiled. 'I promise.'

'Good. We'll crack on, then. But you'll do the reps with me at *my* pace.'

'Why do I feel like I'm one of the kids in my class at school?'

'Because that's what this effectively is. Me, teacher. You, student. Got it?'

'Got it. Good point made well.'

'One thing you'll learn about me is that I always make good points.' She winked at him. 'So, let's talk technique...'

* * *

'I'm really sorry again,' Jay said when the session was over and they'd stretched out.

'I don't understand what happened. You followed my guidance to the letter on Thursday but it was like working with your crazy fitness-obsessed twin today.'

He laughed. 'I assure you there's only one of me. I was being stupid. It's just that...'

Karen steeled herself. It was bound to have something to do with Sophie.

'... Sophie picked out a shirt for me to wear last night but it was too tight. She got upset about me not being that committed to marrying her because I'd put on weight rather than lost it so I was trying to speed things up a bit.'

What was wrong with that woman? Telling him what to wear? Throwing a strop about his weight? Turning him into the obsessive she'd just seen? 'If you want to make decent progress, you'll need to change your diet, and exercise more often,' she said. 'Which means telling Sophie about your plans.'

'I wanted to make it a surprise, though.'

'I know and I get that, but if Sophie's doubting your commitment to marrying her, surely you're better off telling her what you're doing, proving exactly how committed you are and reassuring her of how much you love her. In return, she can give you the support you need like time apart to fit in more PT sessions or even bootcamps. Like helping you make healthy food choices when you're out together.' She paused and sneakily added, 'Like going hiking with you instead of going shopping or drinking.'

She wondered if she'd pushed it with the last comment and felt relieved to see a smile light up Jay's eyes. 'Another good point, well made.'

'I told you.'

They continued to walk in companionable silence.

'I think you need to start charging more for PT to cover the counselling services.' Jay laughed as he nudged her affectionately.

'Ha ha.'

'I'm being serious. Sort of. You're easy to talk to and you make a lot of sense.'

'All part of the service.'

Karen's mobile phone beeped with a text. 'Sorry, Jay, this is probably Ryan. Give me a sec.' She dug her phone out of her pocket. But it wasn't Ryan.

✉ From Unknown
Did you have the time of your life on
Thursday?

Karen stopped dead, her heart thumping. Another message flashed up:

✉ From Unknown
Ryan must have been feeling REALLY GUILTY to
go to all that effort

She felt sick. The anonymous texter knew Ryan. They knew about the *Dirty Dancing* evening. And they knew something about Ryan that she didn't.

'Karen?'

'Hmm...?'

'Are you okay?' Jay asked. 'You've gone pale.'

'Sorry. It's... er... it's a wrong number.' She needed to pull it together. Jay was a client – a new one at that – and this was just... well, she didn't know what it was, but she needed to remain professional.

✉ From Unknown
What could he POSSIBLY have done? Ooh, ooh,

`I know!!!! And soon you will too!`

'It's a persistent wrong number,' Jay said. 'That's three texts.'

Karen sighed. 'They know my name and Ryan's but I don't know who they are.'

'Have they threatened you?'

'No. Nothing like that. Just a bit of silliness.' They set off walking again.

'You could always block them,' he suggested.

'I might do that. It's only the second time they've been in touch. I thought... hoped... they'd got bored. So, subject change. What does Sophie do?'

'Erm... she's sort of between jobs at the moment. She didn't like my kitchen so we're getting it re-fitted and it's handy that she's around for the builders coming and going...'

Karen listened, aghast, as Jay talked about Sophie's plans to refurbish his home. What a piece of work! On top of everything else, she didn't work yet she was freely spending his earnings. Cheeky cow!

They'd reached North Bay Corner and Karen could see Ryan leaning against the railings a little way ahead. He waved and she nodded discreetly, not wanting to stop Jay while he was mid-flow, but he'd obviously noticed.

'Is that your fiancé?' he asked, nodding towards Ryan.

'Yeah. But I don't need to rush off. You were saying...?'

Jay shook his head. 'Nothing. Thinking out loud. Thanks for this evening and I promise I'll behave myself next time.'

'Think about telling Sophie what you're doing so you can fit in some more sessions, won't you?'

'I'll think about it. I know it makes sense, but—'

'It's your decision,' Karen said. 'As your personal counsellor, I can offer you solutions, but I can't tell you what to do.'

Jay laughed and raised his hand for a high-five. Karen responded, smiling. 'I'll see you on Thursday,' she said, 'but get in touch if you want a session sooner.'

Waving goodbye, she jogged over to Ryan, smiling. She leaned in for a kiss but he turned his face away.

'You two looked very cosy,' he muttered. 'Have you been having fun together?'

Karen's smile fell. 'Meaning what?'

'Meaning all the high-fiving and giggling. Very touchy-feely. And you're late.'

She planted her hands on her hips, eyes wide with disbelief. 'Seriously? After all these years you're going to play the jealousy card with one of my male clients?'

'I didn't mean it like that.'

'So how did you mean it?' When Ryan didn't answer, she shook her head. 'I rest my case. Where's the car?'

'Next to Waterfront Lodge.'

Without another word, she strode off in that direction. How dare he accuse her of being anything but professional with a client? She high-fived and laughed with all her clients, regardless of gender.

'Kaz, I'm sorry.' Ryan ran after her and grabbed her hand, but Karen shook him off.

'I haven't seen Jemma in ages,' she said. 'So I think I'll get changed and head over to Little Sandby to see her.'

'Kaz…'

'I'm sure she'll be able to make me a sandwich.'

'Kaz…'

'They've apparently finished the dining room so I'll get to see that.'

'Fine. Do what the hell you like.' Ryan stormed across the road as soon as there was a gap in the traffic. 'You usually do.'

* * *

The ten-minute drive home in silence felt three times that long.

Karen texted her best friend, Jemma, to make sure it was okay to stop by. Jemma replied immediately to say it would be great to see her. Even if she hadn't, Karen would have gone out anyway. She didn't know what was going on with Ryan at the moment but, whatever it was, she needed some space from it. Right now.

21

KAREN

'I love what you've done with the dining room,' Karen said, returning to Jemma's lounge and sitting down on the sofa.

Jemma laughed. 'But that's not why you came round tonight, is it?'

'It is. And to see you, of course.'

Jemma raised an eyebrow. 'How long have we been friends?'

Karen smiled ruefully. Best friends since starting senior school together, Jemma had always been able to read Karen like a book. 'I needed some time away from Ryan.'

'Really? Last time I saw you, weren't you moaning that you barely get any time together?'

'We don't. And any time we do get together seems to end in an argument.'

'But you two never argue.'

'We never used to. It seems to be all we do at the moment.'

'Grub's up.' Jemma's partner, Sam, placed a tray of sandwiches and a bowl of crisps on the coffee table. 'I've got some work to do so I'll leave you to it.'

Between bites, Karen told Jemma about the *Dirty Dancing* fantasy fail, the altercation on the seafront earlier, and the anonymous texts. She passed Jemma her phone.

'What do you make of them?' Karen asked when Jemma had scrolled through the texts.

'I don't know. He or she obviously knows you both. You say you haven't told anyone about the *Dirty Dancing* thing?'

'You're the first.'

'So it has to be someone Ryan's told.'

Karen nodded. 'But who and why?'

'And, more importantly, what did they mean about Ryan being guilty and that first text about you being... what was it?'

'Open-minded,' Karen said.

'Any ideas what that could mean?'

Karen picked up a cushion and cuddled it to her chest. 'I really want to say no, but there's one thing that keeps springing to mind.'

'No! Ryan wouldn't do that to you.'

'Wouldn't he? A few weeks ago I'd have said he'd never forget our anniversary, yet he did.'

'Once in thirteen years, Karen. And he made it up to you. And he only forgot because he was setting up a new arm to the business, giving you both more security for the future.'

Karen covered her face with the cushion. 'I'm making too much of it, aren't I?' She lowered the cushion and smiled at Jemma nodding enthusiastically.

'About the anniversary? Yes. About the texts? No. I'd be disturbed by those, but I'm sure it's just someone being malicious and there's nothing in it. I hate to say it, but could it be Steff? She has got form.'

'It's not Steff. She wouldn't do that. She's my friend.'

Jemma raised an eyebrow again and Karen laughed.

'Okay, she's maybe not a great friend but we get on fine and we got past all that silliness years ago.' Karen scrunched her fingers into the cushion as she mulled over the idea that it could be Steff again. No. She wouldn't.

They'd all met studying Sports and Leisure at the TEC. Ryan and Steff had been best friends since school and Karen found their in-jokes and childish banter too much. At the end of the first year, she worked with Ryan at a sports summer school. Without Steff by his side, giggling and nudging him, Karen discovered a caring, thoughtful individual who she actually liked. A lot.

Returning to college for the second year, Karen started receiving anonymous notes telling her to back off and making out that Ryan hated her. When Ryan caught Steff slipping a note into Karen's bag, they had a huge bust-up. Whilst she didn't condone Steff's behaviour, Karen could see how gutted Ryan was at the loss of his best friend. She met up with Steff one evening to try and fix things. Steff confessed that she was gay and had made the decision over the summer to come out at the start of term. She'd been relying on Ryan – the only person who knew about her sexuality – to be there for her if anyone reacted negatively. She'd convinced herself that Ryan's newfound friendship with Karen meant he wouldn't be there for her so she'd kept quiet about her sexuality and hated feeling she couldn't be true to herself.

With their friendship back on track, it was Steff who finally pushed Ryan and Karen together at the end-of-college party, declaring that it was obvious they both fancied the pants off each other and it was about time they did something about it.

'I really think this is just a blip,' Jemma said. 'You've had thirteen happy years so far. During that time, you've put yourselves under huge financial and emotional pressure by packing in your jobs and setting up a business together. That could have broken some couples but it made you stronger.'

'I know, but now it's tearing us apart. Like I said earlier, we never see each other and, when we do, we argue.'

'Then you have to find a compromise. I'm not saying the running club has to go, but something has to.'

'I know. But I don't know what. It worked before and it doesn't work now and that's the only thing that's different. My mid-morning bootcamp is new but that's part of a normal working day. Ryan does PT then.'

Jemma grimaced. 'Then maybe it *does* have to be the running club that goes.'

'He won't let it go. He'll tell me to cut back on evening bootcamps or PT instead.'

'At the risk of sounding like a stuck record...' Jemma said.

'Yeah, I know. Compromise.' Karen ran her fingers through her hair and shook her head. 'It's such a mess. Oh well, I can't hide here all night. I'd better get home and tell him about the texts.'

They both stood up.

'Make sure you don't accuse him of anything,' Jemma said. 'Just show him them and play the confused card.'

Karen hugged Jemma. 'Thank you so much. I needed that.'

Jemma's phone rang.

'You get that. I'll see myself out,' Karen said.

Jemma gave her a thumbs-up as she answered the phone.

'Bye, Sam,' Karen called up the stairs when she'd closed the lounge door.

She'd stepped outside and was about to close the front door when Sam appeared. 'Just a second.' He stepped out onto the path. 'While Jemma's out of earshot, are you and Ryan free on the first Saturday in July? I want to throw a surprise housewarming party.'

'We should be.'

'If you're not, let me know and I'll change the date. It wouldn't be right to have it without you.'

'Aw, Sam. You're so lovely.' Karen gave him a quick hug. 'I'll check with Ryan and text you later.'

Karen drove home, rehearsing what to say to Ryan about the texts without sounding accusatory. She pulled onto the drive and dug out her phone. One more check on the wording of the texts before she went in. Her stomach swooped as she spotted another one had arrived:

✉ From Unknown
Well, well, well. Seems birds of a feather really do flock together. Can't say I blame you, though. That blond guy in Little Sandby was pretty lush. I'd certainly give him one

'I was being watched,' she whispered, shaking uncontrollably. She twisted round in her seat. Where were they? Were they watching her now? Would they grab her when she opened the door?

'Leave me alone.' She sank down into the driver's seat, too terrified to open the door. 'Please leave me alone.'

22

KAREN

'Urgh! What *was* that?' Karen handed the empty tumbler back to Ryan.

'Jack Daniels. Whiskey's meant to be good for shocks.'

Ryan had seen her pull onto the drive but, when she didn't come inside, he'd come outside to check on her and found her rocking back and forth, pale-faced and shaking.

He sat down at the kitchen table opposite her. 'We'd better change your number.'

'I can't do that. All my clients past and present have that number and it's all over our fliers. I'm not changing it.' Karen banged her fist down on the table. 'And, even if I did, how's that going to stop my stalker?'

'You don't know you've got a stalker.'

'Did you not read that last message? The blond guy in Little Sandby? That's Sam. Did you tell anyone I'd gone to Jemma's?'

'No.'

'Then I have a stalker.' Karen picked up her phone. 'I should call the police.'

'Why?'

'Seriously?' Karen unlocked her phone. 'Because some-one's bloody well been following me.'

'I know, but they haven't threatened you.' Ryan put his hand over hers. 'I know you're upset, and I would be too, but I don't think the police will take a few texts seriously.'

'They're following me!'

'Yes, I know, but it was only once.'

'Which is one time too many.'

'I know you're scared. But look at the texts again. They're rubbish. Probably just some kids mucking about.'

She was about to protest that it couldn't be kids as the sender clearly knew things about them, but her head felt fuzzy and she didn't have the energy to keep going around in circles. She put her phone down again. 'Okay. No police yet, but if I get any more comments about my whereabouts...'

'Then you'll have my full support. I'll even make the call.'

She slumped back against her chair. 'You know I have to ask...?'

'No, Kaz. Really?' Ryan let go of her hand and pushed his chair back.

'Ryan. Don't be like that.'

He rose to his feet, shaking his head. 'No, I don't know who it is. No, I don't think it's Steff this time. No, I'm not seeing anyone else. No, I haven't a clue what any of it means. Satisfied?' Without waiting for her response, he stormed out of the kitchen. Moments later, the front door slammed and she heard his car start.

Slumping forward, she rested her head on her hands. 'That went well.' She sat like that for several minutes. Why was this happening to her? What sort of person sent texts like that? She grabbed her phone.

✉ To Unknown
What a sad little existence you must have if
this is how you get your kicks

✉ From Unknown
You want to ask your boyfriend how he gets
his kicks. I think the answer might surprise
you! Not long now…

23

ALISON

As soon as her alarm sounded on Tuesday morning, Alison grabbed her phone and checked for news from Danniella but there was nothing. Damn.

✉ To Danniella
Just got up. Hoping you'll be at bootcamp this morning. If not, please text me to let me know you're OK xx

After Dave left on Sunday, Alison received a grovelling phone call from her manager asking if there was any chance she could provide sickness cover. Unable to face a week of sitting at home, stewing about everything, she was happy to oblige, as long as they gave her the time off for bootcamp.

Going into work on Sunday afternoon for a late shift, she called Danniella on her break, but the call went straight to voicemail. She also called and texted on Monday morning before work and again during her break, but to no avail. And now she was getting worried.

Driving Dave's van to North Bay, Alison pulled into a space on Sea View Drive. Danniella's car was parked in the same place as it had been on Sunday. She hoped that Danniella hadn't been cooped up in the flat, all alone, for two days solid.

Marching up to the front door of Cobalt House, she pressed the buzzer for number six. After a pause, she pressed it again, eager to hear her friend's voice. Nothing. She hesitated, looking at the other buzzers. Should she ask a neighbour to let her in? Considering how fiercely Danniella seemed to protect her privacy, it was likely the other residents hadn't even met her yet and, if they had, Danniella probably wouldn't appreciate Alison dragging them into her business.

Turning away from the flat, she watched the activity on the seafront for a moment. It wasn't particularly busy yet, probably thanks to the dark grey sky and the forecast for rain. The sky looked to be angry way out at sea but, with hardly any breeze, the downpour would hopefully stay out there at least until the end of bootcamp. A couple of joggers caught her eye. Could Danniella have gone down early for a run?

Alison made her way down the cliff path, muttering, 'Please be there,' over and over.

* * *

'Good morning, Alison,' Karen said, giving Alison a wide smile. 'Did you have a good weekend?'

'Eventful and dramatic but not good.'

'Sorry to hear that.' Karen pushed the flag into the sand then straightened up. 'Must be contagious because that's exactly how I'd describe mine.'

'Really? Sorry.'

Karen shrugged. 'Let's hope this week is better for both of us.'

'Fingers crossed. You haven't seen Danniella, have you?'

'Not yet. Is everything okay?'

'I hope so. She wasn't well on Sunday and I haven't spoken to her since. I'm a bit worried about her.'

'Let me check my phone.' Karen took it out of her backpack. 'No text to say she isn't coming today.'

'Hopefully she is, then. Sorry for turning up early when you're trying to get organised. Can I make myself useful?'

'You can, actually. Can you grab that stick and draw a circle on the sand over there, about four metres in diameter? Thank you.'

Alison obliged. A distraction was good. She could happily concentrate on drawing the perfect circle in the sand because that meant she didn't have to picture Danniella's traumatised expression, speculate on what tragedy she had experienced, worry about her all alone in her flat and what her emotional state of mind might have made her do. And she didn't have to think about her own relationship mess. Dave had sent a text from the airport telling her she was still his favourite girl and he'd pull out all the stops to make it up to her when he got back. Then another one had arrived late that night telling her that the difficulties between them were her fault for wallowing in her family's death. Wallowing? *Wallowing*? How dare he? Well, excuse her for being a bit upset about her entire family being killed. Excuse her for thinking about them on the anniversary of the crash. Excuse her for remembering them on their birthdays, missing them at Christmas, and basically wishing that they were still here.

'I said draw a circle, not dig a trench,' Karen called.

Alison looked down and dropped the stick. Yikes! 'Sorry.'

Danniella didn't turn up to bootcamp and she didn't answer her door afterwards either. Alison tried phoning her once more, but hung up when it connected straight to voicemail again. Shoulders slumping, she reluctantly drove away. There wasn't anything she could do except keep calling and keep texting, hoping that Danniella would finally respond.

24

KAREN

Karen pulled the flag out of the sand then heaved her back-pack onto her shoulder. She'd hoped to catch Alison but, as soon as the session finished, Alison shot off like a rocket with barely a goodbye. That 'eventful and dramatic' weekend she'd mentioned had clearly been as dire as Karen's and it had obviously involved Danniella in some way. Had something happened to break their fledgling friendship already? She couldn't imagine what.

She checked around her to make sure she hadn't left anything on the beach, then set off towards North Bay Corner, wondering whether she was brave enough to check her phone.

'Karen!'

She looked up, startled to hear her name. 'Steff? What are you doing here?'

Steff dropped down from the wall onto the sand. She flicked her long blonde hair over her shoulder and walked the few paces towards Karen. Taller and slimmer than Karen, but with a larger bust and curvier hips, Steff wouldn't have looked out of place in a lingerie or swimwear catalogue.

'I wanted to see you before bootcamp tonight,' Steff said. 'Ryan told me about the texts.'

'I thought he might.'

'I wanted you to know it isn't me. I know I sent you those notes in college but—'

Karen raised her hand to stop Steff. 'I didn't think it was you.'

'But Ryan said—'

'Ryan didn't listen to me. I tried to ask him about the content of the texts and whether there was anything I needed to know about, but he cut me off, saying that he didn't know who sent them and that he didn't think it was you. Then he stormed out and presumably stayed over at yours and I haven't seen him since.'

Steff nodded. 'He only stayed on Saturday, though.'

'And I stayed at my mum's last night.'

'Karen! You can't keep avoiding each other.'

'I wasn't. Is that what he told you? My mum was away at a conference and I was looking after Eden. It was booked ages ago.'

'Okay. Sorry. I don't want to get involved. As long as it doesn't affect our business, the pair of you can do what you like. I just wanted to make sure you know I've got nothing to do with those texts.'

'I know that, so you're exonerated. Feel better now?' She winced at the sarcasm and the shocked look on Steff's face but what did she expect, turning up like that and making it all about her?

'Look, I need to get to a PT session,' Karen said, her tone gentle again.

'Okay. I won't keep you much longer. You know, I sat on that wall and planned what to say to you and none of the variations started with me pleading my innocence.'

'What did they start with?'

'Me asking if you were okay and if I could do anything to support you.'

'That might have gone better,' Karen admitted.

Steff nodded. 'Can we erase the last five minutes and pretend I didn't barge in and make it all about me?' She took a couple of steps back, shook herself, then stepped forward again. 'Hi Karen, I heard about the texts. Are you okay? Can I do anything?'

Karen smiled weakly. 'I'm fine, thanks. Upset, shaken and a little bit scared.' She swept her arm towards the promenade. 'Someone could be along there right now watching me. Or they might be waiting in the car park ready to follow me to my next client.' A shiver rippled down her spine.

'Ryan says you're not going to the police.'

'I wanted to but Ryan talked me out of it. I suppose he's right. Realistically what can they do about a few anonymous texts? I hate the thought of wasting their time.'

'I don't think they'd see it like that,' Steff said. 'There's helplines, you know. If I were you, I'd call one and see what they say.'

Karen glanced at her watch. 'Sorry, Steff. I've got to go or I'll be late. A helpline's a good idea, though. I'll do that. Thank you.'

'Can I walk you to your car?'

'If you want. I'm next to the park. Are you going to be my bodyguard?' Karen smiled and gave Steff a playful nudge. 'Put that karate black belt to good use?'

'Now there's an idea. I could definitely be up for a bit of stalker ass-kicking.'

They walked in silence for a moment.

'Why were you so certain it wasn't me?' Steff asked.

'Because I trust you, and I honestly don't think you'd ever hurt me like that. Those notes in college were thirteen years ago.'

They continued in silence.

'I'm sorry we're not as close as we could be,' Steff said. 'I know that's my fault—'

'It takes two,' Karen assured her.

'We both know it's me who's kept you at arm's length and it's been stupid of me. If you want to talk, shout, scream, I'm here for you. And if you want me to give Ryan an ass-kicking, I can do that too.'

Karen laughed. 'It's tempting.'

'He'd deserve it. He's doing my head in at the moment.'

Karen stopped and frowned at Steff. 'In what way?'

'He's moody, snappy, always criticising me. I've no idea what's going on with him.'

'No. Me neither. He's the same at home. He even got jealous when he saw me laughing with a male PT client on Sunday.'

Steff sighed. 'That's not like Ryan at all. I want my best friend back, and I bet you want your fiancé back too.'

'I do. Very much.' But she had a horrible feeling that he wasn't going to come back. Something had happened to change him and she needed to find out what it was because there was no way they could continue like this.

25

KAREN

'You're really worried about her, aren't you? Karen asked Alison as they untangled some skipping ropes on Thursday morning. Alison had appeared extra early again for boot-camp and the frequent anxious glances back along the prom-enade suggested she was on the lookout.

'I can't help it,' Alison said. 'I haven't heard from her since Sunday.'

'Do you want me to give her a call?' Karen suggested.

'Would you mind?'

'Not at all. Here, you finish untangling this one.' She handed Alison a rope and stepped away with her phone, returning a few moments later, shaking her head. 'Sorry. Voicemail.'

'Yeah, that's what I keep getting,' Alison said. 'Thanks for trying, though.' She looked as though she was about to burst into tears.

'I've got her email address. I can't give you it without her permission, but I don't mind forwarding her an email from you.'

Alison nodded eagerly. 'I never thought about emailing. Anything's worth a try. Thank you. I'll email you when I get home.'

'I'll text her again now,' Karen said. 'Just in case.'

✉ To Danniella
Hope all's well with you. Got a great boot-camp planned using skipping ropes. Just need to untangle them first! Hope to see you shortly

'Do you want to talk about it?' Karen asked. 'I promise I'm the soul of discretion.'

Alison leaned against the beach wall, still working on the knots. 'Long story short. My boyfriend, Dave, and I were meant to be spending this week re-fitting our kitchen only he's bogged off to Ibiza with his mates and I've ended up working. He only dropped the Ibiza bombshell on Saturday and, to put it mildly, I wasn't impressed. Danniella let me stay the night at hers because I couldn't bear to be under the same roof as him.'

'Completely understandable,' Karen said. What was wrong with people? Where was the respect in relationships?

'Danniella let me have a right good moan about Dave on Saturday, even though she had work to do, and she asked me why I stayed with him. I danced around it a bit and, on Sunday morning, I decided to tell her the real reason.' Alison took a deep breath and shook her head. 'I haven't talked about this in years and now I'm saying it twice in the same week. You're from around here originally, yeah?'

Karen nodded. 'Whitsborough Bay born and bred.'

'In that case, you'll probably remember a crash from fifteen years ago. A lorry had brake failure going down Branning Bank and crashed into a car, killing the family in it.'

'Was that really fifteen years ago? Yes, it would be. I was... Oh my God! Alison! Was that your family?'

Alison nodded. 'Please don't be nice to me or I'll start crying.' She took another deep breath. 'Anyway, I told Danniella about my family and... you promise this won't go further?'

'Promise.'

'She had a funny turn,' Alison continued. 'I had to help her back to the flat and into bed. There's no way my family tragedy caused that reaction but I think the story triggered something in her. I know she's recently moved to the area and I know from experience she won't talk about her past...' She shrugged. 'Maybe I'm letting my imagination run away with me.'

'I'm sure she's fine,' Karen said gently. 'What about you, though?'

'Mostly okay. It was a long time ago and, as they say, life does go on. Super cliché but it's true. Weirdly, they've now been out my life longer than they were in it although it seriously messed with my head when I realised that a couple of years back.'

'I can imagine.'

'I don't find it easy to make friends.' Alison picked up another skipping rope to detangle. 'Kids at school didn't know how to deal with the orphaned kid so I got used to my own company. Doesn't mean I don't miss having a close friend. There was this immediate connection with Danniella and I wonder now if it was the traumatised recognising the traumatised.'

'I don't think—'

'Morning campers,' chirped Dawn.

'We'll talk later,' Karen mouthed to Alison before turning round to welcome Dawn and Hailey. 'Good morning everyone.'

As the bootcamp got underway, Karen watched Alison in awe. She was always so bubbly, she'd never have guessed she'd had such a traumatic childhood. How would you even start rebuilding your life after a tragedy like that? And what must Alison's boyfriend be like if he took off on a lads' holiday like that with a day's notice? It certainly put a few cryptic texts and a couple of niggles with Ryan into perspective. It all seemed so insignificant compared to what Alison and perhaps Danniella were going through.

* * *

'Have a great weekend, everyone,' Karen called when the bootcamp was over and she'd taken the Awesome Award photo.

As the others headed off the beach, Alison picked up a skipping rope and started folding it.

'You definitely think something's happened in Danniella's past?' Karen asked.

'Convinced of it and I think she keeps running away from it.'

Karen frowned. 'Could she have left Whitsborough Bay?'

'Her car's still outside her flat so I don't think so. I'm parked up there and I've tried the door several times.'

'Other than the email, I don't know what to suggest.'

'Thanks anyway.' Alison handed Karen the folded rope. 'I'd better get home and get that email done before work. You're sure you're happy to forward it on?'

'It's the least I can do. Actually, let me just check my phone before you go.' Karen checked for messages or voice-mails. 'Still nothing.'

'I'll see you on Tuesday, then,' Alison said. 'Hopefully with Danniella.'

'Fingers crossed. Let me know what happens, won't you? And if you ever want to talk, I'm a good listener.'

Alison looked genuinely touched. 'See you later and thanks for your help.'

'I'm not sure I was much help.'

'You were. More than you realise.' Alison smiled and ran up the steps off the beach.

'Have you been doing your counselling bit again?' said a voice.

'Oh my God, Jay!' Karen clapped her hand across her heart. 'You scared me.'

'Sorry for coming down early, but I've got a proposition for you.'

Karen picked up the flag with one hand and the bag of ropes with the other. 'Sounds intriguing but I need to dump this lot in the car before your PT session so you can either wait for me or come with me and proposition me on the way.'

Jay started laughing. 'I'm not sure Ryan or Sophie would be too impressed if I did that.'

Karen laughed as she thrust the bright orange flag at him. 'Here. Your punishment for scaring me is to be the flag-bearer.'

'It's a bit subtle,' he said. 'I think you should have gone for something brighter.'

'You're hilarious. So what's your proposition?'

They set off towards the car park.

'I run a Scout group and we had the summer term planned out, but something's fallen through. I wondered whether you could save the day and run a bootcamp for us.'

'You're a Scout leader?'

He nodded. 'It's what got me into geography. I joined as a Cub and never left.'

'Sophie doesn't mind you doing that?' Karen bit her lip. That was a bit naughty, but she couldn't help herself.

'She hates it, but I'm not packing it in. She spends Tuesdays – my Scout night – at her sister's which works out great for me because I'm not her sister's biggest fan.'

Karen smiled. 'Good for you.' She'd been worried that Jay was a pushover when it came to Sophie, but she liked this feisty side of him, refusing to let go of something he was passionate about. She'd assumed he'd let go of everything he loved, but it looked like there'd been a compromise after all. Ryan could learn a thing or two from Jay.

* * *

'I've really enjoyed it this morning,' Jay said after they'd stretched out. 'Not that I haven't enjoyed the other two sessions,' he hastily added. 'It's the conversation. It's been good getting to know you better.'

Butterflies fluttered in her stomach as Jay smiled at her, his intense blue eyes fixed on hers. What was that all about? 'And you, Jay. I'm liking the Scouting bootcamp idea but planning it will mean meeting up outside a PT session which means time away from Sophie. Would I be right in thinking you still haven't told her?'

Jay was silent for a moment. 'I tried to but I messed up. I stupidly approached it in a roundabout way. She thought I wanted to start hiking again so we had an argument and I haven't broached it since.'

'Oops. I'm sorry.'

'She's fiery. It's one of the things I love about her. She knows what she likes and what she wants and she gets really passionate about things, unlike me. I'm a bit laidback and indecisive so it's good that she challenges me.'

Challenges? Orders, more like. 'I don't know you well enough to comment on how laidback or indecisive you are but you can't tell me you're not passionate about things, Jay.'

Jay stopped and turned to face her. 'You think so?'

'Oh my God, yes! Everything we've talked about this morning... teaching, Scouting... there was passion flowing from every idea. Don't ever let anyone take that away from you.'

They stared at each other. Karen's pulse raced, her stomach whirred and she felt like she was on a precipice about to jump.

The sound of a text arriving drew her gaze from Jay. 'Sorry. I thought I'd switched that off.' She took it out of her backpack and went to switch it to silent, but the word 'unknown' leapt from the screen.

'No! Not again.'

'What's up?'

Almost as though in a trance, Karen clicked into the text.

✉ From Unknown
You really don't have a type, do you?

Personally, I think you should stick to the
blond. Your new one's a bit podgy

Pulse racing, Karen clutched the phone as she spun around, looking at the beach, the beach huts, the promenade. Who was it? But nobody was looking at them. Nobody was acting suspiciously. Nobody was holding up a placard declaring 'I'm your stalker'.

Another beep from her mobile made her heart thump uncontrollably.

✉ From Unknown
What would Ryan think if he saw this?

A photo appeared of Karen and Jay on the edge of Hearnshaw Park holding on to each other, looking into each other's eyes and laughing. Completely innocent yet that particular image managed to look so intimate.

'Is that us?'

Karen hadn't even registered Jay beside her. Numbly, she handed him her phone and allowed him to scroll through the texts. 'Someone hates me,' she whispered.

'Someone's stalking you,' he cried. 'Are you okay? Do you know who it is?'

Feeling very shaky, Karen made her way to the wall at the bottom of the huts and sat down. Jay sat beside her.

'I don't know who it is,' she said. 'I don't why or what they want but it terrifies me. Someone was watching us earlier, Jay.' Karen's voice cracked and Jay immediately put his arm round her and pulled her to his side.

'Have you been to the police?' he asked.

'Ryan didn't think they'd take a few texts seriously.'

'Someone's watching you and taking photos. I'm sure they take stuff like that very seriously.'

There was another beep. Jay, who was still holding the phone, glanced down at it then leapt up and spun in a circle just like Karen had done earlier.

'What is it?' She grabbed the phone off him.

✉ From Unknown
Aw, how sweet. Did the photo scare you? You play a great damsel in distress. The podgy one will be snogging you next

Hello Friday. Alison sighed. Physically, she felt exhausted, aching from bootcamp and from working instead of taking a much-needed holiday. Emotionally, she was also drained too: worried about Danniella, uncertain of the future of her relationship, and from re-opening old wounds about the crash. Yet would sleep come? Would it, heck. If she could find a way to switch off her mind, she might have stood a chance, but it was like a meme she'd seen on Facebook earlier in the week: *My brain has too many tabs open.* So true.

Tab one had been a text from Dave, sent just before she finished her shift at 10 p.m.:

✉ From Dave
I messed up. I should never have come on
holiday without you. You'd like it here.
It's not just pubs and clubs. Our holiday in
Corfu was better than being with the lads.

Should have re-lived that with you like you
said. Missing my favourite girl xxx

When she read it, a fuzzy 'aw' moment swiftly gave way to
anger and she'd nearly hurled her phone across the
staffroom. Stupid arse. That opportunity had been offered to
him on a plate and he'd turned her down flat. She hoped he
was having a miserable time. She hoped he was lonely. Her
fingers had hovered over the keypad to tap in a reply but she
stopped herself. How could she respond to a text like that?
She certainly wasn't in the right frame of mind to send him a
'missing you too' text but she equally didn't have the energy
to start an argument with someone in Spain.

Returning home to an empty house, she'd felt wide awake
and twitchy. She tried to watch something on TV but couldn't
seem to sit still. A bath perhaps? It might relax her and help
her sleep, particularly if she used some lavender bubbles.

Tab two opened while she lay back in the bubbles, trying
to empty her mind. She couldn't stop thinking about
Danniella, and panic gripped her. What if she'd done something stupid? She clambered out of the bath and, still dripping, and rushed into the bedroom to call her again. No
response. No texts. No emails.

There was a missed call from Dave, though, and listening
to the voicemail opened yet another tab. He was obviously in
a bar or club because she could barely hear him for the background music, chatter and laughter. 'Where the bloody hell
are you? You're with that bloke again, aren't you? That one
you stayed with on Saturday? Well screw you, Ali. Two can
play at that game.'

While she brushed her teeth and got ready for bed, visions of Dave with other women invaded her mind: slow-dancing with a redhead, kissing a blonde, and rolling around on the bed with a brunette. They'd all be slim and beautiful making Dave question why he'd wasted so many years with a 'chubba' like Alison. She grabbed the side of the sink, breathing heavily, stomach churning. She couldn't bear the thought of him with someone else. He was her family and she was his, always and forever. That's what they'd promised each other.

Cue another tab opening around the death of her family.

Crawling under the duvet, she closed her eyes. How different would her life have been if the crash had never happened? She might have had friends, she might have gone onto sixth form with them, meaning she wouldn't have met Dave. Grandma might still be alive; her heart never having suffered the stress and strain of losing her family and having to bring up a teenager alone. Those tabs just kept on opening.

An hour or so later, Alison switched the light back on and padded downstairs. She heated up a pan of milk and made a hot chocolate, adding in a drop of Baileys.

Dave rang again at 2.47 a.m. and she let it go to voicemail. Two hours later, curiosity overcame her and she listened to his slurred message. He'd obviously left the bar or club because there was no music this time: 'I'm sorry, Ali... Didn't mean it... You're my favourite and only girl...'

Alison frowned. Was that a woman's voice in the background?

'Shh... Sorry, Ali. Where was I...? Yes! S'only been you, forever... Don't want anyone else... Hang on...'

Someone was speaking again and, although Alison

couldn't make out what was being said, it was definitely a woman. She sat up straight, heart thumping. Dave's voice came over muffled, as though he'd put his hand over the phone, but she could still hear him.

'I said shh. I'm on the phone to my girlfriend... I told you I had one... Shut up or sod off. You're distracting me.'

A woman giggled in the background and, this time, her words were clear: 'How's this for a distraction? Does your girlfriend do this?'

Then the phone went dead.

What the...? Alison waited for her call to connect without success. She tried again and again but it wasn't working. She flung the phone onto the bed. Probably just as well she couldn't get through because she'd have torn a strip off him without giving him any chance to explain. Could it be innocent, though? There'd definitely been a woman and she'd definitely been trying it on with Dave, but that didn't mean he'd responded. He hated infidelity. His parents had split up after cheating on each other and it had destroyed his relationship with them both. He wouldn't do that to her. Or would he? The last few weeks had been horrendous and they both had a lot of thinking to do about the future of their relationship. Was being with someone else part of his thinking process? She could just imagine the classic cliché: *She meant nothing. Being with her made me realise how much I really love you.* Argh! And would he admit it if anything happened? After all, what goes on in Ibiza...

27

ALISON

There was nothing Alison could do about Dave but there had to be something she could do about Danniella. Should she call the police? How would that conversation go?

Hi, a woman who I hardly know isn't returning my calls and I'm worried about her so I'd like you to break into her flat because I think she's upset about something that happened in her past, although I don't know what...

Yeah, right. That wasn't an option. If only she knew someone who knew Danniella. Of course! Aidan. As Danniella's landlord, he had to have a spare key. Why hadn't she thought of that before?

She didn't have his number anymore and a quick search on her phone revealed he wasn't on Facebook.

Shortly after 8 a.m., Alison parked at the top of Ocean Ravine. She'd remembered Danniella telling her that Aidan's mum ran the B&B where she'd stayed, although she couldn't remember the name of it.

She set off down the road, which featured an eclectic mix of hotels and guest houses of all shapes and sizes. Hopefully the name of one of them would ring a bell. She was near the bottom, not far from Hearnshaw Park, when a name finally seemed familiar: Sunny Dayz Guest House. Was that it? Glancing at the advertising board outside, her heart raced.

Lorraine and Nigel Thorpe would like to extend a very warm welcome to you and hope that, even if the weather doesn't provide you with sunny days, you'll leave with happy memories of Sunny Dayz.

Yes! She'd found it.

* * *

'Morning, my dear, can I help you?' A woman in her mid-fifties wearing a bright yellow apron emerged from what looked to be the dining room.

'I hope so. Are you Aidan's mum?'

'You know my Aidan?'

'I used to. He was a friend at college but we kind of lost touch. I was wondering if you might be able to help me get in touch with him.'

'I'd probably best not hand out his number without checking, but I can give him a message. What's your name?'

'It's Alison and...' She hesitated. 'This is going to sound stupid but a friend of mine is staying in a flat that Aidan owns and—'

'You mean Danniella? Oh, I love that girl. How is she? I haven't heard from her for a while.'

'That's the problem. Neither have I. She was poorly at the weekend and I haven't been able to get hold of her since. I don't want to cause a panic, but I wondered whether Aidan could...'

Lorraine had already whipped her mobile out of a pocket in her apron.

'Have you got a car?' Lorraine asked after she'd briefly spoken to Aidan.

'A van.'

'Good. He'll meet you at the flat in ten minutes.'

* * *

Alison had already parked and was sitting on the steps of Cobalt House when Aidan screeched to a halt behind the van. He ran across the road, a set of keys dangling from his hand.

'I've tried buzzing her and phoning again,' Alison said.

'I tried her on the way over too.' He unlocked the main door.

Following him up to Danniella's flat, Alison's heart thumped with fear as to what they'd find as much as it did from the exercise.

'Danniella?' Aidan knocked on the door and listened, then knocked again. 'Danniella, it's Aidan and I'm here with Alison. We're going to let ourselves in.'

The door opened and a whiff of overflowing bins and stale milk hit Alison.

'Danniella?' she called.

Aidan headed for the lounge and Alison for the kitchen, the aroma making her stomach gag. A pint of milk spilled on the worktop was obviously the source of one of the smells. There were mugs, glasses, empty yoghurt pots, and banana skins strewn everywhere.

'Danniella?' Aidan called, running up the stairs.

'Shit! Ali! Help!' Aidan cried moments later.

She sprinted up the stairs and into the bathroom where Aidan was knelt on the floor, cradling Danniella in his arms, blood on his hands. Danniella's eyes were closed, her face deathly white.

'Call 999,' he rasped.

28

ALISON

'Thank you.' Alison gratefully took the plastic cup of coffee from Aidan.

He sat beside her in the hospital waiting room. 'Any news?'

'No.'

'At least she's conscious. That has to be a good thing.'

Alison nodded. 'I just keep thinking if I'd contacted you earlier...'

Aidan took her free hand in his and shuffled in his seat to face her. 'You can't think like that, Ali. The paramedics reckoned it was an accident, not... you know. Either way, none of this was your fault.'

Picturing Danniella lying on the bathroom floor, she shuddered. What if it had been a suicide attempt? Surely Danniella wouldn't have taken out a three-month lease or enrolled in bootcamp to make a few friends if she was intending to end things. They'd giggled together whilst watching a couple of comedies on Saturday night, as though neither of them had a care in the world. But Alison had plenty of worries that she usually hid really well and, from Danniella's reaction on the seafront, clearly she did too. And, of course, that had been the day after the films. What if Alison's story had been the trigger to Danniella taking that final step?

She shuddered again. The paramedics had asked her and Aidan a stack of questions, but they'd been unable to answer any: had Danniella been drinking, taking drugs, was she diabetic, who was her next of kin?

Aidan had opened the mirrored cabinet above the sink but there was no medication in there other than a packet of paracetamol with only two missing. He'd checked the bin then the bedroom but there'd been no empty pill bottles or packets, no alcohol, no cuts to Danniella's wrists or anything like that, and no note.

The paramedics reckoned she'd either slipped or fainted, knocking herself out on the sink. As they loaded her into the ambulance, she'd started to come round, making Alison feel weak with relief.

'Are you cold?' Aidan asked as Alison shuddered again.

'No. I just keep picturing her and...'

Aidan put his arm around her and she nestled against his side, occasionally sipping on her coffee.

'Are you Danniella's friends?' Alison opened her eyes and sat up. A tall woman stood over them.

'Yes. Is she okay? Can we see her?'

'Soon. I'm Dr Aguda. Your friend is making good progress although she's a bit groggy. One of my colleagues is still with her. Give her half an hour then you may go in. She will be tired so she may not be responsive to a long visit, but I think she will be happy to see you both.'

'Thank you,' Alison and Aidan said together.

With a smile, Dr Aguda strode down the corridor and out of sight.

Alison rubbed her eyes. 'Thank God for that.' She turned to Aidan. 'How long was I asleep?'

'About twenty minutes.'

'Did I spill my coffee on you?'

'I rescued it from your hand as soon as you started snoring.'

She gasped. 'I wasn't snoring, was I?'

Aidan laughed. 'No, but your face is a picture right now.'

Alison gave him a playful shove and their eyes locked as they smiled together.

'It's so good to see you, Ali,' he said, his expression soft. 'I wish the circumstances were different, though.'

She nodded. 'It's good to see you too. It's been a long time. You don't look any different. Not like me.'

Aidan followed the movement of her hands as she indicated her changed body, then shook his head. 'I don't think you've changed at all. You still look amazing.'

'Yeah, right.'

'Yeah, right! You were gorgeous at college and you still are.' Aidan smiled when Alison blushed. 'I'll stop embarrassing you now, should I? So, tell me about life since college.'

Alison shrugged. 'Not much to say. A few years working in the Tourist Information office and now I'm a receptionist at The Ramparts Hotel which I absolutely love. Best job in the world. What about you? Danniella tells me you're a travel writer.'

'Also the best job in the world.'

Alison listened, fascinated, as Aidan listed some of the places he'd visited for his books.

'It sounds amazing. I'd love to travel. I went to France and Germany with my family when I was little but I don't really remember it. I went to Corfu when I was twenty-one and I've barely ventured outside Whitsborough Bay since then.'

'If you get the opportunity, I can't recommend it enough. Whitsborough Bay will always be my home, but the world's my playground.' His phone beeped. 'It's my mum wanting to know if there's any news. Do you mind if I give her a call?'

'Go ahead,' Alison said.

Aidan wandered into the corridor and she sighed. If she hadn't run out of the lesson that day and met Dave while she was at her lowest, could her friendship with Aidan have developed into something more? From that very first day, she had felt a connection that had grown stronger and stronger. They spent study periods in the library, huddled together, whispering about their homework. At lunchtime, they rushed their food, escaped the noise of the canteen, and wandered round the playing fields talking and laughing. She wanted to tell him about her family but she feared that, if she told him the truth, the laughter would stop and, like the others before him, he'd pull away. The thought of losing him as a friend was unbearable, so she never fully let him in. She never explained why she lived with her grandma. She never let on that her heart broke every single day. She never told him that she only felt alive when she was with him. She never admitted that she genuinely believed that he could be her destiny.

Feeling nostalgic, Alison rummaged in her bag for a notepad and pen, scribbled his name on a piece of paper, and placed it on his seat. She smiled as she replayed that first day at college in her mind, then the doubts set in. What if he didn't remember their first conversation and thought she was being weird? She was about to remove the paper when Aidan returned to the waiting room. Too late.

'Sorry about that.' He looked down and laughed. 'I'm hoping that seat has my name on it.'

He remembered. She looked down at the paper then up at him again, smiling. 'So it does. Must be destiny.'

'It looks like I'm all yours, then.' He fixed his dark eyes on hers, a smile playing on his lips. The chatter of relatives and the ringing of phones seemed to fade away and Alison felt like they were all alone. Her heart thumped as he picked up the paper and sat beside her. Butterflies took flight as his leg rested against hers. And, as he whispered, 'Definitely destiny,' all she could think about was his lips pressing against hers.

He kept his eyes on hers and Alison could feel the electricity crackling between them. He leaned a little closer. He was going to kiss her. After all this time, he was...

'Danniella's ready for visitors now if you want to go in.'

Alison stood up quickly, colour flooding her cheeks. Oh, God! Dave! It was fine, though. It wasn't a kiss. It was just a moment. Insignificant.

'Thank you,' she said to the nurse.

Aidan followed her into the ward as her heart raced. Not destiny at all. If they were meant to be, it would have happened at college, not now.

* * *

Tears pricked Alison's eyes as she and Aidan approached Danniella's bed. She looked so small and lost, even in a single bed, connected to a drip and goodness knows what else. Her lips were dry and cracked, and she had dark bags under her eyes.

'Hi,' Alison said.

'Hi,' Danniella whispered.

'How are you feeling?' Aidan asked.

'Like I've got the worst hangover in the history of the world.'

Alison and Aidan sat on the pair of plastic chairs next to the bed.

'Thank you both,' Danniella said. 'You saved my life.'

'What happened?' Alison asked. 'Only if you want to tell us. Remember what I said about my friendship not coming with a full-disclosure agreement.'

Danniella smiled weakly. 'Panic attack. Might have had a few since...' She paused and took a few slow, deep breaths.

'Since Sunday?' Alison asked.

Danniella nodded slowly. 'I didn't try to... I know how it might have looked, but I'd never... You have to know that.' A tear trickled down her cheek and trailed towards her ear.

Alison placed her hand over Danniella's. 'I'm so sorry. It was my fault.'

'No. Not your fault. I need to tell you...' Danniella's eyes flickered. 'I want you to know...' She breathed deeply again. 'Have to explain...'

'You don't have to do anything,' Alison insisted.

'Want to. Need to.'

'You need to rest,' Aidan said. 'Whatever you want to say, it can wait until you're better, can't it?'

'Thank you.' Then Danniella's eyes closed and she drifted off.

* * *

Alison's mobile rang as she and Aidan made their way across the hospital car park. Her stomach clenched when she saw Dave's name on her screen. Without answering, she tossed it back into her bag.

'Dare I ask?' Aidan said.

Alison felt for the tiny ring she always wore on a chain around her neck – the birthday gift she'd given to Fleur on the morning of the accident – and ran the ring up and down the chain, unable to put her finger on why she was suddenly feeling so nervous. 'You remember Dave from college?'

Was it her imagination or had Aidan stiffened at the mention of his name? 'Yeah.'

'I live with him. Well, I do at the moment. He's in Ibiza and I'm here and...' Alison felt the tears well in her eyes and gulped. 'Let's just say it's complicated and leave it there. What about you? Wife? Kids?'

'Single. No kids. I was married, but she—'

Alison's phone rang again. 'Sorry. He'll keep calling. I'll switch it to silent.'

'I can wait in the car if you want to get it.'

'I don't. I wish he'd stop ringing.'

They walked back to Aidan's car in silence.

* * *

'So, how do you know Danniella?' Aidan asked as they set off back to the flat.

Alison told him how they'd met, grateful that he wasn't quizzing her about Dave.

'I'd ask if you want to grab a drink,' he said when they stopped on Sea View Drive. 'But I've got to be somewhere.'

'That's okay,' Alison said. 'Can I have your keys? I don't want Danniella to come back to the mess.'

As he dug in his pocket for the keys, Alison could feel her phone vibrating in her bag. Dave, no doubt. If that nurse hadn't appeared, would she have kissed Aidan earlier? Probably. Which meant she was as bad as Dave. Worse. Because if Dave had been with someone in Ibiza, it really would have meant nothing, but if she'd kissed Aidan, she'd have been kissing the man she used to love.

'If you give me your address, I can call round tonight for the keys,' Aidan said.

'I'll drop them back at your mum's. Save you the trouble.'

'It's no trouble.'

'It's fine,' she insisted, eager to get away before she did something she might regret. 'Thanks for today. See you around.'

'Alis—'

She slammed the car door and ran up the front steps. He hadn't driven off because she'd have heard, but she refused to turn around and look. If she looked, she might run back to him and ask for that kiss.

Hurrying up the stairs to Danniella's flat, she let herself in. The acrid smell of milk hit her and she sank down behind the door, gasping for breath, her body heaving with sobs. Danniella, Dave, Aidan. It was all too much.

29

KAREN

Jay came round on Friday evening to plan the Scouting boot-camp, armed with milk, hot chocolate, and mini-marsh-mallows.

'I called the police today,' Karen said while he brought the milk to the boil.

'What did they say?'

'The woman I spoke to was great. She suggested I change my phone number, but I can't do that because of the business so I've blocked the number again.'

'Again?' Jay took the pan off the hob, poured it into a jug of cocoa, and began mixing.

'I blocked it after you suggested it, but they obviously got themselves another phone because the texts didn't stop. The police said to keep a copy of the messages. If it continues or gets more serious, they can try to trace the caller and prosecute them although if it's a pay-as-you-go they probably won't find them.'

'And you definitely have no idea who could be doing it?' Jay asked, pouring the hot chocolate into mugs.

He passed her a mug and they moved over to the table.

'I didn't think I had any enemies,' Karen said, 'but I've obviously upset someone big time.'

Jay tipped some marshmallows into his mug then handed Karen the bag. 'Not necessarily.'

'What do you mean?'

'I was looking online and it's not always someone who has something against their victim. They could be someone who loves you or even a stranger who's randomly picked you out.'

'They do know me. They know my name and Ryan's.'

Jay grimaced. 'Again, not necessarily. They could have seen you with that extremely discreet bootcamp flag of yours and got your names off your website or social media. Could still be a stranger.'

'I get what you're saying. Oh well, I'm determined not to let them get to me. I'll try to vary my routine where I can, as the police suggested, but I'm not going into hiding.'

'Good for you.'

'And I'm not going to spend any more time talking about them, either. So, let's talk about this bootcamp for Scouts...'

* * *

'My mind is officially frazzled,' Karen said after a couple of hours of planning at the kitchen table. Jay was like a breath of fresh air. Bouncing ideas off each other and building on each other's suggestions, it had reminded Karen of her early days with Ryan and Steff when they'd planned how to run Bay Fitness. It seemed so long ago now and so much had changed between them all since then.

'Are you happy with what we have for the Scouts?' she asked.

'Definitely. They're going to love this. Thank you so much for giving up your time like this.'

'It was an evening well spent,' Karen said rolling her shoulders. 'Do you need to shoot home yet?'

'No urgency, but I can head off if you've had enough of me.'

'I might let you stay a bit longer.' She winked at him. 'But let's have some comfier seats.'

She led Jay through to the lounge, put some music on, and plonked herself down on the other end of the sofa from him.

'Nice house,' he said. 'Have you been here long?'

'About eight years now. We both love it here, but it's rented so there's always that fear that the landlord will announce one day that he wants to sell up. You own yours?'

'It's inherited. It was my grandma's. Probably not what I'd have chosen but I've been steadily modernising it.' He smiled ruefully. 'And then Sophie's been changing all that.'

Karen wasn't sure how to respond without sounding mean.

'Would you mind if I used your toilet?' Jay asked.

'It's upstairs.' She stood up. 'I'll show you. I could do with grabbing a hoodie.'

Karen ran up both flights and switched on the bedroom light, lowered the blinds, then took a hooded top from her wardrobe. Her phone beeped.

⛶ From Unknown
While the cat's away the mice will play, eh?

Can't believe you picked the podgy one
instead of the blond. You'd better make it
quick. Ryan should be home soon. Unless
that's part of your plan. Interesting

She dived for the window and yanked the blinds open, franti-cally scanning the street below. Completely deserted.

'Another text,' she cried, running past Jay as he stepped out of the bathroom.

'You're kidding!' He ran after her.

There was a screech of tyres but, by the time they made it out the door, there were no moving vehicles in sight.

'Damn! Missed them.' Karen pressed down on the door handle then let out a frustrated squeal and stamped her feet. 'No! I've locked us out. I'm so sorry.'

They looked at each other and started laughing.

'At least it's not raining,' Jay said.

Karen looked at her watch and yawned. 10.30 p.m. 'Ryan should be back soon so feel free to head home before you're in trouble with Sophie.'

'I'll stay with you.'

'You really don't have to.'

Jay smiled. 'I do.'

'It's very chivalrous but it's a safe area and—'

'And my keys and phone are on your kitchen table,' Jay finished.

'Ah! Sorry.'

They sat down together on the front doorstep and she nudged into him.

'Will Sophie be mad with you?'

'Probably.'

'Sorry.'

Jay nudged her back. 'Stop saying sorry.'

'Sorry. Argh! Sorry. No! I can't stop!'

Ryan's car pulled onto the drive while they were giggling. He shot them a filthy look as he got out. 'What's going on?'

'We're locked out,' she said as they both stood up.

'We?'

'Ryan, this is Jay. Jay, Ryan.'

Jay reached out to shake Ryan's hand but Ryan shoved his hands into the pocket of his hoodie. Rude. Karen bristled but didn't say anything.

'I'm running a bootcamp for Jay's Scout group and we've been planning it, but my stalker texted. We tried to catch them, but it took too long to run down the stairs and—'

'What were you doing upstairs?' Ryan asked, shooting more dark looks in Jay's direction.

Karen planted her hands on her hips. 'Seriously? We're going to do this in front of a client?'

Ryan pushed past them and unlocked the door.

'I'll get my keys then leave you to it,' Jay muttered, sidling past Ryan.

'What is with you at the moment?' Karen hissed, following Jay towards the kitchen.

Jay retrieved his belongings.

'I'm really sorry about Ryan,' she said. 'He's not normally like this.'

'Will you be okay?'

Karen nodded. '*I* will be. *He* won't be after we've had words.'

'I'd better go before I make things worse. Same time for PT on Thursday?' Jay started walking towards the door.

'Yes. Same time.'

Jay took a step towards her as though he was going to give her a hug then obviously thought better of it. 'See ya.'

She waved him off then closed the door and leaned against it, determined not to confront Ryan with all guns blazing. What the hell was going on? She genuinely didn't recognise Ryan or their relationship anymore so it was time to get to the bottom of it, even if she didn't like the answers. The one thing she was pretty certain of was that acquiring a stalker wasn't just a coincidence. Something told her that Ryan's behaviour and the stalker were connected and she was determined to find out how.

30

KAREN

Karen woke with a start and reached for her phone. 6.21 a.m. Urgh.

The bed beside her was empty and showed no sign of being slept in. She and Ryan had hit a stalemate somewhere in the early hours. Exhausted from going round in circles, she'd given up and retreated to bed. Ryan clearly hadn't followed.

The sound of the front door closing drew her out of bed and towards the window. Opening the blinds a fraction, she watched Ryan get into his car in his running gear, then pull out of Rowan Drive. Were they going to have another weekend of 'conveniently' missing each other due to work commitments?

Karen sighed as she replayed the ugly scenes from the night before. It had been awful. There'd been shouts, accusations, and recriminations. Karen couldn't remember another occasion when she'd felt so embarrassed, especially in front of a client, and she'd never, ever felt ashamed of Ryan before. She therefore knew that if she didn't take a moment after Jay left, her approach would have been like a volcano erupting. When she felt ready for a calm, civilised discussion, Ryan had opened the conversation with, 'I must have missed the email. Are we inviting all our clients back to our house now? And do they all get invited up to the bedroom or is it only the young, good-looking ones?' So the volcano erupted anyway.

Standing in the shower, Karen closed her eyes and let the water cascade over her. Was this it? Was it over? But how had it come to this? Last night, she'd asked him outright if he'd been seeing anyone behind her back, even if it was a one-off, but he'd just turned it back round on her, suggesting there was something going on between Jay and her. She'd felt the gulf between them widen with each accusation.

* * *

Steff picked her up for the Saturday morning bootcamp. 'You look like shit warmed up,' she said when Karen got into the car. 'Ryan?'

'Yep. Massive bust-up last night and we slept in separate rooms.'

'Oh no! Is he still in bed?

'No, I checked. Presumably he's gone for a run. Probably to avoid me.'

'For God's sake, what's wrong with him at the moment?' Steff shook her head as she pulled away.

'If you find out, let me know.'

'Do you want to talk about it?'

'Yes, but it's not fair on you,' Karen said. 'He's your best friend and business partner. Besides, you said you didn't want to get involved.'

'That was silly of me. I'm already involved. As soon as we

went into partnership, our lives became intrinsically linked. I'm all ears.'

Karen smiled gratefully. 'Do you have time for a cuppa after bootcamp? My treat.'

'If you throw in a toasted teacake too, I'm all yours.'

'Deal.'

* * *

Pushing all thoughts of Ryan firmly from her mind that morning, Karen had a blast running bootcamp with Steff. She realised with a pang of regret that she'd stopped making an effort to be friends rather than business partners, she'd stopped noticing the sense of humour and ready banter, and she'd stopped appreciating Steff's gift for inspiring and motivating their clients. All it had taken was for Steff to reach out an olive branch and acknowledge their difficult relationship, and for Karen to accept that branch, and the dynamics had completely shifted.

'Good to see you smiling,' Steff said when the last of the morning's bootcampers wandered out of earshot.

'I really enjoyed that,' Karen said.

'I could tell. It felt like the early days again.'

Karen nodded. 'I hadn't realised I'd got so serious.'

Steff lifted the flag out of the sand. 'I think we're all guilty of that. I don't think the clients would have noticed any difference, though.' She hoisted her backpack onto her shoulder. 'Right. Toasted teacake, tea, and talk...'

* * *

'Sorry to say this, Karen, but what a stupid twat he is,' Steff said when Karen had brought her up to date over brunch. 'He's my best mate and I'd normally side with him on anything, but this is ridiculous.'

'It's not just me overreacting?'

'Hardly. I don't know what's got into him lately. As I said before, he's been really off with me. I can't seem to do anything right when he's around and I've no idea why he's turned on either of us. I have tried to talk to him but I'll try again. I won't let on that we've had a chat, though, or he'll accuse us of ganging up against him or something stupid like that.'

'Thanks, Steff. I really appreciate it.'

'How's the rest of your day looking?' Karen asked as they got ready to leave Waterfront Lodge.

'PT all afternoon and a party tonight. It's a fortieth birthday for one of Mia's colleagues and I really don't fancy it, but I can't think of a good enough excuse to dip out.'

'Tell you what, how about I go to the party and you can spend the evening with Ryan?'

Steff laughed. 'Suddenly the party sounds really appealing.'

* * *

Karen parked outside her mum's house shortly before lunch. Walking up the drive, she spotted Alison watering a hanging basket next door.

'Any news on Danniella?' she asked.

Alison's eyes clouded with tears. 'She's in hospital. I got her landlord to let us in yesterday and we found her collapsed on the bathroom floor.'

'Oh my God! Is she okay?'

'We think so. I'm going to see her at visiting time.'

'Oof.' Something launched itself at Karen. She looked down at the limpet clinging to her waist. 'Hi, Eden.'

'I missed you,' Eden said, hugging her even more tightly.

'And I missed you.'

'Does your sister get all the hugs or are there any going spare?' Alison asked. Eden released Karen and gave Alison a bear hug. 'Can you run a mile yet?' she asked.

'I've only been to bootcamp four times. Give me a chance.'

Eden turned to Karen and proudly announced, 'I bet Alison a lipstick that you'd soon have her running, like, a mile.'

'And I soon will,' Karen said, smiling at Alison. 'She's doing brilliantly so far so she'd better start saving her pennies.' She glanced at her watch. 'Eden, can you tell Mum that I need a quick chat with Alison and I'll be in by twelve?'

Eden nodded towards Alison. 'That lipstick? Totes mine.' Then she ran back towards the house.

'Do they know what happened?' Karen asked when she heard the front door closing.

'A panic attack. She knocked herself out on the sink as she fainted. She was really tired so I didn't get much more out of her. Hopefully she'll be a bit more with it this afternoon.'

'Crikey. Poor Danniella. Will you send her my love? Actually, I'm off to the hospital myself this afternoon to see my great-auntie so I might pop in.

31

DANNIELLA

Danniella couldn't imagine a boxer who'd completed a full twelve rounds feeling any worse than she did. She felt broken physically but also mentally. Hourly checks had made sleep impossible, not that she'd have been able to sleep with so much on her mind. If Alison hadn't been worried enough to alert Aidan... It didn't bear thinking about. Talk about getting the shock of her life and a huge wake-up call. She didn't physically want to run away again – Whitsborough Bay still felt right – but she now knew that running wasn't the solution emotionally either. If she was to have any sort of future, she needed to face the past, and the only way she was going to be able to do that was with professional help. She'd definitely make that a priority.

Another priority had to be a huge apology to Alison and Aidan. If she was going to move forward, it wasn't just professional help she'd need; she was going to need their help which meant she was going to need to open up and hope they didn't hate her as much as she hated herself.

'When do you think I'll be able to go home?' Danniella

asked when a pretty blonde nurse called Kirsty appeared to check her blood pressure and pupil reaction.

'It's not my decision, but I wouldn't be surprised if Dr Aguda releases you later today. Your BP is still low but improving and everything else is looking good. I suspect she'll want to see you have some lunch, though.'

Danniella nodded. 'Fair enough. Thanks.'

She reached for her mobile.

✉ From Alison
Dropped your bag and phone off last night
but you were asleep. Hope you feel rested.
I'll be in at visiting hour. If you get
released sooner or you need anything,
though, give me a call and I'll be straight
over xx

Danniella smiled as she put the phone aside. What an amazing friend. What a lucky day it had been when they'd met. When she'd told Dr Aguda that she had no family in the area, the doctor had looked at her with sympathy and said, 'Just as well you have a couple of good friends, then, because you're going to need them.' She certainly was.

Lunch was hard work, but Danniella knew she was being watched and that her release might depend on what she ate. She managed to force down a small piece of chicken, some vegetables and a yoghurt. *Please let it be enough.* She longed to go back home and start re-building her life. It was funny how she already thought of a rented flat that she'd only lived in for a month as home.

Alison appeared with the first wave of visitors, as promised. Danniella felt tearful at the unconditional support.

'Oh my word, you look so much better than yesterday,' Alison said, hugging her. 'How's the head?'

'Like the hangover from hell, but without the memories of a great night out to make the pain worthwhile.'

Alison sat down. 'When will you be discharged?'

'Hopefully today. They wanted to make sure I ate something first.'

'And have you?' Alison asked. 'Eaten, that is?'

'A bit. Hopefully it was enough.' Danniella sighed. 'I have some issues with food. I'll tell you about them but maybe not here.'

'You don't have to tell me anything.'

'I know, but I need to.' Danniella sighed again. 'I'm going to need to ask for your help.'

Alison shook her head. 'You don't need to ask. Help is here.'

'Thank you. You have no idea how much that means to me.'

'Can I get you anything now? There's a shop downstairs. Newspaper? Magazine? Drink? Chocolate?'

'I'd love a fruity drink if they've got one.'

'Back soon.'

With Alison gone, Danniella lay back against her pillow. She'd binged, hadn't she? Before the massive panic attack, she'd binged on chocolate and ice-cream and goodness knows what else. It had been a long time since she'd done that.

She'd always thought she had a happy childhood until

she was thirteen and her parents announced they'd met other people and were divorcing. Her parents moved in with new partners, she gained five step-siblings, and everyone was happy except her; the outsider with two houses, but no real home. She went from being the centre of her parents' lives – or so she'd thought – to being completely invisible. It was too painful to be part of the family, yet not part of the family, so she completely withdrew. And nobody noticed.

Eight months after the split, the Easter holidays arrived. A load of Easter eggs were stacked on her desk in her bedroom; a poor substitute for love and affection. Rage flowing through her, she punched the boxes and smashed the chocolate to smithereens, then shovelled in chunk after chunk, practically gagging on the stuff, as though it was the only way of filling the emptiness inside her.

Looking at the carnage in horror, barely able to believe what she'd done, she ran to the bathroom and purged for the first time.

Nobody challenged her about the Easter eggs. Nobody asked why the bin was full of wrappers. And, in Danniella's mind, if nobody asked, it was because they didn't care.

For the next three years, bulimia controlled her although, at the time, it felt like the only part of her life that she controlled.

When she was sixteen, her oldest stepsister from her mum's new family, Natalie, turned eighteen. Danniella offered to be on kitchen duty at her party, replenishing the buffet, washing up... and accessing the food without anyone watching.

After Natalie blew out her candles, Danniella took the cake away to cut up for the guests. When Natalie appeared to collect the pieces, she caught Danniella mid-gorge, an enormous chunk of cake in each hand. Danniella couldn't speak, her mouth stuffed full of sponge. She cringed, waiting for Natalie to start yelling at her for ruining her cake and her birthday. Instead, Natalie shut the kitchen door, muffling the music and laughter and looked at her sympathetically. 'My friend Kate is bulimic. You are too, aren't you?'

Danniella made Natalie promise not to say anything and swore that she'd see her GP. She never made the appointment, though.

When Danniella was eighteen, her mum heard her vomiting several times in one week and assumed that she was pregnant. Without giving Danniella the chance to speak, she launched into a bitter tirade about how Danniella was the reason she'd stayed in an unhappy marriage for thirteen years, ruining her life, so there was no way she was going to put her life aside again by supporting her through a pregnancy.

Natalie and her boyfriend, Ricky, had moved in together and they took Danniella in but on one condition: Natalie was allowed to accompany her to her GP and ensure she got the help she needed. It was a tough battle but she finally did win control of her bulimia.

Until that fateful day when her life changed beyond all recognition and her battle with food manifested itself in different ways.

* * *

Alison reappeared with some drinks as the same nurse from earlier stopped by for Danniella's hourly checks.

'Same as before,' Kirsty said, releasing the blood pressure cuff. 'And you ate some lunch?'

Danniella nodded.

'In that case, you're good to go.'

'Really?'

Kirsty leaned in conspiratorially. 'You might want to put some clothes on first, though. Just sayin'.'

'That's brilliant news,' Alison said.

Kirsty turned to Alison. 'Your friend here is going to need lots of support.' She turned back to Danniella. 'What must you do first thing tomorrow?'

'Register with a doctor.'

'And after that?'

'Take all the help I can get. Thanks, Kirsty.'

'Pleasure. And let's not be seeing you again.' With a smile, Kirsty left them.

'Any chance of a lift home?' Danniella asked.

'Of course.'

'And... and I realise this is a *huge* imposition so feel free to say no, but I was wondering...'

Alison gently placed her hand on Danniella's arm. 'I can stay for as long as you need.'

Danniella felt quite shaky with relief. The thought of going back there on her own, with blood still on the sink, the detritus from several binges in the kitchen, and goodness knows what other mess was too much to cope with. 'Thank you,' she whispered.

'You're the one doing me the favour. That bed is ten times more comfortable than the one at home. In fact, *everything* about your flat is ten times more comfortable than my house. How about you get some clothes on then we can get out of here?'

* * *

Later, Danniella curled up on the sofa wearing a fresh pair of PJs, a soft cream throw over her legs.

'I can't believe you came back here and cleaned everything up,' she said, taking a mug from Alison. 'I was dreading coming back to the mess.'

'I couldn't leave it like that.'

Danniella took a sip of coffee. 'I'm really sorry about what happened to your family, by the way, and even sorrier that I didn't get a chance to say that properly before.'

Alison gave her an appreciative smile. 'I don't tell many people but, when I do, they don't usually throw up.'

Danniella sighed. 'I really want to explain it, but I don't think I'm ready just yet.'

'Take your time. I won't push.'

'Let's talk about you instead. Has Dave been in touch?'

Alison's expression darkened. 'Yes, although I haven't spoken to him...'

Danniella sipped on her coffee as Alison told her about the texts, the voicemails, and the mixed messages he'd given.

'He texted this morning. Said he'd ditched the lads and watched the sun set last night, wished I was there, missed me loads, blah, blah, blah.'

'I take it you didn't believe him?'

Alison sighed. 'I don't know what to believe anymore. He was with a woman, but was he actually *with* her? I don't know.'

'What does your heart tell you?'

'My heart says that he'd never do that to me.'

'And your head?'

'My head says what goes on in Ibiza stays in Ibiza.'

'Oh, Ali.' Danniella placed her empty mug on the floor. 'When's he back?'

'Monday.'

'What happens then?'

'He'll get a hell of a shock that I'm not there.'

'You'll let him know where you are, though?'

'I suppose so, although he was convinced you were some bloke I'd hooked up with.'

Danniella paused for a moment. Sod it. She was going to ask. Life was too short for Alison to waste it with someone like Dave. 'What's stopping you from leaving him? Because we both know that you need to say goodbye to him, don't we?'

32

ALISON

Alison's stomach lurched as she looked at Danniella's earnest expression. What was stopping her from leaving Dave? Wow! A million things... and nothing at all.

'I should probably start preparing some tea,' she said.

'If you don't want to talk about it, that's fine. You're speaking to the Queen of Secrecy here so if anyone understands, it's me. I just thought it might help you get your head round things.'

Alison sighed. It would help. Massively. She just wasn't used to opening up to anyone. 'Okay. For a start, there's the practical and financial aspects: a roof over my head and money. I can't afford a place of my own. Well, not yet anyway.'

'I don't mean to sound intrusive or insensitive, but didn't your parents leave you anything?'

'Yes. On paper, I have money. Quite a lot of it.' Alison shook her head. 'But my grandma put it in a trust fund which doesn't mature till my thirtieth birthday. She always believed that the twenties are a funny decade where you're meant to be all grown up, taking on some huge financial and emotional responsibilities, yet most people aren't mature enough or ready to handle them. Yeah, I know. It's ironic looking at it now.'

Danniella raised her eyebrows. 'You're not thirty yet? I just assumed we were the same age.'

'How old are you?'

'Thirty-one.'

Alison shook her head. 'I turned twenty-seven in April. I feel older, though. Rachel next door, Karen's mum, always says Dave and I are old beyond our years. There's nothing like losing your family to age you twenty years overnight and Dave had issues with his family which meant he had to grow up fast too.'

'So you have money,' Danniella said. 'You might not be able to access it, but there are ways around that. You have somewhere to stay too.'

'Where?'

'Here, of course. Obviously we'd need to get Aidan's permission, but it's a big flat for one person and you were saying earlier how comfortable the spare bed is.'

'You'd really let me stay here permanently?' Alison felt so choked with gratitude that the words came out all low and husky.

Danniella placed her hand over Alison's. 'You might have saved my life this weekend. I'd like to return the favour and save yours.'

33

ALISON

Alison had expected her mind to be racing that evening, yet she felt incredibly relaxed. The view from the balcony off Danniella's lounge had her captivated. A canvas of pale pink, lemon, and peach hues swept across the sky, deepening in tone where the colours kissed the horizon. To the right, the castle was silhouetted on the headland. To the left, a string of white lights snaked round from North Bay Corner, past the beach huts, before disappearing beyond the Sea Rescue Sanctuary. A light breeze tickled the sea and danced across the balcony, ruffling Alison's hair.

The gentle tinkling of a set of wind chimes from a nearby balcony stirred a forgotten memory of a six-year-old Fleur hanging some chimes from a hook on the garden fence of their home. She'd informed the family that when they heard the chimes, it meant the fairies were having a grand ball so they needed to tread carefully across the grass. Tears rushed to Alison's eyes and she gasped at the overwhelming vividness of that forgotten memory.

As the colours melted onto the horizon then disappeared for the night, the breeze intensified. She pulled her dressing gown more tightly around her, but had to admit defeat and move back into the lounge. As she stepped off the balcony, the wind chimes tinkled more intensively. Pausing, Alison looked up to the sky and blew a kiss towards the heavens. 'Goodnight, Fleur,' she whispered. 'That's a fine ball those fairies are having, and I bet you're the belle of it.'

* * *

The kettle reached boiling point and Alison was about to pick it up when the door buzzer sounded. Frowning, she tentatively made her way to the flat door.

'Hello?'

'Hi, Alison. It's Aidan.'

'How did you know I was here?'

'I'm all-seeing, all-knowing.'

She glanced down at her PJs. 'It's late. Did you want something?'

'I need my keys back.'

Crap! She'd forgotten to drop them off at Sunny Dayz.

'I'll buzz you up,' she said.

There was a gentle knock on the door moments later and Alison opened it, laughing when she saw what he was wearing. 'Wow! Please tell me you're not a runaway groom.'

Aidan looked down at his morning suit and grinned. 'A runaway best man.'

She closed the door behind him. 'And the DJ has followed up "The Birdie Song" with "Agadoo" so you've made your dash for freedom before "Hokey Cokey" starts and you discover that's what it really is all about?'

'I always loved your sense of humour,' he said, his dark eyes twinkling as he smiled warmly at her.

'Tea?' Disturbed by the butterflies taking flight in her stomach, it was the first thing that popped into her head. 'I was just about to make one when the buzzer went and... of course you don't want one because you've got a wedding to return to. Or I assume you have?'

'Yes I have. But tea would be great.'

'Great. Yes. I'll just boil the kettle. No need. It's already boiled. But I'll make it. You go through to the lounge. It's across the hall.'

'I think I might be able to find it,' he said.

In the kitchen, Alison held her head in her hands, screwed her eyes up, and stamped her feet. What was wrong with her? She'd turned into a gibbering wreck. Fancy giving him directions to the lounge when he owned the flat. Good grief.

* * *

She handed Aidan a mug then shook her head. 'I've just realised that I haven't even asked you how you take it.'

'Milk, no sugar,' he said.

'Phew. Lucky guess.' She was about to sit beside him on the sofa but suddenly didn't trust herself to be in such close proximity to him. She felt all girly and giddy in his presence. It was the morning suit. Definitely. But who was she kidding? Their moment in the waiting room had unearthed some long-buried feelings from college and they were even stronger now than they'd been earlier. When was the last time she'd felt like this around Dave? There'd been moments recently, brief moments, but nothing this intense.

'Ooh. Keys. Let me get you those before I forget again.' She put her mug down next to the chair and retrieved the keys from her handbag. 'Sorry. I collected Danniella today and it went clean out of my mind to drop them at your mum's.'

'It's fine. Thanks.' Aidan's fingers lightly touched her palm as he took the keys and a fizz of electricity shot through her. Gulping, she quickly sat down on the armchair.

'I wouldn't have come round so late but I can't find my garage key and the spare is on here. There's a box in there with cans on strings, shaving foam, an inflatable sheep – best not ask – and other crap to mess up the groom's car.'

'Which is why you've run out on the wedding?'

Aidan nodded. 'Although I think you might have the DJ sussed. It was the "Macarena" when I left.'

He winked at her and Alison felt herself flush from head to toe. 'So Danniella's home from hospital,' she said, 'and she's asked me to stay while she recovers.' She groaned inwardly. Hadn't she already said she'd picked up Danniella earlier and the PJs were probably a big clue that she was staying.

Aidan smiled. 'She called me earlier. That's how I knew you were here. I'm not really Big Brother.'

'Ah! That explains it.'

'She sounded tired but positive. Do you think she's okay?'

'I think she's going to be. She's registering with a GP tomorrow which should get her the professional help she needs. She knows I'm here when she's ready to talk but there's no pressure if she doesn't want to.'

'You're a good friend.' Aidan took a glug from his tea.

Alison sipped on her drink, desperately searching for

something to say that wouldn't make her sound like an idiot again.

'Ali?'

'Yes.'

'Did I say something to upset you yesterday?'

'No.'

He smiled. 'You said that a bit too quickly which confirms that I did.'

'It was nothing.'

'It was obviously something. And I'm not leaving until you fess up.'

'Aidan! That's not fair.'

'Life's not fair, as you've experienced first-hand.'

She narrowed her eyes. 'You know about my family?'

He nodded and hesitated before he said, 'After you ran out of class that day, there were whisperings. I remembered the crash happening and I Googled it to see if it really had been you. I'm so sorry, Ali. I can't imagine what you must have gone through.'

He knew? 'Why didn't you say anything?'

'Because I wanted it to come from you when you felt ready to tell me. You never did, though. I thought I'd failed you as a friend.'

'Oh, Aidan. You didn't fail me. I didn't tell *anyone* at college. I was sick of being Alison Jenkins the-one-whose-family-died. I just wanted to be me. No sympathetic tilts of the head, no sad eyes, no treading on eggshells.'

He nodded. 'I hear you. I was like that when Elizabeth died.'

'Elizabeth?'

'You don't know?'

Alison shrugged.

'Sorry, I assumed Danniella would have told you. Elizabeth was my wife.'

Alison clapped her hand over her mouth. 'Oh my God! You mentioned that you *had* been married but Dave kept ringing and we never finished the conversation. I assumed you were divorced, not widowed. I'm so sorry. When did she die?'

'Three years ago yesterday.'

'No! Aidan.'

He sighed. 'Yeah. Yesterday was a weird day.'

'You poor thing, for yesterday and for losing your wife.'

'I'm okay about it. She was...' He shook his head. 'I'll never get back to the wedding if I start down that road. Worst best man in history.' He stood up and stretched. 'I'll leave you in peace.'

Alison followed him into the hall. What must he have been going through yesterday to have started the day finding Danniella unconscious, all the while knowing it was the three-year anniversary of the death of his wife? Talk about emotional overload!

Aidan reached for the door handle, then turned to face Alison. 'Would you be free for a drink sometime? I know what it's like to have people treading on eggshells around you, avoiding eye contact, stressing over everything they say. We could compare notes.'

Alison nodded eagerly. 'I'd like that. I mean, a drink with you. Maybe not the conversation about dead people although I think it's helpful to talk about it and...' She shook her head. 'I'm so tired. Can you tell? I think I need to stop talking and go to bed.'

He smiled. 'I've got a work deadline coming up so I'll be

holed up in my writing cave for the next couple of weeks, but how about after that?'

'Sounds good. You can get my number from Danniella if you want to text me. Now go and trash the groom's car.'

Aidan leaned over and gave her a gentle kiss on the cheek. 'Night, Alison.'

'Night, Aidan,' she whispered as he ran down the stairs.

She put her fingers up to her cheek. If she closed her eyes, she could still feel the softness of his lips and she could imagine them moving from her cheek to her lips, to her neck. Her heart thudded again. Those long-buried feelings for Aidan? Definitely not buried anymore. Oh boy, her complicated life had just got way more complicated.

34

KAREN

Karen blew her fringe out of her eyes and wiped her sweaty forehead with the back of her hand as she stood up straight. Dropping the scrubbing brush into the bucket of soapy water, she turned around. The kitchen had never looked so clean and, throughout the three hours she'd spent relentlessly scrubbing and tidying, she had absolutely no idea where Ryan was. Or with whom.

Tipping the contents of the bucket down the sink, Karen's emotions switched between anger and fear, as they'd done all evening. It was after 10 p.m., for God's sake. Would it have killed him to send her a text to let her know where he was?

She'd texted him to say that she was staying at her mum's for dinner, but he hadn't responded. She'd texted again when she was at home. Still no response. A couple of phone calls had rung out then clicked into voicemail. She didn't bother leaving any messages.

Removing her rubber gloves, Karen sat down at the kitchen table and picked up her phone again, anxiously

scrolling through it in case she'd missed any calls or
messages whilst cleaning.

✉ To Steff
I know I'm being a pain this evening but I
still haven't heard from Ryan and I'm
getting worried. I take it he hasn't
contacted you????? xx

✉ From Steff
This party sucks so feel free to text me as
often as you want! No word from Ryan,
though. Sorry

✉ To Steff
Thanks. Sorry to hear about the party. Is
there anyone there you know, other than Mia?
Are Jemma and Sam there? I'm sure Jemma said
they were going. I think Sam works with the
birthday boy

✉ From Steff
They were here earlier but didn't stay long.
Had a quick chat with them. A couple of my
PT clients are also here which is just as
well cos I keep losing Mia. She's really
pissed and being all cliquey with one of the
nurses. Wondered if I should feel threatened
but Jemma said she's Sam's ex and a man-
eater. Hoping to leave soon. Need my bed
Zzzzz

✉ **To Steff**
Hang in there. It'll be over soon. Tell Mia
you'll turn into a pumpkin if you're not
home by midnight xx

Feeling restless, Karen decided to run a bath. Sinking beneath the bubbles, she thought about the last bath she'd taken. It had been the rose petal one shortly after their forgotten anniversary, when Ryan had dressed as James Bond. That had been an amazing evening full of laughter and love. The apology had been more than accepted and Karen had thought they'd be back on track. Yet they hadn't been. Had that really been a month ago? Yes. It was mid-June now so a whole month had somehow slipped past.

She immersed herself under the water for a moment, trying to concentrate on nothing but holding her breath. It wasn't working, though. Ryan wouldn't budge from her thoughts. Something had happened, presumably not long after the James Bond night, that had changed things. And she still couldn't shake the feeling that the anonymous texts were related to it. He'd denied it outright and her gut told her that Ryan wasn't the sort who'd have an affair, but what if it had been a one-off? What if something unplanned or unexpected had happened with one of his PT clients or someone from Bay Runners? What if nothing had even happened but there was the possibility that something *could* have happened? Would that have been enough for him to start questioning his relationship with Karen? She sat up again and slapped her hands against the water, splashing it over the sides of the bath. No. Because if he'd wanted out, he'd have broached the subject by now. He wouldn't have gone on for a month, picking fights about stupid things, unless... she grabbed a towel and rubbed her eyes... unless he was hoping that she'd get sick of the tension and arguments and be the one who called time. Was that his tactic? Was he a coward?

Reaching for the plug, Karen remained in the bath while the water swirled down the pipes, leaving the bath empty; a fitting metaphor for her relationship just now. Shivering, she stood up and grabbed a towel. Her stalker knew. Her stalker knew exactly what Ryan had been up to and with whom. Ryan had denied it, but would the stalker deny it if Karen asked them outright? Only one way to find out.

But the stalker had already been in touch:

✉ From Unknown
There was a young woman called Karen
Whose sex life was looking quite barren
Her gorgeous fiancé had decided to stray
Was it Alice or Jessie or Sharon?

✉ From Unknown
Ha ha ha. Bet you're racking your brain
wondering who Alice, Jessie and Sharon are.
They're just random names that happen to fit
the rhyme. But I do know what the last line
should really have said. And you will too.
Very, very soon

Karen slumped onto the edge of the bed, taking deep breaths. Another text appeared:

✉ From Unknown
Where is your young man this evening, by the way? Fancy taking a guess? No point, really. You'll never get it. I know, though. And soon you will. I promise. Enjoy the rest of your evening. Alone. Knowing that the man you love and (used to) trust is not alone

Feeling sick, Karen tried to connect to the number but kept getting cut off.

✉ To Unknown
Why are you doing this to me?

✉ From Unknown
BECAUSE I CAN!!!!!!

35

KAREN

'Do I look like death warmed up?' Karen asked, shuffling into Jemma and Sam's kitchen in her bare feet and PJs the following morning. 'I certainly feel it.' She placed her mobile down on the breakfast bar.

Jemma handed her a glass of orange juice. 'I've seen you look better. I've also seen you look a lot worse although, to be fair, that was alcohol-induced. Did you manage to sleep at all?'

Karen shook her head. 'A couple of hours maybe.'

'Has he been in touch?'

'No.' Karen gulped down her juice. 'I texted to say my stalker had been in contact again and that I was staying with you because I didn't want to be home alone. You'd think that would have generated some kind of response, wouldn't you?'

'Maybe he's lost his phone or it's flat?' Jemma shrugged. 'I want to think the best of him. He's one of the good guys.'

Karen ran her finger around the rim of her empty glass and sighed. 'I used to think so.'

'And now?'

'I don't know what to think anymore. I don't want to believe what my stalker's suggesting but, if he's innocent, where the hell is he? And what *is* going on because he's turned from being the man I love into a stranger who's forgetful, moody, and jealous. It's like we've hit thirteen years together and it really has become unlucky.'

'Are you heading home?' Jemma asked.

'I think I'd better in case he's there and, like you said, he's lost his phone or something. We need to sort this out. If he's changed his mind about being with me, I'd rather know.'

'Have you changed your mind about him?'

Karen ran her fingers through her hair and clasped her hands at the back of her head. 'I've loved Ryan since I was seventeen and I still do, but I don't like him at the moment. I don't know how long I can stay with someone I don't like. And if what my stalker says is true... well, that's it. Over.'

Jemma reached out and gave her a hug. 'I'm here for you, whatever happens.'

* * *

Half an hour later, Karen pulled into Rowan Drive, heart sinking at the empty driveway. She toyed with turning around and driving straight back to Jemma's or going to her mum's, but what if Ryan had been home and left a note?

When she unlocked the door and stepped into the hall, the silence enveloped her like the fret rolling in from the sea and she knew he hadn't been back. Feeling like a stranger in someone else's home, she checked the lounge then the kitchen, but there were no signs of life. The bed was still made, the wet room was dry, and so was his toothbrush. Sitting on the top stair, she leaned against the wall, trying to gather some sort of semblance of a plan. Her phone beeped. Ryan?

✉ From Danniella
Thank you for your kind messages. Apologies for not replying. It's been a tough old week. I know Alison told you I was admitted to hospital. Thankfully it was only overnight, but Ali is staying with me for a bit. I want to get some normality back and would love to return to bootcamp from Tuesday. I might not have much energy, but would it be OK for me to come and try my best? xx

✉ To Danniella
Great to hear from you and I'm so pleased you're home. I was visiting a relative in hospital yesterday and had hoped to say hello but the man on the next bed died while we were there and my little sister had a meltdown! Of course, you can come back on Tuesday. Will be great to see you. We'll take it gently xx

✉ From Danniella
On my goodness, that must have been difficult to see. Hope your sister is all right.

```
Ali and I were wondering whether you have
any plans for lunch today. She's making
roast beef and there's going to be far too
much. We'd love you to join us if you're
free. We'll probably eat at about 1pm but
you're welcome any time from now xx
```

Karen stared at the message. She should probably stick around in case Ryan came home.

```
⊠ To Danniella
That's very kind of you both but I already
have plans. I'll see
```

She stopped mid-text then swiftly deleted what she'd just typed. What would staying at home look like? Going on another crazy cleaning frenzy? Searching Ryan's pockets for evidence of an affair? Pacing the floor, worried sick? Sod it.

```
⊠ To Danniella
I'd love to. That's very kind. I'll aim for
12 xx
```

It was nearly 11 a.m. now. By the time she'd showered and

changed, it would be time to leave. No time to dwell on Ryan. Good.

* * *

'That was probably the best Sunday lunch I've ever had,' Karen said as the three women relaxed in Danniella's lounge. 'Don't tell my mum I said that, though.'

'Thank you,' Alison said. 'I love cooking. Well, I do when it's in a clean, new kitchen like Danniella's.'

'Alison's boyfriend was meant to be refitting their kitchen last week,' Danniella explained, 'but he decided to go to Ibiza with the lads without telling her, using their joint money.'

Karen grimaced. 'Alison mentioned it.' She looked at Alison. 'Dare I ask? Will he still be your boyfriend when he gets back?'

'The question I've been asking myself all week,' Alison said. 'Danniella thinks I should leave him. Not just for this. There've been other things. I don't know what to think anymore. In fact, I'm tired of thinking about it. I'll see what happens when he gets back but, for now, my focus is on Danniella.'

The two friends smiled at each other. 'And you know how much I appreciate your support,' Danniella said, 'but I'm worried about you sticking with Dave out of habit.'

Karen's ears pricked up. Habit? Jay had talked about forming new habits and not doing things just because he'd always done them. Had she and Ryan become a habit? Had their relationship run its course long ago but they were too comfortable in their routine to notice? Scary thought.

'He's changed,' Danniella continued. 'You know that. He's not the man you fell in love with, is he?'

Alison's shoulders slumped as she slurped on her tea. 'No, but I think he's still in there somewhere.'

'What do you think?' Danniella asked Karen.

'Me? You're asking the wrong person. For different reasons, I might be in the same boat as Alison.' She looked from Alison to Danniella. 'What's discussed in the room stays in the room?'

They both nodded solemnly.

Even though she'd only met them both recently, there was something about Alison and Danniella that made her believe she could trust them. 'Okay. Here goes...'

* * *

'Yikes,' Alison said, when Karen had filled them in on the situation with Ryan and her stalker.

'And you have no idea where he is right now?' Danniella asked.

'No idea. He seems to have gone complet—'

She stopped at the sound of her phone ringing. 'Excuse me,' she said.

'Hello? Bay Fitness.'

'Hello. Is that Karen Greene?' Karen didn't recognise the female voice.

'Yes. Can I help?'

'Hi Ms Greene. My name's Daisy Littlewood. I'm a nurse on A&E at Whitsborough Bay General. Please don't panic because he's okay, but we have your fiancé here.'

'Ryan? Oh my God! What's happened to him?' Karen was already on her feet and reaching for her bag.

'We think he was mugged last night.'

'I'll be right there.'

36

DANNIELLA

'Do you think we should have gone with her?' Danniella asked Alison when Karen had left for the hospital.

Alison shrugged. 'We *did* offer. She knows where we are if she needs us. Poor Karen.'

Danniella nodded. Alison and Karen were certainly getting a rough ride from their partners. Whether they'd make it out of the other side as stronger couples was anyone's guess. She hoped they'd make it out as stronger women but, from what they'd said, she couldn't help thinking it would be better if they emerged without their other halves in tow. They both deserved to be treated with a lot more kindness and respect than they were getting.

'Cup of tea?' Alison asked, getting up from the sofa. 'Or coffee?'

'Coffee would be nice. Thanks.'

Danniella wandered over to the French doors while Alison was in the kitchen. It had started to rain. She shivered as she watched the drops splashing on the balcony floor. It was hard to believe it had been blue skies and sunshine earlier that morning. She'd taken a slow walk down the cliff path with Alison and they'd sat on Stanley's bench overlooking the sea, sipping on hot chocolate, while Danniella talked about her family split and her bulimia. It felt cathartic to open up about that chapter in her life, although telling Alison the next part was going to be so much harder.

'Here you go.' Alison handed her a mug and stood next to her watching the weather. 'I don't think I could ever tire of this view,' she said. 'Even in gloomy weather like this.'

'Me neither. I always wanted to live by the sea. When I was little, maybe seven or eight, we went on a family holiday to Cornwall. We hired a beach hut with a turquoise door and I spent every day on the sand. Mum and Dad would take it in turns to build sandcastles with me or play in the sea while the other one sat in the hut reading a book or newspaper. At the time I loved the one-to-one attention.' She took a sip of her coffee. 'Of course, I later realised it was only because they couldn't stand being anywhere near each other.'

She returned to the chair and Alison took up her position again on the sofa.

'Where was home?' Alison asked. 'You never said.'

'Cheltenham, but I wasn't living there when...' Danniella tailed off. Too soon. 'You know what? I might just check my emails. My clients are probably starting to think I've disappeared off the face of the planet. Do you mind?'

'Promise you won't overdo it and start a stack of work?'

Appreciating the concern, Danniella smiled. 'I promise. What are you going to do?'

'It's raining which calls for my PJs and a good book. I know it's still afternoon but, what the heck, it's a Sunday.'

'Don't let me stop you. I might put mine on too.'

Putting her mug down on a side table, Alison left the

room. Danniella moved over to the table where her laptop was waiting. She'd logged on intermittently at the start of last week before things got really bad, but hadn't been able to concentrate for long. Fortunately it had been a quiet week without any deadlines, which was just as well because her business was the only part of her life where she was normally completely in control; everything else was free-wheeling.

She took a deep breath and scanned down the list of senders in her inbox, her heart thumping. Yes, there it was. It had been inevitable really. Sent on Thursday.

Ten years ago today, I saw you for the first time and I knew at that moment that I had to be with you forever. It breaks my heart to be alone on this special day for the first time in a decade. It tears me apart not knowing where you are. Are you safe? Are you well? I know I only have myself to blame. You needed me and I turned on you and drove you away. Please forgive me.
I love you until the wind stops breathing and the sun melts into the sea.
Yours forever
E xx

'"I love you until the wind stops breathing and the sun melts into the sea",' she whispered, her heart melting. It was one of her favourite lines across all of his books. She could remember the first time she'd read it. Her breath had caught in her mouth and her heart had thumped. So beautiful. And then he'd told her the words were written about her.

Her hand shook as she reached out and touched the screen. She ran her fingers down the words, reading them over and over until tears blurred her vision.

'Danniella! What's wrong?'

She hadn't realised how loudly she was sobbing until she felt Alison's arms around her. Tears coursed down her cheeks, absorbed into Alison's PJs.

'Sorry,' she whispered, trying to catch her breath.

'Don't be. Let it out. I'm here.' Alison stroked her back and hair as she cuddled her close.

'Sorry,' Danniella whispered again when the worst of it had subsided.

'What happened? I was gone less than ten minutes.'

'This.' Danniella angled her laptop so that Alison could read the screen.

'Who's E?'

'Ethan. My husband.'

'Your husband? Wow! I wasn't expecting that. Okay. I'm listening.'

Danniella sighed and indicated one of the spare chairs at the table. 'Sit down. You might as well know the full story.'

'You're sure?'

'I'm sure. Although I think you'd better get the tissues. It's not got a happy ending.'

Alison grabbed the box of tissues and her mug of tea and sat down next to Danniella. 'Take your time.'

Closing her eyes for a moment, Danniella took a deep breath. Yes, she was doing the right thing. If she was going to move on, she had to talk about it and Alison had already proved herself to be a valuable friend. She took another deep breath. 'On Tuesday the 6th of September last year, I packed up some of my stuff, got into my car, and I drove. I didn't know where I was going. I just knew that I needed to get away.'

'From your husband?'

'From him. From my stepsister, Natalie. From everyone.' She could feel that same panicky sensation from before and took a few sharp breaths, breathing out slowly each time. 'Ethan and I had a daughter, Abigail. The day I left would have been her first day at primary school. But she never started school. She never made it to her fourth birthday in August. Because I killed her.'

Alison was aware that she was staring, wide-eyed and mouth open, but she couldn't stop. She'd tried not to think too much about Danniella's situation, not wanting to speculate and get carried away with the mystery, but she had wondered if Danniella was running from domestic violence. She certainly hadn't expected this.

'You can't mean that. You can't. The police would have found you. And you're not capable of... You're not.'

Danniella typed something into her laptop then turned the screen round to show Alison again. The website for the *Surrey Mirror* showed the headline: *Local Child Killed by Post Van. Mother Blames Driver.* Alison scanned down the article but it was hard to concentrate. Key words leapt out at her: tragedy, loss, distraught, accident, fatality. Just like all those articles about her own family fifteen years ago.

'You didn't kill her,' she said, gently closing the laptop. 'It was an accident.'

'I killed my little girl. It was my fault. And I ruined some young lad's life.'

Guilt. Alison knew all about guilt. If only she hadn't been ill. If only she hadn't insisted on them going to the cinema without her. But guilt changed nothing; it just destroyed your heart and soul.

'What happened?' Alison asked.

Danniella swallowed the last glug of her coffee and cast her gaze towards the French doors. The rain had intensified, beating on the glass as though desperate to be let in.

'It was Saturday the 23rd of July last year and the weather was just like it is now, only darker, like a storm was brewing. We'd moved to Reigate in Surrey a year earlier and it had been completely the wrong decision. I hadn't settled there or made any friends. I'd tried to strike up conversations with the mums and dads at Abigail's nursery but nobody was particularly friendly. There seemed to be a birthday party every other week but Abigail was never invited. It didn't bother her, but it bothered me. Then one day, the whole class received invites to a party in the next town. Even though two hours in a sports hall full of soft play equipment, bouncy castles, and screaming kids was my personal idea of hell, I was so grateful that somebody had finally invited Abigail that I put my brave face on and took her.'

She ran her fingers through her hair. 'It was awful, Ali. Awful. As if being the newbie and ignored wasn't bad enough, Abigail managed to push one of the other kids over and make her cry. It was an accident but I knew that everyone was looking at me as though I was the mum who couldn't control my own child.' Danniella took several deep breaths before continuing.

'There was food, of course. Tables absolutely laden with party food. Sausage rolls, crisps, chocolate fingers, party rings, cupcakes. You name it, they had it. I kept staring at the plates piled high, salivating, and I knew I was going to gorge the minute they started serving.'

'I thought you'd got your bulimia under control after you left home,' Alison said.

'I still had bad days but, with Natalie's and Ethan's help, I'd taken huge steps. These things never really leave you, though. Food was still my crutch when I felt low or stressed. Instead of gorging then purging, I'd just gorge. When people think of eating disorders, they think of anorexia or bulimia but there's something called binge eating disorder, or BED. It's where you regularly eat huge quantities of food to the point where you feel really uncomfortable and maybe even sick, but you don't actually make yourself sick.'

'Go on...' Alison encouraged.

'They called the kids up for food and, oh my goodness, I had something from nearly every plate. All the other parents were too busy chatting or seeing to their kids to notice me hoovering up the feast. When we were leaving, we collected Abigail's party bag and a balloon and said our goodbyes. I overheard a couple of mums talking. One said they didn't know who I was and the other said that I was Abigail's mum and that Abigail was the "ugly little ginger brat who pushed Courtney over".'

'Oh my God! What a bitch.'

'I know. I should have ignored them but I've always let stuff like that get to me. I strapped Abigail into her car seat and all I could think about was food again.'

Danniella held her hands together against her mouth, as though in prayer. She took more deep breaths. Alison gave her time to gather herself, all too familiar with the pain of saying something like this out loud.

'Abigail was shattered from the party,' Danniella said, her

eyes filling with tears. 'I gave her a cuddle, handed her Bella Bunny, her favourite soft toy, and told her to have a nap while we drove home. We'd barely pulled out of the car park before she was off. As I drove back to Reigate, all I could think of was chocolate. We weren't far from home. The rain was lashing down at this point and any normal person would have looked at the weather and headed straight home. But not me on a binge. There was a newsagent's on the right-hand side of the road but there were double yellow lines in front of it, so I pulled into a space on the left and stopped the car. I turned around to Abigail but she was completely zonked out. I called her name but she didn't respond. So I made the worst decision I could ever have made...'

'You left her in the car?' Alison whispered when Danniella fell silent.

'I kept telling myself that if me stopping the engine hadn't woken her and if the rain hadn't woken her, nothing was going to. I locked the door and checked through the window but there she was, head lolled to one side, mouth slightly open, clutching Bella Bunny.' Danniella let out a strangled sob as the tears tumbled. 'That was the last time I saw my baby alive.'

Alison grabbed a couple of tissues from the box and they both sat there in silence, tears flowing. She so desperately wanted to be strong for Danniella but it had so many parallels to her own tragic story that she felt like she was re-living it all again.

'You don't have to finish,' she said.

Danniella ran her hands through her hair and sighed. 'I grabbed several bars of chocolate and I could have been in and out before the storm broke, but there was a queue and everyone seemed to be making a complicated purchase. The kid behind the counter was so damn slow. I stood in the queue, stomach rumbling, thinking about what I'd gorge on first. The shop lit up with lightning, closely followed by a clap of thunder and I was so focused on food that I barely registered it. It was only on the third or fourth clap that I came to my senses. I dropped my stuff on the nearest shelf and dashed to the door.' Danniella's voice cracked and she covered her face with her hands. 'I was reaching for the door handle when I heard the screech of brakes and then the thud...' Her tears splashed onto the table.

Alison reached over and took Danniella's hand in hers and held it tightly.

'They reckon the thunder woke her and she came to look for me. She was scared of storms. I *knew* there was a storm coming and I left my baby girl in the car alone while I went in search of chocolate.' She looked up at Alison, her eyes red and puffy. 'What kind of person does that?'

'A normal person,' Alison cried. 'Any one of us could have made a decision like that. She was asleep. You'd have only been a few minutes.'

'But a few minutes was all it took.'

'I know. But it was one of those things like a lorry losing control of its brakes on a hill and ploughing into a family car. Seconds either side and my family would have been alive. I know you decided to stop for chocolate, but you didn't order the storm. You didn't know it would wake Abigail and you didn't know that she'd climb out of the car.'

'It *was* my fault. The car wasn't properly locked. I should have checked, but I didn't. All I wanted was food. And my daughter paid for that with her life.'

38

Sleep. Danniella craved sleep but her head was whirring. Shortly after 2 a.m. she gave up trying. Pulling on a cardigan, she stepped out onto the bedroom balcony and took a deep breath of cool, salty air.

Streetlamps followed the curve of the bay, illuminating the deserted seafront, and the moon cast a gentle glow over the castle to the south. A blanket of stars shimmered. *Twinkle, twinkle, little star...* It had been Abigail's favourite nursery rhyme.

'Are you up there?' she whispered. 'I miss you so much. I'm so sorry, baby. I...' Voice catching in her throat, she slumped onto the metal chair. Sorry. Such an inadequate word.

Telling Alison had been the right thing to do. Necessary. Cathartic. Overdue. She hadn't forgotten it. She hadn't blanked it out. She had buried it deep in the recesses of her mind. A week ago, when Alison talked about her family tragedy, she'd felt movement. It was as though her secret was stored in a jack-in-the-box and Alison's revelation had cranked the handle. Over the next few days, the tension grew, the lid sprang open, and the memories overpowered her. Binge, cry, scream, purge, cry, scream, binge. If Alison and Aidan hadn't found her... She shuddered and pulled her cardigan across her chest.

Closing her eyes, she breathed in the silence. Yet it was never really silent. She could always hear the rain hammering on the shop window, the growl of thunder, the screech of brakes... and that sickening thud.

A red postal van was angled across both lanes, the driver's door wide open, air bag billowing in the wind, wipers still swishing. People were running, shouting, crying. A red balloon bounced towards the gutter, a white ribbon trailing in the rivulets.

There was something in the middle of the road near her car. Something small and pink. Danniella bent down and picked up a soggy pink bunny with floppy ears. She fell to her knees, struggling to catch her breath, as she clutched the soft toy to her chest.

'Abi! *Abi!*'

Everything seemed to happen in slow motion. Sirens, blue lights, being pulled to her feet and enveloped in a neon coat, being led to a first response vehicle and lowered into the passenger seat. And a small, pale, freckled arm dangling from under a white sheet.

Abigail hadn't stood a chance, they said; she wouldn't have been in pain. How could they possibly know that?

Ethan was waiting at the hospital and they identified 'the body'. Not their daughter, or Abigail, or a little girl, but 'the body'. As Danniella cradled her baby, she struggled to make sense of how the beautiful face that she knew so well could be attached to a cold, limp carcass. Why wasn't she chatting incessantly about fairies and bunnies? Why wasn't she giggling? Why? *Why*?

There was a funeral. Someone organised a funeral. Ethan? Her? Both of them? A small white coffin draped in a *Disney Princesses* blanket was carried into the church and she reached down to take Abigail's hand; a movement as natural as breathing. The realisation that she'd never hold that warm little hand in hers again made her legs buckle and she sank onto the pew, shaking, whimpering.

There were visitors. Lots of visitors. The house was filled with cards and flowers and casseroles and lasagnes. So much food and yet, for once, Danniella didn't want any. 'You must eat,' people kept saying. 'You must keep your strength up.' Why? What for?

A month after the accident, Natalie and Ricky paid an evening visit. Over coffee, Ricky relayed a story about a friend who regularly worked abroad. He couldn't find his car when he returned to Heathrow and called the police before realising he'd flown out from Gatwick so his car was there. It wasn't a particularly entertaining anecdote but it filled the silence. Danniella nodded and smiled at the appropriate points but something was bothering her. Something to do with airports. Something... *Oh my God*!

'You made me take them off,' she cried, standing up and pointing at Natalie, cutting Ricky off mid-sentence. 'It was *your* fault.'

Natalie looked up at her, clearly bewildered by the outburst. 'Take what off?'

'The child locks.' Danniella backed away from Natalie and looked across at Ethan. 'It was *her* fault. When I picked them up from the airport, she made me take them off. Said she hated feeling trapped in the back.'

'Come on, Danni, that's not fair,' Ethan said.

'Not fair?' Danniella screeched. 'Nothing about this is fucking fair. But you've all been blaming me and it was her. She made me take them off. I said no but she kept going on and on.' She spun round to face her stepsister again, who was clinging onto Ricky's hand, her face ashen. 'You *promised* you'd remind me to put them back on. You killed my baby. *You!*'

'Stop it, Danni.' Ethan was on his feet. 'It wasn't Nat's fault. It was an accident.'

Danniella turned on him. 'Because it was my fault. That's what you mean, isn't it?'

'No. I didn't say that.'

'But it's what you're thinking. It's what you're all thinking. I locked the door, Ethan. Abigail was zonked out and I locked the door, but she got out because the woman with no kids and no sense of safety made me take the bloody locks off.'

Ricky stood up, his arm cradled protectively round Natalie's shoulders. 'Sorry, mate,' he said to Ethan. 'We'd better go.'

Ethan nodded. 'I'll call you later.'

'Oh, that's right!' Danniella cried. 'Just walk away back to your cosy, happy lives, knowing you destroyed—'

'*Enough!*' Ethan bellowed. 'Enough.'

Ethan never raised his voice. Danniella clapped her hand over her mouth as she sank onto the sofa. Had she really just blamed her stepsister for Abigail's death? Had she really just called her 'the woman with no kids and no sense of safety' when Nat and Ricky were still reeling from a failed final attempt at IVF?

The front door closed and, moments later, she heard Ricky's car start and pull away. She knew Ethan was watching her from the lounge doorway, but she couldn't look up at him. She couldn't bear to see the expression of hurt, confusion, or perhaps even hate.

'I don't know what just happened,' he said eventually, his voice cracking. 'But this has to stop. Seriously, Danni. It wasn't Nat's fault for getting you to remove the child locks. It wasn't the postman's fault for driving too fast in the rain. Or the mums at the party who upset you, the people dithering at the newsagent's, or the kid behind the counter serving too slowly. None of them are to blame. It was an accident. A tragic, devastating, heart-breaking fucking accident. But it *was* an accident. Stop looking for someone to blame. Please. Just. Stop.'

But Danniella couldn't stop. Because, if none of them were to blame, it meant that she was.

In the weeks that followed, she soaked her pillow each night as she sobbed, begging Abigail for forgiveness. But even if Abigail, wherever she was, could forgive her, Danniella couldn't forgive herself.

Then came the darkest day of all: what would have been Abigail's fourth birthday in mid-August. When Danniella awoke, the bed was empty. Lying still for a moment, her heart leapt as she heard movement from the next bedroom. Abigail? Had she dreamed it all? But it wasn't Abigail. Ethan was slumped on their daughter's bed, clutching Bella Bunny, tears raining down his cheeks. He looked up at Danniella as she hovered in the doorway and reached out his hand towards her like a peace offering.

If she'd taken his hand, if she'd held him, if they'd cried together, things might have been so different.

But she didn't.

'I know what you're thinking,' she said, her voice bitter and distant.

No response.

'You're thinking we'd be opening presents with our daughter right now... if my wife hadn't killed her.'

'That's not what I'm thinking,' he whispered.

'It is.'

'It isn't.'

'You're thinking that there should be birthday cards on the mantlepiece instead of a jar containing our daughter's ashes.'

Ethan wiped his cheeks and eyes with one hand, still clinging to Bella with the other. 'Why do you keep doing this?'

'Doing what?'

'Pushing me. Trying to get me to say that I blame you.'

'Because you do blame me.'

'How can you think that?' He stood up and placed Bella on Abigail's pillow.

'Because it's true. You, Nat, Ricky... you all blame me. If Nat hadn't nagged me about those child locks, though. And if those mums at the party hadn't been so bitchy and if—'

'Stop it! Just stop it. We can't keep going round in circles, Danni. We just can't.'

'But our baby is dead because of those people.'

'No, she isn't.'

'She is.'

'*NO, SHE ISN'T!*'

'Then why's she dead?'

'It was an accident.'

'And someone's to blame. Why's she dead, Ethan? Why?'

'Why? Because you and your eating are out of fucking control.' Ethan bashed his fist against the wardrobe. 'You left our three-year-old alone in the car in the middle of a storm because you needed chocolate. Who does that? Who in their right fucking mind does that? You killed her, Danni. You. Not the postman, or your stepsister, or the million other people you want to blame. You killed our baby and we're going to have to live with that for the rest of our lives.'

He'd said it. He'd finally said it. She fled back to their bedroom.

'Danni...' Ethan raced after her and grabbed her arm. 'I'm sorry. I didn't mean it. It's not what I think. But you keep pushing me and... It's not what I think. It isn't.'

'Clearly it is.' She shrugged her arm free. 'I think you should stay with your brother. I think we need to be apart. Maybe for good.'

Ethan shook his head. 'Don't say that. Don't say it's over. Don't even think it.'

'You blame me. So why would you even want to be with me?'

'I don't blame you. I shouldn't have said that. It would have been her birthday today, for God's sake. I don't know what to think or say or do. I just want her back. It's like there's a part of me missing and I can't bear it anymore.'

'And you think I can?'

'No. Of course I don't. But we can help each other. We can make it through this together. Because, if I don't have you either, what's the point?'

'I'm not sure there is a point anymore.'

'Danni...' He reached to embrace her, but she dived under the duvet and turned her back.

'Talk to me. Please.'

'I think you've said it all, don't you? I just want you to go.'

He perched on the edge of the bed and placed his hand on her shoulder but she moved away.

'I don't blame you, Danni. I really don't.'

Danniella sighed and pulled her legs up towards her chest in a foetal position. 'We both know you do.'

'I love you.'

Silence.

With a shaky sigh, Ethan stood up. 'If I go to James's, my heart will still be here with you. Never forget that I'll love you until the wind stops breathing and the sun melts into the sea.'

Damn it! Not fair. That line melted her every time. Not today. She scrunched her eyes tightly and turned her head into the pillow. If she released the tears, he'd comfort her, she'd beg him to stay, and nothing would have changed. She'd still have killed their daughter. She'd still have ruined their lives. Ethan was a good man, an amazing man, and he didn't need her around as a constant reminder of everything she'd taken from him. He deserved better. He deserved the freedom to start over.

39

KAREN

Karen handed Ryan a glass of water then curled up at the opposite end of the sofa, frowning. 'Explain it to me again.'

Ryan tutted. 'Do I have to?'

'Not if you don't want to.'

'But...?'

'But I'd like you to, because I'm a bit confused about it all.'

Ryan stiffened. 'You mean you don't believe me.'

'Is that what I said? I'm pretty sure it isn't.'

Karen winced as Ryan took a sip of water, his lips cracked and bruised.

'After my PT session, I went for a drink in The Anchor,' he said.

'On your own?'

'Yes. How many times? I wanted some time alone to think. One drink turned into several. I'd been fiddling with my phone—'

'Yet you didn't think to let me know where you were.' Karen raised her hands in surrender. 'Sorry. Tangent. So you'd been fiddling with your phone...'

Ryan gave her a dark look. Probably best not to interrupt again or she'd never get to the bottom of it.

'Yes, and I might have been staggering a bit so I reckon I was being watched and pegged as an easy target. The seafront was busy so I took the back streets. I had my phone out because I was going to text you when they jumped me.'

'Two blokes?'

'Yeah. And I stupidly put up a fight so they beat me up. Should have just let them take my bloody phone.'

It all sounded plausible so far and there was no doubt that Ryan had been beaten up – his face and the bruises across his arms and chest plainly and painfully proved that – but it was the next bit that Karen wasn't buying. She needed to tread carefully.

'Where does it hurt most?'

Ryan shrugged. 'Everywhere. I feel like I've run five marathons and dropped a stack of dumbbells on my chest.'

Karen gave him what she hoped was a sympathetic look before moving on. 'So what happened after they jumped you?'

'A group of lads saw it. Some of them gave chase and the others helped me. One of them knew me from Bay Runners—'

'But you can't remember his name?'

'He only came for a couple of sessions then dropped out...'

She made sympathetic noises as Ryan continued his bullshit story. None of it added up. Forgetting his helper's name was a little too convenient and made the next part of the story even more implausible. In her head, she felt like a police constable interrogating a witness: *So you went back to this lad's house even though you couldn't remember his name? It didn't seem*

odd that he didn't drop you off home, at A&E, or a police station?
You spent the night at a stranger's house but you can't remember
where he lived because you were 'a bit spaced'? You or he never
thought to call your fiancée at any time? And why didn't the
muggers take your phone? Surely one of them could have grabbed
it? Question after question. Yet she didn't ask any of them this
time because the inconsistencies in his story were already
showing. Proving he was a liar about this would be tanta-
mount to proving he'd been lying about everything, and
Karen didn't want to face that. Not yet.

'I know you don't want to, but I really think we should
report this to the police,' she said.

Ryan quickly shook his head. 'I don't want to make a fuss.
I threw the first punch—'

'After they jumped you.'

'Yeah, but I still fought back. You hear about victims
ending up being the ones who are punished. It's not worth it.'

'It could be connected to my stalker, though.'

Ryan gulped down his water then stood up. 'I don't see
how. You're the one being stalked and I'm the one who was
attacked. It was a random mugging. That's all.'

'Isn't it up to the police to decide that they're
unconnected?'

'Why can't you just leave it? My head's banging and I'm in
agony.' He walked towards the door and stopped. 'You know
what, Kaz? I thought you'd be a bit more sympathetic.'

'I *am* sympathetic. I've been worried sick about you.'

'Could have fooled me. I'm going to bed.' Without waiting
for her to respond, he closed the door and she heard him
limping up the stairs.

Running her fingers through her hair, she slumped back
on the sofa. Could the mugging be related to her stalker? She

felt like there was a connection waiting to be made, but it was just out of grasp.

Her phone beeped and she almost didn't dare look. Thankfully it was only Jay.

✉ From Jay
Hope you've had a good weekend. Took your advice and told Sophie about PT. She laughed. Then she got angry. Fraught weekend but she finally came round and accepted that I need to make a go of it. She's not keen on me having 1:1 time with a female coach but I refused to give up my Thursday session. Cue shouting and being pelted with teaspoons — random, I know. And, more randomly, a packet of Cup-a-Soup! What's that all about? Compromise is I'm keeping Thurs but will sign up for bootcamp on a Mon and Wed evening. So I'll see you tomorrow night, assuming you're running bootcamp that is. Hope you are!

✉ To Jay
Teaspoons and a soup packet? I'm not sure what to say about that so I'll focus on fitness news and YAY! I run all the boot-camps and it varies whether Ryan or Steff run them with me. It would have been Ryan tomorrow but it will be Steff as he's

recovering from an alleged mugging
yesterday

✉ From Jay
Alleged? Sounds like a story

✉ To Jay
The whole thing sounds like a story to me.
Been a hell of a weekend. Stalker's been in
touch again too

✉ From Jay
Sophie's having a bath. I'm free if you want
to share

✉ To Jay
Thanks but I'm tired and emotional. And I
don't want to get you into trouble. If you
don't have to rush off after bootcamp tomorrow, though…

✉ From Jay
Sophie's going out for a friend's birthday
so no need to rush home. Hope you manage to
sleep OK. You know where I am if you want to
talk sooner

✉ To Jay
Thanks. Appreciate it. Get ready for tomorrow. Steff and I are going to put you
through your paces big time!

✉ From Jay
Just as long as you're not going to pelt me
with spoons and soup packets!

✉ To Jay
☺ ☺ ☺

Karen put her phone down, smiling. Seriously, that man was
an absolute tonic. In the space of ten texts, he'd managed to
completely lift her mood. She was thrilled for him that he'd
been given a 'pass' from Sophie to up his exercise to three
times a week, although it disturbed her that it had obviously
caused so much friction between them. It sounded like Jay's
weekend had been as delightful as hers.

It was only 9 p.m. yet it felt like the early hours of the
morning. Time for an early night.

'Are you awake?' she whispered to Ryan when she clambered into bed beside him.

If he was, he was ignoring her. He was lying on his back,
eyes closed. The lamppost outside their house very dimly
illuminated the room through the blinds and she could make
out the dark shapes of the bruises and see the swelling
around Ryan's right eye. Whatever he'd really done to result
in the beating, he hadn't deserved it. He was lucky that they
hadn't done any permanent damage to his eyes, broken his
nose, or knocked out any teeth.

Watching the slow rise and fall of Ryan's chest, an overwhelming feeling of guilt ran through Karen. He was right;
she hadn't been particularly sympathetic. When she'd picked
him up at A&E, she'd been beside herself with relief. All the

anger she'd built up had ebbed away as she'd held him closely, as she'd gently kissed his bruises, and as she'd helped him slowly lower himself into the passenger seat in her car, wincing at the pain of the seatbelt across his bruised torso. But as he'd rattled on about what had happened, the anger started to build again. She felt like she was building a Lego wall as each piece of information spilled out: blue for each lie, green for each inconsistency, red for the anger she felt, and yellow for distrust. And now that wall was like a barrier between them. She loved him so much. Probably always would. But she definitely didn't like him anymore. Didn't believe him. Didn't trust him.

She slowly rolled onto her back, arms by her side, staring at the ceiling. Where could they go from here? Was loving him enough to bury the other feelings?

A tingle ran through her arm as Ryan's fingertips lightly touched hers. Then he took her hand in his.

'I'm sorry,' he whispered.

She was too afraid to ask what he was sorry for.

✉ From Dave
I'm home. Guessing you're at work. Can't
wait to see you. What time do you finish? xx

'What are you going to do?' Danniella asked, handing Alison
her phone back after reading Dave's text on Monday
morning.

'Buggered if I know.' She shrugged. 'What would you do?'

Danniella smiled weakly. 'You're asking the person who
ran away from her problems? What *I'd* do and what I think
you should do are two completely different things.'

✉ To Dave
I'm not at work. I ended up working most of
last week so have some time off this week
instead. I have plans this morning. I'll

```
come to the house at 2pm and return your
van then
```

```
☒ From Dave
That was very formal. What's going on? Where
are you?
```

```
☒ To Dave
The man who spent the last week in Ibiza
without me dares to question my whereabouts?
That's rich. I'll see you at 2. Or not. Your
choice
```

There was a five-minute time lapse before Dave replied. Alison could imagine him starting and deleting several abusive texts before sending his final choice whilst gritting his teeth:

```
☒ From Dave
2 is fine. Can't wait to see you xx
```

She switched her phone to silent and stood up. 'Boring conversation. Let's get you to the doctor's.'

'Because that's so exciting by comparison,' Danniella said.

'The way I feel about Dave right now, a zillion injections would be more welcome than an hour with him.'

'I'll have a word with the receptionist, eh?'

* * *

Danniella returned to the surgery waiting room with a smile on her face. 'She was lovely,' she told Alison as they walked back to Danniella's car. 'She's referring me to an eating disorder specialist and a bereavement counsellor.'

'Did you see a counsellor after Abigail died?'

'No. Probably would have been a good idea, though.'

'Maybe not,' Alison said. 'From what you've said, I don't think you'd have been in the right frame of mind to get much benefit from it.'

'You could be right.'

* * *

'Did you have counselling after you lost your family?' Danniella asked as they pulled out of the surgery car park.

'No. I don't remember it being offered.'

'How did you deal with it?'

'I'm not sure I fully did. Food became my friend and I've never broken that cycle, as you can see. Grandma was amazing. I'll never know where she found the strength to remain positive and strong. She'd tell me tales about Dad growing up. I loved hearing about the early days of his relationship with Mum. Apparently he was a bit of a lad and Mum wouldn't have anything to do with him. It took him a whole year to finally "woo" her as Grandma put it. And, of course, Grandma was able to tell me all about Fleur and Max as babies. It was only recently that it struck me that the reason she talked so much about the happy memories was because she wanted me to remember them as living, vibrant, loving people and stop associating them with the mangled car, the skid marks on the road, the smashed bollards, the bent-over traffic lights and the figures under the white sheets in the hospital. She wasn't daft, my grandma.'

Danniella smiled. 'She sounds very wise. I think you have a lot of your grandma in you.'

'She was. And thank you. That's a big compliment.'

* * *

Danniella needed to do some work when they returned to the flat. 'You know what you could do while I'm working?' She reached across the table for an A4 pad and pen and held them out to Alison. 'Make a list of reasons to stay with Dave.'

Alison smiled at her. 'And reasons not to?'

'Only if you want to. I know it might seem cold and clinical to confine your life together to two lists, but it might help get things into perspective.'

Taking the pen and paper, Alison had to concede that it was a good idea, although she was pretty sure she could guess which list would be the longest. 'I'll do it at the kitchen table so I'm not disturbing you.'

Half an hour later, Alison looked at the two lists, shaking her head.

Reasons to stay with Dave:

1. Somewhere to live
2. Detangling finances
3. Never had another boyfriend – could I really start over?

Reasons to leave Dave:

He's always grumpy

1. He never tells me he loves me
2. He calls me fat but doesn't help me lose weight
3. Laughed at me about bootcamp
4. We barely kiss and never have sex
5. Going to Ibiza without me
6. Paying for Ibiza with our money
7. Nasty phone messages from Ibiza
8. With another woman in Ibiza?
9. Unfinished kitchen
10. Unfinished jobs everywhere
11. We never go out
12. We're not 'together' when we're home
13. I do everything around the house
14. He makes me do the shopping ... on the bus!
15. Forgot accident anniversary
16. Never says sorry
17. Broke Grandma's plates
18. Have to tread on eggshells all the time
19. Where's the relationship going? No sign of marriage or kids
20. I've got to 21 on this list and it took no time!

Were there really seven times as many reasons to leave as to stay? That wasn't good. Those three reasons to stay had been a real struggle and none of them were insurmountable. In fact, they were complications surrounding leaving rather than reasons to stay. Danniella had already said that Alison could stay indefinitely and really, how hard could separating their finances be? They had no credit card debts or loans, having always saved for anything they wanted. Dave had taken a chunk of their savings for Ibiza so the fair thing would be for her to withdraw the same amount and split the rest. The house was his so that was straightforward too.

What about the last point? Could she really start over? Had she written that because life with Dave had become a habit and habits were always hard to break, or was it fear of finding someone new? She wasn't sure it made any difference if it was the latter, because she certainly wouldn't be ready to jump into a new relationship after her experience with Dave. But she *was* scared of being alone. Aidan's face popped into her head and she pushed it aside. Now was not the time. This was about Dave and bringing Aidan into the equation was only muddying the waters.

She picked up the pen and added to the reasons to stay list:

4. Because occasionally – very occasionally – I get glimpses of the man I fell in love with and I can't let go of him because I love him

And that one final point was more powerful than the long list of reasons to leave Dave. It was what had stopped her telling him to shove it years ago. It was what made her hang on and believe that, one day, things could go back to how they used to be.

It would be so much easier if Dave would end it because she was certain she didn't have the strength to do so. He was her family; all she had left. Despite everything, she needed him.

* * *

'Good luck,' Danniella said, hugging Alison goodbye. 'Whatever you decide, or even if you don't decide anything, I'm here to support you and this is your home for as long as you need it.'

Alison couldn't answer. She just nodded into Danniella's shoulders and patted her back, then left.

Driving across town, she felt sick as she muttered to herself, 'Don't demand an apology. See if he gives one and make him work for your forgiveness. Don't say you've missed him because you haven't. Don't act needy. Don't offer to do his washing or to cook for him. Or to come home.'

She reversed the van onto the drive and sat there with the ignition off, eyes closed, focusing on her breathing in an effort to steady her swelling nerves.

A knock on the van window made her squeal.

Dave opened the door. 'What are you doing sitting on the drive?'

'Nothing. I was about to come in.' She took in the colour of his skin and butterflies fluttered in her stomach. It emphasised those gorgeous blue eyes of his. Damn him for looking extra sexy after a week in the sun. 'You're tanned.'

'It was sunny.' Dave stepped back, smiling, to allow her to

descend from the van. As soon as she closed the door, he hugged her. 'I've missed you so much.'

She felt rigid in his embrace, but he didn't seem to notice as he planted a gentle kiss on her lips then grabbed her hand and led her into the house. 'I bought you a present. Well, several.'

'I don't want any presents.'

'You'll want these. Wait in the lounge. I'll be two minutes.'

There was no point in protesting. Alison opened the lounge door and sat down on the sofa, gazing around the room. Something was different. Something was... oh my God! The floating shelves had been put up, with candles and framed photos of her family resting on them. A selection of other pictures and photos had been hung on the walls and the bare windows were no longer bare. He'd actually put the curtains up. Granted, they were very creased after three years in their packets, but they were up. Bloody miracle! There was hope for the kitchen yet.

The frustrating thing about all the part-finished projects was that Alison was perfectly capable of doing all the DIY herself, but Dave was very possessive over his tools. She'd learned quickly that living on a building site was less stressful than the wrath of Dave if she touched any of his stuff; especially his power tools.

The door opened and Dave stepped into the lounge, holding a couple of Duty-Free carrier bags. 'You've spotted the shelves,' he said. 'Do you like them?'

'I do. Which is why we bought them three years ago,' she said sarcastically.

'Yeah, I know. I'm sorry it took so long. Obviously I haven't had time to do anything in the kitchen but I thought if I did a few things in here, you'd...' He hung his head and awkwardly shuffled from foot to foot.

'I'd what?' she said, flatly. 'Forgive you for disappearing on holiday without me or for not spending the week fitting the kitchen?'

Dave looked sheepish. 'Both? I'll have the kitchen done by the end of next month, though. I promise.'

He sounded sincere but she'd heard that one before.

'Presents!' he declared brightly when she didn't respond. 'The lads refused to go shopping so I did my best.'

Alison felt numb as he gradually emptied the bags, starting with the Duty-Free purchases: perfume, a teddy bear, a watch, a bag of miniature Daim chocolates, and a gift set of lipsticks. Then he produced the Ibiza gifts: a silver photo frame with dolphins etched onto it, a necklace with a red heart on it, and a sunglasses case covered in images of books. To be fair to him, they were all good gifts. But it seemed so false. Dave's eyes shone, he spoke with enthusiasm, he kept touching her as he handed her each item, he insisted on putting the necklace on her, pausing to kiss her neck, and he never stopped smiling. He was just like the seventeen-year-old she'd fallen for and yet she knew that wasn't him anymore so it felt like an imposter in front of her. Very unnerving.

'I've got another present for you,' he said, 'but I want to give that to you later. How's your week been?'

Alison raised an eyebrow. 'You really want to know?'

'I asked, didn't I?' Even though he was still grinning inanely, Alison didn't miss the edge to his voice. Was he struggling to keep the nice-guy act going?

'Obviously last weekend was horrendous. I decided there was no point in me spending our holiday moping around the house on my own so I went to work on Sunday to Thursday. I'd been trying to get in touch with my new bootcamp friend, Danniella, all week and was really worried when I couldn't get hold of her. I knew who her landlord was so I got him to let me into her flat on Friday and we found her unconscious on the bathroom floor. Thankfully she was released from hospital the next day but I've been staying with her ever since.' She smiled brightly. 'So how was Ibiza?'

The grin had finally slipped from Dave's face. He took her hand in his, raised it to his lips and gently kissed it. 'I'm sorry about your week. Is your friend okay?'

Feeling wrong-footed, Alison nodded. 'Er, yes, thanks. She's got issues to sort but she's getting help.'

He stroked her hand with his thumb, sending tingles through Alison and setting the butterflies going again. 'She's lucky she's got a great friend like you to be there for her.'

She waited for him to add something negative. But he didn't. Weird.

'You'd have loved Ibiza,' he said. 'I couldn't stop thinking about you while I was there and wishing you were with me instead of the lads. It could have been like Corfu all over again.'

'Yeah, well, I wasn't there, was I?' she snapped.

'I know. I screwed up, Ali. Eggsey told me I was a right twat for doing that to you. His missus was on a girls' holiday and he assumed that's what you were doing.'

'No, Dave, I was expecting to be going on holiday with you or fitting a kitchen but neither of those things happened.'

'What can I do to make it up to you?'

Alison closed her eyes and took a deep breath. 'I don't know if you can.'

He looked genuinely shocked. 'You don't mean that. You

can't. Shit, Ali! I'm sorry, I really am. If I had a time machine, I'd go back to that night when you brought home those holiday brochures. I'd have eaten my dinner instead of making a fuss about the horseradish, then we'd have shared a bottle of wine while picking out where to go before we...'

'Before we what...?'

'You know.'

She knew exactly what he meant, but she wasn't going to make it easy for him. 'You've lost me. Shared some wine and then what?'

'This.' He cupped her face in his hands and kissed her gently on the lips. She didn't respond, but he obviously wasn't going to let it deter him. He ran his fingers through her hair and trailed his kisses across her cheek and onto her neck. Her head was telling her to push him away, but her heart was racing and the rest of her body was stirring with passion.

'You're my favourite girl,' he whispered, moving his kisses back towards her lips and, this time, she responded fully. When he removed his T-shirt then lifted up her top, she released a soft moan then raised her arms so he could lift it off.

Even though her brain was screaming to stop, her body completely betrayed her. She'd never been filled with more desire for Dave. Reaching for his belt, she couldn't get his jeans off soon enough.

The sex was frantic and loud. When it was over, Dave rolled off her and stood by the sofa, his eyes drinking her in from foot to head. Feeling completely exposed she wished they were in bed so she could cover her stomach with the duvet. She folded her arms across herself, trying to hide some of the flesh.

'Don't do that,' Dave said, gently moving her arms to her sides.

'You're looking at my flab.' She steeled herself for some comment about how she'd let herself go, but none came.

Instead, Dave shook his head. 'I'm looking at my favourite girl and thinking how beautiful she is and how good it feels to be with her.' He reached for her hand and helped her to her feet. 'Come upstairs.'

Silently, she followed him up the stairs and into the bedroom where, for the next hour or so, he kissed and caressed and tenderly made love to her. It felt as though he was noticing her for the first time in several years; that he was actually seeing her as a woman instead of a verbal punching bag.

She snuggled against his chest, not daring to speak in case she broke the spell, not daring to move in case she flicked the switch and Grumpy Dave returned.

'Was that okay?' he whispered into her hair as he lightly stroked her back.

'You know it was better than okay,' she whispered back. 'But I don't understand. You've barely touched me for years.'

'I know. There's no excuse for how I've been. I know that I've got lots of making up to do to you. Starting right now.' He tilted her head towards his and gently kissed her again, then moved down her body.

Not sure her blood pressure could cope with any more, Alison gently eased him back up the bed. 'Can we talk instead?'

'Talk?'

'I'd be lying if I said I hadn't enjoyed what we've just done because it was pretty amazing and long overdue. But that's not going to suddenly solve all our problems.'

Dave propped himself up on his arm and gazed at her lovingly. 'Do we have to talk about this now? Can I give you your main present?'

'I don't need another gift.'

He was already out the bed and pulling on a fresh pair of trunks. 'This is the best one. Wait here.'

Feeling very exposed again, Alison leapt out of bed as soon as he left the room, and grabbed a nightie from her bedside drawer. She'd only just pulled it over her head when he returned, holding something behind his back.

He made his way round the bed to her side. 'I don't know why I didn't do this years ago...'

Alison looked from his smiling face to his hand, still hidden behind his back, then to his face again. Shit! He wouldn't, would he? 'No, Dave...'

'I hated being in Ibiza without you and I know that's my fault. I've been taking you for granted and I only realised that when you weren't there. I'm serious about making it up to you. I know I never say it but I...' He cleared his throat. 'I love you, Ali. I'd be nothing without you.'

She nibbled on one of her fingernails, heart thumping as he brought his hand from behind his back and held out a ring.

'What do you think? Could you see yourself doing the marriage thing with me?'

She stared at the silver ring held between Dave's fingers, feeling quite light-headed. If he'd asked the same question a few years ago, or even a few months ago...

Dave looked down at the ring and laughed. 'I should probably have said that this was a quick twenty Euro purchase. If it's a yes, I want to take you into town so you can pick your own. This one might not even fit but I wanted to show you how serious I was about us.'

It was taking every ounce of energy left in Alison's body just to keep breathing.

'Ali...?' His smile faded and he nodded. 'Eggsey said it was too much, but I wanted to show you I'd changed.'

'No. I know. I get it. It's just...' She reached for the chain around her neck and ran Fleur's ring up and down it again.

'Tell you what. Why don't you take it? Don't wear it. Or you could wear it on a different finger if you want.' Dave pressed the ring into her left palm and closed her fingers around it. 'Think about it, eh?'

'I'm sorry. I—'

'No explanations needed.'

The unspoken words hung heavily between them.

'So,' he said, far too brightly. 'What are your plans for the rest of the day?'

'Erm, yeah. I need to pack a few more things then get back to Danniella's and start making tea. She's got a few issues with food so I want to make sure she eats properly.'

'Sure. Yeah. I'll run you back to hers if you want.'

'You don't have to. I can get the bus.'

'I know, but I want to.'

Dave's tone was soft, as though he was offering a lift to be kind, but a thought popped into her head and took root. He was checking up on her.

'I'd introduce you, but she'll either be working or sleeping.'

'Oh, yeah. I wouldn't have expected you to. Do you want a lift now, then?'

'Give me ten minutes to get dressed and pack some clothes.'

'Take your time.' He sat down on his side of the bed.

'You don't have to stay with me. I'm sure you've got loads to get on with.'

Dave shook his head. 'Nothing that can't wait.'

Alison pulled a weekend bag off the top of the wardrobe and placed it on the bed, jaw clenching. There was no reason for him to stick around, but he wanted to see what she was packing: baggy leggings or sexy underwear, not that she actually owned any of the latter. Out of the corner of her eye, she noticed him clocking every item she packed, a frown appearing when she opened her underwear drawer. The cheeky git didn't trust her and that made her angry. Damn angry. Speaking of trust, she hadn't tackled the female on the voicemail yet. That could wait for another day. She was far too mad to tackle it right now.

'When will I see you again?' Dave asked as he pulled up on Sea View Drive a bit later. 'Christ! That sounds like something you'd say to someone after a first date, not after you've been together for ten years. Why do I feel like we're starting over again?'

Despite the anger, Alison couldn't help finding his vulnerability endearing. 'Because, in many ways, we are. And, sorry to say this, but I don't know how long it will last this time.'

Before he could respond, she leaned over and kissed him on the cheek, then opened the van door and stepped down. She picked up the bag and the Duty-Free carriers.

'Have I lost you?' he asked. 'Be honest.'

'Dave, I've always been honest with you and I've always

loved you. But I don't like the person you've become or the person I've become because of it. I liked the Dave I saw today because he reminded me of how it used to be. The problem is that I don't know if it's just an act.'

'It's not an act.'

'Then is it temporary and one day in a few weeks' or a few months' time, you'll be back to being the grumpy git who thinks everything, including me, is "shite"?'

'Ali, I—'

'I know. You're sorry. But it's just a five-letter word and if you really are sorry, I need to see evidence of it. Don't get me wrong. I love my gifts, I love my ring, and I love that you've finally sorted the lounge.' She heaved the bag onto her shoulder. 'But it's been "shite" for four years, Dave. It's going to take more to fix things between us and I don't mean more gifts.'

He shrugged. 'I don't know what you want from me.'

'Remember Corfu?'

'Of course.'

'I want that.' She closed the van door.

'But I've just been on holiday,' he called through the open window. 'I won't be able to get more time off work.'

'I'm not talking about going on holiday, Dave. I want Corfu. You work it out.'

She turned and walked towards the flat, willing herself not to run back to him and shout, 'Yes, I'll marry you.' After all, that's what she'd dreamed of for years: Dave as her family, always and forever. It was still what she wanted. Wasn't it?

DANNIELLA

Hi Danni

I finished my 20th book three weeks ago.
Major landmark. It's called 'It's Always
Been You'. You inspired the title because,
for me, it has always been and will always
be you.

Christina is desperate for it but I keep
stalling. You've been part of my writing
journey since book one and it feels wrong to
submit knowing you haven't seen it and
shaped it into a better story like you
shaped me into a better person. My writing
is lost without you, and I'm lost without
you, Danni.

Christina wants to organise a big party for
the launch and for the milestone but 20
books is nothing to celebrate without you by
my side. I've said no, but I know she'll get

her way like she always does. She'll make me
wear a suit — you know how much I love doing
that — and I'll have to smile and laugh and
schmooze whilst pretending everything's
great. But it's not great because you're not
with me.
I understand that you need time and space. I
know it's my fault that you left and I
berate myself for it every day. It's killing
me not knowing that you're safe and that
you've found some sort of peace. Please, I
beg of you, just get in touch. Just one line
to let me know how you are.
Still loving you more than Christmas, ice-
cream, and fluffy unicorns.
E xx

Danniella smiled at his last line.

'What's amusing you?' Alison asked. She'd been curled
up on the sofa with a book since returning from seeing Dave,
refusing to say anything about how it had gone until
Danniella finished her work. Danniella sensed that the work
thing was just an excuse and something big had happened
that Alison needed to get her head around.

'Ethan's emailed again.'

Alison sat upright. 'But you're smiling.'

'I couldn't help it. He's written another line from one of
his books. It says, "still loving you more than Christmas, ice-
cream, and fluffy unicorns".'

'You never said he's an author.'

'He writes contemporary romance. It's how we met. I edited his very first book, the one that secured him his publishing deal. We'd discovered we lived an hour apart so he asked if he could take me out for a thank you drink.' She smiled at the memory. 'I was so nervous. I kept telling myself that his story was fiction but I knew that, if he was anything like the hero, I was a goner. Turned out he was, so that was that.'

'Aw, that's so sweet.'

'I know. Anyway, I love that line. I remember laughing so much trying to come up with things that someone could love their partner more than that we both got the hiccups.'

'I bet you've got loads of happy memories like that.'

'I have,' Danniella agreed. 'You know what? For so long, I've only focused on the last horrendous months before I left, and not thought about the nine happy years before that.'

'I think you should spend more time thinking about those nine happy years,' Alison said, 'I think it'll help. What else did he say?'

'You can read it if you want.'

'Are you sure?' Alison got off the sofa and moved over to the table to read the email. 'Twenty books? Wow! That's incredible. Ethan Cole? It's not familiar. Does he write under a pen name?'

Danniella nodded. 'Lucas Downey.'

Alison's eyes widened. 'Seriously? Oh wow! He's famous! I can't believe he's your husband.'

Danniella felt herself deflate. 'He's the man I married. Whether he still wants to be my husband is debatable.'

'Read the message again. He loves you "more than Christmas, ice-cream, and fluffy unicorns". I think it's safe to say that the man still wants to be married to you.'

Alison returned to the sofa. 'You might want to drop him a reply to tell him you're okay. You don't need to tell him where you are or even have a conversation. Just let him know you're safe. What do you think?'

'I think I owe him that, don't I?'

'Completely your decision,' Alison said. 'It's easy to give advice when it's someone else's relationship. Not so easy to take it when it's your own.'

Danniella turned back to her laptop and clicked the reply button, but her fingers shook uncontrollably as she tried to type. There was so much to say. How could she apologise for causing him so much pain in one paltry email? She finally managed a few words and quickly pressed 'send'.

```
Send me the book.
D
```

His reply came back within a minute.

```
I can't tell you how relieved I am to hear
from you. I wasn't trying to guilt-trip you
into editing my book, though. I was worried
about you…
E xx
```

Hi Ethan
I know.
Send me the damn book.
Danni

Her fingers hovered over the 'send' button, but her heart started to race and her body started to shake. Beads of sweat pooled on her forehead and top lip as a hot flush overcame her. She couldn't seem to catch her breath. Her fingers tingled, her stomach churned, there was ringing in her ears, then the room started to spin. Oh, God! It had been like this in the bathroom before she'd passed out and hit her head.

'Danni!' Alison rushed to her side. She linked her fingers with Danniella's and looked into her eyes. 'Breathe with me. Deep breath in through your nose... and exhale slowly through your mouth. And again. Deep breath in...'

A few minutes later, Danniella's breathing was back to normal and her heartrate had steadied. 'Thank you,' she whispered.

'I gather that was a panic attack?' Alison said.

Danniella nodded. 'Scary, eh?'

'Too right. I was scared, and it must be ten times worse for you. What brought that on?'

'Finally contacting Ethan, I think. You couldn't get me some water, could you?'

Alison picked up the empty glass and headed to the kitchen.

Looking at the email she'd typed, Danniella clicked 'send', then closed the laptop. That was enough for today. It was short and curt and so much less than he deserved, but it was all she had in her. Would he send the manuscript over? Probably. But, knowing Ethan, it wouldn't be about getting her feedback; it would be about having a reason to maintain contact. How she'd feel reading another of his books was a bridge she'd cross if he did send it over.

Karen left the house at 5.20 a.m. to run an early morning bootcamp with Steff, leaving Ryan sound asleep. Mondays were one of her busiest days. Although she had a couple of breaks, the timings were too tight to nip home to check on Ryan, which was somewhat a relief. She texted to check he was all right and received a short response saying his head hurt, his body ached, and was lying on the sofa watching a series on Netflix. At least he wasn't ignoring her.

Jay arrived for the evening bootcamp and headed straight over to Karen, who lifted one of his arms out to the side, checked it over, then repeated the same with the other.

'Is this some weird bootcamp initiation thing?' he asked.

'No. Just checking for teaspoon and soup packet injuries.'

Jay laughed. 'She might be a bit unpredictable, but at least life's never boring with Sophie.'

'As long as she makes you happy, it's each to their own. Let me introduce you to my friend and business partner, Steff.' Karen waved Steff over. 'Steff, this is Jay who I was telling you about. Jay, this is Steff.'

They both narrowed their eyes at each other. 'Have we met?' Jay asked.

Steff wrinkled her nose. 'I was thinking exactly the same. Have you ever done bootcamp before?'

Jay shook his head. 'Never. Have you ever done anything at Kayley School?'

Steff shook her head. 'I'm normally really good at placing people. Oh, well, it'll come to me eventually. In the meantime, welcome to bootcamp. I hope you enjoy it.'

Despite the worrying situation at home, Karen really enjoyed running bootcamp again with Steff. It turned out that Jay knew a couple of the bootcampers so he quickly settled in and seemed like one of the regulars.

'Have you still got time for that drink?' Jay asked after they'd taken his photo for smashing his first bootcamp and receiving the Awesome Award. 'Or do you need to rush back to Ryan?'

'I've got time,' Karen said. 'I need to put the stuff in my car but if you want to grab us a table, I'll see you back at Blue Savannah in ten minutes.'

'I'll get the drinks in. What would you like?'

'A vat of wine. Although I'd better settle for lime and soda, please.'

* * *

'Ooh, that's refreshing,' Karen said, taking a sip of her drink as she sat down next to Jay. 'Thank you.'

'Pleasure. Are you okay outside because there were tables inside?'

She smiled. 'My office is the great outdoors so it's all good.

Thanks for asking, though. So, what did you think of your first bootcamp?'

'Loved it, although I might not be able to move tomorrow.'

'Great that you knew some of the team already.'

Jay smiled. 'I'd have still loved it even if I hadn't. You and Steff are unbelievable. You're like powerhouses of energy and enthusiasm. It's so infectious.'

She reached across the table and squeezed Jay's hand. 'Aw, thank you.'

'What's going on?'

Snatching her hand away, Karen looked up into Ryan's furious face. Crap timing or what? 'Nothing's going on,' she snapped.

'You were holding hands.'

'We weren't.'

'You bloody well were. My eyes might be black and blue but I'm not blind.'

Jay shook his head. 'Look, mate, we—'

'I'm not your mate.' Ryan glared at Jay.

'People are looking at us,' Karen hissed as she stood up. 'Can we not make a scene here?'

'Fine. I'm going home, but I expect you back within five minutes of me or...'

'Or what? What are you going to do?'

'Five minutes,' he snarled, then stormed off along the seafront.

Karen watched him leave, astonished by the unusual display of hostility. What was going on? Sighing, she slumped back down on her seat, wishing she could curl up into a ball and make it all go away.

'I'm going to have to go,' she said. 'I'm sorry.'

Jay nodded. 'Text me later to let me know you're okay. Or phone me if you need me.'

Karen felt sick as she marched back to her car. Of all the moments for Ryan to appear, it had to be when she touched Jay. A completely innocent gesture, yet she could understand exactly why Ryan had seen it as something more. What was he doing on the seafront anyway? Checking up on her?

Her mobile bleeped as she made it to the car park and opened her car door:

✉ From Unknown
Ooh, that was awkward, wasn't it?

✉ From Unknown
Talk about double standards. He can dish it out but he can't seem to take it. Hilarious

She was being watched again! Karen leaned against her car, her pulse racing as she typed in a response:

✉ To Unknown
This is getting boring. What did he do and who did he do it with?

✉ From Unknown
Ha ha ha. Boring, is it? That's so funny. If you hadn't been so boring, maybe your fiancé

wouldn't have needed to find excitement elsewhere

☒ To Unknown
Just tell me what you think you know. I know you're dying to

☒ From Unknown
Are you sure you want to know? After all, curiosity killed the cat. And what I do know — not what I think I know — is going to kill your relationship. DEAD!

☒ To Unknown
Just tell me

☒ From Unknown
Not unless you ask nicely. Where're your manners?

☒ To Unknown
Please tell me. Pretty please with a cherry on the top. Thank you

☒ From Unknown
Seeing as you've asked so nicely, if a little sarcastically, I will tell you. Tomorrow. Enjoy the rest of your evening

Karen pressed her head against the car door, taking deep breaths, trying to ease the nausea.

'I thought you'd have been long gone by now.'

She looked up to see Jay standing by her car, his keys dangling from his hand.

'Stalker,' she said, handing him her phone.

'Oh, Karen.' He shook his head as he scrolled through the texts. 'This is bad.'

'I don't know what to do or what to think anymore,' she said. 'I know I should believe Ryan, but...' Her voice cracked and tears slid down her cheeks.

'Come here,' Jay said, holding out his arms.

Karen gratefully accepted his hug and the comforting words as she sobbed in his arms.

'I've made your T-shirt soggy,' she said as she pulled away.

Jay looked down at the wet patch. 'That? I hate to say it but I think that's sweat from bootcamp.'

Karen laughed. 'You always know the right thing to say.'

'Not always. I wished I'd known the right thing to say to Ryan earlier.'

She shook her head. 'I don't think there's anything that either of us could have said. He'd already made his mind up about us from the moment he saw us together a week ago. It's so strange because he's never reacted like this to any male clients I've had.' She sighed. 'Which is one of the reasons I don't believe him. I think something's happened between him and a client and his guilty conscience is making him think I'd do the same.'

'Have you any idea who?'

'No. I don't know many of his clients.' She rubbed her hands under her eyes and across her cheeks to wipe away her tears. 'I'd better go. He'll have paced a hole in the carpet by now.'

'Good luck.' Jay opened his arms again.

It probably should have been a quick hug but she didn't

let go and he didn't either. She could hear the leaves rustling in the trees, the cry of a baby, the beep of the pedestrian crossing... and her heart hammering. She tightened her hold, feeling safe and secure in Jay's arms. He did the same and they stood there, locked together, breathing rapidly. She closed her eyes, imagining what it might feel like to kiss Jay. All it would take was a tilt of her head. Electricity zinged through her at the thought of his lips against hers, his hands in her hair. She opened her eyes again and pulled away, confused. Kissing Jay? Where had that come from?

'I'd better go,' she said.

He nodded.

'I don't want to, but...'

'I know.' He held her gaze and she knew he'd felt it too. Something had shifted between them but, right now, she couldn't think about what that meant. Right now, she needed to get home and face the music.

* * *

Glancing at the clock on the dashboard, Karen shuddered. Half an hour had passed since Ryan stormed off. He was going to be livid when she got home. Let him be, though. What right did he have to give her orders like that, in front of a client too? Was Jay just a client, though? He hadn't felt like one when he'd held her that second time. She shook her head. Too complicated. Focus on Ryan. What a nerve he had. She should have told him to stick his demands where the sun didn't shine, but she'd been that surprised and embarrassed that she'd never thought to challenge him. He wouldn't know what hit him when she got home, though.

* * *

He was sitting in the kitchen, nursing a tumbler of dark liquid. A bottle of Jack Daniels sat on the table, and it looked like there were only a few shots left. How many of those had he had already? She dreaded to think. And since when had he started drinking that stuff? He'd given her a glass of it when her stalker had started following her, but she'd never known him to drink it before.

'That was a long five minutes.' He necked the liquid then poured another generous measure. 'What have you been doing?'

Electricity zipped through Karen again as she thought about that hug. She hoped she didn't look as guilty as she felt. 'Why were you on the seafront tonight? Checking up on me?'

'I'd forgotten you were going to be late. I came to see if you wanted to grab a bite to eat.' He took a swig of his drink. 'Just as well I did. Caught you in the act.'

'Oh, for God's sake. There's nothing going on with Jay. He's a client and a friend. That's all.'

'Really?'

'Yes, really. It's completely innocent.' She swallowed hard. It had been a hug. Only a hug. And hugs were innocent, weren't they?

Ryan picked up his phone, pressed a few buttons, then thrust it into her eyeline. 'Doesn't look completely innocent to me.'

Grabbing the phone, Karen's heart raced at the photo of her and Jay in the car park, arms round each other. From the angle it was taken, it looked like they were kissing.

'Oh my God, Ryan! Were you spying on me?'

'No.'

'So where's the picture come from?'

'Your bloody stalker, I presume, deciding to torment me now.' Ryan grabbed the phone back off her. 'I came straight home to wait for you, like I said I would. And I waited, and waited, and waited. Then my phone pinged and this little beauty arrived so I knew exactly why you were late. Care to explain?'

Outraged, Karen thrust her phone at him, the text conversation with the stalker showing on the screen. 'Care to explain?'

She watched his eyes widen then narrow. 'Thanks for defending me.'

'As if I'm going to defend you to some weirdo who's sending me anonymous texts. All I want is for it to end. I thought... hoped... they might admit they were making it up if I pushed them.'

'Looks to me like you believe them.' Ryan downed the rest of his drink. 'So why don't you piss off with your ginger friend, then? I'm sure he'll make you very happy.'

Karen grabbed the Jack Daniels bottle and tipped the remainder down the sink.

'Oi! I was drinking that.'

'I think you've had enough, don't you?'

He stared at her then nodded. 'Yes, I have. I've had enough. I've very definitely, positively had enough.'

'Of what?' she shouted as he stormed out of the kitchen. 'Jack Daniels? Or of me?'

'Of everything,' he yelled, before slamming the front door behind him.

He wasn't going to drive, was he? Karen dashed down the hall and was about to thrust open the front door when she spotted Ryan through the glass, running across the road. At least he wasn't stupid enough to get behind the wheel. Where was he going, though? To see his other woman? Or was he going to Steff's? She was convinced more than ever that he had done something stupid to jeopardise their relationship. Would the stalker be true to their word and provide some evidence tomorrow or would they continue to play games?

Returning to the kitchen, Karen rang Steff to warn her that Ryan might be on his way over and that he was in a dark mood and drunk. Steff assured her she'd text if he appeared. Then she sank down into a seat at the kitchen table, her head in her hands, her mind in a spin. What an evening. What a horrible, awkward, embarrassing evening. Yet that hug with Jay... It had been a long time since Ryan had held her like that or made her feel like Jay just had.

* * *

While Karen was getting ready for bed, a text came through:

 From Steff
No sign of Ryan all night. I'm guessing he's gone to the pub to drown his sorrows, stupid arse. Really sorry xx

 To Steff
Thanks for letting me know. You're probably right. This evening was horrendous. Not sure how much longer I can keep doing this xx

 From Steff
It breaks my heart to read that, but I can't

say I blame you. It's like he's had a personality transplant. I want the old Ryan back

⊠ To Steff
So do I. But I'm worried that he's never going to come back. He's been on the Jack Daniels. Dread to know how much!

⊠ From Steff
Jack Daniels? OMG! Since when did he start drinking spirits? Whatever you decide, I'll support you. I really hope it's not the end for you, though. I always thought the two of you were strong enough to survive anything that life threw at you xx

⊠ To Steff
Me too. And we probably could have done, except I don't know what it is that life's throwing at us and that's the issue. I can't fix the problem when I don't know what the problem is

At about 3.45 a.m., the sound of a key in the lock jolted Karen awake.

'Hi honey, I'm home,' Ryan called, then laughed.

Lying back against the pillows, she clenched her fists. He'd better not think he was crawling into bed beside her, the state he was obviously in. She listened as he clattered about in the kitchen, flinching at the sound of a glass smashing.

Her heart thumped rapidly as she heard his footsteps on the stairs, a thud as he must have missed his footing, then footsteps again. The sound of one of the bedroom doors opening on the floor below filled her with relief. If he'd made it up to the top floor and into their bedroom, she'd have had to go and sleep in one of the spare bedrooms so he'd saved her the bother.

What he hadn't saved her from was a sleepless night yet again. She opened the blinds then lay back on the bed, staring out the window. The inky-blue night sky gradually lightened, then turned into a stunning vista of peach, lemon and baby-pink, with the occasional streak of baby-blue. Birds chirped their morning songs and the world seemed happy and content. The complete opposite to how she felt.

43

KAREN

Karen crept down the top flight of stairs the following morning. As she reached the landing on the first floor, Ryan opened the door to one of the spare bedrooms. A heady stench of sweat and alcohol hit her and she reeled back, fighting the urge to cover her mouth and nose with her hand. He looked at her for a moment, but didn't speak. She wasn't surprised. What could he say after all? Sorry? She had no words either. She had nothing to be sorry for and no idea what to say without opening up raw wounds again.

He crossed the landing to the bathroom and closed the door.

Feeling numb, she made her way to the ground floor, hoping to find the strength to face the day in a cup of coffee and a bowl of porridge. Large chunks of what looked like a pint glass, plus smaller shards were scattered across the tiled floor. Great. First task of the day was to clear up his mess.

As she swept the broken glass into the dustpan, the toilet flushed upstairs and, a few moments later, his heavy footsteps resounded across the landing before the spare bedroom door slammed shut.

She pictured his face as he'd looked at her, his expression completely devoid of any sort of emotion. No regret, no guilt, and no love.

His bruises had started to heal. The deep purple had faded and a greenish/yellowish tint had appeared around the edges. Shame the same couldn't be said about their relationship; it was definitely far from healing. It was in dire need of open-heart surgery and rapidly on its way to flatlining. She glanced down at the fragments in the dustpan. Broken. Just like her trust.

* * *

Karen was on the beach, setting up for mid-morning bootcamp, when Steff joined her.

'I've got the morning free and I figured I could spend it doing the washing and cleaning. Yawn. Or I could come to the beach and see if you could use some moral support. No brainer really.'

Karen smiled gratefully. 'Some moral support would be amazing. Thank you.'

'Did he come home last night?' Steff asked.

'Yes, but not till an hour before dawn. He staggered up the stairs, ricocheting off the walls by the sounds of it, and slept in one of the spare bedrooms again.'

'It's come to that, eh?'

'Looks like it. He didn't speak when I saw him first thing although probably just as well. I couldn't have faced starting the day with a screaming match.'

'I wish I knew what to say, but you're not the only one he's shutting out.' Steff shrugged and shook her head. 'I can't remember the last time I had a proper conversation with him.'

* * *

The session went brilliantly again. The teamwork was amazing to watch and, this time, the dynamic had switched between Alison and Danniella, with Alison being the one supporting and motivating Danniella who was clearly very weak after her ordeal.

Karen looked around the group after their cool-down. 'Steff and I think you were all amazing today but we're unanimous that today's Awesome Award goes to Alison.' She grinned as Alison's jaw practically dropped to the sand and the others laughed and cheered.

'Congratulations, Ali. Five bootcamps in and I can already see a massive difference in you. I'm in awe of your enthusiasm, the effort, the attitude and the amazing teamwork throughout today.'

'Thank you so much.' Alison sounded genuinely astounded. 'I loved today's session. That seedling might have sprouted.'

'Yes!' Karen punched the air. 'I knew you were going to be one of those who grew to love bootcamp. I'll take your photo. Everyone else, I'll see you on Thursday.'

Alison hid behind the flag again as Karen took her photo

'How was it for you?' she asked Danniella.

'Great bootcamp but so frustrating. I feel like I've taken a massive step back in fitness levels.'

'It's inevitable after what you've been through but it'll come back quickly. Don't push yourself too hard too soon, though. Maybe just stick to the bootcamps this week then introduce the running again from next week.'

Danniella nodded. 'Okay. How are you? And how was Ryan?'

'Did they catch the mugger?' Alison added.

Karen pulled the flag out of the sand, shaking her head. 'I'm not convinced he was mugged, especially as he's still got his phone. As for us, it's been a horrendous couple of days and I don't think it's going to improve anytime soon.'

'Have you got time for a coffee back at mine?' Danniella asked. 'You're welcome to join us too, Steff.'

Karen looked at her watch. 'My PT session got rescheduled so I've got a bit of time. Steff?'

'I'm free, if you don't mind,' Steff said.

* * *

When they were settled in Danniella's flat with drinks, Karen updated them on the situation with Ryan and her fears that there was more to it than a mugging. During the conversation, Ryan rang three times.

'You can get it if you want to,' Danniella said after Karen had scowled at the screen on the third call and put the phone back down on the arm of the sofa with a sigh.

'I don't want to,' she admitted. 'I've got nothing to say to him at the moment and, besides, I don't know why he keeps ringing me. As far as he's aware, I'm in a PT session and wouldn't be answering anyway. So, what do you all think? Guilty?'

'Of something,' Alison agreed. 'It might not be that he's seeing someone else, though. I used to work with this lass who was convinced her boyfriend was seeing someone else because he kept getting mysterious texts and calls. Turned out he'd organised a surprise trip to New York to propose to her and an engagement party for when they returned.'

Karen smiled. 'Loving that story, but sadly I don't think we're going to have a happy ending like that. If he was doing something sweet like secretly planning our wedding, we wouldn't be fighting all the time.'

'And he'd have told me,' Steff said. 'Ryan's my best friend. Or he used to be. I don't know who he is at the moment.'

Karen's phone beeped. 'Oh for God's sake. Sorry, girls.' She picked it up and frowned at the screen. 'It's an email this time.'

'He's obviously desperate to get hold of you,' Steff said.

Karen felt sick as she glanced down at her email. It wasn't from Ryan, but the subject header told her exactly who it was from.

`You wanted proof. Hope you can handle it.`

'It's a video,' she said, aware that the others were watching her expectantly. 'I'll grab my iPad and watch it on there. Sorry. Back in a bit. Talk amongst yourselves.'

Retrieving her iPad from her backpack in the hall, she wandered into the kitchen with it, her stomach churning. Sitting at the table, she opened the case and propped it up, took a deep breath, then pressed play.

The words, `In the beginning...` were written on a black screen. A dance track that Karen didn't recognise played in the background.

'What's your fantasy?' an unfamiliar female voice asked,

while the camera panned across a table containing empty bottles of wine, half-empty glasses, a couple of empty tumblers and a bottle of Jack Daniels.

'I'm not telling you that,' a male voice answered. Karen recognised the voice instantly: Ryan.

'Go on. I told you mine.'

'I don't have one,' Ryan said.

The camera continued to focus on the drinks, then moved to some candles flickering.

'Everyone has a fantasy,' the female purred. 'I bet yours is dirty.' There was a pause then the female shrieked with laughter. 'Oh my God! It is, isn't it? You've got a dirty fantasy.'

'I'm admitting nothing.'

The screen turned black again, the words, 'Later that night…' materialising on it.

Karen's heart raced as she kept her eyes glued to the screen.

'It's time to tell me your fantasy,' the same female said. This time the camera focused on Ryan slumped in a chair, barely able to keep his eyes open. He looked absolutely wasted and his speech confirmed it.

'Promise you won't tell anyone?' His eyes kept closing and his head lolling forward.

'Your secret's safe with me.'

'A threesome,' Ryan muttered. 'Would love a threesome.'

The female shrieked with laughter again. 'You dirty dog. Another man?'

'Noooo! Ew. Girls. Karen and… I dunno. Whoever. She won't, though.'

'You've asked her?'

'Mentioned it, but she's not up for it.'

'What's her fantasy?'

Ryan grinned. 'My name's Bond. James Bond.'

'How predictable.'

'She's not 'dictable. Love her. And *Dirty Dancing* fantasy.'

'The film?'

Ryan nodded. 'Lake scene. She loves that.'

'Then why don't you give your boring, predictable little fiancée her fantasies, and maybe she'll give you yours?'

Ryan drunkenly wagged his finger at the camera. 'She'll never do it.'

'Then why don't you find someone who will?'

He laughed. 'You volunteering?'

There was a pause before the female answered, 'I might be. And I know someone else who'd be up for it. Just say the word and it can be arranged.'

Ryan's eyes widened for a moment and he smiled, then his head slumped to his chest as sleep obviously overcame him.

Karen's mouth felt very dry as she struggled to catch her breath. The screen went black again, captioned with: `Well, somebody had to…`'

Heavy breathing emanated from the iPad, seeming to bounce off the walls and fill the kitchen. She knew exactly what she was about to see yet couldn't seem to tear her eyes away from the screen. *Please let it be a prank. Please let it be a PT session.* But her gut told her it wasn't.

Karen started shaking as the caption gave way to film; an erotic film containing two women, one man, one fantasy. She didn't recognise the blonde woman, and the brunette's long hair was obliterating her face. But there was absolutely no doubt who the man was.

'What's he sent you, then?' Steff asked, appearing in the doorway. 'Some soppy apology?'

Karen looked up at Steff, eyes wide, breathing shallow. 'It's not from Ryan.'

At the same time, the heavy panting must have hit Steff's ears as she rushed to the table to look at the film. 'Bloody hell,' she cried.

The other two came rushing in from the lounge. 'What's going on?' Alison cried.

'He's guilty,' Karen whispered, slumping back in the chair. 'Very guilty.'

'Is that...?' Alison asked.

Karen and Steff both nodded slowly.

'Shit,' Danniella muttered. 'I'm so sorry.'

'Do you know the women?' Alison asked.

'No.'

The brunette swept her hair back, revealing her face for the first time. Steff squealed. 'That's Mia!'

'Who's Mia?' Alison asked.

'My girlfriend,' Steff gasped.

'Oh Steff, I'm sorry.' Karen paused the video. 'I didn't see her face. I've only met her once so wouldn't have recognised her.'

'I recognise her,' Danniella said, pointing to the screen which had paused on a clear visual of the blonde's face. 'She was one of my nurses from hospital. Kirsty.'

Steff grabbed the iPad. 'Kirsty? Oh my God, it *is* her,' she sobbed. 'She's Mia's friend from work.' She closed the cover, put the device down and turned to Karen. 'She's the one who used to go out with your friend, Sam. The one who I said was getting too pally with Mia at that fortieth party. Looks like I wasn't being paranoid after all. There *was* something going on between them.'

'And Ryan,' Karen added. She sank back in the chair

again. So they'd been right. All along, the stalker had been telling the truth and now she'd seen for herself how badly Ryan had betrayed her. She'd known there was something but this was far worse than she could have imagined.

Her hands shook as she picked up her phone.

⊠ From Unknown
I promised you'd find out today and I keep my promises. Did you enjoy your home movie, lol? Bet your lying git of a fiancé has been desperately trying to phone you to tell you not to watch it. He was not happy with me when I told him I was sending it. Such fun!

⊠ From Unknown
My work here is done *feels smug*

Steff was sobbing but Karen had no tears. She felt sick, angry and betrayed. Yet, amongst those emotions, she felt relief because now she knew. She knew why he'd turned on her and Steff. She knew where he'd been when he'd stayed out late. She knew why he'd walked away from her in that satin slip. And, because she knew, she could do something about it.

44

Karen sped across town. Ryan had called again as she was leaving Danniella's flat and once more as she got to her car, but she hadn't answered. This was not a conversation for over the phone.

Steff had been inconsolable and Karen's heart broke for her. She'd had double the betrayal: best friend and girlfriend.

Screeching to a halt on their drive, Karen leapt out of her car and stormed into the house. '*Ryan!*'

He stepped into the doorway of the kitchen, phone to his ear, a tumbler of dark liquid in his other hand. As she stomped down the hall towards him, his hand dropped away from his ear and he backed away a few paces. 'Kaz, it's not what—'

'Don't you dare insult my intelligence by telling me it's not what it looks like. I've *seen* the video. I've *heard* the video. I know *exactly* what you've been up to. What I want to know is why you did it.'

He necked back his drink. 'I don't know.'

'Bullshit! Why did you do it?'

'I was drunk.'

She eyed the new bottle of Jack Daniels on the kitchen table, several measures clearly already missing. It was only just lunchtime.

'Also bullshit,' she snapped. 'Why did you do it?'

'We were going through a rough patch. I thought it was over.'

'Oh my God! You are so full of crap. Have you seen the video?'

'No.'

'You should watch it. Very educational. Thanks for sharing my secrets, by the way.'

'Kaz, I—'

'I'm speaking. When it's your turn to speak, you'll know.'

Ryan slumped onto one of the chairs at the table while she paced up and down the kitchen, aware of him pouring another large drink and necking it back.

'So, in this delightful video of yours, Mia suggests that if you give me my fantasies, maybe I'll let you have yours. That part had to have been filmed before you did the James Bond thing. We were *not* having problems back then. You'd forgotten our anniversary and, yes, we'd had a bust-up about that but you made it up to me that night and things were back on track.'

She paused, her mind whizzing through the timeline. 'When we went to the lake to try my *Dirty Dancing* fantasy and it didn't work, you said that some fantasies do live up to expectations. I thought nothing of it at the time but now I know exactly what you meant. You'd already had your dirty little threesome by then, hadn't you? That's what you were talking about. Your fantasy had been exactly what you'd dreamed it would be, hadn't it?' Bile filled her mouth and she swallowed hard, grimacing.

He wouldn't look at her.

Everything was starting to click into place like pieces of a jigsaw. 'When my stalker got in touch, you knew it was only a matter of time before your dirty little secret surfaced. That's why you didn't want me to go to the police. That's why you wanted me to change my number. What did you think was going to happen? That it was all going to go away?'

Ryan shrugged as he stared into his empty glass.

'You stupid prick,' Karen cried. 'So let's return to my original question: why did you do it?'

'I don't know.'

'Not good enough. Why did you do it?'

'I DON'T KNOW!'

'WHY DID YOU DO IT? It's not a difficult question.' Why wouldn't he answer her? Was he hanging on, thinking there was a chance to smooth things over? 'You do realise that we're over, don't you? There is no chance of recovering from what you've done. Our relationship cannot be salvaged. Ever.' Shaking with rage, she leaned on the table and narrowed her eyes at him. 'So why the hell did you do it?'

She could tell from his bloodshot eyes that he was drunk; probably had been all morning.

'Because I could, okay?' Ryan glared at her, his lip curled up as though she disgusted him. 'They threw themselves at me and I was curious. What would you do if someone handed your ultimate fantasy to you on a plate like that?'

'I'd think about the fiancé I loved at home and I'd say no.' Stomach churning, Karen moved away and leaned against the wall, keen to put some distance between them.

'Yeah, well, you would, wouldn't you, Saint Karen?

Because you're always so bloody perfect. Never do a thing wrong.' He poured another drink and raised it to her as if toasting her. 'Have you any idea how hard it is living up to your expectations? Everything in your life has to be so damn perfect.'

'Like what?'

'Everything. You plan your life with military precision. Bootcamp here, PT there, family time here, sex there. Where's the spontaneity? Where's the fun?'

'We've never had a scheduled day or time for sex. Never.'

'Never?' Ryan sniggered. 'Yeah, you're right. We *never* have sex.'

'I didn't say that.'

'But it's true.'

'Only recently and that's because you were getting it elsewhere. So why did you do it?'

Ryan shook his head. 'I've already said. Because of you. It's your fault.'

'How do you work that out? Bloody hell, Ryan. If it makes you feel better about shagging your best friend's girlfriend and some little slapper colleague of hers, then you go ahead and convince yourself that it's all my fault. But we both know the truth. I said no to a threesome and you decided to have one anyway. That's all there is to this. I hope it was worth it.'

He gave her a smug smile. 'Oh, it was. I'm not sure which time was on the video you were sent, but they were all worth it.'

Karen backed against the wall, her hands wrapped across her stomach, her pulse racing. 'It wasn't only once?' she asked in a small voice.

He laughed; a cold, cruel sound. 'If the fantasy is better

than the reality at home, why wouldn't you keep wanting the fantasy?'

Legs like jelly, Karen slid down the wall and onto the cold floor tiles. 'How many times?'

'I lost count. Mia and Kirsty. Just Kirsty. Tell you what...' He wagged a finger at her. 'That Kirsty was an eye-opener. Into everything, that one. Of course, her boyfriend wasn't too pleased when he caught us together.' Ryan laughed again.

Another puzzle piece slotted into place. 'The mugging...?' Which would explain why he hadn't wanted to involve the police for that and why he still had his phone.

Ryan nodded. 'A beating from Kirsty's boyfriend.' He actually sounded proud.

'Where did you stay that night, cos that story about someone from Bay Runners was obviously bullshit?'

'Kirsty's. She's a nurse. She was worried about my bruises the next day and insisted I go to hospital in case there was any internal damage.'

Exhausted, Karen rested her elbows on her knees, her head in her hands. One last question. 'Who's my stalker?'

'I don't know.'

She raised her head and looked him in the eye. 'Don't lie to me. Is it Mia?'

'She says not. I'm guessing Kirsty although Mia says it's not her either. It's not Kirsty's style, apparently.'

'It has to be one of them. Who else would have access to the video?'

'I reckon Kirsty.' His smile faltered. 'You're not going to go to the police, are you?' Was that panic in his voice?

Karen slowly eased herself to her feet. 'To say what? My fiancé is shagging his way round the women of Whitsborough Bay and one of them is sending me video nasties to prove it?'

She turned to leave the kitchen.

'Where are you going?'

'Work. You know me. Bootcamp here, PT session there. Never late. Always reliable. Little Miss Perfect, as you say. I'll be back by eight tonight. I expect you to have gone.'

'And where am I supposed to go?'

'Kirsty's? Mia's? You go ahead and continue to live that fantasy life of yours that's so much better than the reality of the dull existence you had with me.'

'I didn't say that about you.'

'It's what you meant, though.' Head held high, Karen marched down the hall, slammed the door shut, and set off across town to meet her next PT client. Business as usual. Couldn't be late. Structured. Professional. Perfect. Was that really what Ryan had thought of her? And was it such a negative thing?

But she hadn't even driven for three minutes before she was barely able to see the road through her tears. She pulled into a side street, turned off the engine, and clung to the steering wheel as agonising sobs shook her body. It was over. Completely over. The man she'd loved for thirteen years had turned on her, turned to someone else, and turned their lives upside down. Thirteen really was unlucky after all.

45

ALISON

Alison helped a tearful Steff shove her belongings into a couple of suitcases and a stack of black binbags. They dumped everything in the small bedroom at Danniella's then Steff went out to work telling them she'd stay at Karen's that night if she kicked Ryan out or with her parents if she didn't.

'I'm still in shock,' Alison admitted as she wandered into the lounge and pulled on her work blazer. 'Please tell me it didn't really happen.'

Danniella looked up from her laptop. 'I wish I could.'

'Why would he do something like that?' Alison shook her head. 'I can't get my head round it. He's destroyed his relationship with his fiancée *and* his best friend and for what? Meaningless sex? What was he thinking?'

'I don't think he was,' Danniella said. 'Or rather he was thinking with a different part of his anatomy.'

Alison sat down on the sofa, sighing. 'Ryan and Mia have committed the ultimate act of betrayal. There can't be any coming back from that. How could they ever trust their partners again?'

Danniella raised an eyebrow meaningfully and Alison gave her a rueful smile. 'Okay, okay. I know what you're thinking. I'll get him to meet me after work and ask him about the phone call.'

'I don't think you can consider a future with Dave if you don't.'

'I know. You're right.' She sighed. 'Oh, God! What am I going to say about his proposal?'

'I don't think you need to say anything about it until you've found out about the phone call. If he was with that woman, it's over, isn't it?'

'Definitely. There'd be no recovery from that.' Alison stood up. 'I'd best go or I'll miss my bus. Will you be all right on your own?'

'I'll be fine. I've got plenty of work to keep me distracted before my first counselling session.'

'I hope it goes well. Ring me at work if you need to talk afterwards. Or call Aidan if I don't answer.'

Danniella smiled. 'I love that you worry about me. I know it's going to be emotional but I know that I need to do it.' She stood up and hugged Alison. 'Good luck with Dave and don't let him avoid the conversation.'

'I won't. What's just happened with Karen shows how important it is to get to the truth, no matter how painful it is to hear.'

* * *

'I hope you enjoy your stay at The Ramparts Hotel,' Alison said to the couple who'd just checked in. 'And congratulations on your ruby wedding anniversary.'

'Thank you,' they both said, smiling as they headed

across the lobby towards the lifts.

Alison turned to face Chelsea, her brows knitted. 'Why do you keep staring at me? You've been doing it all afternoon.'

'There's something different about you,' Chelsea said, shaking her head. 'It's your uniform! You've lost weight. And you're happy. Your eyes are sparkling.'

'You really think I've lost weight?' Alison asked, pulling at her blouse. Chelsea was right. The buttons were usually pulling but there was actually some give in the blouse. 'I've been going to bootcamp.'

'What's bootcamp?'

Between guests, Alison explained what she'd been doing and about the new friends she'd made, offering them up as an explanation for the sparkle in her eyes. She didn't want to tell Chelsea about Dave, especially as there might be no relationship to speak of depending on how the conversation went after work. Chelsea knew about Ibiza; Alison hadn't been able to avoid that news considering she'd been working when she was meant to have been on holiday or getting the kitchen fitted. Chelsea had, of course, expressed her disgust in no uncertain terms and had made a big assumption that it was over at that point. There was no point in telling her that Dave was back with a bag full of gifts and a marriage proposal. The grief wasn't worth it.

She still didn't know what to make of the proposal. Although she'd been tempted to run back to the van and say yes when he'd dropped her off at Danniella's, that feeling had already subsided by the time she got upstairs, replaced by confusion. Was that a sign that she didn't actually want to marry him or was it simply her being cautious after everything that had happened? And why had he proposed now? Something didn't compute.

46

DANNIELLA

Curled up on her left side on the bed, Danniella tried to empty her mind. The lightest of breezes danced through the open French doors and playfully tickled the cream voile panels.

It was early evening and the warm weather had acted like a magnet, drawing people to the beach. Revving engines, laughter, dogs barking, children's squeals or cries, and the occasional squawk from a gull reminded her that, all around, life did indeed go on; a strong theme from her first session with her counsellor.

A gentle tinkling sound made her lift her head off the pillow for a closer listen. Wind chimes. She laid her head back down and smiled. Alison had told her about her sister, Fleur, and the fairies having a ball when the chimes sounded. She'd cried when Alison had talked about imagining Fleur at that fairy ball; such a comforting thought. Was Abigail with her?

Closing her eyes, Danniella concentrated on nothing but the sound of the chimes.

Darkness had fallen when she opened her eyes again. The breeze had stilled but the room was cool. Shivering, she made her way to the French doors. A full moon cast a silvery glow across the North Sea towards the sand. She paused in the doorway, drinking it in, before the drop in temperature became too uncomfortable and she closed the doors.

Pulling on a cardigan, she checked the time on her phone. Just after 10 p.m. Alison would have just finished her shift and be on her way to meet Dave. As though connected in thought, a text flashed up.

✉ From Alison
Going to meet Dave but I can cancel. How did it go? I can be home in 15 mins if you want to talk xx

✉ To Alison
I was just thinking about you. It was emotional but very good. Came home and slept. Only just woken up! Think I'm going to watch some TV then bed. Relax and enjoy your evening… but make sure you ask him about Ibiza xx

✉ From Alison
Glad it went well. Not sure how long I'll be. Could be ten minutes, could be a couple of hours, but ring if you need me xx

✉ To Alison
I'll be fine. BTW, Karen threw Ryan out and

Steff's staying with her. I've invited them round tomorrow night xx

✉ From Alison
Good for Karen. Got to go. See you later xx

Pocketing her mobile, Danniella padded downstairs and into the kitchen to put the kettle on. While it boiled, she made her way into the lounge, flicked on a couple of lamps, and lit some candles. She gazed around the room. It really was a beautiful flat and Aidan had been so good to her, insisting it was no problem having Alison staying. He was what her grandma would have called 'a treasure'. With a mum as lovely as Lorraine, it wasn't surprising he was so polite and thoughtful. He reminded her of Ethan.

Danniella's counsellor, Marian, couldn't have been a better fit. She was gentle yet firm, empathetic yet businesslike. She'd asked Danniella to start by giving her the basic facts: who'd died, when, and what relation they were to her. Then she'd asked how Abigail had died, not flinching in the slightest when Danniella said, 'I killed her.' She'd simply maintained eye contact and said, 'Tell me about it.' So she did.

Nothing had been resolved in their hour although Danniella hadn't expected it would be; she'd known it would be mainly her talking about the accident and her reactions to it. She'd cried a lot, got angry a couple of times, then cried some more. Marian had let her talk, only stopping occasionally to clarify who certain people were and what their relationship was to Danniella.

Towards the end of the session, Marian asked, 'What do you hope to get from our time together, Danniella?'

'I don't really know.'

'Everyone has something they're hoping to achieve. Some of my clients don't know what it is when they start coming to me, but you're not one of those. Remember, you can tell me anything.'

Danniella nodded. 'I need you to tell me it wasn't my fault, that I didn't really kill my little girl.'

Marian removed her glasses and leaned forward. 'What would happen if I told you that?'

'I'd know that I had the right to go on living. That it's okay to smile, to laugh again, to make some new friends and to enjoy my life even though my daughter is nothing more than a jar of ashes and will never have the chance to life her life to the full.'

'Why would it make a difference if I gave you that absolution instead of, say, your husband, Ethan, or your stepsister, Natalie?'

Danniella shrugged. 'I don't know.'

Marian replaced her glasses and sat back again. 'I think you're going to get a lot from our sessions together, Danniella. It may not feel it at the moment, but the progress you've made in our first hour has been tremendous. It's not me who needs to tell you that it wasn't your fault, though.'

'Is it Ethan?'

Marian shook her head. 'It's you. I think that a big focus of our time together is going to be exploring the guilt that's eating away at you. The guilt that caused you to flee from your husband and the people who care about you. The guilt that's keeping you away from them. And I think that, once you have learned to let go of that guilt, you need my help in reaching out to Ethan and Natalie, don't you?'

Danniella couldn't answer. She hadn't even articulated all that in her own mind yet Marian couldn't have been more accurate.

Marian smiled. 'I'll see you next week, Danniella. Take care.'

Curling up on the sofa now with the TV on low, Danniella sipped on a low-calorie hot chocolate. Would Marian be able to help her shed the guilt that had cloaked her heavily like a suit of chainmail? Would she be able to help her find a way back to Ethan? Ethan. Gosh, she missed him. She'd built up a wall of fear, making him the enemy, always running, always needing to feel safe. It seemed ridiculous now, but it had been easier that way. If she'd stopped thinking of him as the bad guy, she'd have been forced to admit how much she missed him and how devastated she was at losing him as well. And Natalie.

Ethan hadn't sent his manuscript. Instead, he'd emailed again insisting that, much as he would love her input, what he yearned for was her. He'd signed off with another line from one of his books, making her cry.

```
There are three things you need to know
about me:
I'm here for you
I'll wait for you
I'll always love you
```

She hadn't responded.

Danniella glanced over at the table. Her laptop was there, inviting her to make that move. Karen had shown tremendous strength today and, even though she'd crumbled at the time, so had Steff. Alison was braving a difficult conversation right now. She felt herself drawing strength from those three inspiring women as they took control of their lives. She could do the same. She felt ready.


```
Hi Ethan
It's been over 9 months since I packed my
car and fled. Where have I been? Everywhere,
including to hell and back several times.
Towns, cities and villages. North, south,
east and west. England, Scotland, Wales.
Urban, rural, coastal. Running. Always
running. Then about two months ago I stopped
running and I put down some roots. I allowed
myself to breathe. I even made some friends.
Today, I had my very first session with a
bereavement counsellor. Later in the week,
I'm seeing an eating disorder specialist. My
journey around the country may have come to
a halt, but my journey to dealing with life
without Abigail is only just starting. That
journey is going to take me to some dark
places and it's going to hurt.
And I deserve to hurt because I've hurt you,
and Natalie, and so many others. I want to
say sorry but it's such an inadequate word.
I'm hoping my counsellor will help me artic-
```

ulate something more suitable when we work
through my selfish reactions.
Now please send me 'It's Always Been You'. I
could use a Lucas Downey novel in my life
right now. Love the title, by the way. Thank
you for that.
Danni

Re-reading her message with tears clouding her eyes,
Danniella pressed send, then shut her laptop down. Time for
bed and a new start.

47

ALISON

As Alison left the hotel at the end of her shift, a knot of nerves tightened in her stomach. Dave had only proposed the day before. Would he be expecting an answer already? Perhaps she should have made it clearer in her texts that she didn't have an answer yet; she only wanted to talk.

She'd arranged to meet him in The Purple Lobster. They used to be regulars there before life got in the way and they stopped making time for each other. She'd hesitated with the choice, wondering whether to pick somewhere that didn't hold fond memories. It was close, though, and she knew they'd be able to talk in there.

She spotted Dave as soon as she opened the door, sitting on a bar stool, hunched over a pint. He turned and smiled, casting Alison straight back into the past when he used to meet her from work, waiting at the bar with drinks for them both. He'd shaved and was wearing a shirt. A shirt rather than a T-shirt? She couldn't remember the last time he'd made that sort of effort for her.

Dave slid off his stool and gave her a gentle kiss on the

lips, stirring a feeling of longing inside her again. 'I was going to get you a wine,' he said, 'but I wasn't sure if you'd be drinking, what with doing that bootcamp thing, so I thought I'd best wait.'

She smiled, genuinely touched by the rare display of consideration. 'A diet coke would be great, thanks.'

'Do you want to grab a seat and I'll bring them over?' he suggested.

Glancing round the pub, there were several empty tables, including their 'favourite' from back in the day. Alison paused for a moment, looking towards it, then headed in the opposite direction. There was no going back. If – and it was a big if – there was any future for Dave and her, it needed to be about a fresh start and not about hanging onto the past.

'How was your shift?' he asked, placing her drink on a beer mat.

'Good. It was one of those days where it's crazy busy one minute and dead the next, but it's all good. How was work?'

'Not too bad.'

Alison raised an eyebrow as she sipped her drink. Not 'shite', then?

'They've opened up the next phase of houses so we're starting on them,' he continued. 'There's this four-bed one that I reckon you'll love. It's on the end of a cul-de-sac with views over open fields.'

'Sounds nice.'

'I know you've always wanted a brand-new house and that you hate ours...'

'I don't *hate* ours. I just can't stand all the mess and part-finished projects. It feels like we've only just moved in, yet we've been there for years.'

'I know. It's my fault. I...' Dave shook his head. 'Anyway, I was thinking that, if we got the work finished on ours, we could maybe look into doing a part-exchange on this new one. The site manager says I can register our interest and I know it's what you've always wanted.'

True. She'd always dreamed of living in a brand-new property. A fresh start. A blank canvas. No memories of anyone's past, happy or otherwise.

'Say something,' Dave said.

'I don't know what to say.' A proposal? A house move? What was going on?

'I wasn't expecting you to say yes tonight, you know. You haven't even seen the plans. You might not like the house.' Dave sipped on his pint. 'I suppose a decision about the house depends on a decision about the other question I asked you.'

She clocked his eye-line on her bare hands which were playing with her necklace again. The ring he'd given her in a drawer back at the flat, alongside her reasons to stay and leave 'It was only yesterday.' She said sighing. 'You said I could have time.'

He nodded vigorously. 'You can. I'm not pushing you.'

'Good, because this is huge. Marriage? Moving? They're massive steps, and right now, the most critical question is: do I want to be in a relationship with you at all?'

He reeled back as though he'd been slapped. 'You seemed pretty keen yesterday.'

Her cheeks flushed. 'I need to ask you some questions and I need you to be completely honest with me.'

'Okay.'

'Let's ignore the stuff about moving for the moment as you've just sprung that on me. My first question is why do you want to marry me?'

'What do you mean?'

'It's a simple question. Why do you want to marry me?'

'Because you're my favourite girl and I missed you when I was in Ibiza. Eggsey said it's like that saying about not knowing what you've got till it's gone.'

'Why now for a proposal, though?'

'I told you. Ibiza. I felt lost without you.'

'But why now? Why not in Corfu?'

'Come on, Ali. We were only twenty-one and you were still living with your grandma.'

'Maybe not Corfu, then, but anytime in the next six years. My birthday? Christmas? Valentine's Day? A random Wednesday in May? Why not then?'

He shrugged. 'I honestly don't know. I should have done it before. My bad.'

Alison nodded slowly, unconvinced. Her palms started to sweat but she had to ask the next question. 'Have you ever been unfaithful to me?'

His eyes widened. 'Bloody hell, Ali. What do you take me for?'

'Answer the question, please.'

'No, I have never been unfaithful to you. Jesus!'

'What does infidelity mean to you?'

'You're kidding me, yeah?'

Alison shook her head. 'I said I had questions and you promised to answer them honestly. If you don't want to, we might as well call it a night.'

Taking another sip from his pint, he rolled his eyes at her. 'Infidelity is shagging someone else when you're already seeing someone.'

'Just full sex?' she prompted.

'Yes. No. Other stuff too.'

'Like what?'

Dave looked around the pub, as though checking that nobody could overhear their conversation. He lowered his voice. 'You want me to name everything?'

Alison shrugged. 'I'm more curious about where you'd draw the line. Is flirting being unfaithful? Kissing? Touching? Oral sex?'

He looked around furtively again. 'Keep your voice down.'

'Which, if any, of those things do you constitute as being unfaithful?'

'All of them. I think. Maybe not flirting. I dunno. I suppose it depends whether it's a bit of harmless banter or whether it gets suggestive.'

'And have you done any of those things with anyone else since we met?'

'Of course not. What's this about? Has someone said something to you?'

She kept her eyes fixed on his. 'No. Should they have done?'

'No. Nobody's got anything to say about me.'

'Because what goes on in Ibiza stays in Ibiza. Is that the size of it?'

'Is that what this is? You reckon I've been up to something in Ibiza and, I dunno, she was crap in bed and it reminded me of how good it was with you?'

Alison felt a wave of heat flow from head to toe.

Dave took a glug from his pint. 'You want to know what happened in Ibiza? We were typical lads abroad. We had a good laugh, drank too much, ate too much, and were too loud. A couple of the single lads pulled, but the rest of us are either married or in relationships so we let them get on with it. Even though I had a great time, I realised I'd have had a better time if you'd been with me instead. Me and Eggsey sat on the balcony talking one night and he made me see what a total shit I've been to you, so I came back intending to make it up to you.' He took a deep breath. 'Satisfied? Is the interview over now?'

'Not quite. You left me a phone message. You left me several, actually, and they didn't all make for pleasant listening.'

'Sorry.'

'Forget it. This isn't about the nasty ones. This is about a certain phone call in the early hours of Friday. You started off being all mushy, but I heard a woman's voice and it didn't sound good.'

This was the moment. The pivotal moment of truth or lie.

Dave sighed. 'It was Anna. One of her mates copped off with Miggs at the start of the week so she started hanging around with us. She knew none of us were interested but she got hammered that night. We all did, but she was the worst and, for some stupid reason, she decided I was the bloke for her. I was having none of it, like, but the stupid woman wouldn't take no for an answer. She tried to jump me when I was on the phone. I pushed her away which was probably when you got disconnected.'

It sounded plausible. And he hadn't scratched his ear like he usually did when he was lying, although he could have been trying really hard not to because he knew it was his giveaway.

'Why didn't you call me back?' she asked.

'I tried but it wouldn't connect and then we ended up going to one of them foam parties so you'd never have heard me.'

That was plausible too, especially as she'd tried ringing

him after she'd listened to the message and had been unable to connect. 'You're absolutely sure nothing happened?'

'Cross my heart. It was all her. I did nothing to encourage her either.'

Sipping on her drink, Alison replayed every part of that phone message in her head. It certainly fit with his explanation. The choice was hers. She either believed him and they moved on... or she didn't and she might as well end things now because there was no way they could have a relationship if she thought he'd cheated on her. So did she believe him?

She tapped her fingers on the table, watching him glug down the rest of his pint. She wanted to believe him. She wanted to believe that he'd had an epiphany in Ibiza and had come back to make amends. She wanted to believe he loved her and only her. She wanted to believe he was still her family always and forever. So what was stopping her saying yes to this shiny new future he was offering her? Was it the list of twenty reasons to leave him and only four to stay? Was it the exhaustion of four years of treading on eggshells while he took his 'shite' days out on her? Or was it that her heart really belonged to someone else?

'The interrogation's over,' she said.

'Thank Christ for that cos I'm sweating here. If you get sick of working at that hotel, I swear you could get a job with MI5.'

She smiled weakly. 'I'm going to have to go.'

'But you've only just got here.'

He looked hurt and she felt guilty, but she needed time to think. 'I know, and I'm sorry, but I don't want to leave Danniella alone for too long.'

'Okay. Yeah. I get it.'

She bit her lip. He still thought she might be seeing

someone else. She picked up her phone. 'Here. This is my friend, Danniella,' she said, showing him a selfie she'd taken of them next to the giant sculpture of Stanley Moffatt on the seafront. 'She needs me.'

'I need you.' He held her gaze, then nodded. 'I'll drop you off. No point you wasting money on a taxi. I've only had the one pint.'

'Thanks, Dave. All I need is some time. You do understand that, don't you?'

'I do. Take all the time you need. You're worth waiting for.'

48

Karen tentatively glanced through the window of Blue Savannah after bootcamp on Monday evening, her stomach churning with nerves. There he was, all alone at the bar, hunched over a bottle of lager, shoulders slumped. For a brief moment, she felt sorry for him, then swiftly chastised herself. This situation was completely of Ryan's making and he wasn't worthy of her sympathy.

On Wednesday, the day after she threw him out, he'd bombarded her with texts and voicemails begging her to meet up so that he could explain, sober, but she'd refused.

On Thursday, he'd emailed saying she couldn't ignore him forever because they were business partners so she emailed back telling him exactly what she and Steff thought about his role – or lack of it – in the future of the business. Steff wanted nothing to do with him at all. As far as she was concerned, the two people she loved the most had broken her heart and she wasn't going to forgive or forget that ever. It didn't help that Mia had laughed at her for 'being pathetic and overreacting' and then allowed Ryan to temporarily move in, effectively rubbing her nose in it. The email exchange about the business became heated but Ryan finally relented and said he'd think about it.

He stayed away from bootcamps that week and Steff managed Friday night's Bay Runners on her own, but Karen realised she was going to need to meet with him sooner rather than later to discuss officially severing their business ties. She only hoped he'd seen sense because she couldn't face another argument.

She took a deep breath and opened the door.

When Ryan turned around, she could tell that the situation had taken its toll on him too. He was unshaven and there were dark shadows under his eyes.

'You look great,' Ryan said as Karen approached.

'Concealer,' she admitted. 'Without it, I look worse than you.'

'Sorry.'

'Let's not do that, eh? We've said all there is to say and I'm too drained to do it again. I'm only here to talk about Bay Fitness.'

Ryan bought her a drink then they moved to a quiet table in a corner. 'I've made a decision,' he said. 'You're right about the business. The three of us are broken and we can't run it together. You and Steff can buy me out.'

'Buy you out? Ryan! It's not worth anything. The assets are the three of us and the clients. If you set up in competition, which presumably you will, most of your clients will follow you.'

'I'm not going to set up in competition.'

'What are you going to do, then? Surely you're not going to go back to working in a gym.'

He shook his head. 'I'm leaving Whitsborough Bay.'

For a moment, it was as though time stood still. The activity around the pub seemed to halt, the chatter ceasing. 'You're doing what?'

'Our Josh has said I can stay with him for a while. I might set up something like Bay Fitness over there if I like it.'

Ryan's younger brother, Josh, had gone to university in Liverpool and had settled there afterwards. 'Liverpool? You're seriously going to leave Whitsborough Bay?'

'Why not? Unless you can give me a reason to stay...'

But Karen couldn't say it. Over and over, she'd asked herself whether she could forgive him, even if she couldn't forget what he'd done. But there was just no way she could go there again.

'Look, Kaz. If there's any hope for you and I, even the slimmest of slim hopes, you know I'd stay. But there isn't, is there?'

She slowly shook her head. 'I can't. I want to, but I can't. That video. And even before that, the way you were towards me. I don't know you anymore.'

He hung his head. 'I know.'

They sat in silence for a moment, Karen's head still reeling at the thought of him moving to the other side of the country.

Ryan finally spoke. 'When I said buy me out, I meant split up the profits in the business. I trust you to do whatever's fair.'

She nodded. 'I'll speak to Steff and let you know.'

'How is she?'

'Honestly? She's broken. You were her best friend, Ryan. You slept with her girlfriend. Did you never stop to think about the fallout from this?'

He shook his head. 'I didn't think anyone would find out. I know. Stupid, eh? Stuff like that never stays secret. Please tell Steff I'm sorry.'

'She won't be interested.' The pained expression in his eyes was almost too much to take but it was his fault. He was an adult. He'd made the decisions and he had to live with the consequences. 'When will you leave?'

'Not for another month yet. Josh has a mate staying with him but he's leaving mid-to-late July so I can move in then. I reckon Mia will be glad to be shot of me.'

Karen couldn't help smirking. 'Fantasy not such a fantasy after all? There's a surprise.'

'Don't be like that. Sarcasm doesn't suit you.'

'And being a cheating git doesn't suit you.'

He sighed as he sipped on his lager. 'I didn't come here to fight.'

Her shoulders sagged. 'Neither did I. Do you want to move back into the house?'

'With you?' he gasped.

'Don't be daft.'

'Then I'm confused. Where will you be?'

'At my friend Danniella's. There are too many memories in the house. Steff and I boxed up your stuff but it didn't make any difference. We could both still see you everywhere. She moved back in with her parents on Saturday and I moved into Danniella's.' Jemma had offered her a room but Little Sandby was too far out of town for early morning bootcamps.

Karen took Ryan's key out of her pocket and held it towards him. 'What do you think?'

'I think I'm an idiot who just lost his fiancée, his best

friend, and his business.' He took the key from her. 'And in a month's time, I'll lose my home too.'

'Really? Because on Tuesday, I said to you that I hoped it was worth it, and you said it was.'

He shook his head. 'I lied. I've been doing a lot of that lately.'

49

ALISON

✉ From Aidan
I've emerged from my writing cave. Don't
suppose you're free tonight for that
drink? x

Alison's heart thumped as she read Aidan's text a couple of
weeks later, and she immediately felt guilty at her reaction.
Not guilty enough to avoid him, though.

✉ To Aidan
Congratulations! Have your eyes adjusted to
daylight yet? I'm on shift from 2-10pm so
can't do tonight. Lunch instead? Noon in The
Chocolate Pot? x

✉ From Aidan
Perfect. See you then ☺ x

Dashing upstairs to choose an outfit, guilt gripped her

again. She shouldn't feel guilty, though. Nothing had happened between them and nothing was going to happen. He was an old friend and they'd been through a traumatic experience together with Danniella's collapse. A combination of that, nostalgia, and him looking delectable in his morning suit had made her momentarily giddy when he'd kissed her cheek. As for her heart thumping now, it was... it was... well, she wasn't sure what it was but it meant nothing. Definitely nothing. She was with Dave and it was going well. Really well.

* * *

Aidan had already secured a table at The Chocolate Pot when Alison arrived, and those damn butterflies took flight again. Nostalgia. That was all. She'd loved him once and seeing him again after all these years was bound to elicit a reaction.

'You met your deadline, then?' she asked after they'd placed their orders.

'Yes. I've never missed one but this was my closest call yet. I was up till four this morning. I probably look as rough as a badger's arse.' He ran his hand over his stubble.

'No. You look great,' Alison responded, feeling her cheeks colour at the compliment. 'I like it. All tall, dark, handsome, and mysterious...' *Argh! Stop talking!*

Aidan gave her a warm smile. 'Mysterious? I like that. Thank you. So how's the past fortnight treated you?'

'Not so bad. Danniella's doing well. She's had a couple more panic attacks but nothing major. Her counselling sessions are going well and she's in contact with her husband by email. Did she tell you he's Lucas Downey, the author? They've been... What are you smiling at?'

'You. You haven't changed a bit. I asked about you and you told me about Danniella. That's such an Alison thing to do.'

'Is it?'

Aidan nodded. 'Remember when we used to walk round the playing fields at lunchtime? If I ever asked how you were, you'd tell me about something you'd seen on TV or a piece of homework, but you never really talked about you.'

She lowered her eyes. 'I'm sorry I didn't let you in.'

'I wasn't having a dig,' Aidan said, gently. 'I figured it was your way of protecting yourself from the truth. If you don't talk about it, it didn't happen, right?'

Her pulse raced as she looked up again. How did he do it? How did he know her so well? How did he see into her soul? Dave never... No. She mustn't compare. They were very different people and Dave was trying very hard.

'Something like that,' she said.

'So what I'd like to know is what are you protecting yourself from right now? Thinking about those phone calls you were keen to ignore, I'm guessing something to do with Dave?'

Their drinks arrived so there was a natural pause. He'd nailed it again. Should she tell him? He was right about her never opening up but it had helped talking to Danniella. Maybe Aidan could help too. Or, given the way her heart was racing, could he be more of a hindrance?

* * *

'So you're not living together anymore, but you haven't split up?' Aidan asked after she'd given him a potted history, during which lunch had arrived.

'I'm not *not* living with him. I'm just staying with Danniella while she gets back on her feet.'

'And if Danniella didn't need support, where would you be living?'

Alison picked up a forkful of quiche. Good question. And the first answer that came to mind was Danniella's. But that would be like saying it was over with Dave, and it wasn't over.

'It's hard to say because it's hypothetical,' she said. 'Danniella *does* need me.'

'Are you happy?' Aidan asked. 'Really happy?'

'Is anyone?'

He raised his hand in the air. 'I am.'

'Then you're very lucky, Aidan. So, spill it. What's the secret to happiness?'

He smiled. 'Living each day as though it could be your last.'

She wrinkled her nose at him. 'You sound like one of those memes on social media.'

'I know, but it does work. It was how Elizabeth viewed life, even before she was diagnosed with leukaemia, and then it became all the more poignant when she got the terminal prognosis.'

'It was leukaemia? I'm so sorry. How long were you married?'

'About twenty-one hours.'

'What?!'

'I'll tell you the full story in a moment, if you've got time. Going back to the secret to happiness, though, it's about grabbing life with both hands and making it meaningful. That could mean seeing sunrises and sunsets, new places, meeting people, believing in your dreams and going after them, time with friends and family or time alone... Whatever works for you. For Elizabeth, it was all those things. She'd wake up to watch the sunrise from the balcony and, if was pouring, she'd thrust out her arms and let the rain soak her instead. She laughed every day and never let the little things get her down. If there was a moody sales assistant in a shop, she'd make it her mission to make them smile. It never took much – a compliment or asking them about their day – but it lifted them and that lifted her.'

'Elizabeth sounds lovely. But, it can't be that simple.'

'Why not? I'm not saying that life is easy and that there won't be sad moments or hard times, but we all have choices about how the low moments affect us, especially the day-to-day little things. We can let that moody sales assistant dampen our day or we can make them smile. We can moan about the rain or we can splash in the puddles. And we can stay with someone who doesn't make us happy or we can find someone who does.'

Aidan held Alison's gaze so intently that she felt as though he really could see into her soul, and see she was winging it with Dave, uncertain about anything anymore.

'Tell me more about Elizabeth,' she said when their plates were cleared and they'd ordered more drinks.

'We were talking about you.'

She shook her head. 'No. We were talking about Elizabeth.'

Aidan smiled. 'I'll let you off. I promised I'd tell you and I will. But we're coming back to you later.'

* * *

'I can't believe you did that for her,' Alison said when he'd told her about his time with Elizabeth. 'You put your life on hold to make her happy.'

'Which was the secret to *my* happiness at the time.'

'What you did was selfless, romantic, lovely, and very you. But what about you and your future? What if spending all that time with Elizabeth meant you missed out on meeting the person who really was your destiny?'

He shook his head, smiling. 'That wasn't going to happen.'

'How do you know?'

Aidan sipped on his coffee then sat forward in his chair and looked at her intently again. 'Do you know why I never liked Dave back in college?'

'Because you thought he was a tosser?'

Aidan laughed. 'This is true, but the main reason I didn't like him was because he had you.' He smiled ruefully. 'Being with Elizabeth couldn't stop me from meeting my destiny because I'd already met her on my first day at college.'

Alison's heart raced again. 'Me?'

'You were standing in the corridor outside our first lesson, hiding behind your folder, looking like you wanted to run. You had such big, sad eyes. I didn't know who you were or what had happened to make you so sad but I knew that I wanted to be the one to make you happy again.'

'But you never said anything. Even when you split up with Lexie, you never did or said anything to suggest you saw me as more than a friend.'

Aidan ran his hand across his stubble again, shaking his head. 'I know. It was so stupid of me. I was scared that if I asked you out and you said no, you might not want to be my friend. I couldn't bear to lose you from my life so I hesitated and procrastinated and then you met Dave and I was too late.'

Alison didn't trust herself to speak. What was he saying?

He took another sip on his coffee, followed by a deep breath. 'The secret to happiness is living every day as though it's your last. I didn't know that in college but I know it now so I'm going to say what I should have said back then. I love you, Alison Jenkins, and nine years apart has only made my feelings stronger.'

Her eyes widened as she gripped the chair arms. *Oh my God!* All that time when she'd been too scared to say anything, he'd felt exactly the same. He'd loved her and still did. Did she still love him? And, if so, was it more than she loved Dave... if she still loved Dave at all. Dave was her family, though, always and forever, like they'd promised each other.

'I've just dropped that bombshell and realised that you need to get to work,' Aidan said.

Alison glanced at her watch. 'Crap! Yes. I'm so sorry.' She grabbed her purse out of her bag but Aidan placed his hand over hers, sending the butterflies in her stomach on a loop-the-loop.

'It's on me,' he said. 'Maybe we can talk again.'

'Yes. We'll do that.' She stood up. 'I don't know what to—'

'You don't have to say or do anything, Ali. I'm not asking you for anything. We're cool. Get to work and we'll talk again soon.'

* * *

'Are you happy?' Alison asked Chelsea during a lull on reception a couple of hours later.

'Every day since my divorce came through,' Chelsea responded, laughing. 'Now I get to do what I want, when I want, with whom I want.'

'So you don't think there's a secret to happiness?'

'I've just told you. Divorce. I've never been happier. And neither has Jamie the sous-chef.'

Alison's jaw dropped. 'No! He must be about twenty years younger than you.'

'Mmm. I know.'

'You're very naughty.'

'That's the flowers done,' Sarah said, approaching the reception desk. 'What are you two giggling at?'

'I was asking Chelsea what she thinks is the secret to happiness,' Alison said. 'You *don't* want to know her answer. What do you think it is?'

'Ooh, there's a question.' Sarah bit her lip while she pondered. 'Probably different things to different people at different times in their lives. For me right now, happiness is my husband, my friends and family, and my shop. That combination completes me. A few years back, it was less about other people and more about me. For me to find happiness, I needed to let go of a toxic relationship, work out who I was and what I wanted, and learn to like myself again. My best friends helped but, ultimately, it was me who held the secret to my own happiness.' She smiled. 'Was that a bit deep?'

'No, it was actually really helpful,' Alison said. 'Thank you.'

'Any time. See you both later.'

During her break, Alison re-read the text that Aidan had sent shortly after she left him.

✉ From Aidan

Hope you weren't late for work. My timing might have sucked, but I don't regret telling you how I feel. I always wanted to be the person who made you happy but if the secret to your happiness doesn't involve me, I still want to be the person who helps you find your happy. We used to do our homework together in college so let's do that again. Your assignment is: What is the secret to Alison Jenkins's happiness? I'm here for you when you've gathered your thoughts. I'm always here for you xx

The thought of Aidan always being there was very comforting.

✉ To Aidan

Sorry I didn't have time to reply earlier. I accept your homework assignment. It might take me a few weeks to gather my thoughts but I promise I will. Thank you for being honest with me xx

50

KAREN

Three Weeks Later

'Oh my goodness, you guys.' Karen couldn't stop beaming as she gazed round the six mid-morning bootcampers three weeks later. 'That was your toughest bootcamp yet, and that was fantastic. The Awesome Award goes to every single one of you.' She ran along the beach, high-fiving each of them. 'And you, Alison Jenkins, you astound me. Do you have any idea how far you ran this morning without stopping?'

'Do I owe your sister a lipstick?'

'I think you owe her a full set of make-up after that performance. Doesn't she look amazing, everyone?'

The others clapped and cheered as Alison did a twirl. Two pounds short of two stone lighter, she'd confided in Karen that morning.

'Flag and photo time,' Karen called. Tears pooled in her eyes as she watched Alison take a corner of the flag and proudly stand beside it instead of hiding behind it. When Danniella stepped into the photo next to Alison for the first time too, Karen's bottom lip started trembling and she could barely breathe for the lump restricting her throat. Words could not describe how proud she was of the two women who had become like family to her since that terrible day at Danniella's when the truth about Ryan had arrived via email.

As usual, Danniella and Alison hung back to help her gather the equipment together.

'Are you still planning to say goodbye to him?' Alison asked as they walked up the beach together.

Karen nodded. 'I've got Jay's PT session in half an hour then I'm heading over to the house to collect the last few boxes of my stuff. I know I could collect them after he's gone but, despite everything, that man was my life for thirteen years. I can't let him move to the other side of the country without saying goodbye.'

'How do you feel about seeing him?'

'Nervous. Sick. Scared. He broke my heart and Steff's, but...'

'We know,' Danniella reassured her. 'It's not easy to say goodbye to someone you love, is it?'

'Being apart from Ryan this past month has been the hardest thing I've ever done. I can't tell you the amount of willpower it's taken not to scream, "I forgive you" and run right back to him, but I can't run back to him. Being at Jemma and Sam's housewarming without him was so tough. I missed him like crazy that night. I can't forgive him, though, and I can't forget, especially after seeing him on film with another woman. Two women. No matter how hard I try, I can never un-see that.'

'I've got to get ready for work,' Alison said. 'I'll see you tonight, though.'

She headed off towards the cliff path and Karen's heart soared at the sight of her running up the first part. 'Look at her go. I feel like a proud mum.'

Danniella dabbed her eyes. 'Me too. She's done so well.'

They set off to towards Karen's car to put the kit in the boot. 'You're going to miss Ryan, aren't you?' Danniella asked.

'I already do.'

'And there's definitely no going back?'

'No. It wasn't just the sex that hurt. It was the nastiness, the lies, and the jealousy. Much as I'll always love him, it's the Ryan he used to be that I love and not the Ryan he is now.'

'Do you think there are things – terrible things – a person does that can be forgiven?'

'You're talking about Ethan forgiving you?' Karen asked. After moving into the flat, Danniella had shared the full story with her. Karen felt so inspired watching Danniella grow stronger with each counselling session. She still had bad days and she still had panic attacks, but she was tackling each day head-on, refusing to let the guilt drown her. Her strength had given Karen the strength to stand strong against Ryan, even though he'd repeatedly texted and emailed asking for a reconciliation.

'We've exchanged a few emails,' Danniella said. 'Marian reckons I might be ready speak to him.'

'What do you think?'

'I think she might be right.'

'Then go for it. Alison and I will be here for you.'

Danniella smiled. 'I know. I don't know what I'd have done without you two in my life.'

'Same here,' Karen said, placing the kit in the boot before setting off back to North Bay Corner. 'It's been tough for us all in different ways, but we're getting there, aren't we?'

Danniella shrugged. 'You are and I am, but I'm worried about Alison.'

'I thought things were going well with her and Dave.'

'They are. She says she's never been happier with him but if that's the case, why's she still living at the flat? At first, I know it was about not leaving me on my own but you moved in so that wasn't an issue. Yet she stayed. She can stay as long as she wants. You both can. I'm just a bit worried that she's staying to avoid moving back home with Dave.'

'And if she's avoiding that, it's because she knows it's over and she can't or won't admit it?' Karen suggested.

Danniella nodded. 'Exactly. And I think something's happened between her and Aidan. I don't know what, but she gets all flustered when I mention him.'

'So she does. I think we might need a pizza and wine night and a serious talk.'

'I think we might.'

* * *

After saying goodbye to Danniella, Karen found Jay sitting on the wall outside The Surf Shack on North Bay Corner wearing trousers, a shirt and tie.

'Bit formal for PT, isn't it?' she joked, but one look at Jay's face told her that he wasn't in the mood for jokes. With red eyes and a sallow complexion, he looked desperately in need of a hug.

'I need to give training a miss because I need to talk to

you instead.' He nodded towards Blue Savannah. 'Can I buy you a drink?'

'Okay. This is all very mysterious, though. Can you give me a clue?'

'Best not.' Jay stood up and they walked towards Blue Savannah in silence. The cogs in Karen's mind were working overtime. What could he possibly want to talk about?

She perched on the edge of one of the metal chairs outside anxiously awaiting Jay's return. It was the week before schools broke up but North Bay was already busy with holidaymakers. She watched a blonde woman and dark-haired man – similar age and appearance to Ryan and herself – swinging a giggling little girl into the air every few steps. She and Ryan had never discussed when they'd ideally like to have a family but there'd always been an understanding that it would happen, one day, possibly even before the wedding. Yet another thing that he'd taken from her.

Jay re-appeared with two lattes and Karen swallowed on the lump in her throat. 'You're making me nervous,' she said.

'Sorry. This is so hard to say and there's no easy way of saying it.' He paused, worry lines creasing his brow. 'I know who your stalker was.' Karen had told him all about the video and the fallout from that when he'd taken her out for a drink to thank her for running the Scout bootcamp.

'It wasn't Steff's girlfriend or that lass she worked with,' he said.

Karen gripped the arms of her chair. 'Then who was it?'

He winced. 'Sophie.'

'Sophie? As in your girlfriend, Sophie?'

'As in my *ex*-girlfriend, Sophie.'

'You're sure it was her?'

Jay nodded. 'One hundred per cent sure. She admitted it.'

'But why? That makes no sense. I've never met her. And the texts started before I met you so it can't have been a jealousy thing.'

'It wasn't about me, or at least not in the beginning. As you say, the texts were before we met. It wasn't really about you either. It was...' Jay paused, sighing. 'It was pretty messed up, that's what it was, and I'm still struggling to get my head round it.' He sipped on his drink. 'Do you remember me saying that Sophie goes to her sister's when I'm at Scouts and that I'm not her sister's biggest fan?

Karen nodded.

'Well, Sophie's sister is Mia.'

Karen gasped. 'Steff's ex? You're kidding me. Oh my God! That's why you and Steff recognised each other. Because of Mia.'

'It was bugging me for ages as to where I knew her from,' Jay said. 'I avoid Mia like the plague, but I must have seen Steff at some point when I dropped off or picked up Sophie from the flat. It would have been in passing rather than a proper introduction, which is why we couldn't place each other.'

Picking up her spoon, Karen stirred her latte thoughtfully. 'That explains how Sophie would know about what Ryan did with Mia. But why the anonymous texts? I don't know Sophie and I barely knew Mia. There was no bad blood between us.'

'That's where it gets messed up,' Jay admitted. 'Sophie has a lot of issues. I mentioned before that she'd had a rough upbringing. She's always resented people who she perceives have everything, always thinking they're looking down on her. I know this makes no sense when she'd never met you, but she became fixated on you as someone who had everything and therefore was someone to hate.'

'What? Why would she think I had everything?'

'Because you had the "gorgeous fiancé with abs to die for", according to Sophie, whereas she had the "squidgy, ginger, boring twat of a teacher".' He emphasised the quotes with his fingers.

'She *never* said that.'

Jay looked towards the sea and nodded. 'In those exact words. That was me told.' He turned back to Karen. 'Anyway, after she met Ryan, Sophie found you online and to her you had everything: the perfect man, the perfect job, the perfect life and, of course, you're stunning, so she hated you immediately.'

A zing of electricity shot through Karen's body when Jay said she was stunning, and she swiftly brushed it aside. 'That's ridiculous,' she said. 'How could she possibly think she knew anything about me or my life from a few photos?'

'I told you it was messed up.' Jay shrugged. 'You became her obsession and she wanted to hurt you but wasn't sure how. Then Mia showed her that video and suddenly she had the perfect weapon. She sent you the first text soon after that.'

Slumping back against the chair, Karen closed her eyes for a moment while she processed it all. What a mess. From what Jay had told her, she'd already concluded that Sophie was a pretty unpleasant individual, but this was something else. This was vicious. Vile.

'How did you know it was her?' Karen asked, sitting forward again, her heart going out to Jay who was clearly an unexpected third victim of Ryan's little fantasy.

'When I got home from bootcamp last night, she was on the phone arguing with Mia. I heard Ryan's name, then yours, and picked up enough to fit the pieces together. I'm so sorry, Karen.'

'For what? For going out with a headcase? Seriously, Jay, none of this is your fault. She'd have sent the texts and video anyway, whether we'd met or not.'

'I know. She told me everything and actually seemed quite proud of herself. When she met Ryan, she decided she wanted him and was convinced that, if she split you two up, he'd go running to her. She was planning on dragging it out for ages, watching your relationship gradually fall apart, but she's not the most patient of people and, after seeing you and me together, she decided to stick the knife in quicker.' He ran his hand over his beard as he shook his head. 'I knew she had issues, Karen, but I'd never have expected this of her. Sophie told me that Mia knew nothing about the stalking or you being sent the video which is what they were arguing about. I always though Mia was the nasty one but it seems that Sophie's just as bad, so it's good riddance. She's Mia's problem now.'

'She didn't deserve you,' Karen said, placing her hand over his. 'You know that, don't you? You deserve someone so much better.'

'You think so? A "squidgy, ginger, boring twat of a teacher" is hardly the catch of the century.'

'I know so and, if that's how she sees you, she's blind.' Karen gently squeezed his hand, then took hers away, trying to ignore the butterflies doing loop-the-loop in her stomach. 'Besides, I'm supposedly "stunning" with the perfect life, yet my fiancé would rather sleep with a lesbian and the village bike than me. If it's a competition for the worst catch, I think I might have trumped you there.'

Jay's mouth twitched at the corners and, within seconds, the pair of them were giggling helplessly.

'Boring, ginger twat,' Karen spluttered.

'Man repellent,' Jay responded, shoulders shaking.

When they'd finally calmed down, Karen ran her fingers through her hair and smiled at Jay. 'How do you do it?'

'Do what?'

'Make me feel better about everything? Give me some crap news, then have me giggling my head off?'

'Maybe I'm not so boring after all.'

'You're far from boring, Jay.' Their eyes locked and she felt goosebumps up and down her arms as her heart raced. 'Erm... So... What's next for you? Some hiking trips I hope.'

'Funny you should say that. I WhatsApp'd the old gang this morning and we're looking at dates for a trip to the Lakes. It's been a while.'

'Too long, I'd say.'

Karen nipped into the bar to order a second drink and they spent the next half an hour chatting about life for Jay without Sophie, and how Karen was coping with life without Ryan. All too soon, it was time for him to say goodbye and head to school, which meant it was nearly time for Karen to say her final goodbye to Ryan.

'Thanks for telling me in person,' she said, as they stood to leave. 'I know it can't have been easy.'

'It wasn't, but I'd never have given you that news any other way.'

They headed down the steps and paused on the corner, ready to go their separate ways.

'Hope it goes well with Ryan,' Jay said.

'I'm dreading it, but I need to do it.' She lifted up her left hand and gazed at her naked finger. 'I've got the ring boxed up ready to return. Never thought I'd be doing that.'

He put his arms out and she gratefully stepped into his hug. 'New beginnings for both of us,' he murmured. 'Scary, but ultimately for the best.'

'New beginnings,' she whispered back, wishing she could stay in his embrace forever.

51

KAREN

It felt weird pulling onto the drive beside Ryan's car, knowing it would be the last time she'd ever park there. Even more weird was knocking on her former front door. She still had her key, but didn't feel right using it.

'I wasn't sure if you'd come,' Ryan said when he opened the door.

'I nearly didn't.' She followed him into the kitchen.

'I'd offer you a drink but, as you can see, everything's packed.' Ryan's voice echoed around the room.

'I'm not thirsty anyway.' She took in the bare walls, empty shelves, and deserted worktops. It seemed emptier than the day they'd moved in.

'Those are yours.' He indicated three large cardboard boxes on the floor near the door.

'Thank you.'

'My solicitor says everything's sorted with the business, so it's yours and Steff's now. I'm sure the two of you will do brilliant things with it.'

Karen nodded. 'We'll try our best.'

'Have you got plans?'

'We haven't really talked about it. Neither of us expected any of this, you know.' Tears pricked Karen's eyes and she pretended to gaze round the kitchen again, hoping Ryan wouldn't notice, but she'd never been able to hide anything from him.

'If I could turn back the clock...' he said softly. 'If it's any consolation, I'll spend the rest of my life regretting everything I did this year. And everything and everyone I lost.'

The tears wouldn't stay put. She rubbed them away with her fists but, as fast as she wiped, more tears fell. 'I was determined not to do this,' she said, her voice catching in her throat. 'I loved you, Ryan. I trusted you and you hurt me so badly. I really want to hate you for what you've done to me, to Steff, to the business, but I can't. I don't want you to spend the rest of your life regretting what you've done. Kick yourself, but then move on with your life and find a way to be happy somewhere else and, in time, with someone else.'

'I don't want anyone else,' he whispered.

'It's a shame you didn't tell yourself that a couple of months ago.' Karen pressed her fingers to her lips. 'What's done is done and there's no recovering from it.' She pushed her shoulders back and stood up tall. 'I'd better put those in the car.'

'I'll give you a hand.'

* * *

As they loaded the boxes into the boot, Ryan's hand brushed against hers and her heart raced. She looked up and, at that moment, he looked so lost and vulnerable that Karen's heart shattered into a thousand pieces again. One step and she'd be in his arms. A slight turn of the head and she could be kissing him. But she couldn't. She mustn't. She took a step back and closed the boot.

'I guess this is goodbye,' he said, sighing.

Tears welled in her eyes again. This was even harder than she'd expected. 'I wish I could tell you goodbye. I don't want to say it, though. It's so final.'

'What about *au revoir*, like the French?'

'But we won't meet again, will we?'

'Then don't say anything.'

He reached for her hand and tried to pull her into a hug but she stepped back. 'No, Ryan.' She felt completely drained. Her eyes felt gritty, her head thumped, and she felt as though she wanted to curl into a ball like a hedgehog and hibernate.

'I'm sorry for the things I said the day you found out,' he said. 'I'd been drinking and I was lashing out.' He reached out and gently cupped her face in his hands. 'You were always perfect to me.' He gently brushed a tear aside with his thumb. 'You still are.'

'Ryan, I—'

But Karen didn't get to finish the sentence as Ryan's lips gently brushed against hers and she gasped, her heart thumping rapidly. It would have been so easy to respond. So easy. It was over, though. Hard as it was, there was absolutely no going back.

She stepped away from him. 'I can't do this. It's over.'

He stared at her for what felt like hours, then nodded. 'Okay. I'm sorry. Goodbye and good luck.' He retreated to the house.

Sitting in the car, Karen watched him turn and wave then step inside and close the door. It was done. It was properly, finally over. And... damn! The ring. She hadn't returned the ring or the key. Clambering back out of the car, she removed the ring box from the pocket of her hoodie.

Unlocking the door, she was about to call his name when she stopped dead, heart thudding, as she heard a woman's voice coming from the kitchen.

'I found this in the wardrobe,' the woman said. 'Does it suit me?'

'That was Karen's,' Ryan responded sharply.

The woman laughed. 'I kind of guessed it wasn't yours. So, does it suit me?'

There was a pause then Ryan said in a sultry tone, 'You look bloody gorgeous.'

'Get your kit off, then.'

Karen winced. All that talk about trying again and he'd had another woman in the house? What was wrong with him? Cringing, she took a deep breath. She had to know who he was with.

'Ryan,' she called, striding down the hallway. 'I forgot to give you your... oh. Hello.'

A striking woman in her mid-twenties with long, dark, wavy hair sat on the worktop, her legs wrapped round Ryan's waist. She wore the midnight-blue satin and lace slip that Karen had worn the night she'd waited up to seduce Ryan; the night she later discovered he'd lived out his threesome fantasy for the first time. When she moved out, she'd left it hanging in the wardrobe in the master bedroom as a reminder to Ryan of what he'd lost.

'Karen!' Ryan cried. 'I thought you'd gone.'

'Obviously.' She looked from his shocked face to the woman's amused one. 'I don't think we've met. I'm pretty certain you weren't in the video.'

'No, but I watched some of the live shows. I'm Sophie. Ryan's girlfriend.'

Sophie? Jay's Sophie? So, she'd wanted Ryan and she'd got him. If Karen had been a violent person, she'd have walked over and slapped Sophie for everything she'd done to her and to Jay, but she really wasn't worth it.

'Did he tell you I'm going to Liverpool with him?' Sophie continued.

'No, but Ryan's got a track record of keeping secrets. I hope you'll be very happy together. Here's my key.' She dropped it on the floor then, shoving the ring box back in her pocket, turned and left the kitchen. He wasn't having the ring back. She'd sell it and throw a party with the proceeds for all the people she loved who'd been hurt by Ryan.

'You want to know why I sent the video?' Sophie shouted.

'To be honest, Sophie, I'm beyond caring.' Karen stepped outside, but Sophie followed her, laughing.

'You'll want to hear this. You'll like this.'

'Sophie, don't,' Ryan cried, running out the house as Karen opened the car door.

'He knew,' Sophie called. 'Ryan knew it was me sending you the texts.'

Karen turned around slowly and glared at them both.

'Not at the start,' Sophie admitted. 'But he guessed it was me and told me to stop, but I was having far too much fun. Ask him why I sent the video.'

Ryan glowered at Sophie then stepped towards the car. 'Don't listen to her, Kaz.'

'She deserves the truth,' Sophie said, a snide smile on her face. 'I warned him I was going to send you the video, but he said it was too much and I needed to stop. I said that the only way to stop me was to stop seeing my sister and that slag she works with and be exclusive with me. He said he would, but he didn't and, well, you know the rest...'

Karen looked from one to the other and shook her head. 'You're like a match made in hell, you two. Good luck in Liverpool.' She jumped into the car and reached for the door handle. 'Goodbye, Ryan.'

Without a backwards glance, she sped off the drive and out of the estate. Suddenly saying 'goodbye' hadn't been that hard after all.

52

'What *are* you wearing?' Alison stared at Dave, eyebrows raised, as he shuffled into the taxi beside her the following evening.

He glanced down at his bright yellow T-shirt. 'Don't you like it?'

'It's a bit bright.'

'I got it in Ibiza.'

'I gathered that.' His T-shirt was emblazoned with the words: *Ibiza Drinking Team.* 'I'm just not used to seeing you in yellow.'

'I can change it if you want.'

She smiled. 'No. If you like it, you wear it. It's your birthday. I'm not saying I don't like it. It's just very different.'

'You look gorgeous, by the way. You should wear dresses more often.'

For the first time in years, Alison felt good. She'd dropped a couple of dress sizes which had given her the confidence to experiment with colour. She didn't feel ready for anything too bright but a black dress with small red flowers on it was a bold move away from plain, dark colours. In fact, a dress was a bold move. She couldn't remember the last time she'd worn one.

They held hands as the taxi headed for town where they were meeting his partners-in-crime, Greavesy and Eggsey, and their other halves for a birthday meal.

'I wish you'd move back in,' Dave said, stroking her hand with his thumb.

'I told you, Danniella needs me.'

'But that other lass has moved in now. Can't she look after her? Why's she your responsibility?'

Alison looked out of the window, her jaw clenching. 'It's your birthday, Dave. Let's just enjoy the evening.'

'I'd enjoy it more if my birthday present was you moving back in.'

She turned back to face him, her expression soft. 'You promised not to push me.'

'It's been over a month, though.'

'You *promised*.'

He lifted her hand to his lips and gently kissed it. 'Sorry. I just miss you.'

* * *

Alison had met Greavesy and Eggsey before when they'd called round the house, but it had only been brief, superficial conversations. She'd never met their partners. She felt quite apprehensive and also a little uncomfortable about her first night out with them all. Why didn't she know the men better? Why hadn't she met their partners? Why hadn't they been out for drinks with them like a normal couple? Finding time around her shifts was a challenge, but she could have put in for a holiday if Dave had ever suggested a night out. Had it been less about finding time and more about him being ashamed of being seen out with a 'chubba'? Best not to dwell on it. It was in the past and they were focusing on the future now.

'Has Beefy stopped going on about Ibiza yet?' Eggsey's wife, Laura, asked her.

Alison frowned for a moment before realising that Beefy was Dave's nickname; another thing she'd have known instantly if she'd ever spent time with his friends.

'He loved it, but he hasn't talked about it too much,' Alison said diplomatically, not sure whether Eggsey would have told Laura what Dave had done pre-holiday.

'It's all we hear about in our house,' said Greavesy's girl-friend, Tazmin. 'Not surprised, though. Have you seen the photos on Facebook, Ali? The place is gorgeous.'

Alison shook her head. 'Dave doesn't do social media.'

'Are you on Facebook, Ali?' Tazmin asked.

She nodded.

'Right.' Tazmin dug her phone out of her bag. 'What's your surname?'

'Jenkins.'

'Alison Jenkins,' Tazmin muttered as she typed. 'Ooh, there's a few of you. Ah! There you are. I've sent you a friend request. Accept that now please.'

Alison laughed. 'Yes ma'am.' She took her phone out of her bag and did as she was told.

'Brilliant,' Tazmin said. 'I've tagged you into the lads' Ibiza album so you can check out the photos later. It's every-one's pulled together so there are stacks of them. And I should probably warn you, there are a few hairy arses on them. God alone knows why men feel the need to do that.'

'It's not all hairy arses,' Laura added. 'There's some stunning scenery too. You'll be getting Beefy to book you a holiday there next year. I know I want to go.'

'We might go back to Corfu,' Dave said, putting his arm around Alison. 'Or maybe somewhere that neither of us have been.'

He planted a gentle kiss on the top of her head and she smiled but her heart didn't flutter and her pulse didn't race. She'd told Dave she wanted Corfu and he'd given her it over the past month. This was it; the love, the attention, the sense of being a family. It had been like the early days together, dating again, and it had been fun. So why couldn't she take that last step? Why couldn't she move back home?

Danniella and Karen had quizzed her about it over pizza and wine one Sunday evening a couple of weeks back and she'd fobbed them off, just like she'd fobbed off Aidan each time he'd texted and asked whether she wanted to meet to discuss her homework assignment. They'd quizzed her about Aidan too, but she'd shrugged and said she had no idea what they were talking about. Why had she lied to her best friends? She'd opened up to them about everything else, but she couldn't bring herself to discuss her current predicament. Was that because it genuinely was a predicament and she had no idea which way to go. Or was it because she knew and she was scared of the answer?

Dave had done everything possible to show her he'd changed and he genuinely seemed to have done. The thing was, she'd changed too. She wasn't the Alison he'd left behind while he holidayed with his mates. She had new friends, a new home, a new body... and a brand-new outlook on life. She was young and she had her whole future ahead of her. What was the secret to happiness for her? Dave? Aidan? Or was she more like Sarah, needing to let go of the past and learn to like herself again before embracing the future?

53

DANNIELLA

For Danniella there was genuinely no better feeling than running along the seafront as the sun rose. There was something about the tranquillity of the deserted beach and the feeling of being one with nature that was so incredibly uplifting. It was even better on a Saturday in summer, like this morning, knowing that she was experiencing the calm before the tourist invasion.

Today, though, she didn't feel quite as relaxed. Her footsteps were faster, more anxious, more purposeful, because today was the day she was going to speak to Ethan. The following day – 23rd July – would be the anniversary of Abigail's passing; one year exactly since her life fell apart, her family fell apart, and she fell apart. She'd wondered whether that should be the day to speak to Ethan, but Alison and Karen had suggested it might be too emotional for them both and maybe the day before would be better.

After regular email contact, Ethan had eagerly accepted the invite for a phone conversation. The call was scheduled for 10 a.m. She glanced at her watch as she approached Pleasureland, ready to turn around and run back to North Bay. *Four-and-a-half hours to go. Deep breaths.*

* * *

'How are you feeling?' Alison asked as 10 a.m. approached.

'Excited, nervous, and nauseous all at the same time.'

'Do you know what you're going to say to him?'

'I've rehearsed so many variations, but I think I'm best playing it by ear. I'll ask him how he is, pathetic as that sounds, and take it from there.'

'I'm not sure you can rehearse something like this,' Alison said, taking the smoothie that Danniella handed her.

'Marian said the same thing. She suggested I write a few things down that I might want to mention, but not to prepare a speech as such.'

They moved into the lounge.

'Ten minutes to go,' Danniella said, the panic rising. Her breathing quickened and she started feeling light-headed.

'Breathe slowly,' Alison instructed. 'It's only Ethan. It's going to go well.'

Danniella managed to regulate her breathing quite quickly but it didn't always work like that. She'd had several panic attacks since leaving hospital although they were becoming less frequent, which was a good sign.

'Is he calling you or are you calling him?' Alison asked.

'I'm calling him. Marian said it's best if I don't let him have my phone number just yet so I can keep things at my pace.' She nibbled on her thumbnail. 'My stomach's in knots. I need to stop thinking about it. Talk to me. How was the birthday meal?'

'It was good.'

Danniella wrinkled her nose. 'Good?'

'Yeah. Good.'

'Not amazing?'

'It was good.'

Silence.

'I'm worried about you, Ali,' Danniella said. 'Something's not right with you and Dave, is it?'

Alison steepled her fingers against her lips as she shook her head. 'I don't know what it is. I *should* be happy. He's been the perfect boyfriend since he got back, so why can't I take that next step and move back home?'

'Because it's not the right step.'

'It should be, though.'

Danniella shook her head. 'What did Aidan say was the secret to happiness?'

'Throwing yourself into life and living every day as though it's your last. But that's what I've been doing with Dave. He's given it everything and so have I.'

'I know you have.' Danniella smiled gently, her eyes full of empathy. Poor Alison. Danniella was convinced that, deep down, she knew she was clinging on by her fingertips and she was going to have to eventually let go.

'You think I should end it, don't you?' Alison said.

'It's your decision. I just think that, if you're both giving your all and still not finding happiness, it could be that you're trying to find it with the wrong person.'

Alison sighed. 'I don't like being a grown-up. It's too messy and complicated.'

'It doesn't have to be.'

'I know. You're right. Look, it's nearly time for your call. Focus on you and Ethan and we'll talk about Dave and me later.'

'Properly talk instead of avoiding the issues?'

Alison nodded. 'Properly talk. I'll tell you everything about Dave. And I'll tell you about Aidan too.'

'I knew it! Has something happened between you two?'

'No. Well, yes, but not like that. We haven't been up to mischief. It's just... it's a long story and you have a call to make. Do you want the lounge?'

Danniella shook her head as she picked up her mobile. 'I'll go upstairs. I might sit on the balcony and draw some comfort from those lovely wind chimes.' She'd bought two sets from the local garden centre, installing one on each balcony.

Alison smiled, tears glistening in her eyes. 'Abigail will be right there beside you.'

Swallowing on the lump in her throat, Danniella nodded. 'What would I do without you?'

'You'll never be without me,' Alison replied, then she giggled. 'It's taken me fifteen years to find a new friend. There's no escape now.'

Danniella laughed too as she hugged her.

'Can I borrow your laptop?' Alison asked. 'I want to look at Dave's Ibiza photos but they're a bit small on my phone.'

'Help yourself. There's no password.'

'Good luck. Whatever happens, it's a step in the right direction.'

'Thanks.' Danniella headed for the door. 'I forgot to say. The kitchen window's sticking and Aidan said he'd call round at some point this morning. Can you let him in?'

Alison nodded. 'Go on, or you'll be late.'

Danniella smiled weakly, then ran up the stairs to call Ethan's mobile.

'Hi, Ethan. It's me.'

'Danni,' he said, gently. 'Thank God. I'm so relieved to hear from you.'

Oh, that voice! Still so warm, so gentle, so loving, despite everything she'd put him through. 'I'm sorry...' Her voice cracked and the tears tumbled down her cheeks. 'I'm sorry it's taken so long.'

'Hey, let's not start with an apology. And please don't cry. You'll set me off and you know I do ugly crying.'

She laughed through her tears. 'I didn't want to cry but I can't help it. It's been a tough ten months for both of us.'

'I know. But I'm here and you're wherever you are and we're talking. That's a good thing.'

'You think so?' she asked.

'I know so. I've dreamed of hearing your voice for so long and I was beginning to think it wouldn't happen. Talk to me. Tell me anything. Tell me what you had for breakfast or the last thing you saw on TV. I just want to hear your voice, Danni.'

Danniella opened the French doors and stepped out onto the balcony, the sunshine warming her face and drying her tears. 'Okay. I finished reading the most incredible book last night. It was by a writer called Lucas Downey. I don't suppose you're familiar with his work?'

She heard him gasp. 'You read it? What did you think? Be honest.'

'I can summarise it in one word.'

'Crap?'

She smiled. Ethan was always flooded with doubt about every new book, convinced it would be the moment when his enormous fan-base would discover he was a fraud who really couldn't write. 'It was beautiful.'

There was a pause and a sound that could have been a sob.

'Ethan? Are you still there?'

'I'm still here,' he said, his voice heavy with emotion. 'I'm always here. I've missed you so much, Danni.'

'And I've missed you too,' she said, tears tumbling again. 'I've missed us. More than I realised until I heard your voice again.'

54

While Danniella called Ethan, Alison slowly scrolled through the stack of photos on Facebook. Drink, unsurprisingly, was a strong theme. And bare arses, as Tazmin had warned her. Yuck. Interspersed with photos taken in bars and clubs, though, were stunning shots of the coast, beautiful old buildings, and sunsets.

The door buzzer sounded. She jumped up to buzz Aidan in, butterflies fluttering in her stomach. Opening the door to him moments later, they went crazy again, especially when he leaned in and gave her a kiss on the cheek.

'I'm so glad you're here,' he said. 'I was beginning to think you might be avoiding me.'

'I haven't been avoiding you.' She closed the door behind him, feeling guilty. 'I was on shift and I kept meaning to get in touch but...'

'But you hadn't finished your homework?' Aidan suggested.

She nodded. 'It's a tricky assignment.'

'Maybe you need an extension?'

'Maybe. Anyway, Danniella's on the phone upstairs so you've got me all to yourself. I mean, the kitchen all to yourself.'

'Sounds good.'

They stood in the hall, gazing at each other. Alison's heart raced and she felt herself flush from head to foot as she imagined them taking a step closer, lips meeting for the first time.

Aidan cleared his throat and rattled his toolbox. 'Erm. Window. Tools.'

'Yes, right, yes. Kitchen's that way.' She cringed. What was it with her directing Aidan to the rooms in his own flat? 'I'll, erm, I'll leave you to it. I'm in the lounge if you want me. Need me. Need a hand, I mean.' She scuttled back into the lounge, cursing under her breath.

Listening to the sound of Aidan rummaging in his toolbox, Alison took deep breaths, trying to still her racing heart. She might have avoided him but there was no denying how she felt. Was it possible to be in love with two men at the same time? Or maybe it was just one… and that one wasn't Dave.

* * *

'All done,' Aidan said ten minutes later, making her jump. 'What are you looking at?'

'Photos from when Dave went to Ibiza. Have you been?'

He sat down in the chair beside her. 'A few times. There's more to it than most people realise.'

'So I hear. It looks gorgeous. There's a photo I want to ask you about but first, you were right. I *have* been avoiding you. I genuinely was on shift for a couple of dates, but I could have made the others. I'm sorry.'

'Because of what I said?'

She nodded. 'You grabbing life by both hands took me a bit by surprise that day, and things have been complicated with Dave, and—'

He placed his hand over hers and squeezed it gently. 'It's fine. It took me by surprise too. I think I might have gone a little stir crazy in my writing cave to have blurted that out.'

'So you didn't mean it?'

Aidan squeezed her hand again. 'Of course I meant it. Every word. But you're with Dave and, if he makes you happy, then I'm happy for you.' He let go of her hand and sat back. 'I think I need to work on my timing. I didn't say how I felt in college when I should have done, and then I spoke up in The Chocolate Pot when I really shouldn't have. I knew things were complicated with you and Dave and I never meant to add to that. I'm not surprised you were avoiding me. But you don't have to anymore because I'm going away.'

Alison's stomach plummeted. 'When?'

'Not till October but I'll be away for four months. I've been commissioned for a series of books about Europe in the winter. I haven't been abroad since Elizabeth was diagnosed and my feet are so itchy. I can't wait.'

'That's fantastic news. Congratulations.' Alison could feel the tears pricking at her eyes, panic filling her at the thought of Aidan going away.

'So, which photo did you want to show me?' Aidan asked. 'Or I can give you a virtual guided tour of them all.'

Alison forced a smile. 'Virtual guided tour sounds good.'

She scrolled through the photos with Aidan pointing out various landmarks, towns or beaches.

'There are lots of bar shots,' she said, apologetically.

'I love looking at crowd scenes,' he said. 'The trick is to

see what's going on in the background. I've seen some fascinating things in the photos I've taken.'

'Like what?'

'Scroll back a couple,' he said. 'Stop. That one. You're looking at the four lads at the table, but if you look back left, there's someone doing a moony.'

Alison squinted at the screen again. 'So there is! I'd *never* have spotted that.'

'I've taken loads of pictures where someone in the background is pulling a moony or sticking their fingers up. I've also captured a couple of thefts and even someone spiking a drink.'

'Really?'

Aidan nodded. 'Scroll through these and let's see who can spot stuff the quickest.'

'You're on.' Alison scanned round the next photo in a busy bar. Nope. Nothing.

'Got it!' Aidan cried.

'What? You're fibbing.'

'There.' He pointed to the top left corner. 'Bloke having a pee against the wall.'

'Ew! That's disgusting.'

'The grim side of Ibiza,' Aidan said. 'Keep going.'

'Moony!' Alison cried, pointing at the distant bare backside in another one.

'Well spotted.'

'Ah-ha. Check that out,' Aidan said when they'd scrolled through a few more. 'Couple in the background need to get a room.'

'Where?'

'Bright yellow T-shirt. You can't miss him.'

Alison's heart thumped as she looked at where Aidan was

pointing. 'How do I make it bigger?' Not that she really needed to. She recognised the T-shirt.

'Are you okay?' Aidan asked, as her breathing came thick and fast.

'Just make it bigger.'

Aidan clicked a couple of buttons and the photo filled the whole screen, showing a man in a bright yellow T-shirt pinning a woman to the wall of a club. Her legs were wrapped around his waist, her hands in his hair while he kissed her exposed breast. Enough. Alison shut the lid of the laptop and closed her eyes for a moment, shaking her head.

'That was Dave,' she said, opening her eyes and looking at Aidan. 'I am *so* stupid. What goes on in Ibiza stays in Ibiza.'

Aidan stood up, took Alison's hands to help her to her feet, then wrapped his arms around her and held her.

The lying, cheating, devious git. She'd asked him outright and he'd denied it. He'd made her feel bad for asking. If he'd been honest, it would have been over and she might have been able to tell Aidan that his love wasn't unrequited. That's when the tears started. If Dave had been honest with her, Aidan might not be leaving her for four months. How stupid could she be? Danniella was right. Things weren't working with Dave because he wasn't the secret to her happiness, but the man holding her right now was, or at least in part. She couldn't tell him now, though, not after what he'd just told her about his travels. Seems he wasn't the only one with appalling timing.

While Aidan stroked her hair and whispered reassuring words, Alison closed her eyes and held her cheek against his chest. She could hear his heart beating and felt hers racing in time with it. So this was how it felt to be held by Aidan Thorpe. He was slightly taller than Dave but not quite as broad. The way he'd gathered her in his arms felt so different, as though she was precious cargo, to be protected and cherished. She didn't want to let go. Ever.

'Are you okay?' he asked after a few minutes.

'I feel stupid for trusting him again,' she said. 'Especially when...' She stopped herself. It wasn't fair to tell him now. He loved travelling abroad and he'd stayed in the UK for Elizabeth. She couldn't let him stay for her too. If he'd loved her for the past decade, he'd still love her when he got back in February.

'Was that Aidan I heard earlier?' Danniella said, stepping into the room. 'Oh, sorry.'

'She's had a shock,' Aidan said, still holding her.

'Dave was with someone in Ibiza after all,' Alison said, reluctantly releasing her hold on him.

'Oh, Ali,' Danniella said. 'I'm so sorry.'

'Don't be. Deep down, I knew. I just didn't want to believe it. How was the phone call?'

Danniella smiled. 'It was good. Amazing, actually.'

'I'd better go,' Aidan said. 'Leave you two to talk.' He smiled at Alison. 'Would you hate me if I said sorry, not sorry?'

'I could never hate you, Aidan.' *Because I love you.*

'Then I'm sorry, not sorry. You don't deserve for this to have happened, but I'm sort of glad it has because Dave doesn't deserve you.'

'Thank you.'

'I'll let myself out.'

When the front door closed, Danniella turned to Alison. 'How long was I on the phone? What's happened with Dave?'

Alison opened the laptop and pointed at the picture.

'Oh. Is that...?'

'Yep.'

'Oh, crap.'

'Yep.'

'So are you ready to talk? Dave? Aidan? Everything?'

Alison sighed. 'I'm ready to talk.'

* * *

Dave answered the door to Alison a couple of hours later, dressed in his work overalls, a tub of Polyfilla and a blade in his hand.

'Ali! I wasn't expecting to see you,' he said.

'Surprise!'

'You can use your key, you know. It's still your home.' Dave frowned. 'What's with the crates?'

'Danniella's hosting a dinner party for the girls and I need to get my Denby set so this is a flying visit.' Alison smiled innocently. 'Don't let me stop you doing whatever you're doing. I'll shout you when I've packed it.'

Dave shrugged, but headed back upstairs while Alison made her way to the kitchen. She speedily loaded her grandma's Denby dinner service into the two crates, stuffing tea towels round them so they wouldn't slide about. No way was she going to risk leaving them behind in case Dave smashed them. The two replacement plates he'd bought her remained on the shelf, though. She didn't want his guilty purchases; she'd buy her own replacements instead.

Placing the crates by the front door, she retrieved the framed pictures of her family from the floating shelves in the lounge, the photo album from the dresser, and the two wooden boxes containing her family's ashes.

She placed everything outside so that Danniella could

load them into her car, as agreed, while Alison executed the next part of their plan.

'Dave!' she called up the stairs. 'I'm leaving now.'

He ran downstairs. 'You don't even have time for a cuppa?'

'No, thanks. I need to go.'

He looked at the cardboard folder she was holding with 'Exhibit A' written on it in marker pen. 'What's that?'

'I'll show you in a moment. Firstly, this is yours.' She handed him the ring he'd bought in Ibiza.

He stared at it, frowning. 'Ali…?'

'And you remember that conversation we had about what constituted infidelity?' She opened the folder, took out a colour A4 photo that Danniella had printed, and held it up in front of him. 'This. This is infidelity. It seems that, thanks to the world of social media, what goes on in Ibiza doesn't really stay in Ibiza.'

Dave stared at the image, mouth open.

'You know what the funny thing is? If you hadn't worn that God-awful T-shirt last night, I'd never have realised it was you. If you're going to shag other women in public in future, you might want to wear something a little less conspicuous.' She thrust the photo into his hands and yanked open the door.

'It didn't mean anything.' Dave sank onto the bottom stair, staring at the picture.

'Then why do it?'

'She kept throwing herself at me. I said no, but I was really drunk that night.'

'That is such a cop-out. Plus, you forget how well I know you. I've never met anyone who can hold drink like you can. You get pissed, you start slurring, but you never, ever lose control. So don't insult me by pretending you were so drunk that you didn't know what you were doing.' She narrowed her eyes at him. 'Is that Anna or was there more than one?'

'It's Anna,' he said in a small voice.

Alison nodded. 'Your mate Eggsey was right about you. You are a "right twat".'

'Don't leave me,' he begged. 'You mean the world to me.'

'Oh, spare me. If I really meant anything to you, you'd never have gone to Ibiza in the first place.' She stepped outside. 'I'll be in touch about collecting the rest of my stuff. Goodbye, Dave.'

55

DANNIELLA

One Month Later

Danniella sat on the balcony of her bedroom, her hands clutched around a mug of coffee. Karen had left twenty minutes ago to run the 6 a.m. bootcamp and Alison was working the night shift, expected back at about 7 a.m. so the flat was in silence. Tomorrow would signal three months since she'd moved into Cobalt House. Back then, she'd have predicated still being lost and lonely three months later. How wrong could she be?

Moving in wasn't the only anniversary. Today would have been Abigail's fifth birthday. Danniella had come so far since that horrendous day last year when she'd pushed Ethan away, with most of her progress being in the past two months.

As the sun rose over the Sea Rescue Sanctuary, she picked up her phone and called Ethan. She'd hurt him so badly a year ago and it was time she faced up to that.

'Hi, Danni,' he said. 'I thought you might be up.'

'I was watching the sunrise and thinking of Abigail and you.'

'Same here. Not the sunrise bit, but I was thinking of you both. I wish you'd tell me where you are.'

'Why? What would you do?'

'Find the fastest route to get to you, hold you close, and never let you go.'

Tears rained down Danniella's cheeks. 'You have no idea how much I'd like that, Ethan, but I'm not ready. Not yet.'

'I know. I won't push you.'

'Thank you. There is something you can do for me, though.'

'Anything.'

She took a deep breath. 'I need you to tell me what happened to you when I left. I need to understand how much I hurt you.'

'No, Danni. It's in the past. We don't need to go there.'

'But we do. We can't move on if you're not honest with me because, one day, it's bound to come out. It's better that I know everything now and we can heal together. I've talked it over with Marian. She thinks it will help.'

He sighed. 'Are you sure?'

'I'm sure.'

'Okay, then.'

It was difficult to hear about how much pain she'd caused him. How he'd hated her. How, for a short time, he wished she'd been the one who'd died instead of Abigail. How he'd turned to drink but soon realised that the answer wasn't at the bottom of a bottle. Then he'd explained how writing had got him through it. He'd temporarily cast aside his work on *It's Always Been You* to write a new book called *The Secret to*

Happiness, which was essentially their story of life before and after the accident.

'I'm not planning on publishing it, of course, but it helped me come to terms with the situation, my feelings, and my hopes for the future.'

'And what are your hopes for the future?'

'That like my protagonists, Alicia and Will, you and I can find our peace and be happy together again, just like in our wedding song.'

Danniella smiled. Despite being born in the eighties, Ethan was a huge fan of sixties music and 'Happy Together' by the Turtles was his all-time favourite song. Danniella had surprised him by asking the DJ at their wedding to play it for their first dance, instead of the modern ballad Ethan had been expecting.

'How much of the book is fiction and how much is true life?' she asked.

'Everything Will thinks, says, and does is 100 per cent me. Alicia is fiction but, knowing you like I do, parts should be close.'

'I'd like to read it.'

There was a pause. 'I don't know, Danni. There are some dark moments in there. Very dark moments.'

'I've had my own dark moments too so I can well imagine. Please, Aidan. We both need this.'

'Okay,' he said finally. 'But I'll send you it on one condition. You have to promise to tell me your side of the story. I'm not saying you need to do it immediately. I'm saying I want to hear it when you're ready to tell it.'

Danniella closed her eyes and took a deep breath. Yes. She owed him that much. 'I can do that.'

'And I want you to do it in person,' he added.

She gasped. 'Ethan. I don't know. It took me over ten months to contact you. Chatting on the phone is one thing, but face to face?'

'Which is why I'm giving you time. I'm asking for this whenever you and your counsellor feel you're ready. If it takes another year, so be it.'

'I can't ask you to put your life on hold for that long.'

'There's three things you need to know about me,' he said. 'And you know what they are, don't you?'

'Yes,' she said, tears rolling down her cheeks. 'Okay. I agree. I can't guarantee when or where, but I do agree.'

'Then I'll send you the manuscript, but you have to promise me that you'll read it all the way to the end, no matter how upset or hurt you are. You have to find the happy ending.'

'I promise.'

They chatted some more, then said their goodbyes.

By the time she'd showered and dressed, the manuscript had arrived by email. She wouldn't read it today, on Abigail's birthday, but she'd definitely read it soon, maybe when Alison had a day off so she wasn't home alone.

'How do you think the book will end?' Karen asked, sitting beside Alison on the sofa after her Thursday evening boot-camp a week later. Danniella was in her bedroom, reading Ethan's story of their life.

'I'm guessing the two of them getting back together and living happily ever after. I think that's what Danniella's hoping for too.'

'Do you think you'll get your happy ever after with Aidan?'

Alison shrugged. 'Maybe one day.'

'Why not now?'

'He's going away in about six weeks. It wouldn't be fair.'

'On who? I think you should tell him how you feel. Enjoy the next six weeks together and, let's face it, Europe's not the other side of the world. You could fly out to visit him.'

'It sounds so easy when you say it like that,' Alison said. 'But if it was easy, you'd have told Jay you're in love with him.'

'I am not!' But Karen's heart raced at the mention of his name.

'Rubbish. What's stopping you telling him?'

Karen sighed. 'It's only been a couple of months since Ryan. It feels too soon.'

Alison laughed. 'You've just told me to go for it with Aidan and do you know how long it is since I ended it with Dave? A month.'

'But things had been going wrong with him for four years and you'd loved Aidan before Dave.'

'If we're playing that game, then you admitted the last eight or nine months with Ryan had been challenging. If tomorrow was your last day on earth, would you rather spend it with or without Jay?'

'With Jay,' Karen said, without hesitation. 'But I can throw that one right back at you. With Aidan or without Aidan?'

Alison smiled. 'With. And I will tell him – just not now.'

They both looked up expectantly as Danniella wandered into the room and threw herself into the armchair, dabbing her red eyes with a balled-up tissue.

'Dare we ask?' Karen ventured.

'Exquisite. The best thing he's ever written. Oh my God! My heart broke so many times and yet...' She shook her head. 'It was so uplifting. He has to publish it.'

'Have you spoken to him?' Alison said.

'Not yet. I'll be a blubbering, babbling mess if I call him tonight. I've been crying most of the day and I feel drained. It's a soak in the bath and an early night for me. Can I love you and leave you?'

'Of course,' Alison said. 'You can tell us more tomorrow.'

Danniella stood up and headed towards the door.

'By the way,' Karen said. 'What was the ending? What's his secret to happiness?'

Danniella paused, leaning against the doorframe. 'It's my

character, Alicia. Happiness was about her accepting that she wasn't to blame, forgiving herself, and learning to love herself again. And, do you know what, I think he's right. Night.'

'Night,' Alison and Karen said together.

* * *

As Karen loaded the mugs into the dishwasher shortly after, she thought about what Alison said about Jay. After kicking Sophie out, he was a changed man. His confidence seemed to soar as he got his life back. The timing had been perfect for him, heading into the long school holidays, giving him the opportunity to get out and about doing the things he loved. He'd convinced Karen to join him for hikes on Sundays. His enthusiasm for tramping up hills and along coastal paths was infectious and she soon fell in love with walking... and with Jay. It was a massive and unexpected step for her after so many years with Ryan. Or maybe it wasn't that unexpected considering how she'd felt that day in the car park when he'd held her and she'd imagined kissing him.

So why didn't she tell him how she felt? She shook her head as one word sprung to mind: rejection. Ryan had rejected her and had thrown away their love. What if lightning did strike twice? Or what if he didn't reject her but he messed up like Ryan had? It would destroy her.

Alison and Danniella had been through a lot worse than she had, though, and they were working hard on learning to love themselves. She didn't need to do that. She was already happy with herself, her business and her life. Jay could make her even happier, if she could be brave enough to let him in.

'I can't believe how nervous I am.' Danniella's breathing quickened as she stood on the platform at Whitsborough Bay train station a fortnight later.

'Slow down,' Alison said. 'Breathe with me...'

'Thank you,' Danniella whispered, when she'd regulated her breathing again. 'Last thing I need is a panic attack in the middle of a busy train station.

'You haven't had one in weeks,' Alison assured her. 'It's only because you're nervous and that's completely understandable. Seeing Ethan again is a massive step and I'm so proud of you.'

It really was a massive step. When she'd told Marian that Ethan had invited her to his book launch and anniversary celebrations, she'd expected her to say it was too soon, but her counsellor wholeheartedly supported the idea. Over the past month, she'd helped Danniella finally accept Abigail's death as an accident: a series of small, insignificant occurrences that had combined at one particular moment to create a tragedy. Nobody's fault. The next step was therefore to meet with Ethan and, when she felt ready, with Natalie, Ricky, and anyone else she wanted back in her life.

Ethan was thrilled she was coming to the launch. He'd offered to meet her from the station but she was adamant that he should focus on preparing his speech and she'd prefer to see him there and maybe go out to dinner when it was over so they could talk.

As the train pulled in, Danniella and Alison moved towards the doors of the carriage where Danniella had reserved a seat.

'I can't believe that it's been a whole year since I left home,' Danniella said, waiting for the announcement to board. 'Oh, God, Ali. What if this was a huge mistake and I ruin his special night?'

'That's *not* going to happen. He's desperate to see you.'

'But what if I've got it all wrong? I know that the characters in his book get back together at Will's book launch but what if I'm taking that too literally? What if he doesn't really want me back?'

Alison took her hand and gave it a reassuring squeeze. 'You're creating problems that don't exist. He loves you more than fluffy unicorns, remember? So, get down to London and enjoy yourself. And don't forget to keep breathing.'

'The train at platform three is now ready to board,' came an announcement, then the doors opened. Danniella hugged Alison then boarded.

Settling into her seat, Danniella dug out her laptop and scrolled to the end of *The Secret to Happiness* to reassure herself that she was doing the right thing. Will and Alicia, meeting again at the launch of Will's next book, was a beautifully-written romantic and moving moment. She could picture it vividly, but that was fiction and she was about to face reality.

* * *

Danniella felt queasy as she stood outside The Sarrandon Club that afternoon; a private members' club close to Ethan's publisher's London offices and a short taxi drive from her hotel. She smoothed down the chiffon panels of her navy dress. In the book, Alicia wore a floaty, navy dress to Will's book launch. Not normally one for superstitions, she hadn't dared to jinx it by not wearing something similar.

Here goes. Nothing to lose...

She gripped the wooden handrail as she made her way up to the Sapphire Room on the first floor. *Deep breaths. In... and out. This is not the place for yet another panic attack.* She'd already had one in the hotel room, making her late. Hopefully Ethan wouldn't think she'd bottled it.

The door to the Sapphire Room was closed. Damn! It had started. She slowly pushed it open, hoping it wouldn't squeak. These events were usually well attended so she'd be able to slip into the back, unnoticed, until the speeches were over and then she'd try to catch Ethan's eye, just like Alicia did with Will.

The door eased open and Danniella prepared to blend into the crowd. But there was no crowd. There was nobody in the room at all. A couple of large leather armchairs were positioned next to a table in the middle of the room, facing a screen. An ice bucket containing a bottle of champagne sat in the middle of the table, alongside a bouquet of flowers. She frowned and reached for the door again. She'd obviously been told the wrong room.

'Good evening, Mrs Cole,' said a voice.

Danniella turned around to see a suited man in his late-fifties striding towards her, a glass of champagne balanced on a silver tray.

'Welcome to The Sarrandon Club and a very special audience with Mr Lucas Downey.'

'What's going on?' she asked. 'Where is everyone?'

'Everyone on the guest list has arrived. Champagne?'

Still frowning, Danniella accepted the glass.

'Mr Downey has asked that you make yourself comfortable and watch a short film. He'll join you very soon.'

Bewildered, Danniella sat in one of the armchairs. What on earth was going on? In the book, Will and Alicia locked eyes across a crowded room and time seemed to stop as they made their way towards each other. There was nothing about an empty room and a film.

The lights dimmed and the screen lit up. Danniella's heart raced as a mock-up of a test card for a film called *The Secret to Happiness* appeared on the screen. 'Happy Together' by The Turtles played as photographs of Ethan and Danniella together scrolled across the screen: their first few dates, meals out, holidays, moving in together, their engagement party, book launches, their wedding. A lump formed in Danniella's throat and her eyes stung as she watched photo after photo of them quite literally happy together, just like in the song. Abigail appeared on the scene and there were images of her as a baby, then a toddler. More smiles. Two had become three and they were still so very happy together. So many photos, so many wonderful memories.

Then a series of newspaper clippings about the accident, people in black huddled outside the crematorium, and photos of flowers. Tears ran down her cheeks. *Abigail. My baby.*

As the song reached a crescendo, the photos scrolled again, faster and faster. So much happiness and just that one brief moment of absolute excruciating pain that had changed everything.

The song started to play again, quietly this time, as the photos gave way to film. Natalie appeared on the screen. 'Hi Danni. I can't begin to tell you how much I've missed you this past year. I want you to know that I understand and, when you're ready, I want you back in my life. The best news ever was when Ethan said you're safe. Come back to us. I love you, baby sister.' Her voice cracked on that last part.

Nat's husband, Ricky, appeared on the screen. 'Danni-girl. Get your arse back home. We miss you.' He blew her a kiss.

Kristian and Juliette, Natalie's brother and sister, sent messages followed by Ethan's parents and his brother, James. All their messages conveyed the same thing: they missed her, they loved her, they were relieved she was safe. No anger, no hate, no accusations.

The final shot was Ethan sitting in his office, looking directly into the camera. 'There are three things you need to know about me...' he said.

'I'm here for you, I'll wait for you, and I'll always love you,' said a voice from within the room.

Heart racing, Danniella leapt up, her eyes searching the shadows. 'Ethan?'

He stepped into the light and held out his arms.

She ran towards him. 'I'm so sorry.'

'Shh,' he whispered into her hair. 'You read the book. You felt my anger and my pain, yet you still came. That means everything to me.' He cupped her face in his hands and gazed into her eyes. '*You* mean everything to me, Danni.'

As he gently lowered his lips to hers, Danniella knew that she'd found the secret to her happiness. She'd let go of the guilt and forgiven herself, and was ready to rebuild her life with her husband. The road ahead wasn't going to be easy for either of them, but they'd navigate it together. Running away had never been about getting away from Ethan; it had been about escaping from herself and the guilt that would have destroyed them if she stayed. They'd lost their beautiful daughter, but they hadn't lost each other and they never would. And they'd never really lose Abigail. She'd be forever in their hearts and their memories.

As Danniella's train pulled out, Alison blinked back the tears. The strength and courage that Danniella had shown since her release from hospital had been both inspiring and humbling and Alison felt honoured to have been part of that journey. This next step, facing the man she'd hurt so badly, showed such amazing courage and strength of character and now it was time for Alison to take that next step.

✉ To Aidan
I've just dropped Danniella off at the station. I don't suppose you're free for a coffee? I'm on shift at 10pm but I'd love to meet you before then. I'm ready to discuss my homework x

✉ From Aidan
Was beginning to think the dog had eaten it!

Meet you at The Chocolate Pot in half an
hour? x

Alison sipped on her cappuccino, her stomach in knots.
Thank goodness he'd said he could meet her quickly. She'd
have been a nervous wreck if she'd had to wait all day. The
door to the café opened and Aidan looked around the room,
beaming when he spotted her.

'I'm sorry I'm a bit late,' he said, giving her a kiss on the
cheek, sending ripples of excitement through her. He
removed his jacket and nodded towards the chair opposite.
'I'm hoping that seat's got my name on it.'

Smiling, she pushed the chair out with her foot. 'Well,
would you look at that?

Aidan laughed as he picked up the piece of paper.

'Must mean I'm your destiny,' Alison said.

'I always thought so.' He sat down and nodded towards
the americano. 'Is this for me?'

She nodded. 'Saves us being disturbed.'

'Thank you.' He took a sip. 'So you've done your
homework?'

'It's a work in progress but I think you'll like the direction
it's taking.'

He looked at her expectantly and she felt a moment of
panic. What if he laughed? What if he said no? What if he
said he preferred to travel alone and she'd get in the way of
his writing? *No. Stop it. Be more Danniella. What she's doing
today is much bigger than this and, if she can do it, so can you.
And he did say he loves you...*

'I'm going to hand in my notice at work.'

His eyes widened. 'I thought you loved your job.'

'I do, but it's all I know. When things at home turned bad, I threw myself into work and it became like a security blanket. It's time to let go of that blanket and experience something new.'

'A career change?'

'More like a lifestyle change. I've decided to do some travelling. The problem is, I'm not a seasoned traveller so I could really use the services of an experienced travel guide. Perhaps a travel writer?'

Aidan took her hand across the table, smiling. 'I would love to show you Europe, but you need to know something about me before you quit your job, because you may not want to come with me once you know this.'

Her stomach plummeted to the floor. Was he going to tell her that she was too late and he had a girlfriend? Please, no. She nodded, indicating for him to continue.

'I'll have a very fixed agenda, taking you to all the most romantic places in Europe in an effort to get you to fall in love with me.' Aidan squeezed her hand.

Tears pricked Alison's eyes. 'I like the sound of that, but it won't make me fall in love with you.'

Aidan's smile slipped and he loosened his grip, but Alison didn't let go.

'When I was sixteen, I was lost and confused,' she said. 'Nobody wanted to know me, but a lad sat down next to me in my first Travel and Tourism class. I didn't know how to make friends, but he seemed intent on making me feel like I was worth spending time with.' She smiled. 'I fell in love with you back in college, too, but I didn't dare imagine that you felt the same. Back then, I joked that you were my destiny. Turns out you really were.'

'You mean that?'

'I mean it. I love you, Aidan. I always have, but I needed to be happy with me before I could be happy with you.'

'And are you happy with you?'

Alison smiled. 'I am. Finally.'

'Fancy getting out of here?'

'Good idea.'

They pulled on their coats and, hand in hand, ran to the small park at the end of Castle Street, overlooking the sea.

Aidan gently took her face in his hands and lowered his lips to hers. Their kiss was gentle at first. Tentative. Nervous. Then Aidan's fingers intertwined with her hair and he pulled her closer, his kiss deepening. Alison gasped as she ran her hands down his back, pulling him even closer to her.

'Wow! That was worth waiting ten years for,' Alison said, when they pulled apart.

'It certainly was.' Aidan nodded towards the sea. 'May I present the first stop on our tour of the most romantic places in Europe: Castle Park, Whitsborough Bay, North Yorkshire.'

As they kissed for the second time, Alison knew that this was how it was always meant to be: her and Aidan destined to be together.

59

'Where are you taking me?' Karen asked as Jay drove them across town on Sunday. 'You know I'm not good with surprises.'

Jay glanced at her and smiled reassuringly. 'You'll like this one. I promise.'

'Not even a small clue?'

He sighed. 'A tiny one, then. It involves exercise. But that's all you're getting.'

'Jay! You're so mean.'

'It'll be more fun if it stays a surprise.'

Fifteen minutes later, he pulled off the main Whitby road and drove along a bumpy track into what appeared to be the middle of nowhere. Eventually, the track opened into a parking area in front of a series of stone barns.

'We're here. Are you excited?' Jay asked, pushing his door open.

'Erm. Yeah? No idea where we are, though.'

'Jay!' A man in his late-thirties wearing a navy boiler suit and hiking boots strode towards the car and they shook hands. 'Thank you for being my guinea pigs.'

'Pleasure,' Jay said. 'This is Karen. Karen, this is Darius, a former colleague of mine.'

'Nice to meet you, Karen.' Darius shook her hand and smiled. 'You have no idea what you're about to do, have you?'

'None whatsoever. Should I be worried?'

'Nah. You'll love it. And, if you don't, it's Jay's fault, not mine.' He turned and headed towards one of the barns. 'Come on, let's get you kitted up.'

* * *

'Looking gorgeous,' Jay laughed as Karen gave him a twirl in her red boiler suit.

'Looking pretty sexy yourself,' she said and her heart leapt. He did. Who knew that a khaki boiler suit could look so alluring? She imagined herself pushing him against the wall, ripping open the poppers and...

'Are you both ready?' Darius asked. He handed them a crash helmet each, checking for fit. 'Perfect. Let's crack on with the first activity, then. Quad bikes.'

Karen squealed. 'Are you serious?'

Darius smiled. 'Ever been on one?'

'No, but I've always wanted to.'

'We'll be doing two quad bike activities today,' Darius said. 'We'll start you on races round a circuit then go off-roading later. You'll be doing paintballing, an assault course, and a whole lot more. I promise you mud, aching muscles, and lots of laughter.'

'Bring it on!' Karen cried.

* * *

'That was the best day ever,' Karen said, as they made their way back to the changing barn.

'You really liked it?' Darius asked. 'It's not finished yet, but we were keen to test it out and make sure we were on the right lines.'

'I loved it. You're onto a winner here. And it's not just the activities. It's you. You're hilarious.'

'I agree,' Jay said. 'It's brilliant, but you're what makes it. You're what will bring people back for more.'

'I haven't laughed so much in ages,' Karen said. 'As soon as you're up and running, send me some fliers and I'll give them to all my clients.'

'I like you,' Darius said, shaking her hand. 'Your girl-friend's a keeper, Jay. Hang onto her.'

Jay caught her eye and she felt her already flushed cheeks colour even deeper. Did he have any idea how she felt about him?

'I'll leave you to get changed,' Darius said. 'There are crates on the far wall for your kit so shove everything in those and I'll clean it later.'

Still laughing, Karen and Jay headed into the changing barn and deposited their helmets and goggles into the crates.

'Today was fantastic,' Karen gushed. 'Thank you so much, Jay.'

'My pleasure. Although I could have done without the climbing wall. My legs were already on fire from the assault course.'

'Same here, but I was determined to get to the top.'

'You were amazing,' Jay said, then his expression softened. 'You *are* amazing.'

Karen's heart thumped as he took a step closer to her and gently touched her cheek, sending ripples of desire through her. 'You've got a bit of mud on your face.'

She gulped as his fingers gently grazed her lips.

'I'm not sure you've quite got it,' she whispered, closing her eyes as he touched her lips again.

'You're trembling,' he whispered.

'I'm scared.'

'Of what?'

Karen hesitated. Could she do it? Could she tell him? After tough times, her friends had taken control. Danniella had travelled to London and was going to rebuild her life with Ethan. Alison was going travelling with Aidan who she'd been secretly in love with for a decade. It was Karen's turn to bite the bullet. 'I need to tell you something. You know that day in the car park when we hugged?'

Jay nodded.

'I... erm... Something happened. I wanted to...' *Sod it! Actions speak louder than words!* She leaned forward and gently kissed Jay's lips. 'I wanted to do that,' she said, her heart thumping as she waited for his reaction.

For a moment, he looked surprised, then he smiled, flashing his gorgeous dimples. 'And I wanted to do this.' He put his arms around her waist and pulled her close as he returned her kiss with such passion and intensity that she felt quite light-headed when they broke apart, trying to catch their breath.

'And here was me being worried you might not feel the same,' Karen said, running her fingers through his hair. 'I'm not so worried now.'

Jay smiled. 'I already really liked you, but something shifted between us that day in the car park. Things were complicated back then with Ryan and Sophie still in the mix but I figured that, if it was meant to be, it would happen eventually.' He kissed her again, slowly and tenderly this time. 'I didn't think anything could top the quad bikes, but this moment right now has eclipsed everything about today.'

'This moment right now has eclipsed everything,' Karen whispered. And it had. She'd loved Ryan but her feelings for Jay ran so much stronger and deeper. 'I think it's time we said goodbye to Darius and continued this moment somewhere a bit more comfortable. What do you think?'

Jay pulled the poppers apart on his boiler suit and stepped out of it deftly. 'That's me ready. What are you waiting for?'

Karen giggled as she removed her suit. 'Nothing. Absolutely nothing. I think I might just have everything I ever wanted.'

'Me too. I love you, Karen.'

'I love you, too.'

He kissed her again before picking up their boiler suits and throwing them into the crates. 'Ready?'

'Ready.'

'Last one to the car has to wash it.'

'Oi!' She sprinted after him, laughing.

After the toughest few months of her life, she had so much to look forward to now. Steff was back on top form and they'd had some great discussions about how to take the business forward. Sam had proposed to Jemma and they were planning their wedding for next summer with Karen as chief bridesmaid. Danniella and Alison were both facing positive futures too. Three months ago, they'd been strangers facing the darkest of times. They'd all had someone to say goodbye to and it hadn't been easy. Without her friends by her side, she knew it would have been so much harder saying goodbye and moving on from Ryan, that Alison might not have been able to let go of Dave, and that Danniella might have still been running from her traumatic past, unable to say goodbye to her guilt. And now look at them all, and it was all thanks to meeting through that mid-morning bootcamp that Ryan had never wanted her to run. Just as well she'd listened to her heart and gone ahead with it anyway.

She'd always said that individuals could achieve great things, but groups could achieve so much more. And they had. With love, support and friendship, they were all in such different places now, starting exciting new chapters of their lives.

60

ALISON

Four Weeks Later

Alison sat on her bed at Danniella's and flicked through the commemorative album.

'It's a big day today,' she said, lightly stroking her fingers over the final photo of her family by the rock pools. 'I'm flying out to Reykjavik in three days' time and I'll be travelling round Europe for four months with Aidan. How exciting is that? You'd have loved Aidan.' She paused as she dabbed away her tears. 'It's time for me to start living and the only way I can do that is to say goodbye. You're probably thinking I should have done it years ago, but I wasn't ready. I am now.'

She closed the album and placed it back in the bottom of the wardrobe then removed the two wooden boxes. She kissed the lid of each before placing them gently in a bag. 'You'll be pleased with your final resting place.'

'Are you ready?' Danniella asked, poking her head around the door a few minutes later.

Alison nodded. 'It's time.'

'You're doing the right thing.'

'I know.' She stood up. 'Come on, then. Let's do it. Let's say our goodbyes.'

'We've got something for you,' Karen said, joining them and handing Alison a gift bag.

'What's this?

'It's for Europe,' Danniella said, 'but we thought you might want to wear it now. Fresh start and all that.'

Alison gasped as she lifted out a deep-burgundy winter coat with a faux-fur collar and a belt around the waist. 'It's gorgeous.'

'A bright colour for your bright new future,' Karen said.

'I love it. Thank you. Oh...' Her smile fell as she clocked the size eighteen label. 'I'm not sure it's going to fit.'

'Try it on,' Danniella urged. 'I think you'll be surprised.'

Alison pulled the coat on, expecting to feel tightness in the sleeves, but it slipped on easily and the zip pulled up without the need to breathe in.

'Perfect fit,' Karen said. 'You look amazing.'

Alison stepped towards the mirror and ran her hands down the coat, turning from side to side. 'Size eighteen? Oh my God! I can't believe it.' She grinned at Karen. 'Bootcamp did that.'

Karen shook her head. 'No, Ali. *You* did that and I'm so proud of you.'

'Me too,' Danniella said, as they gathered in a hug.

* * *

It was a week into October and the temperature had dropped,

signalling the arrival of autumn. Strong winds over the past few days had caused high tides and over-topping, hurling seaweed, sand, and debris onto the promenade. Alison had been worried they'd have to cancel their plans, but the storm had thankfully subsided overnight. The air was now still and the sky cloudless, painted with a palette of pale greys and blues.

Alison, Danniella, and Karen walked down the cliff path together, took the steps down to the beach, and made their way over to the rock pools below the statue of Stanley Moffatt.

Alison knew she needed to say goodbye to her family before she went travelling, but it struck her that it was so much more than that. She was saying goodbye to the past – to Dave, to her job, and to the guilt that had stopped her from living. And she wasn't the only one who needed to say goodbye to the past. Danniella and Karen had been the ones who'd breathed life back into her and helped her find happiness again so it was only right that the three of them did this together.

There was the gentlest of easterly breezes down on the sand. The three women stood behind the rock pools, facing the sea, Alison in the middle. They didn't have long as the tide was on its way in and would engulf the pools within the next thirty minutes, but they didn't need long. They'd all been building up to this moment for a long time.

'Four months ago, I was lost, lonely, massively overweight, incredibly unfit, and desperately unhappy,' Alison said. 'I was clinging onto Dave because he was all I had left to call family and I was too scared to face life without him, even though life with him was a daily battlefield. The only thing keeping me sane was having a job I loved. Then I met you, Danni, and you somehow managed to talk me into joining you at Karen's bootcamp.'

She smiled at Danniella then Karen who both smiled warmly in return, then she took the two wooden boxes and three cream roses out of a bag. Placing them on the sand in front of her, she reached out either side to take hold of one of Karen's and Danniella's hands.

'Four months on, I've quit my job which is something I never, ever expected to do and would never have been able to do if it hadn't been for the friendship and encouragement you both gave me.' She took a deep breath as the words caught in her throat. 'I was determined not to cry.'

'Me too,' Karen said, blinking back the tears.

'Me three,' Danniella added, wiping her cheek with her spare hand.

'What are we like?' Alison said. 'So, four months on, I can run 10k and I can get into size eighteen clothes for the first time in maybe eight years. I can leave a job I love to go travelling with a man I always loved but was too scared to let in. I'll never be lost or lonely again because I might have lost my biological family, but I've found my new family and they're right here with me in the place where I'm going to say goodbye.' She squeezed their hands as the tears fell.

'Aw, come here,' Danniella said, enveloping Alison and Karen in a hug. They stood on the beach for a moment, sobbing.

'We'd better crack on or the tide will beat us,' Alison said, squeezing them again, then letting go. 'Where were we? Yes. Thanks to you two, I've found myself, my life, and my future. I've found the secret to happiness.'

Danniella and Karen linked arms as Alison stepped forward and picked up the smaller box.

'Goodbye, Grandma,' she said, sprinkling the ashes over the rock pools and into the breeze. Picking up the larger box, she opened the lid, took a deep breath, then released those ashes into the air too. 'Goodbye Mum, Dad, Fleur, and Max. I don't need to keep you in a box anymore because you'll always be in here.' She placed her hand over her heart.

Some of the ashes settled onto the surface of the rock pools while others danced in the breeze, drifting upwards and towards the sea. The sun peeped from behind a cloud, lighting up the dust as it floated away on its final journey.

Alison picked up one of the cream roses and dropped it into the pool. 'A final goodbye to Dave, the past, and my guilt. Life is for living and, from now on, that's what I intend to do, living each day as though it was my last because we never know when it might be.'

She closed her eyes and breathed deeply for a moment, a feeling of peace flowing through her. Turning to Karen, she smiled.

Karen stepped forward with the next rose and dropped it into the rock pool beside Alison's. 'How do I follow that? Mine's a bit shorter. Four months ago, I thought Ryan and I were happy and together for life. Life had other ideas. We were broken and just hadn't realised it. Goodbye Ryan and hello to an exciting new future. That's me. Your turn, Danni.' Karen took hold of Alison's hand as she stepped back from the water.

Danniella stepped forward and dropped the final rose into the pool. 'When Abigail died, a huge part of me died too and the only way I could deal with that was to run and keep on running from the hurt and pain and guilt. At the start of May, I arrived at this beautiful place by the coast and something told me this was the place where I could stop and breathe. I've got a long way to go, but I'm working hard at letting go of that guilt, getting control of my food demons, and rebuilding my life with Ethan. That man is a saint. I must have done something very right in another life to have him. Maybe one day, when we're both ready, we can consider a brother or sister for Abigail but, for now, it's one day at a time.'

She stepped back and took Alison's other hand in hers. 'I used to be scared of the future until I met you two. You quite literally saved my life and I can never thank you enough.'

They huddled together, arms round each other, weeping silently as the tide crept closer. The clouds fully parted and the sun sent silver sparkles down to kiss the gentle waves.

* * *

Back on the promenade, they leaned against the railings in front of Stanley Moffatt, watching the sea creep forward to take the ashes and roses.

'How do you feel?' Karen asked as the roses bobbed on the waves, dipping in and out of view.

Alison paused for a moment. 'I feel liberated.'

Danniella nodded. 'Definitely feeling liberated.'

Alison took her phone out of her pocket and accosted a woman walking a dog to take a few photos of them. The rock pools below were the place where her last ever family photo was taken before life as she knew it ended, so it seemed appropriate to take photos with Stanley where her life started again with her new family.

'We're going to miss you at bootcamp,' Karen said as they huddled on the bench beside Stanley after the photos were taken.

Alison nodded. 'I'm going to miss bootcamp but I'm packing my trainers. I need to make sure I keep exercising while I'm away.'

Danniella laughed. 'You're going away with Aidan. I think it's safe to say there'll be plenty of exercise.'

'Fair point,' Alison said, giggling. 'Make sure you keep a place for me when I return. After all, my life began at bootcamp.'

'Your life began at bootcamp? Oh, I love that,' Karen said.

They sat in silence for a moment, lost in their thoughts.

'I've got something for you both,' Karen said. 'You know how I give out Awesome Awards at bootcamp and the prize is a photo?' She reached into her pocket and took out a couple of jewellery pouches, handing one to each of them. 'You both deserve something you can look at every day to remind you of exactly how awesome you are.'

Alison and Danniella reached into their pouches and both removed a light-grey leather bracelet with a silver star charm attached to it.

'Karen! It's gorgeous.' Alison cried.

'It's your very own Awesome Award. You're both stars.'

'I love it,' Danniella said. 'Thank you. We'll have to get you one too,'

Karen smiled as she pushed up the sleeve of her coat revealing a matching one.

'Oh, Karen. That's the best gift ever,' Alison said, the tears welling again as Karen fastened the bracelet onto her wrist.

'I agree,' Danniella said. 'It's really lovely. Now get off the bench so I can thank you properly.'

'We'd better get to the pub.' Alison said after they'd hugged again. 'I think we've earned a celebratory drink or two.'

She picked up the wooden boxes and placed them in the bin next to Stanley.

As they set off towards Blue Savannah, Alison turned and looked back towards the rock pools, saying one more silent goodbye to her family. It had been her final step in finding the secret to happiness and now she could embrace life to the full. She looked down at her bracelet and smiled. Her life really had begun at bootcamp four months ago, thanks to Danniella and Karen, and she wasn't going to waste another day.

ACKNOWLEDGMENTS

I'm so excited about The Secret to Happiness because it's my first release with Boldwood Books after a few years as an independent author. It has been an absolute pleasure to work with such a talented and supportive team and thank you so much for believing in my manuscript and inviting me to join you. An enormous thank you hug goes to Nia whose exceptional editorial advice and guidance has helped smooth the edges and take my work to a new level. It really has been a joy, Nia. Thank you so very much.

Thank you, as always, to my wonderful husband, Mark, and our daughter, Ashleigh. They are so supportive of my writing, never moaning, especially when I needed to hide away in my editing cave for a few weekends. Big hugs to you both.

An early version of the manuscript was beta-read by my mum, Joyce Williams, my good friend, Liz Berry, and my fabulous writing friends, Sharon Booth and Jo Bartlett. I'm forever grateful to the four of you for your feedback and typo-spotting, especially as it helped shape the book that secured my publishing deal with Boldwood. You guys are the best! Jo and Sharon are both part of my writing support network, The Write Romantics; a 10-strong group of inspiring women who support and guide each other through the highs and lows of being an author. Sharon is also my partner-in-crime in a writing partnership called the Yorkshire Rose Writers. We regularly meet up for tea, cake, and writerly chat and I value her friendship and support so much.

I wrote *The Secret to Happiness* alongside studying a Masters in Creative Writing and used several of the chapters for my fiction assignments. The feedback and encouragement from my tutor group has been invaluable in shaping this book too. It's been an absolute pleasure to be part of such a supportive, helpful and talented group. Thank you so much to Tracy, Janet, Angie, Mandy, David and Georgia. I will be watching your post-MA careers with interest! Also thank you to my tutor, Nicky, for your feedback and patience with my million and one questions.

Thank you also to my cousin, Lisa Lockey, for some really helpful medical advice. Lisa's a nurse so she's become my medical expert. Hopefully I've conveyed everything accurately. If not, it's my mistake; not Lisa's!

I dedicate this book to my dad, Peter Williams. He's not much of a reader, preferring magazines to books, but he's been very supportive of my writing. When my debut book was released, he made me one of those blue plaques that you see on buildings, inscribed with: *Jessica Redland lives here. She was solely responsible for putting Whitsborough Bay on the international literary map.* I love my blue plaque and have it proudly displayed in my office. Thank you, Dad, you superstar xx

Finally, my thanks go to you, my readers. If you've enjoyed *The Secret to Happiness* and any of my other books, it would be amazing if you could tell others by leaving a review on

Amazon. Reviews make a massive difference to an author. You'll see some really long ones on Amazon, but you don't need to write an essay. A positive rating and a short sentence are equally welcome.
Big hugs

Jessica xx

MORE FROM JESSICA REDLAND

We hope you enjoyed reading *The Secret to Happiness*. If you did, please leave a review.

If you'd like to gift a copy, this book is also available as a ebook, digital audio download and audiobook CD.

Sign up to Jessica Redland's mailing list for news, competitions and updates on future books.

http://bit.ly/JessicaRedlandNewsletter

ABOUT THE AUTHOR

Jessica Redland is the author of nine novels which are all set around the fictional location of Whitsborough Bay. Inspired by her hometown of Scarborough she writes uplifting women's fiction which has garnered many devoted fans.

Visit Jessica's website: https://www.jessicaredland.com/

Follow Jessica on social media:

facebook.com/JessicaRedlandWriter

twitter.com/JessicaRedland

instagram.com/JessicaRedlandWriter

ABOUT BOLDWOOD BOOKS

Boldwood Books is a fiction publishing company seeking out the best stories from around the world.

Find out more at www.boldwoodbooks.com

Sign up to the Book and Tonic newsletter for news, offers and competitions from Boldwood Books!

http://www.bit.ly/bookandtonic

We'd love to hear from you, follow us on social media:

 facebook.com/BookandTonic

 twitter.com/BoldwoodBooks

 instagram.com/BookandTonic

Made in the USA
Monee, IL
26 March 2021